Sins
of
Omission

Sins
of
Omission

Randy Roeder

Dusty Typewriter Press • Cedar Rapids

Cover design by Jennifer S. Roeder

The Fisk coffin on cover is in the collection of the Kibbe Hancock Heritage Museum in Carthage, Illinois. Photo by Nancy Kraft.

Dusty Typewriter Press
5001 1st Ave SE
Ste 105 #243
Cedar Rapids, IA 52402
http://dusty.typewriter.press

ISBN 978-1-940509-30-3

First Edition September 2018

Version 1.1.0

For Nancy and Jenn, the women in my life

Notes

Sins of Omission is set in 1975. Although the characters in this novel may appear to be motivated by relatively small sums of money, the figures found in the story are representative of an era when the average Midwesterner earned $11,000 a year, and a new middle-class home cost $30,000. At the time, a first-owner car cost something like $3,400. Two semesters of college—dorm food and housing included—set a family back $2,500; gas was 58 cents per gallon, and bread 29 cents a loaf.

Cell phones and personal computers had yet to arrive on the scene. A typical household contained a single TV set, often black and white, and a land-line telephone. Pay phones were ubiquitous, and charges for a call outside the local area (known as long distance) were considered outrageous. Friends and acquaintances often dropped by when unable to reach someone by phone. Homeowners in small towns seldom troubled to lock their doors.

1

The waves pounded hard against the hull of his wooden johnboat as Blackie Stiles piloted his way downstream. True to form, the Mississippi was acting up again. Every time a stiff south wind blew against the current, white caps popped up. Bad enough if a guy had a v-hull, but a flat bottom did nothing to cut the waves.

A v-hull was out of the question. Blackie was one of a handful of fishermen who still earned a living running nets and trotlines. That meant he spent a substantial part of each day standing on the wooden foredeck of his boat. A flat bottom provided stability, a good thing since he didn't relish the thought of going ass over appetite into the drink. Although he swam like a fish, the odds weren't good if he got tangled in a net while wearing hip boots. Blackie braced himself as the front of the boat crested a wave and pounded back down onto the water.

Up. Pause. *Kaboom!*

Repeat, again and again, catching spray in the face with each wave. Not so bad in the summer when the water was warm. Come November, the droplets would turn his face raw and freeze onto his clothes. He'd been on the river over forty years and hated steering into an upstream wind almost as much as returning home empty-handed.

The boat hit a larger-than-usual wave and came down hard enough to jolt his stomach. He wished he hadn't spent the night at the Bronco Inn. He'd started out playing low-stakes euchre with friends, but things went south when the boys from the Saddle Club blew into town on the heels of a trail ride. The place really got humming when Smiley Koppes bought rounds for everybody. Blackie couldn't remember how he got involved in a pickled egg-eating contest with that guy from Sabula. The kid folded, but Blackie had to finish up the better part of a gallon jar to put him away.

Up. Pause. *Kaboom!*

Fifty-five years old. What in the hell had he been thinking? His head throbbing, his stomach rolling, and anticipating a bout of diarrhea, Blackie adjusted the outboard's tiller, pointing his boat toward Bowman's Island. Between vacationing pleasure cruisers and the roiling waves, he didn't feel much like hanging his backside off the boat. The approaching sandbar beckoned—promising peace, privacy, and a nice willow log back in the bushes. He hoped he'd make it.

He did.

A renewed and better man, Blackie exited the undergrowth a half hour later. He paused at the point where plant life gave way to beach and lit up a Lucky Strike. Nicotine contentment spread its warm glow as he surveyed the scene before him. The blue sky, puffball clouds, and dancing water held the promise of better days to come. It wouldn't take much to improve his fortunes. Divorced and dead-flat broke, he needed a hundred bucks to settle his rent. Thirty more would keep him in gas for a week and a half. Tough as things were, he was sure of one thing—only a fool would trade life on the river for a mortgage and car payments.

Back in the day things weren't so hard. But then a bunch of guys in robes said Catholics could start eating meat on Friday. The Chicago fish markets tanked two months later. Blackie shook his head. He remembered complaining about the twenty-cent profit on each box of carp he shipped. Little did he realize he'd been living in the good old days. At least there'd been a steady market. Things were different now. On Monday, the dealers would be screaming for carp and buffalo. By Friday they'd be next to worthless because everybody wanted sheepshead. The only fish a guy could really count on were catfish and sturgeon.

He'd just started back to his boat when he noticed a dark gray object protruding from the sand beside a massive piece of driftwood. Made of metal and the size of a guitar case, it looked too irregular for an old steam boiler and too small for a cattle trough. Curious, he walked over to the object and kicked some sand away from it.

Whatever it was, it was made of cast iron and old enough to be an antique. No matter, it was sure to be broken. He'd long ago learned the hard lesson that the sands of the Mississippi held little of value. He walked back to the spot where he'd beached his boat. About to shove off, he paused to look out at the water. If anything, the wind was blowing harder than before. His stomach pitched at the thought of going out for another pounding. Better to wait and see if the wind dropped, and if it didn't, head upstream and go on home.

He'd checked his wood-lath fish traps the day before yesterday and anything in them would keep another twenty-four hours. The catfish spawn was at hand, but it was a little early to get excited. When it hit, he'd need to check his traps every day. An egg-laden female could fill a trap with amorous males overnight. Guys who knew what's what harvested the males and left the alluring gal in the trap until the spawn ended. When it came to catfish, Blackie Stiles knew what's what, and what's what meant he had another day or two before things got interesting.

The bow of the boat securely on the sand, he plopped down on the foredeck, lit another Lucky and thought about that old TV commercial. *Lucky Strike means fine tobacco.* Not really so fine, but on the whole, not too bad. If the government really cared about truth in advertising, it'd be *Lucky Strike means good enough tobacco.* He chuckled. Closer to the truth, but the slogan wouldn't sell many cigarettes.

His thoughts wandered back to the object buried in the sand. He had time to kill and might as well satisfy his curiosity about the thing. If it looked good, he'd sell it for scrap. He got up, grabbed an oar, and headed over to investigate.

Using the oar as a makeshift shovel, Blackie began scraping sand away from the side of the would-be treasure. As he did, he discovered scrollwork and leaves cast into the surface of the buried part of the metal. He'd heard that cast iron didn't rust much. From what he was looking at, it had to be true. The patterns were intact and easy to see.

Blackie recognized the object and stopped scraping. He'd discovered a very old and very fancy bathtub—the kind rich people sat in while their maids poured warm water over them. This one wasn't big, maybe a kid's tub. If it wasn't broken, it'd be worth a small fortune, but he'd need help getting it up into the boat.

––––––––

Sitting in his flat bottom, Blackie watched as an apparition carrying a lunch pail in one hand and a spade in the other materialized in the morning mist. The figure revealed itself as male and chose a path through the weed-covered riverbank that led to Blackie's boat. Hank Steines, as good a friend as a man could have, had agreed to lend him a hand with his island discovery, little realizing that Blackie planned to hijack him for the day. Hank whistled softly as he approached and made the step from the bank to the foredeck without breaking stride.

"Morning Blackie," he said, unshouldering the spade and taking the center seat.

Cigarette in his mouth, Blackie mumbled a reply. Though daylight had broken, morning fog still shrouded the river, reducing visibility to the point where navigation became hazardous. There was nothing for it but wait for the sun to burn the mist away. As Hank lit his pipe, Blackie stubbed his smoke. Picking up a thermos, he poured coffee into the lid, then looked across to his friend, waiting for him to speak.

"I don't know how I let you talk me into this," Hank said.

"What, forty percent ain't enough?"

Exhaling smoke, Hank snorted. "Forty percent of nothin' ain't much of anything."

"You're here because you been bored ever since you quit the river."

"Yeah, but the old lady don't rag at me anymore telling me to make something of myself."

Blackie shook his head. "Slingin' trash on the garbage truck is better than fishin'?"

Hank chuckled. "Life on the chow wagon ain't bad. Regular hours, and all you can eat."

"Yeah, but you'll never get the river out of your blood, and the stink of fish will follow you wherever you go."

Hank took the pipe from his mouth, turned it upside down, and knocked it against the side of the boat. Blackie watched as the ashes fell into the water. Hank looked up, met his eyes, and remarked, "At least I still got a wife."

That hurt, but Hank had a point. As far as the good people of Bellevue were concerned, commercial fishermen were worse than the bottom of the heap. Hell, guys who fished for a living were so low they didn't even make the pile. The town's solid citizens wrinkled their noses as they drove by the fishermen's neighborhood and called it Fishville.

At school, the same citizens' children played a game called Fish Fleas. Their kids would walk up to the desk of a fisherman's child, touch it, roll their eyes, and scream, "Oh no, now I've got fish fleas." A variant of the game of tag, the only way for a victim to get rid of fish fleas was to pass them on to someone else by touching them. The kids' parents didn't see anything wrong with the game. After all, they played Fish Fleas when they were young. The lives of fishermen's children were hard, and they soon learned to be tough. What the townsfolk never saw were the tears shed at home. Boy or girl, it didn't matter, the cruelty never stopped.

"Sorry, Hank. I was outta line."

Poor Hank. His wife was from out of town and didn't understand her husband could do nothing to wash the stink of fish away. The only way out was to leave the place, but if he lived to a hundred, Hank wouldn't be able to do it. Though he no longer fished for a living, leaving town would mean leaving the river. Once the river got into a guy, it never let go. Another river, another town, even the same river in a different place, it wouldn't be the same. Hank's river, the place where he knew every rock and recognized the seasons by the smell in the air, where surging floods angrily drove him to shore and midsummer days meant picking fish after fat fish from a trotline, he couldn't escape it. Leaving—a guy might as well gut himself with a dull pocketknife.

"The hell with it," said Blackie. "Let's go. I'll run her out to the middle, and we'll take it slow until things clear up." After pulling the Evinrude's starter rope, he let the engine idle a few seconds and backed away from the shore.

Plumes of wraithlike mist rose from the water, dancing about them as they slowly chugged out to the channel where fog enveloped them like a second skin. Making their way through morning air so thick their outboard sounded far away, the men found little reason to talk. On the river and in their element, the world of wives, rent payments, and senseless chatter fell away. On a half-baked quest for adventure, with the gentle putt-putt of an almost idling motor for companionship, Blackie and Hank felt as content as adult males can be.

———————————

The outboard jerked and clunked. Blackie swore.

Hank addressed his friend. "Sounds like you sheared a pin. Runnin' blind is as good a way to find a wing dam as there is."

He watched as Blackie cut the outboard and tipped it up.

"I expect you're right, Hank. It sounded like rock. Hand me that army surplus box. I keep my pliers in there."

Hank smiled to himself and handed over the ammunition box. His friend was a hoot, always chasing some get-rich-quick scheme. Two years ago, they'd gone up to Hudson's Bay looking for a lost kimberlite deposit. Blackie swore up and down that wherever you found kimberlite, you found diamonds. They spent two weeks up on the bay, looking for an island pictured on a map drawn up by the retired geologist who claimed he'd discovered the deposit. Maybe they found the right island, maybe not, but there was one thing they sure as hell didn't find—diamonds.

Hank didn't care. How many men got to buck the waves in one of the most desolate corners of Hudson's Bay searching for a lost diamond deposit—let alone a deposit marked by a circle on a hand-drawn map. Their boat had been so small they'd nearly swamped it a dozen times. What an adventure. His wife didn't like Blackie, but then, the kind of woman a guy marries wouldn't. Wife be damned. Blackie was a man who knew how to live.

Blackie looked up as he finished his work. The fog had lifted. He handed the ammo box back to Hank, tipped the motor down, and before long, they were running wide open on water smooth as glass. Bowman's Island grew steadily larger, and ten minutes later they found themselves pulling the boat's bow onto the sandy shore.

"How far is it?" asked Hank.

"See that little pile of sand by that big piece of driftwood?"

"Can't believe I missed it," said Hank. "You made one hell of a mess."

"That's why we needed to get here early. I didn't want some camper getting curious about why somebody was digging. Grab a shovel."

Hank shouldered his spade and listened as Blackie described the layout for him.

"It's upside down. I dug far enough to see some of the fancy cast ironwork. If it's in one piece, I bet your lady friend will give us two hundred bucks for it."

Hank smiled at Blackie's optimism. A few weeks after he started on the garbage truck, Marty Efferding, the lady antique dealer, told him she'd buy everything old and interesting he found on the route. Too bad picking junk wasn't as lucrative as his friend imagined. He had to give the truck's driver a percentage of everything he sold, and Marty liked to buy cheap.

When they reached the site, Blackie stuck his shovel in the sand. "Now Hank," he lectured, "we gotta take it easy and not bust anything. You start at the top end, and I'll take the bottom."

"It's probably already busted, but yeah, I'll take it easy." Hank noticed Blackie left him the end of the tub that was completely buried. He'd barely begun digging when Blackie got excited.

"Come here and look at this. You won't believe it. This thing's really something. There's even a fancy handle for dragging it into the middle of the room. Some really rich guy must'a bought it for his kid."

Hank took a few steps to see what Blackie pointed to. The guy was right; the tub looked deluxe. He'd learned a little about antiques from Marty but never heard of a bathtub anywhere near as fancy as this. The thing looked like it belonged to somebody with more money than sense. He imagined a pampered Victorian child dressed in a pinafore, stamping her feet and screaming, "I won't take a bath. You can't make me. I won't. I won't. I won't." Even a fancy tub wouldn't make a kid want to take a bath.

What a weird thought. Last week he'd read a few of the old children's books that he found on the chow wagon and saved for Marty. Now his mind came up with stuff like little girls in pinafores. He'd heard that what a guy reads could affect his mind. He'd better get back to stuff like James Bond and Ellery Queen before he went soft in the head. He returned to his digging and had just uncovered another handle when it hit him. He froze.

"Blackie," he said without looking up. "This ain't no bathtub. It's a coffin."

2

Brute Hinkley was dead. My father-in-law, a man I hadn't seen in ten years, a guy who hated me even more than he hated communists and Democrats, the man who threatened to kill me on sight, had passed over to the other side. I'd read and re-read his obituary in the *Jackson County Sentinel* until I knew it by heart.

Brutus J. Hinkley

Longtime Maquoketa resident and Jackson County Sheriff Brutus J. Hinkley died unexpectedly at his home following a massive heart attack. The son of Myron S. Hinkley and Irma Hingtgen, he was born on the family farm near Andrew, Iowa, on December 17, 1922, and entered the United States Marine Corps after graduating from high school. Hinkley served in an infantry unit where he attained the rank of sergeant and earned a Purple Heart for injuries received during the Battle of Guadalcanal.

At the close of the war, Hinkley signed on as patrolman with the Maquoketa Police Department. In 1952, he won election to the post of County Sheriff and held that position until the time of his death. The longest-serving sheriff in Jackson County history, he was a member of the American Legion Post 57, the National Sheriff's Association, and the Fraternal Order of Eagles.

*Hinkley is survived by his wife Velma, his brother Felix,
and five children: Scott, William, Marilyn (Burleson), Michael,
and Tamara.*

No mention of his son-in-law, Cletus Efferding—no surprise. But no mention of his daughter Myra? My wife? Worse yet, Michael and Tamara were our children, not his. I hadn't seen them since Myra's funeral. Mikey and Tammy had been staying with Brute and Velma the day Myra took her life. Brute blamed me for her death and promised to kill me if I didn't leave the kids with them.

I could have chalked it up to a father's grief, but Brute Hinkley was a man of his word. He didn't just threaten to kill me—he promised. I don't know how many men he shot in the war, but he'd killed two since becoming sheriff, one with his bare hands. The most powerful law enforcement officer in the county, Brute Hinkley never messed around. No ifs, ands, or buts, an attempt to get so much as a glimpse of my children would leave me dead.

There'd be no letters from Dad, no phone calls, no birthday or Christmas presents. I was in no position to make my case in court because I'd been arrested in a prostitution raid the day before my wife drowned herself. She'd been suffering from a crippling depression, and one day I realized we hadn't had sex in over a year. Unhappy with the situation, I made my first and last visit to a house of ill repute.

Myra's suicide devastated me. I figured the kids were better off with the Hinkleys than the guy responsible for their mother's death. Forced from my hometown Bellevue by Brute's threats, I sold my business at a loss and started drinking. When the notification for the hearing to terminate my parental rights showed up in the mail, I didn't fight it.

Fence posts and telephone poles whipped by as I drove through the verdant Iowa countryside. My hands gripped the steering wheel. The words in the obituary rankled. His kids, not mine. I didn't like it, not a whit. Myra's omission ate at my core. Mikey and Tammy were under three when Myra took her life. They'd have no memory of her, no memory of me.

There could be just one reason Myra's name didn't appear in the obituary. Brute and Velma had raised our children as their own. The effort required must have been phenomenal. Photos tossed, scrapbooks purged, friends and family warned. Whether from misplaced intentions or outright meanness, the Hinkleys had erased Myra and me from the kids' lives.

Brute's obituary left me so upset I visited a psychologist, an older gentleman who told me to put the kids' best interests first. Although the current recommendation was to tell children about their natural parents when they were old enough to understand, some old-school practitioners recommended hiding the fact until adulthood. Though my shrink wasn't one of them, he wasn't on my side.

"This isn't your decision, Cletus," he counseled.

"Even if it means my kids are living a lie?"

He raised his eyebrows and peered at me over the top of his half-frame glasses. "You haven't been part of your children's lives for ten years. You've done it because you believed it best for them. Why do you think it would be okay to waltz in now against the family's wishes?"

I wasn't that noble. I hadn't told him about Brute's death threats.

"You see, I couldn't visit because—"

He held up his hand. "Couldn't or wouldn't, it makes no difference. Unless the family is on board, you'll do nothing but create problems for your children."

"But—"

"But nothing. Tearing your children's lives apart because you're upset about an obituary is irresponsible—especially after they've just lost their father."

Father. Leaning back in his chair, surrounded by his credentials, my personal Sigmund Freud had lobbed the hand grenade without warning. It hit like a blow to the kisser, shocking me into seeing the situation from the kids' point of view. Their dad had died, the only father they'd ever known. I was peanuts by comparison.

"The Hinkleys may not have made the wisest choices," he continued, "but you have no right to make the situation worse."

I didn't argue. My Sigmund wannabe had it right.

Lost in thought, I breezed down Highway 64 barely aware I operated a motor vehicle. The need to slow down for the little town of Wyoming brought me back to the present. The place marked the midpoint of my journey. Bellevue, my hometown, lay another forty miles away, but I planned to break the trip at Maquoketa, the seat of Jackson County—the place where my kids lived and my wife was buried.

Stunned, I sat on the ground trying to process the scene. I'd come to Mount Hope Cemetery to see what the Hinkleys had inscribed on Myra's marker. I'm not keen on cemeteries, but I made the side trip because I had to know. Brute had given me his ultimatum on the day of the interment, and I'd spent ten years wondering whether my wife had been buried under her maiden name or as Myra Efferding. Prepared to see the Efferding name missing from the marker, what I discovered instead was beyond comprehension—nothing.

I replayed the day of Myra's funeral. I could see it like it happened yesterday. We buried Myra in the first plot to the right of her uncle Lucius Hinkley's tall marble marker. I was sure of it, but instead of a gravestone, I saw only grass. To the right of the empty spot stood a new marker inscribed with the names Brutus and Velma Hinkley. Brute's dates were closed; Velma's death date was open. My father-in-law died two months ago, and a granite monument already marked his passing. Myra died a decade ago, and nothing?

I got up and circled Lucius Hinkley's marker, making a larger and larger circumference with each rotation. I found no indication that Myra had been buried anywhere within one hundred-fifty feet of her uncle. I stopped walking. Spotting a caretaker in the distance, I headed over to ask about the cemetery records. Preoccupied with one of those new weed whackers, he was unaware of my presence. I put my hand into his line of sight and waved it. He looked up and shut down the trimmer.

"Good morning," I said, "can you tell me who has access to the cemetery records and where I can find him?"

The caretaker wiped his face with a red bandana. "Yup, I can. It's me, and I'm standing in front of you."

"I need to know if somebody is buried here."

"The early bird gets the worm."

"How's that?"

"I leave in another half-hour. Get in the cart. We'll drive over to the shed."

We climbed into his golf cart, drove something like half a block, and pulled up to a maintenance shed the size of a double garage. We entered through the side door. Though there wasn't a soul in the place, the voice of John Denver thanking God he was a country boy greeted us from a battered radio. We walked through an assortment of lawn equipment to a gray steel desk with a couple of shelves above it. My companion pointed to a row of ring binders. "Here's where we keep the lists. I don't know where the official records are. What's the name?"

"Efferding, with two effs."

He pulled down a binder marked E-G and began riffling the pages. "Nope," he said. "No Efferdings buried here."

"Try her maiden name—Hinkley, Myra."

"Hinkley, now there's a name I recognize." He pulled another volume, flipped a few pages, and having settled on one, ran his finger down a list.

"Yup, here it is, Hinkley, Myra. Section C, number E-189. I'll take you over in the cart."

We got into the golf cart, and he drove me back to the spot where I'd begun my search.

"Here it is," he said. "It's unmarked."

I climbed out of the cart, shaking my head. "Ten years and no marker, you've got to wonder why somebody would do something like that."

I turned to thank my driver. When I finished, he removed his cap and scratched his bald pate. "Mister, all kinds come through here, and each one is hoping to find something. I can tell you're not collecting dates for a family history. I saw you sitting over here crying. The person buried here meant something to you. No marker, it doesn't mean anything, and it happens more than you think. Some people don't order the stone right away. They don't know what kind to get or maybe they want to ask a relative about what to put on it. Maybe they can't face up to it. Maybe they're short on money. Time goes by, and they move to another town or somebody else dies. Maybe there's nobody left."

"You forgot the big one," I said.

"The big one?" he asked.

"Maybe they want to forget."

Hank watched Blackie straighten up, put his hands on his back, and stretch. His friend removed a blue bandanna from his hip pocket, wiped the sweat from his face and smiled. "Looks like we're in for a payday, Hank. It's not busted at all."

"We still got a problem, Blackie. The sucker ain't empty."

"Ah, old as it is, there won't be nothin' left but bones, we can just dump 'em."

Hank scratched his chin, hoping Blackie knew what he was talking about. "Kinda spooky you know. Ain't superstitious or anything like that but opening this thing up ... that's like robbin' a grave. Sort of gives me the willies, what with that little window above where the face used to be and all."

Blackie didn't seem to share his reservations. "Now that I see how nice it is, I figure we can get three hundred bucks. Tell you what, seein' as how this wasn't what we thought, we'll go fifty-fifty. Spend it on your wife. Maybe she won't think I'm such a bad guy after all."

"The last thing I'm gonna do is tell my wife is we robbed a grave."

Blackie gestured at the mud and sand around them. "Do you see a cemetery? This thing washed in here. It don't belong to anybody, and nobody cares about it. It's ours for the pickin'. Let's go, Hankie. I got fish traps to run and trotlines to pick up."

Blackie usually called him Hank. He didn't use Hankie unless his patience was wearing thin. Hank didn't like the nickname but considered it a lot better than Snot Rag, the name he'd been tagged with as a kid. He'd given and received more than a few black eyes over that one. His parents had named him after his grandpa, Henry E. Steines, but he'd insisted on the name Hank. Things went fine until fourth grade when one of the guys discovered his middle initial. He'd blackened enough eyes to put the Snot Rag name to rest, but he'd been Hankie ever since.

Well, a hundred fifty bucks was a hundred fifty bucks. When Blackie bent over to take one of the handles, Hank joined him, and they dragged it back to the boat. The cast iron box wasn't light, but the sand provided little resistance. "Heavy, but not too bad," observed Hank. "At least it's not full of water."

"Heavy enough," grunted Blackie. "Slide 'er into the water a couple inches, and we'll wash the mud off. Don't wanna mess up the boat."

Hank couldn't believe his ears. Coated with sand, algae, dead minnows, fish scales, and slime, the inside of a commercial fisherman's boat gave new meaning to the word filthy, and Blackie's flat bottom was worse than most. Well, to each his own. In Blackie's world, coffin mud didn't belong, and there'd be no talking him out of it.

As Hank washed away the mud, the extent of the casket's ornate cast iron artwork became clear. The box was in beautiful condition, right down to the glass faceplate. Hank knelt in the water, put his hands on the glass to block the sunlight and looked inside. A thick brown stain inside the glass obscured his vision. He thought he saw the dim outlines of a face.

"See anything?" asked Blackie.

"For a minute there, I thought maybe I could see a face, but now I don't. Lookin' into a coffin can get to your imagination. You look."

Blackie held his hands around his eyes and tried to look through the glass. "Nothin," he said. "The glass is too dirty to make anything out. Besides, the thing floated down the river and washed in upside down. Whatever's left has gotta be all mixed up. I didn't hear anything movin' around inside when we dragged it. There can't be much left."

Hank massaged his lower back. "Wider at the shoulders than at the head and feet. Looks like something they'd carry up Boot Hill in a western movie."

Blackie yawned and rolled his neck. "Dang thing must weigh a couple of hundred pounds. None of them boot-hill coffins ever looked this fancy. This one's more like one of them mummy cases, taller up at the head than down at the ankles. Then it gets taller again to make room for the feet."

"You gotta admit the little foot compartment is nice," said Hank. "Who wants to go through eternity with cramped feet?"

"Like a dead person's gonna care. Let's get 'er up in the boat. I got work to do. You can run the traps and trotlines with me."

They struggled but managed to get the cast iron box into the boat. Soaked with sweat, they took their seats—Blackie in the back and Hank in the center alongside the casket. A break was in order. Hank lit his pipe while Blackie silently puffed a cigarette.

Hank spoke first. "You see that little plate below the face window? It's got some kind of hen scratch on it."

"I did, and we'll have to do something about it," Blackie replied. "If it's a name, we won't be able to sell it. People will think it belongs to somebody and try to track it down."

"The plate's pretty tarnished, they might not be able to read it."

Blackie grabbed an oar, pushed the boat out, and let the outboard down. "You want to take a chance they'll think we stole it?"

Hank rose from his seat and examined the plate. He removed a pocketknife from his jeans and opened it to the screwdriver blade.

As Blackie started the engine, Hank began working on the four screws holding the plate in place. He removed one but snapped another off when the boat encountered the wake from a passing cabin cruiser.

Blackie yelled over the sound of the motor. "Wait until we're on shore."

Hank nodded. No need to hurry, they had a big day ahead of them. By the time they'd run Blackie's traps and trotlines, the floor of the boat would be full of slippery, flopping fish. The catch, combined with the weight of the coffin, would leave the boat riding low in the water. They'd need to run slow, and when they got back home, the fish came first. He'd be expected to help ice them down before unloading the casket.

No way around it, Hank would get home late, and his wife would be honked. He hated it when she threw things. Knocking the ashes from his pipe, he decided to wait until she was asleep before he set foot inside. Mornings agreed with her. Better to sack out on the couch and face the music later.

He and Blackie could take their time with the cast iron box.

3

With the radio playing Captain and Tennille's "Love Will Keep Us Together," I crested Baker Hill and sped down into the valley that was home to the town of Bellevue. The sun shone brightly, Nixon was gone, and the Viet Nam war had ended in April. To heck with the National Speed Law and its mandatory fifty-five mph speed limit. I rapped the Nova up to seventy-five and let out a whoop. Brute Hinkley had driven me from God's Country ten years ago, and it felt good to be back. I blew through the double bridges over Big and Little Mill Creeks at almost eighty.

Though my ancient Nova was up to the task, I had to slow down when I realized I was in a school zone. I'd forgotten they'd plopped a new high school out on the edge of town and a car wash a little farther in. Other than that, it didn't appear as if much had changed since 1965. When I hit Front Street, the town's breathtaking view of the Mississippi nearly brought me to tears. I was home.

But of course, I wasn't. Armchair philosophers are right—you can't go home again. Once I'd been back a while, I'd realize I wasn't the person who left here a decade ago, and neither was anyone else. I'd left town with a cloud hanging over my head, and people wouldn't have forgotten. Myra's suicide, a prostitution arrest the newspaper wrongly played up as a visit to a sadomasochistic dungeon—scandals cling like leeches in small towns.

I'd come back for a vacation, the first time I'd taken off two consecutive weeks in seven years. Though I didn't expect to be run out on a rail, I doubted the townsfolk would roll out the red carpet. The fishing trip hadn't been my idea. A couple of friends back in Cedar Rapids heard the pool below the lock and dam was lousy with catfish and wanted to test the waters. Though I hadn't fished in years, I agreed to go along and drove over a day early because I had waters of my own to test. I thought it best that the town's citizens know of my return before my friends arrived—maybe we'd avoid at least some of the craning necks and whispered asides.

They say small towns never change, and except for the new school, it looked like Bellevue had changed less than most. Fine with me, I don't like change. Maybe the sameness would reduce the shock of encountering familiar faces, faces once friendly that would now view me with suspicion. But I had a plan of attack. If I wanted to spread the news of my return, the best places to start would be the Super Value grocery and Bub's, the town's busiest barbershop.

My first stop was the Big D Super Value. I walked in and picked up a sixteen-ounce Pepsi bottle. The owners had modernized things a bit, but the place felt familiar. Viola Till stood at one of the cash registers dressed in a navy-blue smock. Ten years and she hadn't changed a bit. I picked her register, an easy choice because there were just two, and put my soda on the counter.

"Hello, Vi. Do you remember me?" I asked.

She tried to look friendly—almost made it.

"Cletus Efferding, of course I do. It's been a long time. So where are you now?"

Viola didn't beat around the bush. She'd collect as much gossip as she could before I left the store. "I live in Cedar Rapids and work at Killian's Department Store. I run a dance studio on the side."

She nodded, looking pleased that her simple question had elicited so much information. "You're just passing through?"

"I'm back on vacation. A couple of friends and I are going to do some fishing. We thought we'd take in the big Fourth of July celebration next week."

"Not a family trip then." She was fishing to see if I'd remarried.

"No, still single. The kids are living with Velma Hinkley. You know, Brute passed away a couple of months ago."

"I heard," she said.

I picked up my change and soda pop. "Good to see you."

"Bye," she said.

I didn't expect a warm smile and didn't get one. Okay by me, my mission didn't involve winning a popularity contest. Viola Till now knew where I lived, that I had a respectable job, that I was unmarried, and where the kids were living. By suppertime tonight, all the women in the extended Till, Sieverding, and Kilburg families would have the poop on Cletus Efferding. Before morning, the Catholic half of the town's population would know. Add to that every third person to pass through the store, and my public relations plan was well underway. Viola and the Big D represented the first step in my plan of attack. I left the store, walked by my car, and dropped the soda in it. Time for step two, a haircut.

I headed in the direction of the river, rounded the corner, and turned up the sidewalk toward Bub's Barbershop. There'd be at least a half-dozen people inside to spread word of my return. Still thinking about what I wanted to say, I put my hand out to reach for the door handle and froze. Racks of women's clothing looked back at me through the glass. I'd walked up to the wrong entryway.

Not just any entryway, but the door of what was once Efferding's Menswear. Between my grandfather, my father, and I, we'd thumbed the latch and put our fingers around the handle for something like ninety years. My father loved the door so much he'd refused to replace it when he put a modern, pigmented-glass front on the business.

The sight of the worn, familiar oak panels ripped the heart from my chest. Stumbling out of the entrance onto the flat and even sidewalk, I grabbed a nearby parking meter to steady myself. Why did I think I could just breeze back into town, a place so thick with memories that every step reminded of what I'd lost—roots, my family, a third-generation business. I turned, walked back to the car, and drove down Front Street, heading for the park on the palisade south of town.

Leaving the town behind me, I blasted across the overhead and drove up the winding road to the top of the bluff. My trustworthy Nova didn't mind the sharp curves, and what better place to pull myself together than the spot where I escaped the social pressures of my teen years and found solace during the darkest days of Myra's depression. I parked and exited. As I took in my surroundings, a cloud-dappled patch of sky greeted me.

Somehow the sky looked wrong. Then it hit me; it shouldn't have been there. The stone and timber lodge, a wonder of architecture that opened onto a vista spreading for miles, a rustic masterpiece with twenty-foot ceilings and a fireplace a man could stand in —it was missing. I stood on the drive, trying to make sense of the void.

I don't know how long it took to recover. When I did, I found myself walking toward my original goal, but instead of skirting the park's stunning answer to a chalet, I trod over a concrete slab, the hideous remains of a building once the pride of a community.

I hadn't seen the building in years. Why did its absence affect me so much? I searched for an answer, found none. Putting my hands in my pockets, I walked over to the edge of the bluff and turned onto the well-worn path that led to Pulpit Rock. When I got there, I had the place to myself.

If there's a more beautiful spot on the face of the earth, I don't know it. As a brisk wind ruffled my hair and wayward gulls circled a hundred yards away, I looked out over the town and the Mississippi. To the right, a dozen wooded sloughs crisscrossed a floodplain that reached to the tree-lined hills of Illinois and stretched as far north as the eye could see. A towboat and barges slid downriver. Below me, its streets laid out like rows of corn, lay my hometown, the place I was born and where I hoped my bones would one day lie. Bellevue, the closest God came to creating paradise on earth.

The gulls broke up and flew back to the river. I took it as a sign it was time to go. I filled my lungs with some of the freshest air on the planet, embraced the view one last time, and climbed off the rock. Not quite finished with my Efferding-is-back project, I had things to do, starting with the haircut. This time, I'd approach Bub's shop from the other direction. I didn't want to walk by the old store again.

As I cruised down Second Street, I looked up to see a flashing red light in the rearview mirror. Muttering under my breath, I pulled over. Back in town for a couple of hours and already harassed by the police? When Viola Till put the word out, she didn't waste time.

I cranked the window down and watched the cop approach. I didn't recognize him.

"You just ran a stop sign. Can I see your license, please?"

As if I had an option. "Stop sign, what stop sign?" I handed him my license.

"You can't see it from here, but you ran a stop sign two blocks ago."

I didn't understand. "There aren't any stop signs on Second Street."

He ignored me and studied my license. "Clete Efferding? I didn't recognize you. You've been gone a long time. They put the stop sign in five years ago."

I looked at the officer but couldn't place him.

"William McCard," he said.

I should have known, but ten years, sideburns and a mustache had moved him into adulthood.

"Wiley McCard. I remember ordering extra-long suits for you at the store. I spent so many years driving around this town my brain was on autopilot. A stop sign on Second, I would never have guessed."

Wiley scribbled on his citation book, tore off the sheet and handed it to me. "This time, I'm giving you a warning, Clete. Things change."

———————————

I put my hand up to my forehead and peered through the plate glass window of Bub's Barbershop. An empty room rewarded the effort. No moose head on the wall, no football-shaped wasp nests hanging from the ceiling, no red vinyl chairs filled with guys bemoaning the fate of the Cubs, no Porter Wagoner on the radio, it wasn't possible. How could the town exist without a barbershop with a nickel nailed to the floor and idlers laughing at the unsuspecting boys who tried to pick it up?

"No, Cletus, there is no Santa Claus." My father's startling revelation echoed across the decades as I shook my head in disbelief. I felt as disappointed now as I did then.

I felt a hand on my shoulder and turned. An older man with a bad case of the shakes leaned against the plate glass. I recognized the tell-tale signs of severe Parkinson's and put a name to the face—Zeke Vaughn.

I extended my hand. "Hello, Zeke, Clete Efferding here."

He didn't take it. Probably embarrassed he'd have trouble returning my grasp. I could see he didn't recognize me.

"Bub, Bub closed the shop … last fall."

"That's too bad. I used to live here and wanted to gossip and get a hair trim. Where does a guy get a haircut now?"

"… um-uh, Razor Ray's."

Though he had difficulty staying upright and speaking, Zeke seemed inclined to chat. I learned Bub closed his shop when he found a good-paying job with fringe benefits. If I wanted to spread the word of my return among the men-about-town, I'd need to visit Razor Ray's shop. Zeke let me know that Ray, new to town, ran an up-and-coming business, one that sold hairpieces.

The thought of a barber selling wigs must have appealed to Zeke, a smile lit up his face as he shook his head side to side. "Next thing you know … selling makeup."

We shared a laugh. As fine a man as you'd want to meet, Zeke's condition left him a shell of what he'd once been. I hated seeing him reduced to his current state, and though I knew he enjoyed our bit of socialization, I had a task to complete.

"It's been good talking to you Zeke, but I need to get going. Gee, it doesn't seem like Bellevue with Bub's Barbershop gone."

Zeke extended a faltering hand and smiled. "Still ... um, the same old town."

I put one hand on his elbow and used the other to give his oversized mitt a warm shake.

———————

Razor Ray had a client in the chair when I entered the shop. "About five minutes," he said and turned back to his customer.

I hung my suit coat on the rack, took a seat, and checked out my surroundings. Except for the posters advertising hair pieces, the place looked familiar enough. Ray had taken over Buzz Lucke's old barbershop. Back in the day, I usually got my hair cut at Bub's but made it a point to patronize Buzzy as well. A small-town clothier needs to be careful about playing favorites if he doesn't want to lose business. Buzzy must have retired, but the shop's honey-colored paneling still gleamed, containers of pomade and hair tonic stood at attention in front of the mirrors, and overgrown philodendrons and mother-in-law's tongue still filled the large clay pots in the front window.

I'd have enjoyed the pleasant atmosphere a lot more if there'd been a half dozen guys in the chairs lining the wall. Ray's may have been a great place to get a haircut, but a community gossip center it was not. I'd have to look elsewhere for scandalmongers eager to spread the news of my return.

The chit-chat at the chair didn't engage me, so I picked up a copy of the *Herald-Leader* to catch up on the happenings around town. The front page led off with a story about a project to paint the town's fire hydrants to celebrate next year's Bicentennial of the United States. Below the fold, I learned the County Magistrate had sentenced somebody I didn't know to three days for stealing a cop's hat from the town's patrol car. Interesting, but not much of a conversation starter.

"Next."

I looked up to see Ray whisking the barber's cape off his freshly trimmed customer. "Right with you," I said, folding the paper and returning it to a stack adjacent an ashtray promoting the Bob Ernst Insurance Agency. On my way to the chair, I loosened my necktie and undid my collar button.

"You must wear a tie a lot," said Ray.

"A tie and jacket almost every day. I used to own a men's store."

Ray tucked the little towel around my neck and spread the cape. "Most guys don't know enough to loosen their collar button when they get a haircut. I need to remind them. What'll it be?"

"Same as now, but a month shorter."

He picked up his electric clipper and flipped the switch. "Will do. Where you from?"

"Bellevue, originally. I used to run a store called Efferding's Menswear, but now I'm in Cedar Rapids. Back to do some fishing." I waited for Ray's reaction. None came.

"Too bad we don't have a store like that now. I've got boys, and we have to buy their clothes in Dubuque."

Ray had been in town long enough to know about the death of my wife, yet he treated me like a human being. Apparently, he didn't care about my past. Too bad—his acceptance of events past made it less likely he'd spread the news of my return. I decided to see what I could learn from him instead. "I still have a cousin here, Marty Efferding. Do you know her?"

"Oh, the lady antique dealer. I know her by sight but can't say we're acquainted. How's she doing?"

As if I knew. We hadn't spoken in ten years. When Brute Hinkley threatened me, I had to leave town on short notice. Marty knew of my predicament and offered to buy Efferding's Menswear. Though she wasn't the most reliable person in town, she came up with a modest down payment, so I agreed to sell the store on contract. Not one of my better decisions.

Devastated by my wife's suicide, I sold cheap, and when I tried to cash the check a couple of weeks later, it bounced. After apologizing profusely, she made a few installments on the down payment. Then the money stopped, but by that time, I'd started drinking more than was good for me. Eventually, I was sober enough to care, but Marty had bankrupted the place. A three-generation business, destroyed by my neglect in a little over a year.

Lost in thought, I'd almost forgotten Ray's question. "Marty and I haven't talked for a while. She took over the family store after I left town, and I sort of lost track of her. Still using her maiden name ... do you know if she ever married? What with women's lib and all, you can't always tell these days."

"Nope, she's single. Doesn't have a store. Runs her antique business out of her house and garage. Takes her pickup and trailer to every auction in this part of the state. They say she knows her stuff and ships to big dealers all over the country."

And screws them all, financially and otherwise.

Marty came to live with us after her widowed mother abandoned her. For reasons none of us knew or understood, Aunt Kate walked out of the house one day leaving her fourteen-year-old daughter to fend for herself. Marty's arrival turned our home into a war zone rivaling anything in the European Theatre. A rebellious teenager, she screamed at my parents, stayed out half the night with older guys, and earned a reputation as the town tramp. I didn't know if she deserved the rap, but gossip about her loose morals caused me no end of embarrassment at school. When she left home the day after her high school graduation, my mom celebrated by cooking a turkey dinner with homemade bread and sweet potato pie. Marty eventually returned to Bellevue when I was in my twenties—a sadder, but not much wiser, woman.

Ray must have noticed my cousin didn't make for cheerful conversation. He changed the topic. "You didn't say, what kind of fishing? Bass? Panfish?"

"A couple of friends are coming over, and we're going to set out a few trotlines for catfish."

"It's a good time for catfish. Trim around the ears, or shave?"

"Some people still get their ears lowered? I never imagined."

Ray chuckled. "A few die-hards still go for the white sidewalls. I take it the answer is 'trim.'"

I shook my head. "Sidewalls, will wonders never cease. But back to the catfish, why so good right now?"

"We haven't had any big mayfly hatches."

"Ah, the fish bugs. Who could forget 'em, but what do they have to do with catfish?"

"I thought you were a fisherman."

"Not really, I'm more interested in spending time with my friends. One of them is a catfish fanatic."

Ray stopped scissoring and swiveled the chair toward the mirror, so I could inspect his work. "Catfish gorge on mayflies and quit biting for a week or two after a big hatch." He paused. "There, now. How's the length?"

I studied Ray's work. "Great length and a nice haircut. I remember now. Nobody caught much after the fish bugs showed up."

Ray reached for a bottle of Irish Rose tonic, spread a drop or two on his hands and rubbed it into my hair. "You'll be glad to hear there aren't as many fishflies as there used to be. Blackie Stiles told me it's because the river is changing, He says the last really big hatch was something like a dozen years ago."

I watched Ray put the knob of his round plastic grooming brush between his index and forefingers. "Glad to hear it," I said and looked in the mirror as he gave my hair a deft brush or two. "I remember the time I parked under a street light overnight. When I picked up my car the next morning, I had to clean twelve inches of dead, stinking fishflies off it."

Ray put his brush back on the counter. "They sure are attracted to light. The city usually douses the streetlights when they get bad, so they're not that much bother."

"Weird. They only live a day. Did you ever wonder if it feels like a whole lifetime to 'em?"

"No."

I waited for a follow-up. Apparently, my question held little interest for Ray. Then again, it wasn't one of the brighter things I'd ever come up with. Maybe my off-the-wall comment would help spread word of my return. I imagined Ray talking to his next customer. *That Cletus Efferding, nice guy, but a little strange. You know his wife killed herself.*

Thank goodness, the sound of the blower masked the need for further conversation. Little bits of hair flew in all directions as Ray gave my neck, ears, and barber's cape the treatment.

"Well, looks like you're good to go," he said as he removed my neck strip. He unsnapped the cape and whipped it off with a flourish. "That'll be four dollars."

So much for my plan to spread word of my return at a barbershop. After paying up, I tightened my tie, slipped into my jacket, and made for the door. Although the shop's front window offered a panoramic view of the Mississippi, the scene didn't hold my attention. I'd been back in town just a few hours and had already adopted the local mindset—taking the river for granted.

4

Voices drifted from the darkened garage as a sickle moon crested the top of the bluff. Blackie Stiles and Hank Steines had covered the windows and were ready to get to work. Hank flipped the light switch, and the men studied the ornate casket they'd pulled from the sand. Once out of the boat, the box hadn't been hard to handle. It now rested on a sturdy pair of sawhorses they'd set up on the concrete floor.

"Hey, Hank," said Blackie, "what happened to that thing that looked like it had a name on it?"

"I took it off while you were messing with the gas tank."

"Where's it now?"

"I tossed it out on the bank, into some weeds. That a problem?"

"Don't think so. Anybody sees it, they'll think it's just another piece of river junk."

"I can look for it tomorrow."

"Nah, don't bother. I'll get us some beer."

Hank smiled, happy that Blackie didn't get bent out of shape over a tarnished brass plate and content to let his friend make the decisions on their project. He'd learned adventures with Blackie worked best when he let his strong-willed companion take the lead.

When Blackie returned, he handed Hank a Schlitz. Free beer was always good, but Hank couldn't help but wish his buddy would stock up on better brew.

"What about Marty?" asked Blackie. "Think she'll want it?"

"Sounded pretty excited. She's got something to do but said she'll be over later."

"Guess it's game time."

"How's that?"

"Jesus Christ, Hankie. We gotta dump the bones before she gets here."

"We got a couple of hours. She's gonna make a delivery first. Said it would be about midnight."

Blackie walked to the workbench and retrieved a Crescent wrench. "Must be two dozen nuts on this thing."

Content to let Blackie do the work, Hank tipped his cap back, seated himself on the fender of a boat trailer and pulled on his beer. "More like a dozen," he said as he watched as his companion twist off the first bolt to come under his wrench. When it snapped, Blackie's knuckles made hard contact with the cast iron.

"Goddamn it! Jesus Christ, you sonofabitch!" Thankfully, Jesus chose not to strike Blackie dead on the spot. A powerful overhand throw sent the wrench rocketing toward the far wall where it ricocheted off a door hinge and landed on a stack of hoop nets. Dancing and cursing, Blackie managed to buck his shin on the boat trailer, an action that resulted in further antics.

Hank took in the show, chuckling to himself as he wondered if Blackie's battered shinbone was heaven's revenge for his friend's blasphemy. Blackie's anger would soon pass. In the meantime, silence seemed the best option. When Blackie stormed out the side door, Hank wisely chose to remain seated.

Five minutes later, a smiling Blackie returned with a bottle of Black Velvet. "Hard liquor for hard work," he declared.

"You got glasses?" asked Hank.

Blackie looked puzzled. "Grandpa always said it was bad luck to drink a glass of whiskey in the company of the dead."

"Never heard that before."

"Me neither," Blackie snorted.

Blackie's lame joke diffused the tension in the air. The men shared a laugh and swigged straight from the bottle. The bottle passed back and forth a half dozen times before Blackie set it on the floor. "Time to get back to work," he said and turned to his workbench.

Hank watched as his partner returned with a second wrench and a can of penetrating oil. After dabbing a dozen bolts with oil, Blackie began working them loose. Hank shifted on his boat-fender seat. "We still gotta get that thing ... Hey, what's that smell?"

Blackie sniffed. "I don't smell nothin'."

"Ever leave a garbage can full of fish guts in the hot sun for two weeks with the lid on?"

Blackie sniffed again, shrugged.

"It's coming from the coffin, Blackie. I never noticed it when we were outside. You must'a broke some kind of seal messing with those bolts."

"Can't be. It's just dust and bones."

Hank stared down at the floor, rubbed his face with his hands. "Somebody's still in there. And whoever it is, ain't dried up. Smells like dead fish, worms, and rotten meat."

A loud knock came from the door. It opened to reveal a smiling, petite blonde in form-fitting jeans and high-heeled boots. She waved as she entered. "Hey guys, what's that ... e-e-e-yew!"

Hank watched as she looked at the burial case, the whites of her eyes dwarfing the irises.

"Oh my God, it's not empty!" she shrieked

Hank cleared his throat. "You're early, Marty. We didn't get a chance to clean it out yet, but we will."

Marty pulled a handkerchief out of her green leather purse and held it to her nose. "Are you guys crazy? Robbing graves. What the hell's wrong with you? You think I'm going to buy a second-hand coffin?"

Blackie tried to reassure her. "We didn't dig it up. It got washed up on an island. We'll empty it out and take a hose to it. Be good as new."

Still holding her handkerchief to her nose, Marty began backing out of the garage. "I don't want anything to do with this, and I'm not about to go to jail over a rusty, stinking coffin. If you're smart, you'll get rid of it fast. Even if you do get the smell out, the first thing any buyer will want to know is where it came from."

"Aw, cast iron don't rust, it's just a little stain on the surface," said Blackie. "Bead blast it and it'll clean right up. You ain't ever gonna find another one like this."

Marty backed through the door. "Good," she replied as her heel caught on the threshold. Grabbing the door frame, she re-adjusted her boot and disappeared into the darkness.

Blackie and Hank looked at each other in silence. Blackie spoke first, "Don't smell *that* bad."

"Well, you're around fish all the time, and I toss garbage cans. Maybe our sniffers ain't up to snuff. Anyway, your get-rich-quick scheme just fell through. Now we gotta get rid of this thing."

Blackie picked up the Black Velvet, upended a pail and sat on it. He took a few swallows. After removing a Lucky from the pack, he put the unlit cigarette in his mouth and mumbled, "Sniffers up to snuff ... Hankie, sometimes you sound pretty damn dumb. Got a light?"

Hank pulled a pipe and lighter from his overalls. After torching the end of his friend's cigarette, he lit his pipe and reached for the bottle. "Pretty damn dumb, eh? Before I got married, I had a thing with her. Those high heels and tight jeans, she's a hot little spitfire. I wanted to make it permanent, but she wouldn't have any part of it."

"Then you're dumber than I thought. Half the town's had a thing with her."

"And most of them are liars. Underneath all that hair and makeup is the finest woman I ever was with."

Blackie shook his head. "Then I feel sorry for you."

"Yeah, you're the expert on women. Anyway, tell you what. If Marty ain't interested in this cast iron bucket, I expect nobody else will touch it. We might not be able to sell the thing, but we can sure as hell have some fun with it."

"Nothin's good as money."

"I got an almost as good," Hank smiled.

"Ain't no almost."

"Free beer."

"You may not know much about women, Hank Steines, but there's one thing I like about you. You always got a Plan B."

5

Friday morning, just past midnight, my second day back in town. A noisy mosquito buzzed my face as I tried to sleep. It had already nailed me once, and that made it hard to relax. Like anybody with half a brain, I'd brought along a good supply of mosquito repellant for my fishing trip. I climbed out of bed, turned on the light, and anointed myself with the stuff.

I'd rented the smallest cabin on the lot, a diminutive building that looked even smaller without sunshine streaming through its windows. There were two of them, if you included the one in the door, and two rooms if you included the bathroom. A worn foldout couch doubled for a bed. I had an upholstered chair, a nightstand, swag light, and dresser with a decrepit television on top.

The far side of the room served as a kitchen. A pair of well-used cabinets hung over the stained porcelain sink, and next to it sat a two-burner gas stove. An empty space that once housed an apartment-sized refrigerator now held my suitcases. I'd folded the card table and chair that served as a dining set and leaned them against the wall this morning. The change allowed me to move my ice chest in from the trunk of the car. The owner referred to my digs as the economy cabin.

Packing for a fishing vacation made me realize just how long it had been since I'd had anything to do with the so-called great outdoors. I had to buy what most people call "old clothes" for the trip. Since I worked in a menswear department and owned a dance studio, my everyday attire made me something of a clothes horse. A jacket and tie six days a week and a pair of pleated slacks with a Ralph Lauren polo on the seventh felt as natural to me as overalls on a farmer.

There was more to it than that. At five feet eleven inches and trim, I had a body made for the traditional look, and sentimentalist that I am, I must have been the last guy in Cedar Rapids to regularly wear a hat. Still, the all-too-human desire to fit in had left its mark, and in these more casual times, I'd begun wearing a sports coat on Saturdays. I'd stepped it down a bit, but I still had my standards.

One of the newer styles left me feeling positively ill—leisure suits. Made of hideous, cheap polyester, not only were the damn things ugly, they didn't breathe, and if one ever caught fire, the poor schmuck wearing it would have the privilege of feeling the fabric melt into his skin. Between synthetic safari jackets, white patent leather shoes, and putrid checked pants, I'd begun to wonder if there'd ever been a worse period for men's fashion. Periwigs and pantaloons had one up on a full Cleveland.

Since I was awake anyway, I decided to break out my new fishing clothes and go for a late-night walk. I opened the dresser and pulled out a pair of blue jeans, the first I'd owned since high school. Without a doubt, they looked better on me than the average guy. After topping them off with a white, fresh-from-the-package pocketed t-shirt, I could have passed for a casual Warren Beatty. Not a bad looking guy as far as movie stars go, though I had a bit of an edge on him. I bounced out of the door of my cabin in new Adidas sneakers, crossed the street, and headed up the block towards Milt's Conoco, a convenience store where I hoped to find a cooler full of beer.

I did, and after the clerk put my six-pack in a bag, I continued up the main drag in the direction of L & J's Maid-Rite Shop. It was closed, of course, but when I got there, I crossed over to the river side of the street. Bellevue sits on a high bank with a park that stretches for a mile and a half along the Mississippi. From my vantage point, I could see three-quarters of a mile upstream and a mile down. To the south, broken slivers of moonlight reflected off the river's surface; to the north, the lights of the lock and dam cast eerie shafts of light onto the water below.

As I stood between a picnic table and a wooden stairway that led down to the water's edge, I wondered if it was *the table*. Whether the same or not, it was in the right place and looked like it—the table where my late wife spent the last half hour of her life.

"I'm sorry, Myra," I said. "Sorry for all of it, the hooker, not being a better father to the kids, not taking better care of you when you were sick. In spite of all the hard times, I know you loved me, and I hope you know I loved you. I'm forty-three years old now, Myra. It's been a long time, and of course, there have been others, but you were the one—the mother of my children, the love of my life. You mattered. You counted. Forgive me."

By no stretch of the imagination would anyone call me a religious man. But like almost everyone, I sometimes pray when things go bad. Though Myra died a decade ago, I find myself talking to her rather than God. Maybe it's because I learned God won't help you if you give in to grief. You can roll in it until you're moaning and rocking, pounding the earth in a misery as old as humanity, weeping until you're dehydrated, and he won't lift a finger. I could be off my rocker, but when I feel blue, a little chat with Myra does more for me than all the prayers in all the churches on the face of planet Earth.

Cradling my six-pack, I started down the set of steps Myra used as she walked to the river to drown herself. When I reached the bottom, I perched on a fragment of an old wooden barge, a vessel pulled ashore and left to rot when operating it became unprofitable. An empty coffee can and a forked stick pushed into the gravel at water's edge told me someone had been fishing there.

I settled in, maybe a dozen feet from the spot where Myra entered the water and twisted the cap off a bottle. A dog barked; crickets chattered. Stars twinkled overhead, and a soft breeze blew in from the river. As I looked to the far shore, I made Myra a promise. When the time was right—our kids would know. I wouldn't let their grandmother erase us from their lives.

———————————————

I'd just reached the top of the stairs when I noticed someone sitting on Myra's picnic table. A nearby streetlight provided all the illumination I needed to recognize Wiley McCard, dressed in his civvies with his backside on the tabletop and feet on the seat. He waved a cigarette-bearing hand at me. "Clete, I wondered who was down there. You're out late."

"I couldn't sleep so thought I'd take a walk."

"Me neither. I usually work night shift, and the wife and kids are in Des Moines visiting her mother. Put the two together, and it's hard to sleep."

I had to smile. "Night shift in Bellevue must be pretty quiet."

"Most nights." He pointed to my bag. The contents: three bottles of Bud and three dead soldiers. "That beer?"

"Sorry, Wiley. I didn't know the city's jurisdiction included a federal shoreline."

Wiley laughed and shook his head. "Don't know if it does and don't care. Doesn't seem like a crime for two guys who can't sleep to share a beer."

I took a bottle out of my bag, handed it to Wiley and sat—not next to him on the table top, but a table-length away, on the seat. We faced the river.

"Of course, we're on city property now," Wiley observed.

"Sounds like Bellevue must be one of those no-beer-in-parks places."

"Only if there's a problem. The chief believes in small-town policing."

"Never heard of it."

Wiley set his beer on the table. "We don't broadcast it, but the chief's got it down to one sentence: 'We're here to solve problems, not arrest people.'"

I twisted the cap off my fourth bottle. "Makes sense to me."

"Yeah, but sometimes there's no alternative. That's why I switched shifts today. Tiny Mootz is gonna have a hayride tonight. He's planning to drive the wagon through town, and if I know Tiny, things will get noisy, and there'll be a keg of beer stashed between the bales. We have a new guy on the force who's gung-ho—let him handle it if things get out of line."

"I still can't believe I ran that stop sign today. Thanks for not giving me a ticket. I thought everything would be the same, but the town's changed more than I imagined."

Wiley slapped at a mosquito. "Really? Feels the same to me."

"Maybe, but the high school is west of town now, Bub closed up shop and Buzzy retired, and the State Park Lodge—don't even get me started. What kind of bureaucratic, State-of-Iowa jackass would decide to tear it down?

"The state didn't tear it down. Somebody burned it—arson."

I shook my head. "I can't believe it. Hope you caught the bastard."

Wiley finished his beer. The guy could put 'em down.

"Half the town knows who did it, but we didn't have enough evidence for an arrest. Got another?"

"Last one," I said and handed the bottle to Wiley. "So, if somebody does something minor and it's not a problem, you try not to arrest him. Does it follow that if somebody does something big, and you don't have enough evidence for an arrest, you make him miserable?"

My question must have made Wiley uncomfortable, he didn't answer. Instead, he stood and chugged his beer—the whole bottle in something like six swallows.

"Let's put it this way, if anything ever happens to Canker De-Cook, this is one cop who's not going to lift a finger."

"Canker DeCook? Figures. The slimy bastard never was happy unless he was up to no good."

Wiley handed me the empty bottle. "Forget it, Clete. I shouldn't have mentioned anything. Like I said, we couldn't make a case. It's just what people believe. Well, take it easy now." He paused, waiting for a response.

Inwardly fuming over Canker DeCook and at a loss for a reply, I nodded. "I'll take it any way I can get it."

A lame sign-off, but in a small town, it still works.

6

His elbows propped on the hood of the Ford F-100 pickup, Herman Cohen peered through the eye-pieces of his binoculars. He rotated the focal adjustment until the farmer atop the green and yellow John Deere tractor came in sharp and clear. The driver, heading his way, wore blue bibbed overalls, a red bandana around his neck, and a cap matching the green of his tractor. The guy wasn't taking in the scenery but looked down at the dark brown earth, as if the only thing that mattered was keeping his tractor in a straight line, so the points of the metal apparatus attached to it didn't uproot the small green plants growing in orderly rows. Old MacDonald was overweight.

Herman smiled. Irv had picked a beautiful piece of German optics for him. He'd selected the best Zeiss binoculars in the sporting goods store. Guys like Irv didn't grow on trees.

Irv's rifle barked, and the man in the tractor slumped in his seat. "Got him," he said as he raised the gun. He worked the Winchester's bolt and the empty casing dropped to the ground.

"You sure he's dead?"

"Hear the shot? A solid hit in the trunk with a 150-grain load behind a .270 hollow point. Nobody survives that."

Herm continued looking through the binoculars as the tractor, its driver still slumped in the seat, began quartering across the field, tearing up shoots of young corn, heading for a fence. "Take an insurance shot. Then let's get the hell out of here."

Irv rested the rifle back on the top of the pickup's cab, carefully lined up another shot, and squeezed the trigger.

Herm peered through the binoculars. Though the slumping man barely stirred, he could detect the hit. No doubt about it, the guy was a goner.

Their task complete, the men picked up the casings and slid back into the pickup. Irv took the wheel. After looking in both directions, he pulled out, turned west at the first intersection, and drove carefully away. They rode quietly, Irv paying attention to the road, Herm looking out the side window at the young corn dotting the fertile fields.

Herm took in the sights for something like ten minutes before breaking the silence. "I wonder where the Johnny Popcorn will end up. With no driver, it won't go far."

"It'll go until it tips over or hits something. A green tractor's a Poppin' Johnny, not a Johnny Popcorn. We've been in Iowa five years, and you don't know that? If we're gonna blend in, you'd better start getting things like that right. They call 'em Poppin' Johnnies because the two-cylinder engines make weird noises when they run."

"OK, Poppin' Johnny then. I wish I could handle a rifle like you. You're one helluva shot—as good as they come. I can deliver a bullet face to face, but unless it's an easy shot, I'm not so good. Sometimes I wonder why you stuck with me all these years."

Irv looked at his companion. "You're cute. Besides, if you hadn't come along, I'd still be thumping low rollers for Big Angie. I offed a couple of guys, but they were accidents—lightweights who couldn't take the abuse. Then Angie would get mad at me because deadbeats who don't breathe, don't pay. You taught me everything I know. This self-confidence thing, Herm, it's time to work it out. It rips me up to see you so down on yourself."

Herm unfolded a highway map and studied it. They were eighty miles from their home in Cedar Rapids. "I liked the work. I was good at it, and I still miss it. Today is like old times; maybe we got out of the game too early. Take a right when we get to the high-way."

"If we didn't get out, we'd be dead. Eighty-one hits in twelve years, and who knows how many guys we put in the hospital. Sooner or later, somebody was going to figure out our little secret. Once they found out, we'd have been dead in a week. Like they say, we were living on borrowed time."

Herm folded his arms. "Those were some damn good days. You know, I don't feel like I'm holding up my end anymore."

"I can't believe I'm hearing the Blowtorch talk like that." Irv shook his head. "People were so afraid of you all Angelo had to do was to mention the Blowtorch, and he got whatever he wanted. I hear that Valium stuff can help a guy when he gets down. Maybe you should try it."

"All this time and you really don't know me," Herm's voice cracked. "I'm not the man you think I am. I never told you, but the whole blowtorch business was an accident. I burned off Joey Snowman's face and hands after he was dead, not before. Without a face or fingerprints, nobody should have been able to identify him. There must be thousands of dentists in Cook County. Who'd a thought, the cops would visit 'em all?"

Irv sighed. "Shut it off, Herm. It's no big deal, so what if that pile of blubber Angie told the losers he'd have you burn 'em if they don't go along. We saved our money and got out of that life. Now we live in a big Victorian house in Cedar Rapids, have season tickets to the symphony, and sell antiques. We're livin' the dream, and if you'd just pick your chin up off the floor, you'd learn to appreciate it."

"I'd like to pull off one more score like you just did. One that involves me."

When Irv didn't answer, Herm looked back out the window at barbed wire fences, telephone poles, and the occasional woodlot. When you threw in a farmstead or two, the Iowa countryside made for a pleasant enough drive. His feeling of contentment didn't last. When the pickup halted at a stop sign, the dust that had been trailing behind the pickup caught up with them.

Irv raised his hand to his mouth and coughed. "These gravel roads. I don't know how the people out here can stand it. I can taste the dust, and look at the truck, it's covered."

Herm peered through the grimy windshield. "Turn right onto the blacktop. We'll go to a carwash tomorrow and vacuum out too. Right now, we want to look as dusty as every other truck out here."

As the truck picked up speed, the worst of the offending dust blew off the glass. Smooth blacktop replaced rutted gravel, the quality of the ride improved, and with it, Irv's disposition. "That had to be the easiest ten grand in history."

"I still can't believe it," said Herm. "Ten big ones for whacking a farmer."

"I guess the guy was a tightwad who owns four farms. He worked his son-in-law like a slave and wouldn't let him buy new equipment. There's just the one girl, so they're in line to inherit the works. Sonny Boy finally got tired of waitin' for the old guy to kick off. That's why it had to be today. He and his wife have a bullet-proof alibi. They're at something called a cattle congress with a neighbor who's a deputy sheriff."

A tear rolled down Herm's cheek. "I shouldn't have to ask you about the job, Irv. We used to share everything. This was a big decision, and I wasn't part of it. You just tell me we're doing the hit, and that's that. It's always been about us, but this one feels like it's about you. Why'd you take the job? We agreed we were done."

His face set in a frown, Irv didn't respond.

Herman began to sob. "You've been shutting me out. It's over, isn't it?"

His face the picture of misery, Irv turned to Herm. "It's not like that. I don't know how to say it because your trust means more to me than anything. You've been so upset lately, and the stress just got to me. I hope you can forgive me, but one thing led to another, and in a moment of weakness, I—"

"Don't say it, Irv. I can't take it. After everything we've been through ... I'll die. I'll just die."

"I lost the money for our place in the Bahamas in the commodities market, all of it."

"That's all?"

Nearly in tears himself, Irv looked at his partner. "I went in over my head on pork bellies. I'll never eat bacon again."

Herman put a hand on Irv's shoulder. "Don't worry, Big Guy. It's okay."

"I took the job because I wanted to make it up to you. You've been down so long and wanted that vacation home in the worst way. The money from the hit makes up for half the loss."

"You could never let me down. You didn't need to do this, I know much you wanted to walk away from that life."

"The deal just fell into my lap."

Herm re-folded the map. "It's good, Irv. We'll earn the money back eventually. That's our motel down the street. Think about it, ten grand for picking off an old man. These Iowa people are sure nutty about their farms."

Irv pulled into the center lane and flipped his turn signal. "Good thing for us they don't know anything about antiques. I wish you'd let me sell that secretary's desk we picked up last month."

"That desk is prime Eastlake. The best I've seen, and we'll never find anything like it again. You know how I love Eastlake. Tell you what, sell the fainting couch, I'm tired of it."

Irv steered the F-100 into the deserted Howard Johnson's parking lot and backed up to a horse trailer. "I'm glad you're ready to let go of it. The color isn't right for the drapes and a fainting couch is an easy sell. Let's get this trailer hooked up and get on with our buying trip."

Herm put his hand on the door handle and smiled at Irv. "I really get pumped when we go on these road trips. After we're finished in Dubuque, let's head over to Wisconsin. That dealer in Mineral Point might have some more of that dreamy Roseville."

"That's more like it Herm. Think about happy things instead of mooning around. After we pick up that Tiffany lamp at Elkhart Lake, we'll have a nice dinner at the Osthoff and head down to Bellevue.

And I have a surprise for you. Marty Efferding called yesterday and said she might have a fancy Victorian coffin for us. Says it's shaped like a mummy case."

"Oh, we gotta buy it," Herm said as he pushed the door open. "Ever since I joined the American Association for Gravestone Studies I've been fascinated by mortuary antiques. No normal person is gonna buy a coffin and working the freak trade would be fun." After exiting the truck, he walked to the back of the vehicle to direct Irv toward the hitch.

Irv reversed and stopped at Herm's hand signal, then got out to help position the trailer tongue over the hitch ball. "Marty says the thing's probably a hundred years old and might be as fancy a box as they made back then. She hasn't seen it, but the guy who has it says it's shaped like a mummy case and has vines and drapery cast into it. I guess there's a little window, so you can look at the dead person's face. Angie would buy something weird like that in a heartbeat."

Herm cranked the hitch down onto the ball. "Too bad we can't go back to Chicago to sell it to him. A little window where you can see the dead person's face, that's so sick. He'd have loved it."

"Funny," said Irv as he fastened the safety chain. "All our years together, and I find out you blowtorched Joey Snowman after he bought it. I wonder if Angie knew and started the story just to scare people."

"I wish now that I torched the Snowman when he was alive, but it never occurred to me. Being the meanest guy in Chicago, now that woulda been something to be proud of. I always wanted to be the best at something, but here I am, fifty-two years old and still a nobody."

Irv shook his head. "You're somebody to me, Herm. Besides, running the most successful hit operation in the city's history is a big deal."

Herm looked at Irv morosely. "You're just trying to cheer me up. I bet Capone had solo guys who did that many in five years."

"Not the same. It was easy in the old days. Jeez, when you give me those puppy eyes, it breaks my heart. You're retired, Herm. All that doesn't make any difference now."

"It does to me."

7

Russell Jameson looked out at the placid Mississippi from his aluminum-framed lawn chair and sipped a late-morning Budweiser. Playing hooky at age sixty felt as good as it did when he was twelve, but if his congregation had any idea he'd substituted a bachelor week on the river for his annual minister's retreat in Texas, there'd be hell to pay. A week at St. Paul's Retreat House in Arlington, Texas, or a week in a trailer at Shady Haven Court in Bellevue, Iowa, did it really make any difference? One hundred fifty miles away from his congregation and traveling on his own dime, the distinction seemed small.

Russ jumped as a voice interrupted his reverie. "Hey Russ, thanks for the fish. We're having people over for a fry up tonight, and you're invited."

Relieved the speaker didn't belong to his congregation, Russ relaxed. A shirtless druggist named Mel ducked under the awning and settled into a vacant chair.

"Great offer, Mel. I haven't started the car in four days and was afraid I'd have to go to the store for canned goods. Beans, fried canned potatoes, and fish, I could live on that for a month. The only motor I want to deal with is an outboard, and the only sound I want to hear is a bass flopping in the bottom of the boat."

Ah-oo-gah, ga-ga-oo-gah. A horn blared over the water as a flat-bottom boat approached the nearby dock. A beer in one hand, an unsteady figure stood on the watercraft's generous front deck with outstretched arms, apparently moaning from a case of abdominal pain.

Russ spoke first. "What the heck's that noise, and what's he doing?"

Mel laughed. "Sounds like the horn from a Model A Ford, and I think he's trying to sing."

Oo-gah. The klaxon wailed, and as the boat touched the dock, the swaying figure in the bow nearly tumbled into the water. The driver laid off the horn and cut the motor, allowing Russ to listen as the star of the show bellowed like a bull with his equipment caught in a barbed wire fence.

> *Oh, bury me not, on the lone prairie*
> *Just sink my bones in the Mississippi*
> *Down in the mud, where the turtles play*
> *I'll sleep in my coffin as cold as the clay.*

The singer repeated his four-line ditty while his companion tied off the boat. The task complete, the men exited the watercraft, paused to roll their hip boots to their knees, and strode down the walkway to the shore. After a brief pause to take in their surroundings, the pair made a beeline for Russell's trailer.

Russ watched them approach. "Hip boots and a straw hat with golf tees on it. There's a combination you don't see every day."

"And I felt bad about not wearing a shirt," quipped Mel.

Still trying to take it all in, Russ watched as a half dozen of his neighbors, curious about the noise, made for his trailer. They were still arriving when the boat's pilot stopped outside the awning and announced, "We found an old coffin down on Bowman's Island and brought 'er back in the boat with us. Must'a floated down the river. Hank here got a little excited, so I gave him a beer to calm him down."

More than one, thought Russ as he looked at the speaker's tottering companion.

"You gotta see this thing," the pilot continued. "Must be a hundred years old and looks like one of them fancy mummy cases you see on television." He gestured toward the boat while eying Russ's six-pack cooler. "Course, Hank drank up my share, what with worrying about dead bodies, ghosts and all."

The guy in the golf-tee hat chimed in, "You don't look none too steady yourself, Blackie. A little beer would settle you right on down."

Mel burst out laughing. "You guys are good. What do you think, Russ? They deserve a beer?"

Russ wasn't sure that he wanted to encourage the pair, but then again, he didn't have anything better to do. He reached into his cooler and retrieved two cans of Schlitz—no sense giving them the Budweiser. Extracting just a bit more pleasure from the situation, he paused before handing them their beverages. "I'm a minister, boys. You two gonna be in church on Sunday?"

Blackie raised his eyes on the heavens. "I'll be there. On my soul, Reverend. On my soul."

"Me too." Hank crossed his heart. "Right there in the pew next to Blackie."

"I expect no less," Russ replied. "Just promise you won't sing when it's time for hymns."

The remark brought a round of laughter. Russ smiled and almost felt guilty about the cheap beer. His fishing retreat had done much to restore his tattered soul. He hadn't enjoyed himself so much since seminary. After handing over the Schlitz, he picked up his Bud and raised the can to Blackie and Hank.

"That was a good one, guys," said Mel, "but a lot of work for a free beer."

"Not as much as haulin' a coffin out of the mud and gettin' it up into the boat," Blackie replied.

"I nearly busted a gut," complained Hank. "Cast iron ain't light. On top of that, the darn thing is startin' to smell a bit. I'm gonna have nightmares for a month."

Russ looked at his companions and then back to the newcomers. "Wait, there's really a coffin?"

Water still dripped from Blackie's boat and trailer as Hank leaned against the fender of the pickup. His pipe in his mouth, he struck a farmer's match against the zipper of his fly. It flared, and he raised the matchstick to his pipe. Five or six puffs later, the tobacco caught.

Seeing Marty Efferding last night unsettled him. It had been ten years since their affair, and though he saw her often enough, sometimes she really got to him. He'd been a confirmed bachelor wanting nothing more than to spend his life on the river, hunting and fishing, chasing the sunrise, and enjoying the occasional woman who wandered into his life. Then she came along and spoiled it all.

He'd fallen and fallen hard. The trouble was, she hadn't. When she let him down, she left him low. So low, he shut himself up in his trailer and missed most of a season on the river. So low, he married the first woman who'd have him even though he didn't love her. His wife was a good enough woman; she had to be to put up with him. But to this day, he'd change everything and anything in his life to be back with Marty again.

He swatted a mosquito. Smoking a pipe was supposed to keep the little boogers away. Whoever made up that fairy tale must have spent his life inside. And now Marty's cousin, pretty boy Cletus Efferding, was back in town. Everybody was talking about it. How he left town after he drove his wife to suicide. Those Efferdings sure knew how to make people miserable.

When they brought Marty home to live with them, she wanted to fit in so bad she asked to have her name changed from Hillman to Efferding. Not that it helped any. No matter what she did, it was never good enough. The Efferdings rode her and picked at her until they made her crazy. Made it so she could never trust anyone, even a man who loved her.

Hank sighed. He'd been so distracted he'd let his pipe go out. Taking another match from the box, he moved to strike it on his zipper, about the only way you could get the dang things to light when you got a bad box.

"Playing with yourself again, Hankie?" Blackie had rounded the corner of the garage, accompanied by his son Terry and carrying a six-pack.

Hank groaned inwardly. Schlitz on the boat this morning, Schlitz with those guys down at the dock, and now Schlitz to ride around Bellevue. Didn't anybody in this town drink Pabst?

"Terry's gonna drive us," Blackie announced. "Normal-wise, I don't worry about drivin' and havin' a few. But drinking beer, pullin' a boat with a coffin in it, and honkin' an oo-gah horn is a damn good way to lose your license. Ain't that right, Terry?"

Terry didn't answer. Hank wasn't surprised by his silence. Unlike his old man, the kid didn't know how to have fun. Maybe he still felt bad because his ma didn't take him with her after the divorce. The boy needed to buck up and realize how lucky he was to have a dad with a sense of adventure.

Blackie looked from Terry to Hank and shifted the six-pack to his other arm. "Between the two of you, I don't know which one looks grouchier." He glared at Hank. "It was your idea, Hankie. This is supposed to be fun."

"I still don't see why we had to load that damned thing back in the boat and pretend we just discovered it," Hank complained.

"Because it's a better story. People wanna be in on things that are fresh, not when they're a day old. Didn't you have fun this morning?"

"Yeah, but we were up late last night, and now I'm getting a headache."

"Only one solution for that," said Blackie, "more beer. If you start in the morning, you gotta keep at it."

"Guess you're right," Hank sighed. "Don't know what came over me."

As if what came over him wasn't Marty Efferding. Ten long years, and he still couldn't kick it.

"Okay, Terry. Now here's the deal. Hank and me are gonna ride back in the boat with the coffin. You drive up Front Street, and whenever you hear us toot the oo-gah horn, stop. We'll show people the coffin, and when we're done, we'll honk again, and you can drive on."

Terry stared at his feet. "Sure," he said.

"Then when you get past the lock and dam, turn over onto Second Street and drive down to the newspaper office. We're gonna get our picture in the newspaper."

Terry looked back up. "Correction. You're gonna get your picture in the newspaper. Leave me out of it."

Hank wondered if Blackie noticed his son's lack of enthusiasm. He doubted it, but hey, whether he liked it or not, it would do the kid good. Terry needed to wise up and enjoy life.

Blackie shoved a beer in Hank's face. "Ready Hank? Bottoms up and chug-a-lug."

Hank emptied the can. The stuff wasn't so bad if you swallowed so fast you couldn't taste it. He tossed the empty container in the driveway.

Blackie handed him another. "Into the boat, and let's get the show on the road."

Hank climbed into Blackie's boat and sat on the bow platform. His friend stowed the remaining beer in a bait box and took up position behind the casket.

"Bottoms up," cried Blackie. While he and Blackie chugged, Terry cautiously pulled out of the driveway. Half-lit and prepared for glory, Hank sang of coffins as Blackie tested the oo-gah horn.

Standing outside the Herald-Leader office later that afternoon, Hank smiled yet again, as the photographer called out, "One last shot." He'd lost count, but Hank estimated Tom was on his sixth last shot. Between buddy-buddy photos with Blackie and pictures of the coffin and boat, the guy shot more than two rolls of film.

"Well Blackie, Hank, that just about wraps it up. I've got as many pictures as I need and almost enough notes to do the story. I'd like to be there when you turn the box in. It'll make for a nice wrap-up."

Hank took an involuntary step sideways as he looked at the photographer in disbelief. "Turn it in? The fun's just getting started. We're gonna have Terry park it outside Portz's Tavern and drink for free until suppertime."

"You guys look pretty well-oiled already."

"Only on the outside, Photographer Tom," said Blackie. "Only on the outside. The noontime crowd at the Bronco Inn got pretty generous buying us rounds. But Portzie's is gonna be a different story. It'll be full of farmers from Springbrook. Tight as ticks. They lose a buck at cards and whine the rest of the night. No-sir-ee, Bob. We're gonna insist on mixed drinks if they wanna see a genuine antique coffin. Why—"

Bwee-oop! A single blast of a whooper and flashing lights announced the arrival of the town's police car. A tall, uniformed officer exited the vehicle. A shorter dark-haired man wearing a navy-blue sport shirt and gray slacks followed. The officer gestured toward the trailer with his thumb, "Looks like a coffin there in the boat."

"It looks like a coffin because it is," replied Blackie. "We dug it outta the sand on Bowman's Island. Probably floated down the river."

"We have a complaint that you've been driving around town with a coffin scaring little kids to death."

Blackie's face darkened. Hank knew the look and jumped in to defuse the situation. "Good to see you, Wiley. Workin' days, huh? We were parked outside the Bronco, and some kids wanted to see it, so we lifted the tarp and showed it to 'em. We didn't tell any boogeyman stories. You know how kids are. They probably scared themselves talking about it later."

Blackie put his hands on his hips and pushed his chin forward. "Since when is it a crime to show somebody a coffin? Not a law on the books says you can't. You know that as well as me, Wiley McCard."

Wiley adjusted his sunglasses and put his hands on his hips. "I also know when somebody's been drinkin,' Blackie, and you and Hank are two and a half sheets to the wind."

"Well, we ain't three sheets, and we ain't drivin'. Terry here is our chauffer and ain't touched a drop. Ain't that right Terry?"

"I'm driving, Wiley," said Terry.

Wiley looked unimpressed. "OK boys, here's the deal. The chief told me in no uncertain terms that when I find you, I am to seize the coffin." He pointed his thumb at his companion in the Izod shirt. "You know Ray Gallagher here. He'll take possession of the casket and keep it until the county medical examiner makes his investigation on Monday."

Blackie hooked his thumbs in his belt and jutted his chin. "I know my rights. The coffin is mine by the Law of Salvage. You can't take it without a warrant."

"I don't know anything about the Law of Salvage, and I don't have a warrant. But if I have to get one, the chief's not gonna be happy about it. Unless you guys can prove that it's empty and you didn't steal the thing, there's gonna be an investigation. You don't want him mad at you if it comes to that."

"Wiley," said Hank, "you know we didn't rob any grave. I can show you the spot where we pulled it out. We're just taking it around town to have a little fun. How about we take it to Ray after supper?"

"Shut your mouth, Hankie Steines," snapped Blackie. "We're fifty-fifty on this, and you can't give my piece away—not unless you wanna saw the damn thing in half."

Hank sighed. "We had our fun, just let Ray have it."

Blackie removed his cap with a flourish, bowed to Wiley, and as he straightened, almost lost his balance. "Officer, with all undue respect, I insist on my legal rights under the Law of Salvage. Possession is nine points of the law. To release my personal property to you would weaken my claim to the item in question."

"You're quite the lawyer," Wiley replied. "You've got two options: deliver the casket to Ray Gallagher now, or I run you and Hank in for public drunkenness and disturbing the peace. While you're cooling your heels, I'll get a warrant and seize the coffin, your truck, your boat, and your trailer as evidence relevant to the investigation of a crime. It'll be a month before you see them again."

Blackie tipped his head back, raised his right arm, and pointed an index finger into the air. "I insist on my God-given rights under Common Law, the Declaration of Independence, and the Constitution of the United States of America."

Terry rolled his eyes. "Shut up, Dad. You lost."

"Your boy's a smart one," added Hank as he watched Terry head for the truck.

Blackie nearly fell as he climbed up onto the trailer and into the boat. "I insist on my—"

"Where do you want me to take it, Ray?" asked Terry as he craned his head out the driver side window. "The funeral home?"

"I don't want that rusty hunk of junk anywhere near the home. Take it to the alley behind my furniture store and back up to the garage door."

Blackie called out to his son, "Terry, don't forget when you back the trailer you have to turn the wheel in the opposite direction from normal."

"I know, Dad."

"Kid thinks he knows everything," Blackie muttered as Terry started the truck and pulled away.

Hank watched as an unsteady Blackie stood in the boat, gesticulating and shouting to a passing couple, "I insist on my rights under the—"

A passing feed truck drowned out his diatribe.

Randy Roeder

8

"Here you go, Cletus."

"Thanks, Loretta."

I stared in happy anticipation at the skillet-browned potato patty and slab of fried meatloaf. Only in Bellevue would the combination earn billing as the special of the day. I'd arrived at the Riverview Hotel late for lunch and almost missed the dish that said "hometown" to me as much as any other. The hotel had been serving it since time immemorial, and given the place dated back to the 1860s, that might have been a long time indeed.

My relationship with the eatery dated all the way back to junior high. My folks didn't want me hanging out there because they worried about the bad influence of the pinball machine near the front window. "Pinball machines teach young people how to gamble," my mother lectured, and as a result, the hotel became the image of sin incarnate and the place I longed to be. The guys I ran around with heard that professional women stopped there from time to time to dispense their erotic favors. The rumor fueled our adolescent imaginations, and we began referring to the establishment as the "Whoretel," wishing desperately we might lose our innocence in one of the rooms at the top of the stairs.

Alas, I fear our imaginations had gotten the best of us. As I grew older, I came to understand the operation's business model depended on the sport fishermen and vacationers stopping by to enjoy the splendors of the Mississippi. The realization that a traveling hooker would have to be brain damaged to set up shop in downtown Bellevue remains to this day a significant marker on the path to my adulthood.

My fishing companions would be joining me tonight at the Log Cabin Motel down in Fishville. They were renting the two-bedroom unit next to mine, and we intended to share a fire pit and outdoor table.

Lumir Sedlak, Eddie Brada, and I were as unlikely a group of friends as you'd expect to meet. I haven't fished in over two decades. Lumir doesn't fish much but enjoys working wood with traditional hand tools. He'd recently turned seventy-five. Eddie, a few days short of twenty-one, lives for hunting and fishing. He had just turned fifteen when Lumir discovered the young man's parents spent more time drinking and gambling than they did with their son. He stepped in to provide Eddie with the guidance that got the boy through the shoals of a rocky adolescence. They've been friends ever since.

I snarfed my meatloaf and potato patty and considered another helping, but asked Loretta for a piece of rhubarb pie instead. Gossip had it that she'd served lunch at the hotel since the first World War, but I didn't buy it. She didn't look a day over sixty.

Halfway through my pie, I heard the bleat of a Model A horn out on the street. One of the customers went outside to investigate and came back in with the news that Blackie Stiles and Hank Steines were parked outside displaying a coffin they found on an island south of town. Half the room left to investigate, but the fishermen's find didn't excite me. Weird stuff washes up along the river all the time.

I checked the notice board on my way out of the dining room. Apparently, Butch Scholtes had some calves to sell, and Goose Roling wanted to buy walnut logs. We'd missed the Volunteer Firemen's pancake breakfast last week, but an adjacent notice for an upcoming auction proved more interesting.

Helen Nicholson had classified her last book and passed on to the other side. A friendly, intelligent woman, she'd presided over the town library for decades and lived across the street from the house where I grew up. As I scanned the auction bill, I spied a line mentioning "two antique carpenter's chests, filled with tools." Since they'd scheduled the auction for tomorrow, I'd bring the sale to Lumir's attention tonight. He bought more old tools than he could ever use, but for some reason, he bristled if I referred to him as a collector.

I picked up the Nova and drove west. I'd expected a trip back to my old stomping grounds would help me accept the loss of my wife and kids. It didn't. Yesterday's stop in Maquoketa and my evening at the spot where Myra drowned herself had done nothing for my peace of mind. I fiddled with the radio until I found KMAQ, the local country station. In twenty-five minutes, I'd be back in Maquoketa, with no plan for what I'd do when I arrived.

Except I did. The Nova didn't pick an itinerary and drive me there. A destination had been in the back of my mind since morning. Unable or unwilling to control myself, I found myself driving toward the Hinkley house, the place where my children lived with a woman they called Mom, the woman who had erased Myra and me from their lives.

I got there, slowed, and took a long look as I drove by. I didn't know what I expected to see—maybe the kids out on the lawn, Tammy having an afternoon tea party with friends or Mikey tossing a basketball through a hoop in the driveway. I didn't see a soul, but the house looked nice. Brute and Velma had kept it up.

My emotions started to get the better of me, so I turned onto a side street and parked. Ten minutes later, I had myself back under control and rounded the block. I'd pass the house one more time, and that would be it. Spying on the kids felt creepy.

About to pull out, I saw a boy on a bike pedaling down the street in the direction of the Hinkleys' as fast as he could go. It had to be Mikey. The kid had Myra's hair and looked to be the right age, but of course, he'd be Mike now. Getting his learner's permit next year, and after that, girls and dating. No doubt about it, my boy could handle a bike. When he rode by the house without so much as looking, my heart fell to the floor.

A sigh passed my lips, leaving me as shriveled as a balloon from last week's birthday party. I pulled away from the stop sign defeated, a lonely, irrational wreck bent on intruding into his children's lives. If a nutcase is somebody who doesn't understand his actions, my behavior didn't speak well for my mental health. Shaking like a leaf, I drove to the first tavern past the courthouse and made for the door.

The décor wasn't much. Dilapidated plywood booths lined a wall covered with standard-issue black paint. A narrow aisle divided the box-like accommodations from a row of un-upholstered stools bordering a bar with a grimy Formica top. The place didn't have a kitchen, so the couple sharing a pizza must have made do with one of those frozen jobs fresh from the microwave. After my delicious fried meatloaf and potato patty lunch, the thought of nuked food didn't appeal to me, so I opted for a bar stool.

My presence brought the resident population to three, four if you counted the guy polishing a glass behind the tappers. I ordered a Pabst and slumped over it when it arrived, the do-not-disturb posture of drinkers the world over.

Getting hammered doesn't help when I'm down. It had taken some hard lessons, but sometime around age forty, I finally made the connection. Not there to get smashed, I hoped a quiet seat, a little peace, and a beer or two might help me get a grip on myself.

Halfway through my second glass, things began to get clearer. I knew Velma Hinkley. My former mother-in-law wasn't the brightest woman in the county, but she had smarts enough to take good care of the kids and a good heart to boot. Misguided she might be, but I had no doubt she loved Mike and Tammy. As much as I might not like it, my shrink had it right. I needed to stay out of their lives until they were eighteen. No more driving past the house, no more trying to sneak a peek, no attempt to say hello.

I finished my beer and didn't want a third, so I reached for my wallet. Instead of making a quick and easy trip to the cash compartment, my fingers strayed to the photo section. The only picture in it was one of Myra, taken when we were dating. The plastic compartment facing it contained a newspaper clipping. I pulled it out and unfolded it. If I'd done it once, I'd done it two hundred times, but despite the care I lavished on it, this time the paper separated along the crease. I lined the pieces up on the bar, looking at the grainy photo that was more dots than image and read the text beneath.

Michael Hinkley, aged ten, smiles as he receives his Webelos badge from den mother Ronda Easton. His parents Brutus and Velma Hinkley and his sister Tamara, stand in the background.

"Another example of the way I manage to destroy everything I touch," I muttered to myself.

"You say something, Mister?" the bartender asked. "My hearing ain't what it used to be."

"Sorry, I need to learn to speak up. How much?"

"That'll be one-eighty."

I carefully returned the fragments to my billfold. Small-town papers are noted for covering the mundane, but eight years of subscribing to the weekly *Jackson County Sentinel* had yielded just this one snippet. I put two dollars on the bar and walked out into the blinding sunlight.

The woman behind the counter adjusted her glasses. "You're lucky we're slow today, I have time to help."

After I'd left the bar, I didn't feel like driving back to Bellevue and didn't need the upset of a return trip to Myra's unmarked grave. I walked instead to the county courthouse to see if they had a record of my Grandpa Efferding's first marriage. My parents didn't talk much about the founder of Efferding's Menswear. He died before I was born.

It didn't occur to me to ask about him when I was younger, and now with the folks dead, I didn't have a source of information. A vague recollection of visitors stopping by the house when I was a kid, speaking in hushed voices about "his other wife" and how "he used to be a Catholic," left me with the impression there was much I didn't know.

"If you want a certified copy of the record, the fee is five dollars. If you don't need anything official, and I can put the volume on our copy machine without damaging it, the charge is just a dime."

"I don't need a copy, the names and dates are just fine," I replied.

She grabbed a piece of paper and removed the pencil from behind her ear. "And the name is?"

"August Efferding."

"There's a name you don't see every day. Could you spell it for me?"

I did and watched as she wrote it out. Her coral red nail polish matched the color of her lipstick. Normally I don't care for bright red lips, but hers looked nice. I didn't mean to make eye contact but did. We both looked down. My chest buzzed. I could see she felt it too, but the ring on her finger meant it wasn't going anywhere.

She looked up. "Do you have an idea of the year? Each of our indexes covers a decade."

I took a step back, didn't let my eyes focus. "Sometime between 1870 and 1890. There may have been more than one marriage."

She smiled, apparently enjoying our connection. Some people like the buzz, and I'm one of them, but the roller coaster I'd been on today left me in a bad state. One more eye lock and I'd end up making a stupid pass. One she hadn't bargained for, one I'd regret.

"Three indexes, that'll take about fifteen minutes. Have a seat," she said. Her scent hung in the air as she disappeared into the back room.

Still keyed up from my drive by the Hinkley house, I spent the time thinking about the kids. One thing I could do for them would be to make it easy to learn about the side of the family they'd never known. Though they might not want the information when they turned eighteen, sooner or later, it would mean something to them.

My clerk came back more quickly than anticipated. "Found it," she announced bringing a heavy leather-bound volume over to the counter. She turned it to face me and pointed to the record. "August Efferding and Gertrude Meyer, September 3rd, 1876, married by M. T. Shiffmacher, a Catholic priest."

I bent over to look at the record. She didn't step back. Determined to avoid looking at her face as I straightened up, my eyes landed on her neck. She had short hair, and I could see the pulse beating just above her collarbone. As I leaned back, she tilted her head and a dangling earring came to rest against the soft skin of her neck.

I stepped back again, at least two feet from the counter. "Thanks for the help, but this isn't the one. I'd heard Grandpa had another wife and maybe she was Catholic."

She gave me the hundred-watt, full-blown smile. Damn it! Eye contact again. Eyeliner with two shades of shadow and blush on the cheeks.

"Well, I guess that's that," I said.

She gave me the hundred-watt again. "There could be more to this, you know."

The lady was killing me. "I don't see how."

"Way back when, fire damaged some of the courthouse records. It happened before they wrote up the indexes, so not every marriage was included. If your grandfather's other marriage took place in a church, you could check there. They may have the records."

"Thanks, I just might just do that."

I stumbled down the hall and out of the building. I hate it when a woman who is unavailable does that to me. I just hate it.

I heard my friends Lumir and Eddie pull up to their cabin before I saw them. They must have had the truck's windows down, for the sound of Frankie Yankovic's accordion preceded them. Lumir didn't hear as well as he once did and liked his music loud. Unlike Lumir, Yankovic was not Czech, but my friend liked his music and considered him an honorary member of the brotherhood.

Lumir believed the eight-track tape player in Eddie's pickup ranked as the seventh wonder of the modern world, and in happy anticipation of the fishing trip, had purchased a three-volume set entitled *All-Time Polka Greats* for the ride over. Poor Eddie. Though of Czech descent, his idea of good music involved concert recordings of rock bands like Deep Purple. The ninety-minute trip from Cedar Rapids must have felt like a lifetime.

I helped them unpack and get their gear stowed. Since my companions had planned to arrive late in the day, they'd delegated the Friday night meal prep to me. I left them to their own devices while I put foil-wrapped potatoes into the coals of the fire I'd started earlier. As the heavenly smell of baked beans with bacon, brown sugar, and molasses drifted from my cabin window, I began oiling the lovely twelve-ounce rib-eye steaks I'd brought with me from Cedar Rapids. The task complete, I popped them on the grate, spread the plastic cover on the forest-green picnic table, and put out the plates and utensils.

The meal didn't disappoint. By the time we'd pushed our plates back and polished off a six-pack, twilight had set in. To my surprise and delight, I discovered that Lumir and I would have the morning to ourselves while Eddie scouted locations to set our trotlines tomorrow evening.

"We'll want to set the lines in the pools below the wing dams," Eddie explained. "I'll be looking for the ones where the catfish congregate in weather like this."

"Wing dams?" asked Lumir. "I have not yet heard of these wing dams."

I had to smile. Though born in the United States, Lumir spoke with a Czech accent. "Underwater rows of rocks that the government put in in the 1930s," I replied. "They help keep the channel clear."

Eddie drained his can of Milwaukee's Best and announced, "I won't need you guys until late tomorrow afternoon when we get the trotlines ready. Clete, where can we seine minnows?"

"Seine minnows?" I asked.

Eddie smiled and continued, "We're running a hundred ninety-five hooks tomorrow night. We have to seine. Nobody can afford that many minnows."

"I've been away from here a long time," I replied. "Some of the guys used to seine the riffles behind the Dyas Mill. We could try there."

Eddie stretched and yawned. "I worked a double shift and running on four hours' sleep. Tomorrow's a big day. Time to turn in."

Lumir got up to join him. "It has been a big day, Clete. Get me for breakfast, and we will go to that auction you told me about."

Age had started to get to Lumir. Five years ago, we'd have been drinking coffee and playing double solitaire until one in the morning. Though I hated to see him growing older, he remained vital and fit, and truth be told, my habit of staying up late owed more to frequent catnaps than any inherent stamina. Certain I'd go to bed with the chickens at Lumir's age, I doubted I'd have anywhere near his energy.

I could understand Eddie's exhaustion. A double shift snatching guts at Wilson Packing would be enough to knock anybody back. Eddie worked like a dog, taking as many hours as he could get and then spending his paycheck freely. The unionized plant's high wages allowed him the luxury of a new pickup, fishing boat, and trailer. While I'm sure he made monthly payments on all of them, the rig represented an impressive achievement for a twenty-year-old.

My wristwatch read 10:30 by the time I finished cleaning up the dishes. With my friends asleep, I'd have to come up with my own recreation. Though the sign in the courtyard advertised "Free TV," watching television was out of the question. The clunker in my cabin got one channel, and even that was snowy. Not ready to turn in, I fired up the Nova and made for the bar at the Riverview Hotel. Though old enough to know better than to expect it filled with cheap and wanton women, the possibility of chatting up an old acquaintance or two had its allure—assuming, of course, that time had dimmed the memories of my infamous past.

9

I'd been at the horseshoe-shaped bar for forty-five minutes, long enough to realize the barstools on either side of me were going to remain vacant. Not that I recognized everyone in the room, but something like half the faces looked familiar. I couldn't place the barmaid or waitress, but the customers who recognized me did their best to avoid eye contact. I'd have left after my first beer but for my interest in the person sitting directly opposite me on the horseshoe.

His face sporting a three-day growth and his body grease-stained coveralls, Canker DeCook was whooping it up with a couple of friends. He looked every bit the loser I remembered. Drunk, mean, and hanging out with lowlifes even drunker and meaner, the guy who torched the beautiful lodge on the state park bluff hadn't troubled to bathe or put on clean clothes before stepping out on a Friday night. He and his buddies spilled as much beer as they drank and repeatedly bumped into the customers on the stools next to them.

"That was some fart, Canker," one of his companions roared.

Canker slapped him on the back. "There's more where that came from," he snorted, and from the look on his face and reaction of his associates, I realized he'd managed to repeat his earlier effort.

I looked at the vacant stools on each side of me. I hadn't donned a jacket and tie, but I'd showered and put on a fresh shirt before going out for the night. Canker DeCook looked, and probably smelled, like he'd crawled out of a trash can. While I sat quietly at the bar, Canker spilled beer, noisily passed gas, and jostled those next to him. Despite his oafish behavior, the hotel's customers tolerated him, while they viewed me as an outcast because my wife had taken her life a decade ago. Time to leave.

About to re-enter my eight-year-old car, I noticed a late-model pickup across the street. So well-scrubbed it gleamed, its lavish chromium trim gave testimony to a major effort to deplete the mines in South Africa. Not my style, but nice wheels indeed. The fly in the ointment was the lettering on the door: C. A. DeCook, Contracting and Grading. The contrast between the tidy vehicle and the slimeball in the hotel bar could not have been greater.

It didn't take a genius to realize Canker's pickup had never been anywhere near a construction site. The lettering on its door told me he'd elected to charge the expense of the purchase and maintenance of his personal toy to his business. The gleaming hot-wax job, the chrome spotlights and winch, the oversized tires and wheels—all subsidized by tax breaks from the federal and state governments, breaks unavailable to me due to the nature of my career.

I'd just depressed the door latch on my rusted-out Chevy when the injustice of it got to me. Sure, I'd inherited a nice chunk of change from my spinster Aunt Millie, but I'd been responsible and invested it in trust funds for my children, kids I couldn't visit. As a result, I still lived in a one-bedroom apartment and maintained an "until death do us part" relationship with an increasingly unreliable vehicle. Meanwhile, Canker DeCook, a coarse, unkempt, flatulent lowlife who torches an iconic lodge and cheats on his taxes, drives a flashy new vehicle. Worse yet, he's more socially acceptable than I am.

In a fit of anger, I crossed the street to the sidewalk opposite. After checking carefully in both directions, I reached into my pocket, extracted my car keys, and carefully arranged the two longest so that they protruded from my fingers. Starting at the front fender and pressing hard, I scored two ugly marks in the paint as I walked the length of the vehicle.

"Take that, you dirty firebug," I muttered to myself.

God, it felt good, but the damage didn't begin to satisfy my urge for revenge. I turned around and headed back in the direction from which I'd come—this time waving my hand up and down to create a pattern with ten-inch undulations. Still not happy with my efforts, I leaned over the hood and began scribing circles in the paint.

"I don't think Canker is gonna be very happy when he finds out what you did to his truck."

Caught! I nearly jumped out of my skin. Shaking like a leaf, I turned to locate the source of the voice. My cousin Marty—tight jeans, big hair, and all—materialized out the of the shadowed alley next to the Big D Supermarket. Marty, the trampy teenager whose reputation hung like a lead curtain over my adolescent years. Marty, the woman who cheated me out of the family menswear store.

"Uh . . . hi Marty. How've you been?"

With one hand on her hip and the other clutching the strap of her green shoulder bag, she looked me up and down. "Little Cletus Efferding, just look at you. What would Mama say if she knew her darling boy had grown into a middle-aged man who spent his nights sneaking around town vandalizing other people's property? Better yet, what would that ornery S.O.B. Canker say if he knew what you did to his wheels?"

Stunned that I'd been discovered, and even worse, that it had been my cousin Marty, I couldn't think of a response.

"This is the second time I've caught you with your pants down, Cletus. Do you remember the first?"

How could I forget? Memories of her barging in on me came flooding back. My tongue froze to the roof of my mouth.

"You owe me, Cletus."

Her comment got the juices flowing, and I found my voice. "I owe you? After what you did to me? Cheating me out of the store? I don't owe you a thing."

"You owe me more than you think, Mama's Boy, and you can start paying me back by buying me a drink and listening to what I have to say. Otherwise, you and your friends at the Log Cabin Motel can expect a visit from Canker and his buddies."

"Log Cabin?" I asked, "What makes you—"

"Cut it, Cletus. Everybody knows you're staying down in Fishville."

Reluctantly, I followed her around the corner to Portz's Tavern. The venue hadn't changed an iota since my last visit. In fact, the boys from Springbrook playing euchre at the back table looked identical to those who sat there a decade ago. Marty and I took seats at the bar.

"Hello, Cy," Marty said to the barman. "Cletus here is buying, and I'll have two Tequila Sunrises. I expect he's gonna have two as well. We'll be at the front table."

"Cancel that," I replied. "I don't drink spirits. I'll have a draft— Old Style."

Cy nodded, and Marty and I made for the well-worn table. I don't know why I didn't catch it earlier, but Marty had already had a few—actually, more than a few. I considered calling her bluff and walking out, but the woman was just crazy enough to tell Canker I'd tampered with his truck. I didn't feel conversational so decided to let her take the lead.

Cy brought the drinks and set them down with a flourish. "Run a tab?" he asked.

"I'll settle now," I said and paid up. I didn't plan on hanging around longer than necessary.

When Cy left, Marty downed her first Tequila Sunrise in two gulps and stared at me. "Cletus Efferding," she said, shaking her head. "Perfect little Cletus, the apple of Mommy and Daddy's eye. I used to hate you. Every day, all I heard was 'Why can't you be more like Cletus? Cletus is polite and gets good grades. Cletus helps around the house and at the store.' If I had a buck for every time I heard how wonderful you were, I'd own the town."

I didn't have a response, but then again, I don't think she expected one.

"When my mom abandoned me, I was a scared fourteen-year-old who just wanted to fit in with my new family. Louie and Joan—what kind of idiot social worker thought your parents would take good care of me? I thought I did the right thing when I asked to have my name changed to Efferding. Well, that was the biggest mistake of my life. They said it was a good idea, but little did I know when I became an Efferding, nothing I did would be good enough. 'Efferdings don't talk like that. We don't dress like that. You're an Efferding, act like one.' Over and over again, world without end. Amen."

"They took you in, Marty. They couldn't let you go to a home. What would people think?"

"What would people think? Did you hear what you just said? They didn't want me. They never wanted me. All I amounted to was an embarrassment—the snot-faced brat of a sister your dad was ashamed of. Why do you think Mom and I only visited twice in all those years? She was never good enough for her sanctimonious brother and his wife."

"Marty, you got things all wrong. Mom and Dad wanted to help you out."

"You've got your head up your ass," she snapped. "You had it there then, and you've got it there now. Help me out! All I learned from Louie and Joan is that the only thing worse than being abandoned is being taken in by people who don't want you."

I looked down at my beer and took a deep breath. Her take on what happened when she lived with us didn't square with mine, and I was tired of her beating up on the folks. They'd driven into the side of a train car at an unmarked crossing almost twenty years ago. No time for farewells. There one minute and gone the next. The loss still hurt like it happened last week.

I'd resolved to be civil, but it took every ounce of restraint I possessed. "Let's get back to why we're here. You wanted to talk about who owes who on the store. As far as I recall, you left me holding the bag."

Marty twisted one of the rings on her fingers. "I did, but it's not what you think. Right after I took over, I had a nervous breakdown … lost it completely, and I blame Louie and Joan."

I glared, and she dropped her head. "That's rich," I said. "You cheat me out of the men's store and blame it on my parents."

"It's not like you think, Cletus. About the time you left town, I fell in love and got pregnant, but he fished for a living. He wanted to marry me, asked again and again, but I said no. Not married and my belly starting to show, I felt so worthless I tried killing myself with sleeping pills. All I got out of it was a miscarriage. I couldn't stand it anymore and took every penny I could out of the store and got out of Bellevue. Six months later, a nun in Milwaukee found me shivering in an alley, and I couldn't remember anything that happened after I left town."

Marty shook with emotion. Anyone who didn't know the woman would be ready for the waterworks, but I grew up with her and recognized the emotion—rage. A human volcano, ready to blow.

"The man who loved me, the man who fathered my child, wasn't good enough for me. Where do you think I learned that? I'll tell you where—from Louie and Joan. They taught me how to be an Efferding. Well, I learned my lesson and got a dead baby out of the deal."

My anger flared. "Mom and Dad should have left you rot in some godforsaken orphanage back in Prairie du Chien. You were selfish and ungrateful then, and the years haven't changed you any. Attacking people who can't defend themselves, acting like the town tramp, cheating me out of the store . . . what's wrong with you?" I put my hand down on the table, hard. Beer sloshed out of my glass.

Marty erupted and screamed, "I had that money coming! After the way they treated me, I deserved it. Every single goddamned penny. All I ever heard is what a disappointment I was. How I'd never amount to anything—that I was a tramp like my mother."

As I looked around, I realized every head in the bar had turned to us. I didn't care and raised my voice to match hers. "You're a liar!

They took you in because you're family. They just wanted you to make something of yourself."

"Family!" she shouted. "There's not a day that goes by but that I don't thank God that you and I are the last of the Efferdings. You think I don't know about Aunt Millie? The woman's got two blood relatives on the face of the earth, and she leaves everything to you. She made sure that the lawyer sent me a copy of the will even though I didn't get a damn thing. Remember what she had him put in it, Cletus? Well, I do. 'To my niece Martha Efferding, I leave nothing. Blood will out.' Another crazy Efferding. I'm glad she's dead."

The jukebox had gone silent, I realized someone had unplugged it to better hear what we had to say. I didn't care. "Don't confuse us with Aunt Millie. You're wrong about the folks and wrong about the Efferdings. You and I are not the end of the line. I have a son and daughter."

"Thank God the Hinkleys took them," she shouted. "Maybe they'll have a chance at a decent life. You made your wife so miserable she killed herself. Do your kids a favor. Stay away from them."

And with that, she stood and tossed her second Tequila Sunrise in my face. I rose and without thinking, picked up what was left of my beer and returned the compliment. Throwing a defiant look at the gawking customers, I made for the door before she could recover. At least I had the satisfaction of being the first to leave—only a loser leaves second.

My hand on the latch, I turned to face her. "Bitch," I bellowed.

"Jerk," she sobbed.

I left her there to cry it out, and blotting tequila from my cheek, walked to the car. I should have felt victorious, but Marty's face, the picture of abject misery, wouldn't go away. As my anger began to subside, I got the sickening feeling that on some level, Marty was right. I couldn't put my finger on it, but even as a child, I understood that she and her mother were an embarrassment to us. Still, we took her in and hoped she'd improve herself. Not that it did any good. Memories of the constant bickering between Marty and my folks began playing themselves out in my mind. The scenes weren't pretty but weren't anywhere near as nasty as she made out.

Or were they? As I started the car, half-forgotten memories of the sound of a slap and my mother's voice screaming the words *tramp* and *slut* came back to me. I remembered my father shouting about shame and reputation. Though my parents never treated me with anything but love, kindness, and respect, the intensity of their reaction to Marty's shortcomings had terrified me. I remembered lying in bed the night of the big blow up, shaking and asking the man upstairs to restore our happy home. The words of my petition rushed back to me.

"Please, God, make her go away forever, and please, whatever happens, don't ever let them do that to me."

10

Sunrise found me on the Presbyterian side of the cemetery south of town, sitting on the ground, staring at my parents' headstone. My dew-soaked clothes clung to me, an unwanted second skin that looked as though it belonged to someone else. No surprise, I'd come to the grave last night after leaving Marty and hadn't returned to the cabin. Too upset to sleep, I spent the night searching for answers, but rosy glow of dawn found me with nothing but questions.

What on earth caused my parents to distance themselves from the other Efferdings? Why had they taken Marty into their home when they obviously didn't care for her or her mother? Why did Aunt Millie, unhappily absorbed in her career, choose to remain single, living with neither man nor woman?

There was too much about my family I didn't know. Over the years, I'd told myself I'd been too busy growing up to ask my father about the home he'd lived in. A convenient self-deception, but wide of the mark. My queries had not been infrequent, and my father's responses were repetitive and anything but enlightening.

"Your grandfather was a wonderful man who worked hard to build a business we could all be proud of. He loved his children, and Sunday dinners were the highlight of the week. He made good money and bought the best that Koppes Grocery had to offer. Father owned the first Oldsmobile in town, and we rode to church in style. Working with him at Efferding's Haberdashery taught me everything worth knowing. You know, I never wanted to change the name to Efferding's Menswear, but I had to keep up with the times."

After that, nothing.

Questions about my mother's family, on the other hand, elicited long stories filled with practical jokes, Sunday picnics, ne'er-do-well cousins, and a stubborn Ford that spent most of its time in the shop. She'd laugh, get misty-eyed, bring out her scrapbook and photograph album, going on so long I'd get restless. My boredom aside, I envied her carefree childhood.

Things were different for me. I started ringing up sales on Efferding's cash register as soon as I could stand on a stool to reach it. No after-school baseball for me, I swept, dusted, unpacked, folded, and wrapped every afternoon—not to mention Friday evenings and all-day Saturday. Lectures on family reputation, the necessity of sitting in the front rows at church, the importance of *Yes, sir* and *Yes, ma'am* became an integral part of my life, and heaven help me if I were ever seen on the street in a pair of blue jeans. The son of a shopkeeper, I accepted it as my lot in life and didn't mind, but it did seem strange that I was the only kid in class with his own cemetery plot.

My thrifty father presented it to me as a fourth-grade birthday present. I can't say I was impressed. We'd just finished the cake and ice cream when my father left the room and returned with a brown paper envelope for me.

"You're ten years old now, Cletus, and before long, you'll be a man. The way you help around the store, I don't know how I'd ever get along without you. If your Grandfather Efferding were alive, he'd be proud of you, but not as proud I am. Now that you're older, I'd like to give you something that lasts, not a toy that breaks and wears out in a year or two. Inside this envelope, you'll find the deed to a cemetery plot, one right next to your grandfather's. Your mom and I will be on the other side of you. Never forget, conservative, long-term investment is the key to good money management."

My mother's fork dropped, hitting the side of her plate and bouncing onto the floor.

"Gee, thanks, Dad," I stammered.

"That's your father, always looking at the big picture," said my mom as she blotted her lips with her napkin. "Louis, don't you think it's time to tell Cletus about the other part of his present?"

I might have been ten years old, but it didn't take a genius to understand there was only one answer to that question. The edge in my mom's voice would have cut glass.

My father's shirt collar must suddenly have grown tight. He put his finger inside, readjusted it, and smiled. "Of course, Dear, saving the best for last. Go ahead."

"Cletus, tomorrow you father is taking you to the Western Auto store to pick up that new bicycle you've been wanting."

Although the expression on my father's face left no doubt he hadn't been consulted, he didn't miss a beat. "A bicycle is an expensive gift, one we can barely afford, I'll need you to put in extra hours at the store."

Mom reached over, took my father's hand, and gave it a squeeze. One of her nails caught him just inside the thumb, drawing blood. "Since your father depends on you so much, it's important that you're on time. After you're done at Western Auto, he'll take you to the store, where you can pick out a wristwatch—any one you want."

My father paled. Mom might have been easy going, but you didn't mess with her.

I stared at the void between Grandpa Efferding's grave and my parents' monument, the only piece of real estate I owned. Who'd be there to mark my grave when I was gone? Marty, the cousin who already hated me before I called her a bitch in front of a room full of people? My kids, raised as Hinkleys, would they care enough to bother? Maybe it didn't make any difference. My wife Myra had a husband, parents, children, and siblings but the location of her burial remained unidentified.

Eventually, I drifted off. Perhaps Marty knew more about the family than she let on. Unreliable Marty—we'd driven each other so far apart that reconciliation seemed impossible. Was the price of a small-town men's store worth alienating the only adult member of my family? Not that it mattered. Marty and I made as unlikely a pair of candidates for friendship as ever crossed paths. No wiser than when I'd driven through the gates the night before, I left the cemetery and pointed the Nova in the direction of the cabin.

When I pulled into my graveled parking space, I saw Lumir, already awake, enjoying a cup of coffee at the picnic table. A fly swatter lay within easy reach. The picture of contentment, he looked at me with raised eyebrows as I slid out of the Nova. "You look worse than a dead man," he said as he swatted at a fly. "Coffee?"

He didn't wait for an answer but rose and headed for his cabin. I hooked a leg over the plank that served as the table's seat and plopped down opposite his steaming cup. The lack of sleep, fight with Marty, and night in the damp had taken their toll. I felt a headache coming on and wished the sparrows fighting over crumbs a few cabins away would just shut up.

As I waited for Lumir to return with a giant mug of caffeinated ambrosia, I'd reached the logical endpoint of any serious attempt at woolgathering: the sniveling pack of creatures collectively known as mankind could go to hell. They didn't deserve me. I'd buy some scrubland and move to a shack in the woods, where secure in my superiority, I'd commune with Mother Nature. The human race, add them all together, and they don't amount to a pile of cat scat.

Cradling my throbbing head in my hands, I grunted when Lumir thumped a mug of coffee on the table.

"One of these days, you must teach yourself to face the new day like a man," he lectured. "Buck up, learn not to drink so much, and get on with your life."

I wrapped my hands around the mug. "Not drinking, worse."

Lumir didn't sit, but leaned back, stretched, and proclaimed, "Not drinking? Why then, what's wrong with you is nothing a good breakfast won't cure. Look around you. It is a beautiful morning, the birds are singing, the sky is blue, and you are on vacation. It is a fine day to be alive."

"At your age, any day's a good day to be alive," I muttered.

"And that is why I enjoy them. You believe you will live forever, so you do not appreciate the time you have. One day, before you know it, you will be dead as roadkill. All the hours you spent moping will be wasted, and you will have nobody but yourself to blame."

Great, just what I needed.

"You see—" Lumir cut himself short, stooped to pick up the swatter, and flattened a fly. He levered the flat edge of the flap under the remains and flicked them off to the side.

"So goes a man's life," he continued. "One day he is the swatter, and the next, he is the fly. Now take your coffee, haul your carcass into the cabin, and get cleaned up. We have breakfast, an auction, and fishing ahead of us. The day is young."

I didn't reply but uncoiled my legs and hoisted them over the bench seat. Muttering to myself, I grabbed my coffee and trudged back to my cabin to remove the limp and grimy clothes donned with so much hope the night before. Sometimes well-adjusted friends can be a pain in the patoot. I truly love Lumir, but the guy simply cannot understand that a good portion of humanity needs to sulk. It's the way we make sense of the world.

I left the cabin a half hour later in fresh duds, showered but unshaven. I'd be damned if I was going to take the extra effort to make myself presentable for the multitudes. If not at peace with the world, I was willing to meet it a fourth of the way. Maybe.

I found Lumir waiting for me in the Nova. A straw hat pulled down over his face, his hands folded across his belly, he gently nodded his head, bopping along as Glen Campbell's "Rhinestone Cowboy" drifted from the radio. A snort escaped his lips as I opened the door. "No need to scare a man half to death," he said.

"One minute you're the swatter, the next you're the fly," I replied.

He straightened up as I got into the car. "I do not know why I waste my breath on you."

As we turned onto Front Street, an announcer let us know we were listening to "1320 on your dial, station KMAQ, Maquoketa, Iowa," and told us we wouldn't want to miss tomorrow's special edition Polka Party program. Scintillating stuff, I was about to change the station when he broke into the news report. The lead-off story caught my attention.

> *Officials in Bellevue, Iowa, remain puzzled over the discovery of a mysterious coffin reportedly pulled from the sand on an island in the Mississippi several miles south of town. Discovered by local fishermen, the ornately decorated cast iron coffin appears to be at least a century old and currently resides in secure storage at a facility maintained by the Gallagher Funeral Home.*
>
> *According to Gallagher, the coffin is a deluxe "shoulder box," wider at the shoulder than at the head and feet, that cost fifty times as much as the two-dollar wooden burial cases in common use back then. "It has the same basic shape as the mummy cases you see in museums," he explained.*
>
> *The highly decorated casket features an intact glass window located just above the location where the deceased's face would be. Years of dirt have fogged and etched the glass so that the contents, if any, are no longer visible.*
>
> *Police spokesman 'Mac' McLean says an investigation is underway, and the coffin will remain in storage until Monday, when it will be opened in the presence of representatives of the Department of Natural Resources and the Jackson County Medical Examiner. "We don't expect to find much," said McClean, "but we need to be sure the coffin is not concealing evidence of a more recent crime. We also need to be very careful. One of the experts we talked with suggested the unusual airtight coffin and its isolated location may hint at the burial of a victim of smallpox or another communicable disease.*
>
> *In other news—*

Lumir reached over and clicked off the radio. "Strange goings on in your hometown. There are many hills around here, and the area is rural. Things like this do not happen in Cedar Rapids. The situation reminds me of that hillbilly movie *Deliverance*. You know, pretty country, lots of trees, peace and quiet, but the people are strange and abnormal."

"*Deliverance*? A couple of fishermen find a coffin on an island, and suddenly we're all homicidal rednecks?" I sputtered. "What about the head at the Linn County Assessor's Office? Now that's big-city twisted."

Lumir stroked his mustache. "The head of the Assessor's Office, I do not recall. What did he do?"

My friend really needed to do something about his hearing. Lord knows I tried to convince him to get a hearing aid, but the man still went out on dates. His social life, coupled with his innate vanity and stubborn Bohemian pride, made for a hard sell. Though I argued his good looks and manly physique outweighed any effect a tiny piece of plastic might have on the fair sex, he persisted in his belief that putting one in his ear qualified him for the nursing home. I didn't have the guts to come out with the brutal truth—the primary concern of women his age was that the guy be breathing.

I spoke louder. "Not the head of the Assessor's Office, the human head somebody sent to the Assessor's Office. Remember? The *Cedar Rapids Gazette* reported on it a while back."

"I am not deaf, and of course, I remember. The poor woman who opened it mistook it for a moldy grapefruit and almost threw it away. The police eventually arrested a young man who stole it from an aboveground crypt in Marion."

I slowed to twenty-five as we entered the downtown. "And you think Bellevue people are strange? At least when we find a coffin, we don't decapitate the corpse and mail it to the assessor because we're mad about our taxes."

Lumir had a ready response. "Yes, but the situation is different. The man used the dead woman's head to make a political statement. Why, it is almost a free speech issue."

As I pulled into a metered parking spot across the street from the hotel, I realized nothing would shake my friend's belief that the citizens of Bellevue were a debased race of hillbilly ghouls. A change in the direction of the conversation appeared to be in order.

"By the way, I had the chance to see the casket yesterday but passed on it because I wasn't interested. The guys who found it were hauling it around on a boat trailer, blowing an oo-gah horn, and showing it off."

Lumir huffed. "And this is normal behavior? It is as I said, like the movie, *Deliverance*. Still, it is too bad you missed your big chance. A man does not get to see a hundred-year-old mystery coffin every day. I would like to have been there."

Apparently, showing off an antique burial case indicated a sordid backwoods degeneracy, but gawking at one was okay. I switched off the ignition, happy we'd soon be inside discussing the menu.

11

We arrived for the Helen Nicholson auction nearly an hour and a half in advance because Lumir wanted to "look around." He immediately wanted to register as a bidder.

"They usually sell the tools first,' he explained. "I do not want to be standing in line, waiting to register when the bidding starts."

"Bidders don't register here," I replied. "Everybody already knows everybody."

"I am not from here. How will they know who I am if I do not register?"

"Don't worry, they already know you're staying at the Log Cabin Motel and traveling with Clete Efferding. If you win a bid and they ask, just tell them your name is Lumir Sedlak and you're from Cedar Rapids. I doubt they'll ask."

Shaking his head, Lumir began making the rounds of the goods displayed on tables and hay racks. I dutifully followed him as he went from one display of merchandise to another. My friend examined Christmas decorations, pots and pans, and jigsaw puzzles. His straw hat pulled low over his eyes, Lumir seemed intent inspecting every item he passed—every item except the tool chests, that is.

"Lumir, I thought you came here to bid on the tool chests?" I asked.

"Sh-h-h," he said, glancing furtively over both shoulders. Holding his hand close to his chest, he gestured with his thumb that I was to follow him. I did, and we walked over to the edge of the property.

"Don't give me away," he cautioned. "I do not want the other bidders to know I want to buy the tool chests. If they see someone is interested, they will think the chests are valuable and bid on them." He put his finger to his lips as a pair of men in bibbed overalls approached. I recognized Wally Daugherty and Vin Feltes and was about to say hello.

I didn't get to. Lumir roughly pulled me away and led me across the street.

"Don't draw attention to yourself," he hissed. His eyes shifted from side to side as he checked our surroundings before continuing. "I do not want anyone to notice me. That way, they will be less likely to notice when I do look at the tools."

Trying to appear casual, I put my hands in the pockets of my jeans and turned outward so that we stood side to side, rather than facing each other—the way farmers do when they're watching the world go by. "Ah yep," I said, "but you better get lookin' at them tools before this here auction starts, else you be missin' out on 'em."

What seemed like an entire paragraph of the Czech language issued from Lumir's mouth.

"What'd you just say?" I asked.

Lumir turned to face me and clapped a hand on my shoulder. "After the swear words, I said if I miss the tool chests because of you, I will gut you like a fish, cut you up in little pieces, and use you to bait Eddie's trotlines."

A vivid, if idle, threat.

"If you don't look at them, how will—"

"Clete, you told me you have been to auctions before. That may be true, but I can see you know nothing about them. It is better if you avoid me until the chests are sold. If you want to go downtown for coffee and come back later, I will not be offended."

The idea of going back to the cabin for a nap sounded better, but after my miserable night outdoors, I knew I'd just lay down and sleep the day away. "I'll stick around," I said. "I haven't been to an auction in years, so it should be interesting."

Lumir nodded and slid away. "I will see you later then. In the meantime, do not act stupid."

I watched as my friend returned to the auction displays, making surreptitious passes by the tool chests, failing miserably in his attempts to appear inconspicuous. The entertainment value of Lumir's cloak-and-dagger operation diminished after his sixth pass, so I returned to the merchandise tables looking for treasures I might purchase for pennies, sorting through the detritus of the town librarian's life. While there are those who consider the public display of a deceased person's belongings tacky, I find them endlessly fascinating. Who would have thought the town librarian owned a bustier, derringer, poker chips, and roulette wheel? And what on earth was the local purveyor of fine literature doing with stacks and stacks of true crime magazines?

A tap on the shoulder interrupted my musing. I turned and looked up to see my old high school friend Dale, larger than life and sporting a grin that said no matter what had happened since we last met, he was happy to see me.

"Dale! Oh my God, I can't believe it's you."

He grabbed my hand, shaking it vigorously. Except for the mustache and sideburns reaching down to his chin, he hadn't changed a bit. If anything, he looked bigger, younger, and healthier than ever. Age does that to a fortunate few; the really unlucky fall apart quickly. Me, I'm somewhere in the middle—still trim, but with a touch of gray in the temples.

We started chattering away and within minutes were seated on the grass in the shade of a maple tree, the years falling away as if they'd never happened. Seeing no ring on his finger, I wondered if he was single or perhaps living with someone. Feeling no need to pussyfoot around the question, I asked.

Dale responded to my query with gales of laughter. "You're never gonna believe this, but I'm getting married in two weeks. Forty-two years old and tying the knot for the first time to a woman named Clara."

"For the first time?"

"Yup, and never even lived with somebody. I asked her if she knew what she was getting' into, and she said no, but I didn't either."

"Tell me more," I said. "She divorced? Are there kids?"

"Nope, a widow lady. She's twenty-six."

I did a double take. "Twenty-six? Talk about robbing the cradle. You're going to kill yourself trying to keep up with her."

"Then I'll die with a smile on my face. But hey, ya gotta come to my bachelor party. It's gonna be a blowout. Rick's renting a farmhouse up along Spruce Creek."

My heart sank. "I don't know, Dale. Maybe it isn't such a good idea. Myra's suicide didn't make me the most popular person in town. I'd hate to be the one to throw a wet blanket on the celebration."

Dale dismissed my concern with a wave of the hand. "Well, it's time they got over it and time you did too. How long you going to be in town?"

"Through the Fourth of July, maybe a day or two longer. After that, I need to get home. I work two jobs you know; I doubt I could make it."

Dale stood, grabbed me by the arm, and pulled me upright. "Damn," he said. "I'm the first guy in history who has a bachelor party on a Monday night, and you're gonna be in town." He slapped me on the back. "Talk about dumb luck."

I wasn't certain about the "luck" but felt sure about the "dumb." "I don't know, I have to be up early the next morning to run trotlines. My friends are counting on me."

"You've gotta come, Clete. It's on a weeknight, so the guys will have to be to work the next day. I'll only get married once."

Against my better judgment, I promised to attend the party. After some chitchat that included a rehash of the antique coffin story, Dale left to pick up his fiancé for lunch. I walked back to the site of the bidding to look for Lumir.

I'd gone maybe seventy steps before I saw him, leaning against an almost empty hay rack, a foot or two away from the tool boxes. The contents of the rack had been sold and carted away. Only larger items like the tool chests remained. From the smile on his face, I could see Lumir had been the high bidder. All in all, a perfect scene—save for one small detail. Lumir happened to be chatting with my cousin Marty. Sure she'd leave before long, I pulled up short and made for the thick of the bidding.

The auctioneer was going great guns, his unamplified singsong filling the entire backyard. I didn't recognize him, but he was knocking the lots down faster than anyone I'd seen and had the crowd's undivided attention. The ring man stirred old memories. Hickory Smith had been working the area's auctions for decades. He'd aged since I'd last seen him and had taken to wearing spectacles. As wiry as the trees for which he'd been named, I doubted he'd ever slow down.

A gnat buzzed my ear, and I swatted at it.

"Sold, to the guy who looks like Warren Beatty," the auctioneer called. "Don't believe I know you. Name?

"Mark it down for Cletus Efferding," said Hickory as he handed the runner a box containing an oversize doll wearing a pink dress. "Looks like he needs a girlfriend."

The crowd laughed.

I didn't want the doll, but I'd have made a bigger scene if I didn't accept it when the runner handed it to me. Doing my best to appear as if I bought dolls every day, I gradually edged my way out of the throng.

Still carrying the doll, I started for Lumir only to discover that he and Marty were still at it. Not only were they still at it, but they'd removed tools from the chests and were looking at them, pointing out features and talking. I desperately wanted to leave, the sooner, the better. The hell with Marty. Throwing caution to the winds, I walked up to the hay rack.

Lumir was the first to speak. "New girlfriend, Clete?"

Marty looked at me without rancor, as if last night's argument had never happened. "Hi, Cletus. I hope you didn't pay over two dollars for it. Everybody thinks Kissy Kathy is worth a lot because she is so large, but nobody buys them because they look cheap."

Not knowing what else to do, I set my doll on the rack.

"I got them, both chests, full of tools" crowed Lumir. "They did not sell the tools separately. I got the whole works. Forty dollars for one box, and twenty-five for the other.

"Swell," I said, trying to muster up some enthusiasm.

Lumir couldn't control his excitement. "These tools are very old. They may date back to the time of the Civil War. There are saws, chisels, and gouges, but mostly they are wooden planes. I never dreamed I would own anything like this. Marty here has been trying to buy them from me. Already she has offered me six hundred dollars, but I do not want to sell."

"Six hundred bucks?" I felt my enthusiasm for the tools grow.

"Marty tells me she is your cousin," Lumir said. "You are lucky to have such a nice relative, and I am lucky she slept late and was not here to bid on the tools. I have invited her to have fish with us as soon as we catch enough for a meal, and she is coming."

The prospect of a meal with Marty nearly put me over the edge. I hadn't enjoyed accidentally buying an oversized doll in front of a bunch of people who already thought I was strange. Dale's kindhearted invitation meant I'd be attending a party in the boondocks with guests who wouldn't like me. To top it all off, I was short on sleep and obligated to seine minnows and impale their broken bodies on barbed hooks later this afternoon.

Battered and taking hits on all sides, I clung steadfastly to the secret that holds the key to human survival and provides succor to the downtrodden. Come what may, I intended to take a nap.

12

Herman Cohen pressed the doorbell of the white one-story house. A chime sounded, followed by the excited yap of a small dog. A minute passed. The door opened, and as it did, he turned his head and called to the man sitting in the car. "She's home, Irv."

Marty Efferding appeared on the other side of the door, cradling a squirming dachshund. She didn't invite him in but pointed to her left. "Meet me in the garage. It's open. I'll be there in a couple of minutes."

Between the glass and the barking dog, Irv could barely make out what she said, but the pointed finger and the word "garage" told him all he needed to know. He turned and made his way down the steps. "Garage," he called to Irv and walked to the side of the house.

He and Irv had visited Marty Efferding's digs last summer, so the tiny house with a three-stall garage next to it didn't surprise him, but the discovery that the garage now boasted a second story did.

Irv stepped up beside Herm as he was still taking it in and let out a low whistle. "The town must have no zoning. Try that in Cedar Rapids, and you'd be tearing off the top before you got it framed." He paused. "From the looks of the thing, her carpenter didn't do her any favors."

Herm looked at gaps between the second story's mismatched pieces of wooden siding. Since the boards weren't parallel, he found it hard to determine if the workers had set the windows properly. Somehow, they looked crooked. Maybe the pieces of tarpaper protruding from the edges of the frames created the illusion of crookedness. "She got took," he said. "Not even a year old, and already it looks bad."

Irv opened the hollow-core door, and Herm followed him inside. Marty had filled almost every inch of the structure with the detritus of years gone by. Except for a path leading to the stairway and another pointing to a card table and four chairs, precarious stacks of clutter held sway.

They made for the table where Herm grabbed a rickety ladderback chair and gave it a twist. "You better test yours before you use it. One of these collapses, you could end up butt down on the concrete."

Irv tested his chair. "You know, that's what I like about this business, you meet all kinds. It's not like when we worked for Big Angie. Back then, we knew what to expect. Everybody we met was a snake in the grass, out to cheat everybody else and ready to smack 'em if they complained. So predictable, it got boring."

"I gotta agree with you, but the upside was anybody who got too weird got whacked. Here in Iowa, most of the people in the antique business are nuts to begin with. Normal people who get into it end up going broke. You and me, we're the exceptions—not crazy, and we make money.

Irv leaned back in his chair, wiggled a bit, and leaned forward again. "Think Marty's nuts?"

"Like a squirrel on cocaine. You're taking a big risk with that chair, Irv."

A creaking door announced Marty's entrance. "You guys want some coffee?" she asked as she approached.

Irv glanced at a nearby shelf. A chipped enamelware pot sat atop a hotplate. An open jar of Folger's Instant with a plastic spoon protruding from it stood alongside. The shelf below the first displayed a ceramic dish filled with packets of artificial sweetener, and next to it, a pale green ashtray shaped like the state of Florida over-flowed with lipstick-stained butts.

"We'll pass," said Irv, secure in the knowledge that Herm wasn't interested. "So, where's the coffin?"

Marty took a seat at the table. "There's a problem. The seller didn't tell me it was still in use."

Herm waived off a fly and chuckled. "No problem. Irv and I can evict the current occupant. Some of our customers are so strange, they'd like a used one better than new. Do you know if we can get the headstone? We could jack up the price if we sell 'em as a kit."

Irv leaned back in his chair. It creaked in protest. "Herm's got a point. Can you get the marker? Maybe it'll have angels carved on it or something. A lot of those Victorian stones are ornate."

Chuckling, Marty pulled a pack of Salems from her purse. "He didn't have the stone, just the coffin."

"You know, Irv," said Herm, "maybe we shouldn't dump the contents. Whoever takes it might want the original owner. Even though we'd have to be careful about who we sold it to, people still collect mummies and stuff. I hear there's a whole museum of 'em in Mexico. Imagine an American-made mummy case with a mummy inside"

"Maybe we can make a market in Victorian stones," observed Irv. "I know American colonial is hot right now. Pickers are ripping off cemeteries by the truckload."

Herm scratched his chin. "Just think about it, those Victorians took the cake when it came to shelling out for fancy markers: lambs, tree trunks, crying angels, weeping willows, the whole shebang. And the kids' markers—empty cradles, chubby little praying hands, baby shoes with no feet in 'em—"

"Guys!" Marty interrupted. "I'm not in that kind of business. I thought the coffin was empty when I told you about it. I tried to phone you a dozen times to say the deal fell through, but nobody an-swered."

"You didn't get us because Irv and I are on a buying trip. Just put us in contact with the seller, and we'll deal directly with him."

Marty lit up a mentholated joystick. "I can't do that because the police confiscated it yesterday."

"Oh, the coffin on the radio news." Herm stared at the floor. "Too bad, it sounds like a Fisk. The poor schmuck died right after he patented it, so he never got the chance to get in on the money. They're rare because they were so expensive. Worse yet, most of 'em are six feet under and nobody knows where to dig if they want one. We'd have paid you a thousand."

"It smelled funky. The guys who found it tried to open it. They must have sealed it back up somehow, otherwise nobody would be able to get near it."

Herm twisted his pinky ring. "With the corpse, we could have gone another five hundred. The stiff would be in great shape because they sealed Fisk boxes to make 'em airtight. A buyer could put the body someplace, let it dry out, and *presto*! A month or two later, he's got a mummy."

"Might take longer," said Irv, "what with all the preservatives."

Marty fetched the Florida-shaped ashtray and stubbed her barely smoked Salem.

"You don't get it," said Herm. "A cast iron casket with shrouds, vines, and lilies on it floats down the Mississippi River. Every radio station we listened to is carrying the story. Your little town is famous, and on the underground market, a box with a history like that would sell like hotcakes."

"Damn," groaned Marty. "Business is slow, and I could have used the cash. The last few days have been hell. First the coffin deal disappears, and then I miss out on the biggest score of my life."

Irv's eyes widened. "Biggest score of your life? I like hearing stories about the big one that got away. Maybe Herm and I will have some of that coffee after all."

Herm waved a hand. "Don't b—"

Irv kicked him in the ankle.

Marty stood, pulled another cigarette from her pack, and faced the hotplate. "I put some water in the pot last night but never turned it on."

The possibility of a dead roach floating on the day-old water nearly made Herm retch. "I could go to the house and get some fresh —"

Irv kicked him again, rubbing his thumb and fingers together behind his back in the universal sign for money. After turning to check that Herm understood, he extracted a silver cigarette case from his shirt pocket. "Sounds great. You know, I used to smoke Salems too, but I'm a Benson & Hedges man now."

The hotplate switched on, Marty set the jar of instant, its plastic spoon still protruding from the top, and three reasonably clean mugs on the table. The discolored bags of artificial sweetener followed.

"So, about the big score," asked Irv, "what happened?"

Marty shook her head. "The deal of a lifetime and I missed out on it. I overslept this morning and was late for an auction. They sold two chests of antique tools that had been in the hands of a local family forever. When I got there, the old guy who bought them was standing at a hay rack unpacking the tools one at a time and grinning from ear to ear. I could tell right away. Eighteenth-century, early, from the years before the Revolution. Two chests of colonial tools in unbelievable condition.

"Old tools are popular now," said Irv. "I know a guy out in New York who pays big money for the things. He's some kind of rich brain surgeon. Still, a couple of chests of antique tools, who'd want to risk hauling 'em out to New York if he might not want them."

"He'd sure as hell want these. I spent a couple of hours this afternoon reading about early tools in the *EAIA Chronicle*. The tools in the chests are stamped with the names Francis Nicholson, I. Nicholson, and Cesar Chelor. Francis Nicholson is the father of the American hand plane, born in 1683 and died in 1753."

Irv nodded, his face a blank.

"You still don't get it, do you? He's absolutely the biggest name in early American hand tools. The I. Nicholson tools were made by his son Iohn, who took over the family business. Chelor was the old guy's slave, a black man who made tools right alongside him."

Herm cracked his knuckles. "Those Southerners always had an angle. Free labor, how you gonna compete with that?"

Her shoulders slumping, Marty rose to check on the water. "It's boiling," she said. "Nicholson wasn't southern; he lived in Massachusetts. Owning slaves was legal there back then."

"Slaves in Massachusetts," Herm replied. "Who'd a thought it?"

Returning with the pot, Marty poured steaming water into the cups.

"Thanks, Marty," said Irv as he spooned the brown crystals from the jar into his cup. He gave Herm a no-nonsense look. "Two spoons, or three?"

Herm couldn't believe it. Irv expected him to drink the stuff. "Two," he mumbled.

After setting the pot back on the hotplate, Marty returned to her chair. "It gets even worse. The guy who bought the chests kept waving his arms around, so excited he could hardly talk. He said some of the planes cut patterns were backward. Then he started holding different ones together and he showed me how the old man's planes were used to make the ones that belonged to the son. Turns out the father's planes are something called 'mother' planes—specialized tools for making other planes."

Herm remained unimpressed. "Father planes, mother planes, other planes, who cares?"

Marty didn't notice. "The old man kept saying he'd never seen anything like it. His mother lode, my disaster."

Trying hard to look as if he was enjoying himself, Herm managed a few sips of Marty's swill without gagging. As much as he cared for Irv, when he got something fixed in his head, the guy could be unreasonable. Like today, trying to poison him with Marty's coffee. "Gee Marty, this coffee hits the spot," he lied.

Irv set down his cup, pulled out a handkerchief and blotted his nose. "Damn allergies. So, what do you think the chests are worth? We've sold a few old tools, but they never brought much."

Marty peered at her companions over the rim of her coffee cup. "Really, these chests are priceless, but except for museums, there's only a handful of buyers with that kind of dough."

"In the Nicholson family all these years," mused Irv. "You're talking provenance and authenticity up the ying-yang. Just the kind of stuff museums eat up, but museums are cheap. Unless they had somebody donate the tools, they wouldn't be interested. In the long run, you're back to what an individual buyer is willing to fork out."

Marty's slack posture revealed the extent of her disappointment. "I knew they were good when I saw them but didn't know they were the find of a lifetime. I offered him six hundred, but he wouldn't take it. I didn't want to go any higher. I've been building my inventory, and right now six hundred is my entire business account."

Herm wrinkled his nose as streams of smoke poured from Irv's nostrils. He'd tried time and again to get the man to quit smoking, and he hated the way cigarette smoke clung to Irv's clothes. Sometimes his partner's breath smelled worse than a dog's.

"Tell you what, Marty, I'd like to help out," said Irv. "Introduce me to this guy, and if I can make deal a with him, you can have a ten percent finder's fee."

"You think I'm born yesterday?" she sputtered, squaring her shoulders. "No, way. You want the tools, so that makes you my customer. Since you have cash, I'll have room to deal. Call your rich brain surgeon and come back to me with an offer."

Irv dropped his cigarette onto the growing heap in Central Florida. It rolled from the summit to the edge of the ashtray.

Miami, thought Herm.

His hands on his knees, Irv leaned forward. "If I needed a brain surgeon to tell me what something's worth, I wouldn't be in this business. Ten big ones."

"I may not have been born yesterday," a reinvigorated Marty replied, "but I wasn't born the day before either. Twenty thousand."

Irv's chair started to sway. He stood in time to avoid crashing to the floor. "You're on," he said.

"What?" Herm leapt from his seat, put his hands on his hips and glared at his partner. "Outside, Irving. Now, and I don't mean maybe."

Irv paled. "We'll be back in a minute, Marty. Herm and I have business to attend to."

Herm didn't wait for Irv, but strode to the door, leaving his partner to follow. By the time Irv caught up with him, Herm was a good twenty feet from the garage, with his hands clasped behind his back and looking as angry as the Lord God preparing to loose fire and brimstone on Sodom and Gomorrah.

"You're gambling again, Irving. You promised after you lost our condo money you'd never do it again. You don't have any idea of what those tools are worth. And what about me? Don't I have a say in our business? This coffin thing gave me an idea. I want to build a sideline in mortuary antiques. It's easy entry and low risk. You keep telling me I should do something about my self-confidence. How can I do anything about it, if the business is always about you?"

"How could I know you were interested? You never told me you wanted to get in on the ghoul trade."

Herm put his hands on his hips. His voice grew louder. "I never used to have to tell you anything. Before you started taking me for granted, I didn't have to. You picked up on my signals, but now I'm a doormat. I don't want to deal in any goddamn tools. I want to make a name in funeral parlor collectibles, and I want that Fisk coffin. Make it happen, Irving. Financial infidelity is just as bad as the other kind and just as hard to forgive."

"But the police have the coffin, and the whole world knows about it. Think of the risk. We'd never be able to sell it."

"The people we know, that box wouldn't be any harder to sell than those damn tools. I want it. If you care about me, Irving, find a way to get it, and then you can buy your stupid tools."

"I care, Herm. Really, I do. Anything you want, it's yours. I'll find a way to get the casket and the tools. Just don't call me Irving anymore. Please?"

13

Lumir and I took the last two seats at the Riverview Hotel restaurant. I couldn't remember seeing it so busy. It took all of ten minutes for the indefatigable Loretta to appear.

"What'll it be, Cletus?" she asked, pulling the pencil from behind her ear.

"I'll have coffee and the liver and onions. Say, you're doing a bang-up business. Is Saturday always so busy?"

"What with all the reporters in town, things are poppin'. You going to the press conference?"

My jaw dropped. "Press conference?"

"Blackie Stiles and Hankie Steines are having a press conference at 1:30 in the parking lot by the seawall. That's when the TV trucks will be here. Blackie and Hank are having the time of their lives, walking around town in their hip boots, signing autographs for kids, telling ghost stories."

"Hmph," I sniffed, "the things people get interested in,"

Loretta looked over her glasses at Lumir. "You?"

"I will have the Salisbury Steak. And coffee, too. Too bad that I missed the chance to see that coffin. Something like that does not turn up every day."

Loretta scribbled on her pad and returned the pencil to her ear. "You just might get your chance. Ray Gallagher has it locked in the garage behind his furniture store, but so many people showed up wanting to see it, he finally started letting them in. When word got around town, more people kept showing up. He tried to keep count, and after three hundred people went through the store, he said 'enough.' Now everybody who didn't get to see it is mad, so he said he'll open up again tomorrow."

"Poor guy," I said, "running a funeral home in a small town. He can't afford to have people mad at him. One big mistake and he's out of business."

Loretta ripped the order from her pad and looked down at me. "I expect you'd know all about that."

Nice dig, Loretta. I doubted the reason my sudden exit from my hometown would ever be forgotten. For generations to come, children and grandchildren would hear of the nefarious Cletus Efferding, the haberdasher who drove his wife to suicide.

Lumir's expression indicated he'd caught Loretta's slight. "These hill folk have long memories," he said after she left. "They are not tolerant like the Czech farmers I knew as a boy."

"You see too many bad movies. People who live along the Mississippi River are not hillbillies. Bellevue is a small town, a place where people know and tolerate each other in ways outsiders find difficult to understand. It's not so much what I did, the problem is I did the worst thing imaginable. I surprised them."

"They are surprised when a depressed person takes her life?"

"No, they are surprised when someone they've known for years visits a prostitute and his wife kills herself afterward. It would have gone down better if I had a reputation as a philanderer, but they thought of me as a church-going family man."

Lumir stroked his mustache. "I still do not understand."

"I'll give you an example. There was an older gentleman in town, the last of the steamboat captains. Everybody called him Cap. Pretty well along in years, he went into his second childhood. One day he began walking around town in his boxer shorts. His neighbors tried to talk him out of it, but he insisted there was no difference between his boxers and a pair of Bermuda shorts. When he first started going out in his skivvies, he wore them with a nicely pressed, collared shirt tucked into them. The next summer the collared shirt disappeared, and he took to a wife-beater shirt and suspenders. The summer after that, he got more basic—boxers and suspenders."

"What happened then?"

"He died."

Lumir shook his head. "I do not understand the point you are trying to make."

"Old Cap got strange little by little, so people got used to it. That last summer, when he'd show up in the grocery store wearing his boxers and suspenders, the clerks were nice to him, helped him out, and called him Cap or Mr. Beckman."

When Loretta brought our coffee, Lumir took a sip and remarked, "The townspeople are kind to a respected citizen when he loses his memory. The story does not prove your point."

"The point is the change was gradual. They gossiped about him, but they weren't shocked. Besides, Cap wasn't a respected citizen; he was a crotchety old coot who slowly went dingbats. Then there was Ardelia Krumbatey. Crazy as a loon. Invented the miniskirt forty years before the British and walked around town in skirts that barely covered her butt. Walked stooped over, but with five pounds of makeup on her face, and ten pounds of jewelry, you've got to expect that. Never dated anybody and lived alone her whole life. Older than dirt when I left town and still wearing anklets and swinging her fanny in short skirts. A total nut job, but people were polite and called her Miss Krumbatey. They felt comfortable with Ardelia because she was born nutty."

Lumir picked up his knife and fork. "I still do not understand your point."

"I saw her yesterday. She's ten years older than when I left, but now her skirts don't quite cover her underpants. The kids in town call her the Underwear Lady, but as sure as I am sitting across from you, her fellow citizens treat her with respect. Most of them are willing to accept a complete whack job but cross the street to avoid me. The moral of the story is that people who live in small towns are nice to their neighbors as long as they think they know them."

Lumir returned his utensils to the table. "Running around in their underwear, dragging coffins behind boat trailers, torching historic buildings . . . the moral of the story is the people in your hometown are crazy as bat poop."

As I turned over, my arm flopped against something unexpected. I woke with a start to find Kissy Kathy sharing a pillow with me. Confronting a pair of glass eyes from a distance of four inches didn't make for an easy return to the world of the living. I gave Kissy a hard shove, propelling her out of the bed and onto the floor.

"Damn Eddie," I muttered.

I'd wanted to leave the doll back at the auction, but Lumir wouldn't hear of it. Apparently, some unwritten rule of auction etiquette requires the purchaser to haul his junk away, so Kissy accompanied Lumir's tools back with us to the Log Cabin Motel. Exhausted by the previous night's lack of sleep, I'd gone directly to my cabin, leaving the oversized plaything back in the Nova.

I hoisted myself off the mattress and stretched. When I stumbled out of the cabin door, I found Lumir and Eddie at our outdoor table playing double solitaire. I glared at Eddie. "Cute," I said, taking a seat. "Really, cute."

After a bit of ribbing about middle-aged men who slept with dollies instead of dolls, we got down to the business of the day. Eddie had decided to concentrate our fishing efforts on a stretch a few miles downstream, close to a federal campground. After scouting some likely looking sites, he'd left his flat bottom pulled up on a sandy beach next to a boat ramp. We'd drive there to set our trotlines, but first we'd need to seine our bait.

Our plan of action complete, Eddie swung his legs over the table's seat. "Time to get going," he announced.

I stared in disbelief. "Already? I just got up."

The sounds of the carillon at the Lutheran Church drifted through the air. Six o'clock, I'd slept the afternoon away.

"You looked so happy cuddled up with your dolly that we did not want to wake you," Lumir teased.

"Let's go," said Eddie. "We've got three and half hours 'til dark."

We drove to the Dyas Mill riffles. The reality of the task hit home when we reached water's edge. We'd be wading upstream against a strong current, over a rocky, unstable stream bed, stretching our seine across the rapids. Eddie and I had already agreed Lumir would watch from the bank. Miraculously, our older friend seemed content to let us do the work.

Since I've never been comfortable with the idea of men wearing shorts, Eddie had reserved our sole pair of hip boots for me. He'd seine wearing a pair of cutoffs and a near-death pair of canvas deck shoes. I felt sorry for him. Given the number of cold-water springs that flowed into it, Mill Creek would be chilly.

Our first pass through the riffles produced something like a hundred shiner minnows. If the gods smiled on us, another pass would do the trick. The gods had other ideas.

As we began our second pass, the heel of my boot snagged a rock ledge, and I lost my balance. Letting go my end of the seine, I tried to step onto the bank. My foot encountered a slippery patch of clay and I fell chest first onto the slimy incline. Cold water poured into my boots.

I returned to the perpendicular to find the lower half of my face, my arms and my torso covered in mud. Eddie stood midstream laughing so hard I thought he'd wet himself.

Cupping his hands, Lumir called from the opposite bank. "Are you okay, Clete?"

"I'm fine," I yelled.

"We should have known better than to let a man who plays with dollies seine minnows."

I crawled up on the slippery incline and walked to a log where I took off the hip boots and dumped them. Gingerly re-entering the stream, I retrieved my end of the seine and took up my former position. The rest of our bait-gathering went off without a hitch.

When we got back to Eddie's pickup, I sat on the tailgate, removed my cold, soggy footwear, and slipped into my Adidas sans socks. Feeling a little more human, I made for the door of the pickup.

Eddie blocked my way. "No way," he said.

Lumir edged in front of me and closed the door. Once inside, he rolled down the window. "He's right, Clete. You are a disgusting mess, and it is better for you to ride in back."

"For Christ's sake, it's a fishing truck."

"A very nice fishing truck," Lumir replied. "You can ride in back."

Truth be told, nobody in their right mind would let me anywhere near the inside of a vehicle, so I hoisted myself into the box of the pickup and settled in among the bait buckets, trotlines, and wet seine.

I wasn't angry, but I still owed Eddie for his Kissy Kathy trick. As the wind ruffled my hair, I spent the four-mile drive happily plotting my revenge. We arrived before I had time to settle on a plan, but since the best part of getting even is the anticipation, the failure didn't concern me.

When we reached our destination, Eddie drove over the pebbly beach, right up to his boat, and parked. I hopped out, took off my once-white shirt and picked dried pieces of dirt off it. The mud would wash out, the green stains—not so likely.

A smiling Eddie hopped up into the box of the truck and began sliding the trotline boxes and minnow buckets toward the tailgate. No doubt about it, the guy enjoyed fishing. His infectious enthusiasm sidetracked my thoughts of retaliation, and within minutes, Lumir, Eddie, and I were comfortably ensconced on overturned buckets, sipping beer, and impaling minnows on barbed hooks.

Eddie baited five hooks to my one. "Did you know this is the place where those fishermen brought in that old coffin?" he asked. "Right at that boat ramp. Wish I'd have been there to see it,"

I fumbled with a recalcitrant minnow who believed drying out on the sand was a death preferable to that of hanging on a hook. "You got in last night, spent the day on the river, and already you know all about the coffin?"

Eddie swatted a mosquito. "I was back in town by noon and drove to that lot by the dam to watch a towboat go through the locks. What with all the cars, TV trucks and microphones, I could barely find a place to park. The guys who found the coffin were giving a press conference."

"What did these men say?" asked Lumir.

"Just about how they found it half-buried in the sand. But then the second one got to talking, a guy named Blackie. That's when things got weird. He said that they might have found the grave of the Old Hag."

I raised my eyes skyward. "Oh, for the love of Mike. If a word of truth ever passed Blackie Stiles' lips, it'd be a slip of the tongue."

Lumir shushed me. "I want to hear what Eddie has to say."

Eddie continued. "He said that after the Civil War, a couple named Bowman lived on the island where they found the box. One day the woman rowed up to the fish market with a pair of hundred-pound catfish in her boat. Of course, everybody wanted to know what she used for bait, and she said, 'My husband. I cut the drunken sonofabitch up in pieces, put 'em in crocks, and left 'em in the sun. When those chunks of 'im got good and ripe, I used 'em in his very own hoop nets.' According to Blackie, nobody ever saw the guy again."

"The story is interesting," said Lumir. "We should have attended this press conference."

I couldn't understand how a sensible man like Lumir could be so interested in Blackie's balderdash. "The Old Hag story has been floating around town forever. Blackie dressed it up and fed it to the press."

Lumir put his hands on his knees. "Clete, you think this little town of yours is some snow-white piece of heaven. Why is it not possible that someone from Bellevue chopped up her husband?"

"And used him for fish bait? To catch hundred-pound catfish? You've gotta be kidding. At one time or another, every kid in Bellevue has been scared silly listening to talk about a boogeywoman called the Old Hag. Whenever there's a full moon, she's supposed to crawl out of the river looking for children to feed to her pet snapping turtles."

Lumir smiled indulgently. "Many of these old folk tales have a basis in fact. Perhaps the fisherman did find the grave of a woman named Bowman who murdered her husband. She may have killed him in a rage, stabbing again and again until he was almost in pieces. From there, it is not such a far step to cut him up to dispose of the body."

I finally got my sand-covered minnow on a hook. "I don't get it, Lumir. You think the local people are strange because they're excited about this fancy casket. You're just as interested as they are, but somehow you think you're different."

"It is as I said earlier, my interest is historical. I will go to see the coffin tomorrow if the line is not too long."

"Me too," enthused Eddie.

My friends' excitement proved infectious so, putting my pride aside, I gave in. "Thunderation," I said in my best hillbilly accent. "No sense a man feudin' with his partners. I'm gonna get me a look-see at that goldarn box too."

Lumir looked at me with concern. "Clete? Ever since you have come back to your hometown, you are acting strangely."

14

A trotline is a thing of beauty: forty hooks attached to foot-long leaders tied to a three-hundred-pound-test cord. Every seven feet, a baited hook floats just off the river bottom waiting for a fish to pass by. Because of its location, a trotline is well-suited for the capture of the Mississippi's scavengers: carp, sheepshead, sturgeon, and catfish.

In a river culture, poor folk eat carp and sheepshead. The middle class eats catfish and sturgeon. The rich eat beefsteak. Though the old ways were dead, my companions and I were conventional in one respect. We'd set our trotlines to catch catfish. Everything else would go back in the drink.

We pushed off in Eddie's boat as the morning sun hovered just over the horizon. Last night's set had gone like clockwork. This morning, we'd pick up our six lines. Since Eddie had the luxury of a two-man crew, he assigned me the task of raising the lines and Lumir that of handling the dip net.

My job entailed grabbing the buoy, pulling the first anchor, and piling the wet trotline in its wooden box. When we reached the far end of the line, the second anchor would go into the box, and the buoy placed atop it.

It didn't take long to get the hang of it, but I kept getting interrupted by fish and soon grew to hate them. I had to hold each slimy fish with one hand and unhook it with the other.

"I don't know if I like this, Eddie," I complained. "If one of these hooks goes flying through my fingers, I could get sliced. What with river water, gook, and fish slime on his hands, a guy could get an infection."

"You got a tetanus shot?" he asked.

"Yeah."

"No big deal."

We raised three lines without incident. Things went haywire on the fourth.

"Eddie, the line seems stuck on the bottom, I can barely pull it in."

"You're hooked on a snag. Lean back hard and give a good pull. If we're lucky the leader will break. If the main line is wrapped around something, you're in a pickle. It's three-hundred-pound test and won't break. You might pull in a sunken outboard motor or a piece of a boat."

"Or another coffin," snickered Lumir.

I gave a tremendous yank. Whatever we'd snagged moved. The damn thing proved hard to raise. The first few pulls were beastly, but after a bit something gave, enabling me to switch to a hand-over-hand pull. A section of sunken tree limb became visible in the murky depths.

"What do I do now?" I asked.

Eddie reached into his jeans and pulled out a pocketknife. When you get it up to the surface, I'll cut the leader, and we'll let it go."

Just then, the tree limb dove for the bottom, slamming my arms against the oarlock.

"It's alive!" Eddie screamed. "A fish, a fish!"

I worked the monster back to the top.

"This fish will not fit in the dip net," observed Lumir.

"A carp," said Eddie.

I breathed a sigh of relief. "A junk fish. You can cut the leader, and he's out of our hair."

Eddie looked at me as if I were daft. "Like hell we will. A fish that big is not going back in the water."

"But it's a carp," I insisted.

Eddie put the outboard in neutral. "Hand me the line. I'll work him close to the boat. You kneel down and put your hands in his gills. Just heave him into the boat."

"Put my fingers inside him and heave that ugly hunk of slime into the boat?"

Lumir cleared his throat. "This is what we can expect from a man who plays with little girls' toys. We can change seats, and I will bring in the fish."

"No way," I said, passing the line to Eddie. I knelt and worked a hand into a gill. I had to lean out so far over the side to reach the other gill that I nearly lost my balance. If the fish dove again, I'd be taking a bath.

He didn't. Eddie cut the leader, and I pulled with all my might. I heaved so hard the monstrosity not only cleared the gunwale, it cleared my face. Unprepared for the sudden shift in weight, I fell backward onto the floor of the boat. The god-awful piece of ugliness landed on top of me, its scaly belly pressed against my face. I pushed the thing off, rubbing its foul juices from my lips.

Eddie sat at the motor laughing so hard he couldn't speak.

"Clete," said Lumir, "we have misjudged you. All this while we thought you were interested in dollies, but instead we learn you like kissing fish."

I rose, soaking wet and covered with detritus from the bottom of the boat. "Lumir and I are changing places. He can pull lines, and I'll man the dipnet."

Eddie found his voice. "Hate to say it, Clete, but looks like you've been carped."

"I did not like the look of the brown stuff hanging from the fish's belly," Lumir added. "Maybe Clete got crapped."

I took Lumir's seat. Eddie didn't know it, but the revenge, I'd extract for his heckling had increased proportionately.

Lumir proved an adept trot-liner, and the rest of the morning went off without a hitch. After we landed, Eddie and I loaded our gear and fish into his truck while Lumir stepped off into some high weeds to commune with mother nature.

The look on Eddie's face told me he considered the morning a huge success. "Seven catfish, and a monster carp," he said. "I bet the biggest cat will go four pounds."

"Yeah, but what are you going to do with the carp?"

"Take it to Junnie's Fish Market and get it weighed. After that, I don't care, somebody will want it."

Lumir returned from his trip to the weeds carrying a rectangular piece of oxidized metal. "Looks like I found a piece of old brass. It might come in handy. I could polish it up and use it to make inlays for one of my projects."

I had to laugh. Lumir's shop was filled with such odds and ends as buckets of bent nails that could be straightened and used again, bolts without nuts, used chicken wire, and broken appliances —all carefully stored in the event they "might come in handy."

"Wonder what it was," mused Lumir, turning the scrap over in his hands. "A brass plate with a hole in each corner for mounting it to something. Must have been a sign or nameplate. I think I see some sort of writing on it, but it's too faint to make out." He took his treasure to the cab of the truck and got in.

"Let's go," said Eddie. "We have fish to dress."

"We?" I asked.

Eddie looked me up and down. "You might as well help, you can't get any dirtier than you are already."

As I headed for the cab, he held up a hand. "You better ride back in the box. I never fished with anybody who manages to make such a mess of himself."

15

Herman took in the action at the busy, well-run restaurant just off Highway 20. Waitresses bustled, bus boys quietly cleared tables, coffee cups seemed to refill themselves. No doubt about it, a Sunday morning breakfast in Dubuque made for a great finish to a buying trip. He and Irv had ended their antiquing expedition at the Julien Motor Inn, a stay that didn't disappoint. Amazing that anyone would saddle a grand old hotel like the Julien with the title "motor inn." A nice place, but he and Irv wanted a change of scenery for breakfast and had stopped here on the way out of town.

He looked away as Irv upended a ketchup bottle, dosing a perfectly good plate of scrambled eggs with a river of goo. Fifteen years and he still couldn't get over the way the guy poured the stuff on his breakfasts. Ketchup on eggs, ketchup on ham, ketchup on bacon, and ketchup on toast. In most matters of life, his partner had good taste, but when it came to breakfast, all bets were off. Herm shuddered as he remembered the time Irv had slathered the stuff on an order of biscuits and gravy, a sight so terrible that he had to leave the table lest his stomach turn.

Breakfasts overrun with pureed tomato guts were a small flaw in an otherwise decent partner. At least Irv's passion for the sauce didn't extend to other meals, a fact that kept the situation tolerable.

He'd once asked Irv about the eccentricity. His query resulted in three days without a word passing between them, so he never mentioned it again. Determined to ignore the man's assault on common decency, he picked up the copy of the Sunday morning *Telegraph-Herald* from the chair beside him and buried his face inside.

He'd just made it to page two when Irv addressed him from the other side of the newspaper divide. "Anything in there about the coffin?"

"Half a page."

"What's it say?"

"Don't know yet, I just got started."

Herm continued reading. "They don't know it's a Fisk. Even the local undertaker has no idea. I guess the town is swarming with reporters. Hundreds of people stood in line yesterday to get a chance to see it. Marty might have a tough time getting hold of the thing. The local cops are gonna keep watch on it overnight."

"She's a smart girl. I gave her enough ideas, so something should work out. Still no idea where it came from?"

"Nothing solid. Says here some locals believe it washed out of the grave of a crazy woman who lived there on an island a hundred years ago. They say she chopped her husband up in pieces and used him for fish bait."

Irv snorted. "A real amateur. Cuttin' somebody up is a lot of work, not to mention messy. Remember the time we did Brownie Boccero? I told Angie: I don't care how much you pay, never again."

"Well you gotta admit, Angelo knew how to send a message. Little wifey findin' pieces of her husband scattered across the front porch, no way she was gonna talk. Wish I'd been there to see the look on her face. I heard after that nobody in the neighborhood could remember anything about anything, not even their own names. If that old lady on the island had a brain, she'd just have dumped him and let the current take him away."

"I don't know, Irv. It says here she caught some really big fish afterward. So, a lot of unnecessary work, but at least she got something out of it."

"Anything else good in there?"

Herm heard Irv put down his fork and knew he could safely fold the paper. "No, that's it," he said as he returned it to the chair.

Irv blotted his mouth with his napkin leaving a healthy red stain behind. "It's a good thing that the kind of people who buy this stuff don't ask many questions. That coffin is going to be hot. Are you sure about this mortuary antiques thing?"

"It's like a calling. I know this is what I want to do with my life, and for once, I'm gonna be the best. You have no idea how disappointed I'll be if Marty can't pull off the heist."

Irv removed a Benson & Hedges from his case and lit up. "For twenty grand, the lady will do it."

"We could do it for a lot less if we swiped the coffin ourselves. And after that, we could find out who that geezer is and buy your old tools directly from him. We don't need the woman at all."

"And we don't need the risk. You're a city boy, but I grew up in a small town before the old man moved us to Chicago. Everybody knows everything about everybody in these rinky-dink places. Marty would know we made off with the casket in a heartbeat. Sooner or later she'd blab, and one day, an investigator shows up at our door. With our past, we can't afford that. That's why she's bringing the coffin and the tools to us."

Herm scratched his chin and narrowed his eyes. "A lot could go wrong without somebody down there to protect our interest. Marty's an experienced dealer, so there won't be any problem with the tools. I'm worried about my coffin. What if she can't pull it off?"

"Already thought of it. Remember when I did that year in the Joliet lockup and met a guy from Iowa called Canker?"

"How could I forget? It's the longest we've ever been apart."

"Well good old Canker likes to think he's big-time bad, and guess what? He's from Bellevue."

"No crap?"

"No crap." Irv crushed his cigarette, grabbed a packet of saccharine from the caddy in the center of the table and began fiddling with it. "I checked the phone book. He still lives there."

"You're—" Herm paused, waiting for a customer to pass. "You're talking about risk. Bringing in another guy is riskier than handling it ourselves."

Putting the pseudo-sugar packet on the table, Irv placed his hand behind it and flicked his index finger. The packet arced through the air and landed in the center of his partner's lap. "Field goal," he announced.

"I'm serious, Irv. The guy's an amateur, and that means risk big time."

"Canker's smart enough to iron out any problems. I doubt we'll need him. You never used to be so high-strung. Don't worry so much."

Herm picked up the sweetener, poured, and stirred it into his coffee. "You're right, I need to relax. By the way, the coffee here is outstanding. And not just the coffee, my Eggs Benedict were to die for."

"What'd you expect? The sign outside says *Fine Dining*."

What's the name of this place again?"

"The Bridge."

"Next time we're in Dubuque we've gotta eat here again. Maybe come in the evening for steaks. The Bridge, I'll try to remember, but it's such a short name."

Irv raised an eyebrow and pointed to a nearby window. "See that big steel thing just outside? The one that goes across the Mississippi River and has a million cars on it? Should be hard to forget."

Herm felt his face grow red and changed the subject. "We've had a good trip. Even though gas here by the river is sixty cents a gallon, the truck and trailer are full, and we've got a line on some of the best stuff to ever show up in this part of the country. To top it off, I know what I want to do with the rest of my life. When we get back to Cedar Rapids, I'm going to get new business cards with engraved gothic letters—Herman Judah Cohen, Specialist, Antiquarian Mortuary Artifacts. I'm thinking textured off-white cardstock, maybe one hundred percent rag content with an embossed crest."

"I didn't know the Cohens had a crest."

"You got a hole in your education because you never went to *shul*. Cohens come from a line of priests going all the way back to Aaron. We're practically royalty."

A look of contentment spread across Irv's face as he stubbed his cigarette into a clear glass ashtray. "It's nice to see you excited about something instead of feeling bad about yourself. We'll make this new thing of yours work out. They say the future of the antique business is specialization. We could have three: nineteenth-century pottery, Eastlake furniture, and mortuary artifacts."

Herm felt his stomach tighten. "I don't know how to say this. I want the mortuary thing for my own."

Irv looked crestfallen. "What's wrong? I thought we were partners in everything. Share and share alike, respect and trust, mutual support, the whole ball of wax."

"We are, but let's face it. It's hard for you to step back and not try to control everything. Case in point—you gamble in commodities with our money and contract for a hit without telling me. Then you offer twenty grand for some tool chests and don't include me in the decision. You think you're a great guy, but I'm suffocating. I need this."

Looking as if he'd been slapped, Irv averted his face and sat in silence. Herm sipped his coffee and said nothing. Minutes passed.

Irv spoke first. "I'm sorry, Herm. I know you're right, but I just can't help myself. I don't know what it is, but for as long as I can remember, something hasn't been right with me. I never learned how to take other people's feelings into account."

"How would you feel if you were me? You make thirty thousand in business decisions with no more consideration for me than you would for a pet dog. The mortuary line is mine, or I'm leaving. I don't want to, but if you horn in, so help me God, I will."

Irv pushed his chair back, rose, and left the restaurant without a word. Herm threw a ten spot on the table and followed. By the time he reached the truck, his partner was already inside, staring straight ahead, his hands on the wheel. Herm barely had time to get into his seat before the truck began rolling. Forty-five minutes into the drive back to Cedar Rapids, Irv broke the silence.

"Fifteen years. Fifteen years and you'd throw the whole thing over because of a second-hand casket? Fifteen years, I don't look at anybody else, and just like that, you're ready to waltz on out. Over a chump change deal with Marty Efferding?"

"Chump change? I was there, Irving. I heard it. Twenty grand for a bunch of dried-out old tools, and you have no idea if they'll bring half that. You risk everything for a bit of fun and meanwhile, our island hideaway drifts away on the tide."

"Okay, Herman. If that's the way you want it, go your own way. But if you do, it'll be too damn bad because you were too impatient and thin-skinned to understand a good deal."

Herm was having none of it. "A good deal, like the pork bellies? This time it's worse. We're talking twenty thousand, not ten."

"Who said anything about paying Marty twenty grand?"

"I heard—"

Irv slapped the dash hard. The sharp crack reverberated through the cab. "You heard, but did you trust me? Did you respect and support me? Who said anything about paying Marty a dime?"

"But—"

"Think, Herman, think. Who's been moaning around feeling worthless because he misses our old way of life? Who wants to pull off one last hit so he can feel better about himself?"

Herm suddenly understood his partner's plan and felt small. Worse than small. A bacterium belly-up in a Petri dish had more on the ball than he did. For the first time since entering the car, he understood his partner's intentions.

Irv sat rigidly in his seat, his hands gripping the wheel so hard the knuckles showed white, his jaw clenched so tightly the muscles of his cheek stood out like rope. The redness in his face and the unshed tear in his eye testified to the depth of the man's emotions.

Hern swallowed hard. Why had he ever doubted Irv? The man couldn't help it if he had trouble communicating. How could it be otherwise, when his so-called father took a leather shaving strop to him every day?

"I'm sorry, Irv. I don't know what came over me. I get it now. Zero percent investment and one hundred percent gain. The whole enchilada, we get all of it. I don't know how I could have doubted you.

Filled with remorse, he gently touched Irv on the shoulder.

Randy Roeder

16

Back in my cabin, I stripped off my carp-befouled clothes, climbed into the shower, and stood under the life-giving spray until the water grew cold. When I went to the bureau to retrieve a fresh set of boxers, the dire reality of my clothing situation hit me. I retrieved the last of my new white t-shirts but had exhausted my supply of jeans. No doubt about it, this fishing business had taken a toll on my wardrobe. Stepping over the cabin's tiny closet, I took an inventory of my options. Summer-weight gray and tan suits, brown and black wingtips, four dress shirts, a pair of charcoal-colored pants and a collection of assorted neckwear greeted me. I selected the charcoal pants and black wingtips. Not something you'd typically pair with a white t-shirt, but since I picked my ensemble wisely and know how to carry myself, I had no doubt but that I looked good.

I stepped out into the mid-morning air and found Lumir and Eddie seated at our shared picnic table, unpacking the Nicholson tool boxes and discussing the contents. When Eddie was in high school, he'd spent hours with Lumir learning everything there was to know about hardwoods and working with traditional hand tools. Though his interest had waned somewhat, he and Lumir had spent the last several months working on a joint project. Eddie's father suffered from an incurable stomach cancer, and he and Lumir were building a walnut burial case in anticipation of the man's demise.

Eddie's dad didn't know about the project, an omission which made sense in a way. It's hard to give it your all and stay optimistic about the future if you learn someone is building a coffin for you. Though Lumir had doubts about the wisdom of the endeavor, he went along with it. My friend treasured the time he spent with Eddie and believed the activity served as good therapy for a grieving young man who'd received little attention from his parents.

Built of the finest walnut lumber from Lumir's stash, the casket featured hand-carved columns on each of the corners and exquisitely shaped sprays of ivy leaves on each of the narrow ends. "That Eddie can carve," Lumir once remarked, and I must say I had to agree with him. Beautifully varnished, the box now rested in Lumir's shop, undergoing the ministrations of a lady friend who had nearly completed the lining.

"You look like a new man," Lumir said as I approached the picnic table.

"Just as good-looking as the old one," I replied.

"At ten o'clock, we're going over to the fish market to weigh the carp. Want to come along?" asked Eddie.

"Can't," I said. "Time to do laundry."

Lumir looked me up and down. "When a man's down to wingtips and a t-shirt, it's past time. We are going to lunch at noon and then going to see the mystery coffin. Don't be late."

I allowed as how I wouldn't and went back to the cabin to retrieve my bag of dirty clothes. For some reason known only to God, I'd parked the Nova behind the cabin last night rather than outside the door. When I rounded the corner to pick it up, I dropped my laundry bag and let out a string of swear words that would have sent a lesser man directly to hell. Somebody had spray painted my car, covering it with graffiti. Nothing fancy, just crude lettering in basic black.

Wife killer! the driver's side advised me.

I walked around back, looked at the trunk. *Whore bait!!* Then around to the passenger's side: *Pervert!!!*

Whoever did it went all out on the hood. A stick man with a tiny erect penis hung from a gallows. Alongside it, the vandal had scrawled *Little-dicky Efferdong.*

Unable to comprehend the scene before me, I circled the car again, my guts tied in knots, cursing all the way. I must have been louder than I thought. Lumir and Eddie rounded the cabin, stopped in their tracks, and stared.

Lumir broke the ice. "It looks as if the townspeople have not forgotten you."

Eddie patted me on the shoulder. "Clete, I'm sorry I talked you into coming back to your hometown. Why don't we pick up the boat, pack up the trotlines, and go home? Pole-and-line fishing is good on Lake McBride right now."

Lumir removed his hat and stroked his hair. "Your town gets more like the *Deliverance* movie every day. I can see why you left. These are not normal people."

I squared my shoulders, leaned forward, and stuck out my chin. "You're both wrong," I said. "Eddie, you're wrong, because there's no way in hell I'm cutting my vacation short because some idiot vandalized my car. And Lumir, I know the people who live here; the town might be home to a jackass or two, but the people are not dim-witted rednecks. They're decent people living in a quiet, peaceful town who want nothing more than to keep it that way.

Eddie looked as if he didn't get my point. "Okay, so the town has some swell residents. We can take your car to a dealership tomorrow. They can buff most of it out. It may be eight years old, but a '68 Nova is still worth it."

"No," I said with conviction. "It stays the way it is. I don't want to give the jerk who did this the satisfaction of thinking his artwork upset me."

"Are you sure, Clete?" asked Lumir.

"Sometimes you're the swatter, and sometimes you're the fly. Today, I was the fly," I replied as I picked up my bag of clothes and headed for the Nova. "When we get back to Cedar Rapids, I'll get an Earl Scheib paint job for $49.95. See you for lunch."

I started the engine and turned onto the drive. My friends didn't know I'd vandalized Canker DeCook's truck, and he'd probably paint my Nova again if I cleaned off the artwork. Though I didn't believe Marty had ratted me out, I knew she had trouble keeping her mouth shut. She must have spilled the beans somewhere along the line. Still, I had to laugh. If the barely literate scrawl on my car amounted to Canker's idea of revenge, I didn't have much to worry about. The handwriting on the car was consistent and as such, the work of one hand. Canker hadn't even taken the trouble to enlist his friends in the activity.

I turned onto Front Street and headed toward the laundromat. Two blocks up, I spotted a man standing on the sidewalk in front of a white house, gesticulating wildly. As I passed, I noticed a woman on the porch, her arms waving as rapidly as the man's, obviously agitated and obviously shouting. With my windows up, I couldn't make out what the fuss was about, but the visuals said it all. Hankie Steines had just been thrown out of the house—possessions, clothing, and all —very publicly, on the town's main drag, on a Sunday morning. He must have had a hell of a night, and secretly I hoped whatever he'd done to rate the expulsion was worth it.

Still chuckling over the incident four blocks later, I almost missed the laundromat. Though I try not to rejoice in the misfortunes of others, the scene was a classic. I pulled into the small gravel lot in front of the building, grabbed my laundry, and entered. As the door closed behind me, my light-hearted reaction to Hankie's problems evaporated. The reality of my new environment hit home. Laundromats are seldom cheery, but the prospect of an hour and a quarter in the slag heap on Front Street was enough to suck the joy out of a lifetime of intimate Sunday mornings in bed.

Located in a 120-year-old stone granary, the operation's concrete floor and plaster walls screamed for paint. Alcatraz had nothing on the tomb-like space. Spider webs hung from cement posts, fluorescent lights buzzed and flickered, dead crickets lay in corners, and rivulets of rust-colored water trickled from broken machines. Thank God, the place was empty. Three-quarters of the world's child abuse takes place in laundromats, and I wasn't in the mood to watch a screaming mother gobsmack her kids.

After getting ripped off twice by the change machine, I accumulated enough coins to buy soap and plug the slots of a still-functioning washer. I'd just reached the half-way point of a story in a three-year-old *Reader's Digest* when I heard the front door open and looked up to see my cousin Marty walk in.

Great. Now what? Yesterday Marty had been as pleasant and cheerful as apple pie. The night before she'd been a screaming harpy ready to pick me to pieces and carry the remains off to the gates of the underworld. Consistency had never been the woman's high point.

Her presence unnerved me so much I had trouble getting back to my article on Thad, a mountain climber whose dead mother's wind-driven voice convinced him to keep walking toward base camp rather than settling in for a nap in the snow. After Marty had loaded a pair of washers and seated herself in the chair across the low table from me, I realized the suffering mountaineer and I were about to part company.

"You're a popular guy," she said. "Nice paint job on your car."

"No thanks to you. You spilled the beans on my messing with Canker's truck, so he paid the cabin a visit last night."

"I didn't blab. If Canker DeCook knew you had anything to do with the scratches on his truck, you'd be in traction and hooked up to a monitor—if they got you to the hospital on time. What on earth possessed you to do anything so stupid?"

"The guy burned down the State Park Lodge for Christ's sake, and people treat him better than they do me. It's not fair."

"Was it fair to cheat on your wife when she was down in the dumps?"

"You've got me. Still, Canker did it deliberately. His way of giving the whole town the finger. I never intended to hurt Myra."

Marty didn't seem interested in my rationalizations.

"Cletus, why did you sell Efferding's Menswear to me?"

I put down my magazine. "I've asked myself a thousand times, and the answer is always the same. When Brute Hinkley threatened me, I had to leave town in a hurry. You were working for me and knew the business."

She rummaged through her bright green purse and pulled out a lipstick. "I figured as much but hoped there was more to it."

I watched as she colored her lips. "How so?"

"I hoped you sold it to me because the sale would keep the store in the family."

"I needed a buyer—fast. You were there. As for keeping the business in the family, it would have been nice, but I guess we know how that worked out."

She returned her lipstick to her purse. "You might think you know how it worked out, but you don't. Ever try to kill yourself, Cletus?"

I'd once been close but wasn't about to bare my soul. "Nope," I said.

"Well, when you're upset enough to do the deed, you're not thinking about invoices, inventory, and discounts."

Marty had a point. Actually, she had two. I'd never considered that selling the store to her would keep it in the family because I thought of her as an outsider. And while I'd once contemplated taking my life, I didn't try to follow through. Though she'd bumbled the job, Marty had taken the despair thing a step further than I.

At a loss for words, I made no response.

"And I lost a baby. Do you know what it's like when one day there's a child inside you, and the next day it's gone? I didn't plan it that way, but when I took those pills, I murdered my baby."

Her words hit like bolts of electricity. Though I managed to keep my grief under control, not a day passed that I didn't feel responsible for my wife's death. I didn't like Marty feeling the same way about her baby, and I didn't like her feeling the same way I did about losing the family business. We may have shared similar life experiences, but I possessed sound judgment and reliability, qualities

Marty lacked. Certain the differences between us outweighed any biological similarities, I hurried to put the conversation on a more comfortable basis.

"That was a long time ago," I said. "We all make mistakes, but we move on. Say, I was driving down Front Street and saw Hankie Steines standing out on the sidewalk with his clothes scattered all over the front yard and a woman on the front porch screaming at him. Looks like his old lady tossed him out on his ear."

My diversion worked. Marty always enjoyed a good piece of gossip, and the look that crossed her face indicated avid interest.

"Have you heard anything?" she asked. "Have they been fighting? Is there another woman? There's got to be a reason."

"Hey, this is my third day back in town. I have no idea of what's behind it. I hoped you'd have the hot poop and clue me in."

Marty popped out of her chair, gathering up her purse in such a hurry its contents spilled onto the floor. She knelt to retrieve them. The task completed, she looked up at me red-faced and said, "I just remembered. I left coffee on the stove with the burner on. I need to run back pronto and turn it off. Don't worry about my clothes. Nobody will bother them while I'm gone."

As if I'd worry about her laundry. I watched as she rushed for the door. She'd just put her hand on the glass when I remembered Lumir wanted me to invite her to our fish fry that evening. I called after her.

"Hey Marty, before I forget, we caught a bunch of catfish this morning and are having a fry-up at the cabins tonight. Lumir says I'm supposed to phone you, but this is better. Can you make it around 7:30?"

"I'll be there," she called over her shoulder and pushed her way outside.

Good old unreliable Marty. She forgets she has coffee on the stove and then leaves her clothes behind, taking up machines others might use. Talk about scatter-brained. Still, I understood I'd been too hard on her. She'd had a rough life from day one, and having her mother walk out when her father died didn't help any.

After idly wondering why my news of Hankie's domestic woes reminded her of an overheated coffee pot, I returned to my story of Thad, the steadfast mountaineer. When I finished, I understood that he and I had a lot in common, ordinary guys heroically marching on despite obstacles and setbacks encountered along the way.

Marty could have learned a lot from us.

17

Hank Steines managed to get his wife quieted down. She agreed to let him back in the house to fetch the rest of his belongings, but the way she kept pouring it on convinced him he'd be an absolute fool to put up with her longer than necessary. The dingbat kept talking about divorcing him as if it was the worst punishment known to man. Not even close. Then the nutcase swiped the keys to his truck while he was busy carrying his stuff out. She could have the damn thing. The engine needed a rebuild anyway. All this fuss because she didn't want him hanging around Blackie. Well, a man who can't pick his own friends might as well turn in his gonads. No way Hank was ready for that.

He'd just added his double-barrel shotgun and duck decoys to the curbside heap when Marty Efferding pulled up with her pickup and trailer. She rolled down the passenger-side window and gestured.

"Need a hand?" she called from inside.

"Could use some help moving my stuff," he replied, leaning on the edge of the window.

"Where to?"

"Blackie Stiles doesn't know it yet, but he's got himself a new roommate."

"You could move in with me."

Hank swallowed hard, pushed his hat back on his head. "I don't know. I thought we had something once, but you kept sayin' you weren't interested. I don't need that again."

"I made a mistake, Hank. A big one. Let's get your stuff loaded and off the sidewalk. We can talk later when you've had time to think about it."

"I'm tired, Marty. Right now, I don't know if I'm ready for another woman."

Marty made no reply but got out of her pickup, walked to the back of the trailer, and opened the doors. Blackie, still standing at the cab, watched as she began moving his possessions inside. When Marty picked up his double-barrel, he found the motivation to speak.

"Be careful with that, it belonged to my grandpa. Between him, my dad, and me, that gun has popped more ducks than Bellevue has people."

"I don't see how. It's so old, it has hammers on it. By the time you'd get it cocked, the ducks would be gone."

"I'll show you how to use it sometime. Once you get the hang of it, you can set both hammers before you get it to your shoulder. Course, you've got to be careful. If the hammer doesn't lock in place and snaps forward while you're bringing the gun up, it'll go off."

"So?"

Hank walked back to the trailer. "It can kick back in your face, and you'd get pretty bruised up. I got a case for that thing somewhere if I can find it in this mess."

He took the gun and began searching for its case. Though he didn't say so, he'd never been so happy to see a friendly face, and to top it off, the face belonged to Marty Efferding. Maybe, just maybe, one of the worst days of his life would turn into one of the best.

They worked in silence, loading the trailer. The task didn't take long. The load was small because he kept his tools and fishing gear in a rented garage near Blackie's. As he added his now-cased shotgun to the top of the accumulation, he heard footsteps tromping down the sidewalk. He turned in time to see his wife storm up to Marty.

"I knew it!" his irate spouse screamed. "It figures that worthless piece of crap would have a creampuff on the side. You proud of yourself, home wrecker? The whole town thinks you're a slut, and now you just proved it."

Hank moved to put himself between the women but didn't make it in time. A resounding slap split the air as an open hand nearly sent Marty to the ground. He stepped between them, facing his wife.

"There's nothing going on," Hank said, grabbing his spouse's arms. "You hit her for nothing. She's just helping me get my stuff moved. You threw me out, remember? She just—"

Screaming pain shot through Hank's groin. He let go of his wife and folded like a tissue. The snot-faced shrew had kneed him in the balls. Shouting and curses filled the air as he straightened up and saw Marty, her face bloody, plant a haymaker on his old lady's chin. She fell back onto the lawn. Still recovering from the blow to his testicles, he was unable to stop Marty from delivering two sharp kicks to the woman's backside—one with the pointy toe of her shoe, and the other with her four-inch heel.

"Don't you ever, ever call me a slut again," Marty fumed.

"We better go Marty," counseled Hank, "before the law comes."

I found Lumir seated at the table outside our cabins, busy polishing the piece of brass he'd discovered in the weeds near the boat ramp. I don't know where he'd managed to locate a piece of fine steel wool, but the scrap was beginning to shine. As I approached, he turned the piece over, exposing the oxidized side then covering it with his forearm. We all have our quirks. If Lumir didn't want to show me the result of his efforts before it had reached a blinding gleam, okay by me. Shiny objects don't do much for me, but Lumir liked his glitz.

"How'd the big carp weigh-in go?" I asked.

Eddie answered, calling out through the screen door of the cabin he shared with Lumir. "Fifty-seven pounds. Biggest the guys at the market have ever seen."

"Big, but they didn't want anything to do with it," Lumir added.

Eddie joined us at the table. "That's true, but I got lucky. Some guys over at Shady Haven Resort came into the fish market to buy sturgeon and said they'd take it. They're gonna cut that big baby into four monster fillets, smoke 'em, and have a party."

"I'm just happy we don't have to get rid of the thing," I said. "But hey, it's time to go see the coffin. I'll drive."

Lumir grunted. "I do not wish to ride in your car."

"I'm not so hot on the idea either," Eddie added. "It says you're a small-dicked wife killer for Christ's sake. Doesn't that bother you?"

"Not really. Neither statement is true. I'm more than happy with my equipment, and my wife took her own life."

Eddie folded his arms over his chest. "Yeah, but I don't want people staring at us wherever we go."

Lumir nodded in agreement. "I will be uncomfortable as well. I don't know why you will not ask the police to investigate."

An outstandingly bad idea given that I'd trashed Canker's truck —time for a diversion. "I ran into Marty at the laundromat. She's coming to our fish fry tonight."

Eddie held up the keys to his truck and motioned for us to join him. "Glad to hear it," he said. "Let's go."

A five-minute drive brought us to Ray Gallagher's furniture store. A small knot of people stood in front awaiting their turn to ogle the burial case. Eddie parked the pickup, and the three of us crossed the street to join them. We soon learned that Ray, a bit cranky yesterday, had undergone a change of heart and greeted today's visitors with a warm smile and the occasional handshake. The news of Ray's good mood and a sunny June day made for a casual, almost festive atmosphere, one oddly suited to viewing a coffin. Oblivious to their own mortality, people chatted amiably, as if waiting in line for a turn on a Ferris wheel.

It took all of three minutes for Lumir to strike up a conversation with a retired schoolteacher and her daughter, and a minute longer to charm the mother into a weak-kneed appreciation of his manly virtues.

"You can learn something from him," I whispered to Eddie.

"More than you could teach me," he whispered back.

Eddie's riposte reminded me that I'd yet to exact vengeance for his Kissy Kathy caper. I let his comment ride but resolved to remedy the situation within the next twenty-four hours. The heck with tit for tat, this haberdasher intended to escalate.

"Hi Clete, how's it going?"

I turned to see an-off duty Wiley McCard approach. His neon-blue leisure suit and wide-collared polyester shirt suggested he'd spent his Sunday morning in a house of God. I hoped the two were on good terms. Were I the Almighty, I might have forgiven the leisure suit, but his choice of a white patent leather belt with matching shoes would have earned him a black mark in the Book of Life. While not grounds for an automatic damnation, when Wiley met St. Pete at the Pearly Gates, he'd have some explaining to do.

"Wiley," I asked, "what are you doing here? Working undercover?"

He laughed. "No. I just want to see the coffin like everybody else."

"I thought you'd have been crawling all over it and have your fill by now."

"It's not a police department case," he replied. "Blackie and Hank found the thing on an island outside the city limits, so the County Sheriff and Department of Natural Resources have jurisdiction. Our only involvement is to make sure nobody steals it. I spent the entire night parked out back looking at the garage door from inside the patrol car."

"Can't imagine who'd want it. Must have been a boring assignment."

"A couple of cats got into a real tussle around four a.m., otherwise not much going on. Speaking of catfights, your cousin Marty got into a humdinger this morning. She's lucky she didn't end up in the county jail. I didn't know she had something going with Hankie Steines."

I remembered Marty's reaction to my report that Hankie had been thrown out of the house. "News to me too," I replied. "Getting into a fight over somebody like Hankie is hard to imagine."

Wiley shrugged and hooked his thumbs into his patent leather belt. "Like my ma used to say, there's somebody for everybody."

I grimaced and looked away. If Efferding's Menswear were still open, there'd have been no way Wiley would have been walking around town in an outfit like that.

"Take your thumbs out of your belt, Wiley." I couldn't help myself. "When a man's wearing a suit, he doesn't hook his thumbs in his belt. It's a fashion rule." One I'd made up on the spot, so he wouldn't call attention to the eyesore encircling his waist.

"Didn't know," he said. "Anyway, when Eldon called it in, the dispatcher made it sound like such a big deal the chief showed up in his own car. By then, Eldon had the women separated, and each one wanted the other charged with assault and battery. That would have meant figuring out who was at fault, making an arrest, and delivering 'em to the lockup in Maquoketa. No way the boss wanted the patrol car out of town what with all this coffin business going on."

Wiley started to move his thumbs in the direction of his belt but caught himself and tugged at his jacket sleeves instead, an unfortunate move that called attention to his ruffled cuffs. Compared to the belt and shoes, the shirt seemed a small trespass indeed.

"He had Eldon put Hankie and his wife in the patrol car and drive them to city hall. Marty rode with the chief."

"Arrested all three. Easier than sorting them out."

"We didn't exactly arrest them. The chief sat them down in his office and read them the riot act. Told them if they didn't cooperate, he'd charge Hankie with assault and battery and the women with assault with the intention to do great bodily harm."

"Whoa, sounds like the chief is a tough cookie. I thought he believed in small-town policing. You know, solving problems, rather than going overboard."

"He's a genius. The magistrate wouldn't have put up with the great bodily harm thing, but the chief scared the living bejesus out of them. You know—felonies, incarceration, a five-digit bail bond ... After that, nobody wanted to press charges."

"Then no problems, and everybody gets off scot-free?"

Wiley reached for the bill of his patrolman's cap, realized he was in his civvies and made a move for his belt. He stopped before he got there and put his hands in his hip pockets instead.

"Wiley," I said. "The rule goes for the back pockets too."

Another lie, but the belt was an obscenity.

"You can be a pain, Efferding."

"Good fashion sense doesn't come easy."

Wiley ignored my remark and finished his story. "The chief wrote citations for all three. Disturbing the peace. They'll have to go to Maquoketa for a hearing tomorrow, but the lesser charge means transportation is their problem, not ours. They'll be looking at fines and court costs. The magistrate is death on disturbances to the public order."

"Good solution. Say, Eddie and Lumir are already at the door. I better get going."

I joined my friends just as Ray opened the door to let them in. After six of us had passed, he closed the door again. Wiley didn't make the cut. Our group included three teen-aged girls. None of them looked old enough to be there.

When we entered the attached garage, the scene didn't meet my expectations. I'd imagined a funeral director would have done something to soften the experience, maybe place the box on a fabric-covered bier and set out a flower or two. No dice. Apparently, even the simplest niceties were reserved for paying customers.

The coffin rested on a trio of sawhorses. Naked incandescent bulbs hung from the ceiling. The oil-stained concrete floor and a grimy, rag-covered workbench didn't do much for the overall atmosphere. Empty cardboard boxes and furniture crates filled one of the two stalls.

I don't know how many ways there are to spell weird, but the casket exhausted all of them. The part that got me was the size of the thing. It looked to be a bit over five feet long, small for a full-sized adult. I couldn't imagine anyone breaking a cadaver's legs to force a fit, and the thought of a child inside the grotesquely ornamented box gave me the willies. Death is bad enough, but the cast-iron shroud adorning the lid served as a stark reminder of the coldness of the tomb and the likelihood the departed would rise to haunt the living.

I gave the air a good sniff but didn't smell anything out of the ordinary. Ray noticed but didn't say anything until Eddie followed suit.

"No smell," he explained, "but somebody messed with the closure bolts. One's twisted off, and someone loosened and re-tightened a few of the others. I suspect whoever did it broke the seal and gas started leaking out, so they tightened them back up again."

I chuckled. "Sounds like Blackie and Hank got a bit curious."

"We don't know that," said Ray. "But somebody tampered with it. When you think about it, the box is a good product: over a century old, dunked in the Mississippi, and the seal still tight—and with a glass viewing window over the face, yet. Too bad the nameplate is missing. Unless somebody reports a suspicious excavation, we're unlikely to ever know who's inside."

Our group stared at the burial case in silence. Ray soon cleared his throat and began a spiel he must have given a hundred times.

"The vines, cocoons, and butterflies at the foot of the casket symbolize death and rebirth. Though they seem strange to us today, Victorian funeral customs were elaborate. Symbolism played a big part in the way the people of that era dealt with death. Locks of the departed's hair, photos of the deceased in their coffins, and baby shoes framed in black crepe seem morbid to us today, but back then that sort of sentimentality was part and parcel of everyday life.

"What's the deal with the baby shoes?" asked Eddie. "I don't get it."

"Although infant death was common in the nineteenth century, it hit the parents just as hard as today. Some families found it comforting to have the shoes mounted in a shadow box along with a picture of the deceased. They'd hang the arrangement on the wall, often for as long as a year, although some families never took them down."

"Weird," said Eddie. "Too bad the glass is so cloudy. It would be cool to see the face. Maybe it's a deformed, stunted kid or a little old lady."

Ray looked appalled. Eddie's enthusiasm must have offended his sense of decorum. He'd barely recovered when, for reasons I couldn't fathom, Lumir walked up to the coffin, spread his fingers, and pushed them against its surface, just below the glass window. He followed by cocking his index finger and pushing it against the casket yet again.

"No touching," an authoritative Ray announced. "The coroner's office and sheriff haven't completed their investigation."

Lumir, his face the picture of innocence, shrugged. "Just an old Czech tradition. Hand signs to protect against the Evil Eye."

I couldn't believe my ears; Lumir didn't have a superstitious bone in his body. His antics, coupled with Eddie's morbid curiosity, must have been a bit much for Ray. He shooed us out the side door and closed it firmly. I couldn't be certain, but I thought I heard the sound of a bolt sliding through its barrel. Without a doubt, we'd met the funeral director's criteria for oafish behavior.

"Thanks for getting us booted early," said one of the girls who had accompanied us into the viewing.

The remark must have irritated Lumir, for he turned on his heel and began speaking Czech in a singsong I'd never heard him use. After blessing them with a cross-like motion, he shifted to a lower register and growled, "I have saved you from the Evil Eye, but I cannot save you from the curse of The Hag." He raised his index finger into the air. "When you walk in darkness, beware. She who is dead shall rise again."

The startled girls froze on the spot.

18

I couldn't sleep, so the wee hours found me seated on Myra's picnic table, staring out at the Mississippi. Not that I could see much. Fog shrouded the river, and the rising mist had begun pouring up over the high bank and settling in around me. The soup-like conditions meant we'd have a heck of a time finding our trotlines in the morning. Not that it would bother my friends any. They'd be perfectly content to blunder aimlessly between shore and the channel in vague hope of finding our buoys.

The events of the day had left me so keyed up my overactive mind wouldn't allow blessed slumber to overtake me. Someone had vandalized my car. The malice behind the activity bothered me more than I'd let on. I suspected Marty was right, that Canker hadn't done it. The juvenile insults and images hinted at a perpetrator in his early teens. Reality sucks. Myra's suicide had become so embedded in the town's folklore that young people heard about it as matter of course. Layers of exaggeration and misinformation stick like glue to oft-repeated stories, and God only knows what tales they heard. Nothing I could do would set the record straight.

Lumir's odd behavior during our inspection of the mysterious casket didn't do much for me either. My best friend's inexplicable conduct had me concerned. His mumbo jumbo about the Evil Eye and Old Hag had been so out of character I feared the onset of dementia. When I broached the topic with Eddie, he laughed and brushed off my unease, telling me to lighten up. We were on vacation, he said, and if Lumir enjoyed tweaking the locals, more power to him. I suspected he was right, but I knew one thing he didn't. Binge worriers are more important than youngsters like Eddie realize. Without us, mass chaos might erupt and wipe civilization from the earth. On duty tonight, I had the responsibility to take the little things seriously lest they get out of hand.

The high-powered searchlight of an approaching towboat swept the river below me, methodically moving back and forth as the pilot searched shore and water for navigational markers. Normally bright enough to illuminate anything within a half mile, the fog-dimmed beam played across the water uncertainly. A dangerous night to be on the water, but the captain had a schedule to keep. I shivered and wished I'd brought a jacket.

My worries ping-ponged back and forth, giving me no peace until the mystery that was my cousin distracted me. Marty had surprised us by bringing Hankie Steines to our fish fry. A nice enough guy I guess, but he'd managed to drink as much as Lumir, Eddie, and me combined. Halfway through the evening, Marty pulled me aside to emphasize she and Hankie were friends, and any rumors about them having an affair had no basis in truth. I didn't believe a word. She hadn't changed since high school, and her obvious affection for the guy told me all I needed to know.

Though I take a dim view of extramarital hanky-panky, her carrying on with Hankie didn't bother me. For reasons I didn't understand, my cousin and her eccentricities had begun to grow on me. Marty couldn't live a normal life; she was incapable of it. Though she'd cheated me on the sale of Efferding's Menswear, her actions paled in comparison to what my folks did to her. Though I expected I'd live to regret it, I'd done something tonight I never dreamed possible. I agreed to lend Marty six hundred dollars.

She wanted to buy the Nicholson tool chests in the worst way. She offered Lumir twelve hundred dollars—six hundred immediately and another six after she'd delivered the tools to a buyer. Though I saw the glimmer in his eyes, Lumir didn't bite. His "once in a lifetime" find had a price, and Marty had just met it. Sensing his refusal had more to do with my tales of her financial irresponsibility than an attachment to the chests, I offered to lend her the second six hundred. When she left for home, Lumir looked at me as if I were the one whose erratic behavior forecast impending senility.

"Are your sure, Clete?" he asked.

"Of course." I spread my hands magnanimously. "If Marty manages the first six, I'll lend her the rest. She can pay me after she makes the sale."

Although the four beers I'd consumed may have clouded my judgment, I wanted to do something for Marty—something to make up for my parents' callous indifference to her. Call me a sap, but I liked the woman in spite of myself. At the time, the possibility I'd never see the money again didn't seem to matter.

Lumir lectured me. "She's a nice girl, but she will never repay you. I took the deal to teach you a lesson you should have learned the first time around. Never lend money to a freeloader."

The towboat had reached a point directly across from me; its feeble searchlight now played on the lock and dam. What with the noise of its engines, I missed the sound of someone climbing the wooden stairway that ended a few feet from me, the structure I thought of as Myra's stairway. Through the fog, I could barely make out the figure standing at the top. Someone had wrapped themselves in a blanket to ward off the chill.

"Good evening," I said. Though nearly three a.m., a cheery good morning would have sounded ludicrous.

No answer. As the person approached I saw the blanket was dripping. It came to me in a flash. The damn fog. Someone had been in a boating accident and was in shock. I rose. "Are you okay? There's a phone booth outside Milt's Conoco. We'll call and get help. Are there others?"

A shake of the head. The sole survivor, wrapped in a blanket so tightly I couldn't tell if I was speaking to a man or woman.

"The Conoco is about two blocks. Can you make it that far?"

Trembling hands lowered the blanket to shoulder level.

Myra!

She stepped closer. I couldn't move. Though I recognized her, Myra didn't look like herself. She looked dead. Dead, but pale, beautiful, and wet. She came no closer but stood keening, an otherworldly wail filled with misery, a disconsolate testimony to the twin miseries of mental illness and an unfaithful husband. Her eyes rolled back in her head, leaving only the whites. Entranced, I couldn't look away.

"Cletus" she sobbed. "Come with me."

"It's not time, Myra. I can't."

A howl, filled with all the pain of every suicide since Adam, erupted from deep within her. I watched as she crossed the few feet between us, pursing her lips, closing in for a kiss. I turned my face aside. I couldn't do it. I couldn't kiss a cold, wet corpse with barren eyes.

She screamed. I looked back to see her face rotting before my eyes, exposing bone and muscle as skin peeled away. My ears rang. The smell of mold and decay overwhelmed me. I couldn't breathe.

Not Myra, the Hag!

She grabbed my shoulders and sank her teeth into my cheek. I tore my face away and fell through space as pain unlike any I had ever known tore my soul into a thousand pieces. Centuries passed, and the excruciating torment disappeared. Cold and damp became my bed.

———————

I'd taken quite a fall, and though the drop from the top of the picnic table was less than three feet, I must have pinched a nerve in my upper back. Damn, right between the shoulder blades. I managed to right myself and crawled back onto the seat. Myra's ghost and the Old Hag, figments who had stalked my nightmare, had disappeared in the manner such apparitions do when a troubled sleeper awakes.

I rolled my neck to uncoil the kink in my back. It didn't help. I tried putting my hands over my head and stretching but got no relief. At least I'd been able to complete the two activities. With any luck, I'd be stiff for a day or two and then be back to normal. Chilled and uncomfortable, I pulled myself erect and set off in the direction of the cabin.

When I reached my destination, I realized the movement had done me good. The small improvement in my back meant the day had ended on an up-note. Nothing to crow about, but I'd started out this morning on the bottom of Eddie's johnboat with a glob of carp offal in my mouth. I took my small victory as a sign that tomorrow would be better.

Except it already was tomorrow. Eddie and Lumir would be picking me up in an hour and fifteen minutes to pull trotlines. No point in going to bed, so I picked up an abandoned copy of *Destry Rides Again* that lay next to the Gideon's Bible in the drawer of the nightstand. I tried to get involved in the story, but my picnic table nightmare had left me too keyed up.

Myra, my kids, the way my parents treated Marty; Aunt Kate abandoning Marty; my weird aunt Millie; Grandpa Efferding, I cycled through memories like slides on a screen. Did I ever know a normal family life? The whole kit and caboodle felt like a horror show.

The Efferding family, not much to be proud of. What had I been thinking when I decided to put together a family history for the kids? What would I say when I handed it to them?

Hey kids, you come from a long line of wackos. You're probably messed up too. Enjoy.

On the other hand, I doubted I'd pass this way again. I could write the thing up and hang on to it. If the situation presented itself, I could pass it on. If not, I'd have satisfied my own curiosity. The Efferding family, a cardboard front presented to the world, a fiction designed to hide the dysfunction lurking within. Though the original motivation for the project lay in tatters, my vacation would soon reach the halfway point. Before long, I'd want to take time away from fish and friends and get started.

Lumir and Eddie surprised me by showing up on time, filled with their customary good cheer. Apparently, they'd been up and drinking coffee for the last half hour.

"Guys," I said, "Lumir will have to pick up the trotlines this morning. I pinched a nerve in my back last night. Bending over and pulling lines out of the water just isn't going to happen."

Eddie smirked. "Sounds like Kissy Kathy got the best of you last night."

"No, I fell off a picnic table."

Eddie whistled. "You lead a dangerous life, Clete."

"If you only knew, Big Boy."

"Knew what?"

"You'll find out."

And he would, as soon as we got back from picking up the lines. I'd agreed to make breakfast: oatmeal with whole milk, butter, brown sugar, and raisins. Late yesterday afternoon, I'd picked up a little something extra for Eddie's bowl.

We made it through the fog-covered blacktop down to Eddie's boat and set out onto the water. As I expected, the pea soup rising from the river made it difficult to get our bearings and almost impossible to locate the gallon jugs that served as our buoys. After wandering aimlessly for forty-five minutes, things began to clear, and the task went off without a hitch. We returned to the cabins with a half dozen catfish. Lumir and Eddie set to work dressing them while I made breakfast.

Whistling happily, I stirred as cereal bubbled on the hot plate. None of that quickie one-minute stuff for me. My friends and I would be enjoying the real McCoy. I managed to time the meal exactly, putting the coffee on the table just as Lumir and Eddie sat down.

"We're having another fish fry tonight," Eddie announced. "I've already invited the families in the other cabins."

"Can't make it," I replied. "I'm going to Dale's bachelor party. You, Lumir, and the trotlines are on your own tomorrow morning."

I watched as Eddie dug into his oatmeal with gusto.

"How is it?" I asked.

"Wonderful," he replied. "Raisins are a great idea."

I frowned. "This oatmeal doesn't seem quite right. Mine tastes fishy."

"Not mine," Eddie replied.

He'd nearly finished the bowl when his spoon stopped mid-air. "Now that you mention it, something does seem off."

I pointed to his spoon. "What's that, next to the raisin? Looks like a fish eye. Not a catfish, maybe a sheepshead."

Eddie froze.

"I put four in your bowl. Looks like you don't have that many left. I was going to use three, but Kissy said to go for broke. She thought you deserved it."

Eddie didn't say a word but picked up his bowl and made for the trash can where he dumped oatmeal, bowl, and spoon.

I didn't expect him to rejoin us at the table, and though I hoped he'd lose his breakfast, he didn't. Still, I was satisfied.

Nobody messes with Cletus Efferding. Nobody.

Last night's half hour of sleep caught up with me after my oatmeal breakfast, so I returned to the cabin and racked out. Although Dale promised his Monday night bachelor party would break up early, I suspected the event would go on longer than anticipated. Somewhere in the middle of a dream in which I got rich selling Helen Nicholson's tool chests, a banging noise interrupted my slumber. I checked my watch. Two in the afternoon. Turned out the noisemaker was the guy who owned the cabins. Somebody had called his office, wanting to speak to me.

I struggled out of bed and crossed the gravel lane between buildings in my stocking feet. My pinched nerve seemed to be getting better. When I got to the office, Dale was on the line.

"Clete, Dale here. I heard somebody spray-painted your car with all sorts of nastiness."

"How'd you know? It's spent most of the past day and a half parked down here behind the cabin."

"Duh, you parked it in front of the laundromat yesterday. You didn't think you could leave it on Front Street on Sunday morning without a hundred people seeing it? Everybody knew about the paint job by this morning. That's why I called."

"You know who did it?"

"No, but I don't think you should drive it to my bachelor party. After a few beers, the guys might think that comment about the size of your equipment is funny."

I sat in a nearby chair, picked up a pencil, and began adding doodles to the impressive collection on its wooden arm. "That comment was painted on the hood. I don't understand how people could see it when they drove by."

"I heard it from Orville Schab; Hankie Steines told him. If Hankie and Orville know, that means it made the rounds at Junnie's Fish Market and P. J.'s Woodshop. I'll pick you up at 7:30, and you can ride in my new truck. I might need you to drive me home later."

"Where are you having it?"

"Out on Spruce Creek Road where Hap Herrig used to live."

I added a mustache to the leering devil I'd just drawn. "Hap moved away?"

"Died last winter. The house is empty right now. The furniture is still in it, so his grandson Jay said it would be a good place to have the party. Nobody within a mile to complain about the noise and traffic."

"Okay, you drive. See you later." I hung up the phone.

Lumir and Eddie were nowhere to be found, so I retrieved *Destry Rides Again* and settled in at the picnic table for a little reading. I'd just finished chapter five when Lumir and Eddie pulled up.

"What you been up to?' I asked.

"Coffin patrol," replied Eddie. "The Sheriff and Deputy County Medical Examiner are here today, and we got to be part of the big parade."

I put my paperback down. "Parade? What parade?"

Eddie looked at me with wonder. "If you didn't sleep all day, you'd know what's going on in your own hometown. They put the box in Ray's hearse and took it down to the Conservation Commission lab south of town to see if it would float. Of course, the television trucks and reporters had to follow them to see what was going on. People have been staking out Ray's store, so when the hearse, police car, and TV trucks took off, they pulled in behind them. We saw the line and joined in."

I raised my eyes to the heavens. "The coffin again. It figures."

"See," said Lumir as he settled onto the plank seat across from me, "I told you Clete wouldn't be interested. "There was no point in stopping to pick him up."

Eddie put his hands into his hip pockets. "Guess I'll stop by the fish market to see what's going on."

Eddie left, and I turned my attention back to Lumir. "Did it?" I asked.

"Did it what?"

"Did it float?"

"It did, but very low in the water. Only an inch or two broke the surface. That means it must have floated onto the island."

"Then what?"

"For someone who thinks he is above the rest of us, you are very curious."

"So, shoot me," I said.

"You are not very perceptive. Since the coffin floats, they don't believe it was buried on the island."

"I already figured that, Lumir. What happened then?"

"They put the thing back in the hearse, drove it back to the store, and backed into the garage. After that, they locked themselves inside and would not talk with anyone. People kept trying to peek through the window panels in the door, so they covered them with paper. A while later, the Deputy Coroner came out and said folks should go home and wait for the TV reports and newspapers to find out what's going on. A policeman told everyone to go home, so we left."

"Hmph," I grunted. "All that to see if it floated. Who cares?" I picked up my paperback. That Max Brand guy could tell a story.

Lumir didn't let me get started. "I want to look through my tool chests one more time before I sell them to Marty. Will you help me bring them out here to the table?"

My pinched nerve squawked as I helped Lumir carry the chests. I toughed it out. We put the first on the table top and the other on the ground. I sat down opposite him and watched as he lovingly unpacked them. He handled each tool as if it were a treasure: turning it in his hands, remarking on its construction, pointing out how it might be used. I couldn't miss his fondness and respect for these objects from long ago and began to feel guilty for my part in helping Marty buy them.

"Lumir," I said, "if you enjoy these tools so much, why are you selling them to Marty?"

My friend was silent for a moment, then put down the plane he held. "Clete, it is very hard for me to part with these treasures. I may not understand the ways of the antiques market, but it is obvious that these tools are something special. Your cousin offered me twelve hundred dollars for the chests. The offer represents a profit of over a thousand percent on something I have owned only a few days. I cannot turn it down."

"Marty is no fool when it comes to antiques. She's going to sell them for a lot more than she paid."

"And I hope she does well on them. We have a fund at Saint Wenceslaus Church that is used to buy food for women and children from broken homes. Often, the families are divided because the man drinks and becomes violent. Twelve hundred dollars is a windfall and will triple the size of the fund. I cannot keep the tools."

Lumir would regret missing the opportunity to help others more than he'd miss the tools. The man had a heart as big as Minnesota. Still, that didn't make the impending sale easy for him, so I spent the next few hours sharing the excitement of his find. After we'd returned the chests to his cabin, Lumir left me with one final bit of wisdom.

"You can kiss your six hundred dollars goodbye. Nice as Marty is, you will not see a cent of that money, but at least you'll have the satisfaction."

His remark puzzled me. "What satisfaction?"

"The satisfaction of making it possible for me to donate twelve hundred dollars to our fund for needy families."

19

... and that's the lunchtime news, weather, and sports on this twenty-ninth day of June, 1975, on station KMAQ, Maquoketa, Iowa, 1320 on your radio dial and the home of all your country hits. Next up, the farm market report with Bob Mayhew.

Sitting in an overstuffed rocker behind the counter of Five Seasons Antiques, a decidedly unhappy Herman Cohen stared down at the floor.

Irv dialed down the volume on the radio. "I was sure happy when I found out I didn't have to understand the farm reports to blend in with the people here in Cedar Rapids."

Herm didn't respond.

Irv returned to his seat at the shop's roll-top desk, the crowded repository of inquiries, invoices, and receipts that served as the hub of their antique business. "Kinda interesting, though, how we both learned to like country music. The stories in the songs are incredible. They go right to your heart."

Herm, staring off into space, folded his hands over his belly and sighed.

Irv tried again. "I heard Willie Nelson's new song yesterday, 'Blue Eyes Cryin' in the Rain.' Really tore me up."

"It wasn't on the news, Irv. If Marty had my coffin, news that somebody swiped it would be all over the place by now. We shoulda done it ourselves."

"Don't worry, I already took care of it. When Marty didn't call this morning, I got hold of Canker and asked him to get it for us. He runs a construction company, so I offered him enough to make it interesting, two thousand."

Herm felt as if he'd been slapped. "You did what?"

"I figured if we had two people trying to steal the damn thing, we'd double the chances of getting it."

"You just did it again, Irving. You made a business decision without consulting me."

"I'm doing my best to put that box into your hot little hands."

"I'm not a baby, and I'm not stupid. Like Angelo used to say, there are fifty ways to spell mistake, and guess what? You just made all of them. When we ran our Chicago operation, we were the best in the business because we collaborated. Twice the brainpower, twice the experience, and twice as successful as anybody else."

"But I—"

"Hold on, I'm not finished. You think retirement hasn't been easy for me, but at least I haven't lost my edge. You're making mistakes that'd embarrass a fourteen-year-old. I've kept my mouth shut, but you've lost it. Maybe I'm getting soft too, trying to appreciate the little things in life and focusing on our relationship. Five years ago, I woulda called you on it. I see now I should have been less concerned about us and more concerned with survival."

Irv glared at his partner. "Go ahead. What mistakes? What have I done that's so terrible I can't fix it?"

Herm stood to make his point. "Just this once, hear me out. Mistake number one, asking Marty to do the job. Not only is she not a thief, but she'll have to get somebody to help with the coffin because it's so heavy. That means two people in on the job. Let's say we take Marty out so we can keep all the money. There's still a loose end, a partner who can rat on us. We gonna kill 'em both?"

"If we hit Marty, her partner will be too scared to talk."

"Really, Irv? You sound so sure of yourself. Mistake number two, getting your buddy Canker involved. We barely know the guy, and guess what? He's gonna need a helper, just like Marty. Are we gonna whack four people from one little town? Talk about risk, the place will go nuts. The news will all over the country. I can see the headlines already. *Killing spree on Iowa border. FBI called in. Manhunt begins.*"

Herm waited for Irv's response. Got none.

"You're makin' me crazy, Irving. You don't listen to me, even when I know what I'm talking about. You think I'm stupid? You're the one that's gonna get us caught. I don't think I can take it anymore."

"Ya gotta slow down, Herm. You're all wound up over nothing. Nobody said we were gonna whack four people, and we're not gonna end up in prison because some small town nobody made off with an old coffin."

Herm covered his face with his hands and began sobbing uncontrollably. "I'm at the end of my rope. My whole life is going to hell, and I don't know what to do about it."

Irv left his chair and went over to put an arm around Herm's shoulders. "Hey," he said, "you're the Blowtorch, the best in the business. This is nothing compared to the jobs we did for Big Angie. Remember the time we iced the Grillo brothers? Now that was risky."

Herm turned, grabbed the edges of Irv's cardigan, and buried his face in his partner's chest. "It's too much for me. It's just too much."

Irv gave his partner a hug, then gently pushed him away. "You're a nervous wreck, Bud. Let's close up shop and go home. I'll fix a nice lunch, and then we'll go see Doctor Bob. He'll be happy to work you in. He owes us because we gave him a deal on that Queen Anne dining set. Maybe it's time to try that Valium thing we've heard so much about. Come on Herm, you're not in this alone. We'll get through it together. You'll see."

Irv squeezed Herm's arm, then stepped to the front window where he flipped the hanging sign to the *Closed* side. Thinking he heard a news bulletin in the background, he turned up the radio.

> *. . . and here she is, the First Lady of Country Music, Tammy Wynette, with a 1320 KMAQ country classic, "Stand by Your Man."*

The sounds of Wynette's anthem filled the room as Irv took his partner's hand. "She's right, Herm. Thick or thin, I'm in this with you all the way."

Eddie returned from the fish market with happy news indeed. A couple of boys had approached him offering to sell him several hundred nightcrawlers they'd picked up. Wanting to try a different bait, Eddie bought them. The transaction meant I wouldn't have to seine minnows before I went to Dale's bachelor party.

My new-found freedom had me singing in the shower, thinking about my attire for a big night out. Dale warned me that the evening would be causal. After four days in jeans and t-shirts, I was ready for a jacket and tie. Still, it wouldn't do to outshine the guest of honor, so I settled for tan slacks and a pastel-yellow oxford cloth shirt. My brown Italian loafers and matching belt added just the right touch, and though I yearned to add a sport coat, I didn't want to be overdressed. I checked the mirror. God, I looked good. Worried that I still might be overdressed, I undid the collar buttons on my shirt.

Dale showed up wearing jeans and an Allman Brothers concert t-shirt, looking like he intended to mow the lawn. The illusion that I'd dressed appropriately for the party in tatters, I hopped into the spacious cab of his new truck, and we were off.

Our destination, a two-story farmhouse, sat on an alfalfa-covered rise. Once as pretty as a postcard, the house had undergone one of the modifications common to the area. Hap, the former owner, had excavated the earth on the downhill side of his home and built a two-stall garage that opened into the basement. A concrete slab level with the first floor served as a combination garage roof and patio.

Far from the first to arrive, Dale and I parked on the sloping lawn amid a colorful assortment of cars, pickups, and motorcycles. We ascended the hill to the house amid congratulatory shouts, cheers, and insults. I surveyed the crowd and realized Dale and I might have been oldest people there.

Great minds think alike. "Most guys my age have three or four kids," Dale said. "Their wives aren't happy to see them going to a bachelor party, so a lot of the people here are Rick's friends. It's a younger crowd, and some of them, I don't know."

"No problem," I said, "we'll show 'em how to have a good time."

When we reached the top of the hill, a crowd of well-wishers surrounded Dale. The raucous, well-oiled participants were a bit enthusiastic for me, so I broke from the group, and after a visit to the keg, grabbed a chair on the patio. I had a great view, though the music was too loud. Small wonder, a wall of J. B. Lansing speakers six feet high lined the back wall of the house.

I'd just settled in when our host tapped me on the shoulder and handed me a joint. I'd heard a lot about marijuana and didn't think of it as the Devil's weed, but I declined. A good chunk of the town already thought of me as a depraved wife killer, I wasn't about to do anything to generate more negative publicity. Since I didn't know many of the attendees and already had lost track of Dale, I decided to spend the evening observing human behavior. The partygoers had a hard time believing I didn't smoke pot so kept offering me their funny little cigarettes. I kept declining. I'd been at it for an hour when the music stopped, and a derelict-looking young man walked to the center of the patio holding a peanut butter jar high over his head.

"A present from our old buddy Canker," the guy announced. "He couldn't make it tonight, so he sent this instead and said we're supposed to have a good time."

"What is it?" somebody in the chair next to me yelled.

"Downs! Canker sent us a jar full of downers."

The crowd whooped and followed Shabby Guy into the house. I wasn't about to go inside and didn't have a way home. I checked the view from all sides of the patio and couldn't see Dale anywhere. Alone on the patio and with no idea where to find my ride, I went to the keg for another beer.

People started drifting back onto the patio. When I got button-holed by a guy who wanted to know if I was the real Cletus Efferding he heard so much about, it was all I could do not to push him over the patio railing. The music came back on, and I started drinking from nervousness—more than I should have.

Somewhere along the line, I quit turning down the funny little cigarettes, and the party got strange. I didn't recognize most of the music, and the heavy drums and bass guitar started getting on my nerves. I'd just decided to hitchhike back to town, when a song I knew, Jimi Hendrix's "Purple Haze," began pouring from the wall of speakers.

"Chair dance!" someone yelled and began pounding his steel folding chair against the cement surface of the patio. As he pounded he began hopping like a demented man, jumping up and down to the music. "Chair dance!" he cried again.

The cry was taken up by a half dozen revelers, who whirled and pranced, madly thumping their chairs on the patio in time to the music. At the end of the song, a dancer threw his chair over the railing of the raised patio. The others followed suit, and metallic clanks filled the air as chairs hit the cars parked below. Another deafening song came on. Time to go home.

Guests were still arriving as I made my way through what had become a tightly packed throng. Someone slammed into me and slid to the floor.

"Another one down," came a voice from the crowd. The other revelers cheered.

Dale appeared, elbowing his way through the ring of spectators and said, "Give me a hand with him, Clete."

I was never so glad to see someone in my life. Happy to lend a hand, I positioned myself at the casualty's feet while Dale hooked his arms under the armpits. The crowd parted as we worked our way toward the house. Someone held the door for us, and we made our way inside.

A biker-type munching a donut pointed to the left. "First-floor bedroom, over there."

When we entered the room, I did a double take. Our fallen soldier wasn't the first. Three others lay sideways on the bed. We deposited our burden alongside.

The biker's voice came from the doorway. "Hey, there's still room for one more."

I wanted to punch him, and I wanted to take a baseball bat to Canker DeCook. Disturbed by my anger I said, "Dale, let's go home."

"My thoughts exactly," he said.

Easier said than done. We'd had far too much to drink and had trouble finding Dale's truck. When we did, he couldn't remember how to unlock his new vehicle. I wanted to drive, but in truth, was in no better shape than my friend. When we managed to get underway, Dale drove slowly. With luck, we'd make it back to town in one piece.

We were poking along, minding our own business, when I noticed the road getting narrower and narrower. It should have been getting wider.

"We're going the wrong way," I said. "You should have turned right when we left the party. Pull into that lane and turn around."

Dale did and had just completed a three-point when a pickup swerved right in front of us. The driver braked hard, blocking the roadway. I knew the guy who got out. Six-six and maybe 270 pounds, a bar fighter short on brains and long on mean, a visibly angry Ronnie Redmond stormed up to our truck.

"You been stealin' my hogs!" he screamed.

A hot-tempered piece of business ten years ago, and just as volatile now, he reached through Dale's open window, unlatched the door, and dragged him onto the gravel. Dale is big, almost as big as Ronnie, but he's one of those gentle giants. He might have had a chance in a fair fight but was too drunk to take care of himself. Fearing for my friend, I leapt out of the pickup and rushed up to the seething madman.

"Wait," I shouted.

Redmond turned and glared at me. "Efferding, you dirtbag, I heard you was back in town. When I'm done with you, there won't be enough left to bury."

I held my hands in the air. "Wait," I shouted again. "We're not stealing anybody's hogs. Look at our pickup. No racks, no gate, no way to haul a hog."

He glowered. Behind him, Dale lay on his side, uninjured but barfing.

"Look at my shoes," I pleaded. "Nobody wears Italian loafers in a hog lot. We were at a party and drank too much. We're trying to get back to Bellevue, but we took a wrong turn."

"Somebody's stealin' my hogs. What the hell you doin' in my lane? Scouting 'em so you kin come back later?"

He took two steps toward me, grabbed my shirt and raised his hand. I stared at a fist the size of my face. One last chance.

"I know who it is. He doesn't farm, but he's been selling hogs over in Jones County. People in town are starting to talk about it."

"You lie."

"It's Canker DeCook."

Redmond lowered his fist. "That worthless piece of crap. Figures it's somebody like him. If you're lying Efferding, you're gonna know hurt like you don't know from what."

Time to reinforce the message.

"Canker's from Cottonville," I said. "You know how they are. Canker did it. It's Canker."

20

Hank sprawled on Marty Efferding's couch watching *All in the Family*. Archie Bunker was a hoot. Everybody seemed to think the man was a redneck caveman, but Hank didn't. He felt sorry for the guy. The country was going to hell in a handbasket while ordinary guys like Archie paid the bills for protesting college students who collected government food stamps. Talk about the working man of America getting the shaft. Right now, if it weren't for Marty, he'd be riding the shaft along with them.

"I brought you a ham sandwich," Marty said as she handed him a plate and snuggled in next to him.

His wife never brought him a ham sandwich unless he asked for it.

Marty rested her hand on his chest and kissed his ear. "We have to keep your strength up," she whispered. "You have your work cut out for you if you want to keep this lady purring."

"I can handle it, but explain this coffin thing again. It doesn't make sense to me."

"What's so hard? Twenty thousand for coffin and tools."

"I get that, but if the tools are worth a lot more than the casket, why do we have to bother with it? Better yet, why don't we just sell the tools to somebody else?"

"Eat your sandwich. They have a rich buyer. I don't. The best I could get is something like ten."

"We're lucky that the coffin is still at Ray's. As sure as the sun rises, it'll be gone by tomorrow night."

Hank bit into his sandwich. Mayo, butter, tomato, lettuce, and Swiss cheese. On the rare days his wife made him a sandwich, she might add grape jelly to the meat. No doubt about it, life was looking up. A hot little number like Marty in love with him, bringing him sandwiches, treating him like a man instead of nagging all the time. Still, breaking and entering and burglary seemed a bit much.

Marty placed her hand on his thigh. "I'm sorry I didn't marry you when I could have. I've regretted it ever since. Stay with me. Married or unmarried, I don't care. Whatever you want."

Marty's hand felt warm on Hank's leg. He swallowed hard. "She threw me out. I gotta get a divorce. They're expensive."

"Move in with me. Take your shotgun and let her have the rest. We'll get you a boat and a pickup. Chuck the job on the garbage truck if you don't like it. You can fish again. Partner with Blackie if you want. Do your guy things; go look for diamonds. I don't care. Just come home to me when you're done."

Visions of paradise unimaginable flooded Hank's mind, but common sense soon dispelled them. "They'd walk away from the deal without the coffin? If they can make so much on the tools, that doesn't make sense."

"They're originally from Chicago, Hank. City boys, who knows what makes guys like that tick? What this girl knows is how to recognize the gravy train when it heads her way."

"Your hair sure smells good," murmured Hank. He sighed, and as he did, the cares and worries of a lifetime floated away. "You're my gravy train, Baby," he whispered as he pulled Marty onto his lap. She began moving rhythmically.

"Choo choo, Hankie. Choo choo!"

Hank played his flashlight over the iron coffin. The thing looked spookier in Ray's darkened garage than under the fluorescent lights in Blackie's shed. The diversion he'd created had gone like clockwork. He'd been worried he'd meet with the town's police car driving north from Ray's to check on the fire he'd set. There were three routes to choose from. Since he'd torched an abandoned building behind the old piano factory, Second Street was the logical choice for a cop driving to the fire. He took Third and hadn't seen a soul. By the time he got to the garage, Marty had already removed the glass panel from the side door and unlocked it for him.

He pointed his flashlight to the floor, then back up to Marty. Dressed in black, with burnt cork rubbed on her face, she looked so good he couldn't resist grabbing a nice handful of her soft, warm bottom the second he got close enough to touch.

"Business first, feel-copping later," she warned.

He'd been against the burnt-cork thing, but there was no way out of it. Marty insisted that blackface and a stocking cap would be a good disguise. When he pointed out that most of the town could identify her truck, she still didn't budge. Some fantasy thing on her part he guessed. Like the way she kept saying they were pulling a caper. Hank had refused to darken his face. The nickname Hankie was bad enough. He'd rather be caught looking like himself than have people calling him stupid for the rest of his life.

"Wouldn't be half so weird if the body wasn't still inside," said Marty. "The truck's backed up to the door. Go open it."

Wonder of wonders, Ray kept the fiberglass door's rollers lubricated. It raised so easily that Hank had to grab the bottom edge to keep it from getting away from him. The sudden movement didn't startle the cat waiting outside. It walked into the garage without hesitation and hopped onto the coffin.

"You think the cat smells something?" asked Marty. "I think I do, maybe a little."

"I don't," said Hank as he reached to push the animal off the box. He gave it a gentle shove, was rewarded with a hiss and a scratch on the back of his hand.

"Here, let me," said Marty. She extended a hand only to have it lacerated.

Hank directed the beam of his light to a wall and located a broom. "That's it," he snarled as he used the broom handle to take a swing at the animal. The makeshift bat made contact and sent the feline hurtling into the air. The ensuing shriek nearly deafened him. "That come from the cat?" he asked.

"Let's get out of here before that damn animal wakes the dead," she replied.

Hank stared at the casket. He could have sworn the noise came from inside.

"Focus," said Marty. "We need to get out of here."

The effort required to move the coffin surprised Hank. Since it was already on sawhorses, he assumed they'd simply grab the handles on each end and walk it the fifteen feet to the truck. Marty's lack of upper body strength became apparent when she began to waver before reaching their destination. Though close to dropping it, they managed to get the burial case into the pickup without incident.

Marty drove the pickup home while Hank stayed behind to close the garage door and fetch the car. He'd been in and out of Ray's garage in something like five minutes.

Miracle of miracles, I woke up the morning after a bachelor party with no hangover. Sleeping until eleven helped. After running a comb through my hair, I slipped into a pair of jeans and peered out the screen door.

My friends sat in their usual spots at the picnic table. An unopened newspaper lay in front of Eddie. Lumir fiddled with the radio. I noticed they'd brought the boat back with them. It rested on a trailer alongside their cabin.

"How'd the fishing go?" I asked.

Eddie grunted but said nothing, so I turned to Lumir and raised my brows.

"No catfish. We got skunked," he said.

Eddie grimaced. "We brought the boat back because we're going to try the north side of the dam tomorrow."

Lumir held a finger in the air. "Sh-h-h. Here it is," he said and upped the volume on the radio.

Police in Bellevue, Iowa, are red-faced after an antique coffin was reported stolen from Gallagher's Furniture during the night. The coffin, a century-old artifact found on an island in the Mississippi, disappeared last night after the on-duty officer assigned to keep watch over it was called to a fire in another part of town. The ornate cast iron casket, the focus of media attention since its discovery, had been opened just hours earlier as part of an investigation by the Jackson County Medical Examiner. Prior to its disappearance, officials had planned to re-bury the casket and remains at an undisclosed location to keep the body from being disinterred.

According to police spokesman 'Mac' McClean, the department believes the fire, which consumed an abandoned building, was an arson designed to lure the town's sole night officer away from his watch on the furniture store. "We're operating under the assumption that the crimes are linked," said McClean. "When we solve one crime, we'll have the solution to the other."

Yesterday afternoon, a seven-man team wearing surgical masks ground off the bolts holding the casket's lid in place. When the last bolt was removed, investigators found the barefoot body of a woman wrapped in a white burial cloth and wearing a brown dress with a lace collar. The Medical Examiner found no evidence of foul play.

According to local funeral director Ray Gallagher, the body was in remarkable condition. "We weren't really looking at a skeleton," he said. "We were looking at skin, eyelids, and curly hair. Based on the size and condition of the teeth, the Medical Examiner believes she was in her thirties. She wasn't badly decomposed because the coffin was so airtight, and as far as it goes, I've smelled worse."

> *A spokesman for the Jackson County Attorney said the*
> *perpetrators of the theft would be prosecuted to the fullest extent*
> *of the law.*

"What the hell?" I said.

Lumir acknowledged me with a lift of his coffee mug. "You miss out on a lot by sleeping so much. But what do you say for the people of your town now? Eddie and I may have wanted to see the coffin, but we never thought of stealing it. As I said before, the people here are strange. I was wrong to call them hillbillies, but I have a better understanding now. They are a folk stranger than I ever imagined—riverbillies."

"It's a good thing you got out when you did," said Eddie. "You might have ended up with one of those riverbilly names like Goose, Skillet, or Steel Belly."

"Kid around all you want," I huffed. "With all the publicity the box has gotten, it's probably somebody from out of town."

Lumir rubbed his chin. "Maybe Eddie and I shouldn't go to see the strippers in East Dubuque tonight. All the excitement is here in Bellevue. Maybe the Underwear Lady will forget her panties."

"If Ardelia Krumbatey goes that far," I cautioned, "you don't want to be here to see it. Besides, I have my heart set on Razor Ray's dance at Lombardi's."

I'd learned about the dance when Marty and her beau came to our Sunday night fish fry. Apparently, Ray played keyboard and knew how to deliver a country song. The event, advertised as an early warm-up for the Fourth of July, was a doubleheader and included a band known as the Undecided Decision. The name didn't do much for me, but who was I to judge. Back in the day, I danced to Dick Buscher and the Clichés.

"You'll be missing a good time," said Eddie. "You ought to come along. We—"

Lumir cut him off. "Where is this Lombardi's again?"

Eddie didn't know it, but Lumir was trying to save me from an explanation I'd find difficult.

"It's okay, Lumir."

Eddie looked puzzled.

"Eddie, I haven't been in a strip club since Myra died. The dancers remind me of the mistake I made the day before she took her life."

"Oh."

Lumir put down his mug with a thump. "Well, it's Eddie's birthday, and I want to celebrate and see the pretty ladies dance naked."

I doubted Lumir cared much about the entertainment, but he'd mentioned a night on the town would do Eddie some good. Though Eddie's father hadn't given him the attention he deserved, the man's cancer weighed on his son.

"And I need that ride to Lombardi's," I chimed in. "My vandalized car might be alright for tooling around Bellevue, but I can't very well drive it to a big dance. Just don't get so carried away with the ladies you forget to pick me up on your way back."

Eddie picked up Lumir's earlier question. "Where is this Lombardi's, anyway?"

"Fifteen miles north, on your way to East Dubuque," I replied.

Eddie picked up his newspaper. "Strippers dance to pretty good music—a lot better than you're going to hear."

"Don't be so sure," I countered.

"Whoopie!" Eddie snorted. "Waltzes and foxtrots."

I rolled my eyes. "Not by a long shot."

"Polkas, and two-steps?"

"Too advanced for the local crowd. At Lombardi's, they play riverbilly music. What'd you expect?"

21

"Herm, Herm. Wake up."

"Um, yeah. I'm awake, just resting my eyelids."

As Irv's face came into focus, Herm realized he'd dozed off in the recliner. The Scotch after lunch must have laid him out.

"We got the coffin," Irv said rubbing his hands together. "I told you not to worry. We got it just like I said."

Irv yawned. "That's nice. I wonder where I left my Valium."

"Who cares? We did it. The casket, the tools, they're ours."

Herm stretched and tipped the recliner into the upright position. "Last I noticed, we didn't do anything. Who grabbed the coffin, Marty or Canker?"

"I don't know, but it's all over the news somebody stole it."

Herm rose, shuffled to the dining room and began pawing through the detritus on the large mahogany table. "Then we don't have the merchandise and don't know who has it. I expect it'll all work out. I know I left that thing here somewhere. It's almost medication time."

"Maybe you should skip the next one. They're really knockin' you out.

"Nothing to worry about. Doctor Bob said I might be fuzzy the first few days. I'm supposed to keep on a regular schedule until I see him next week. He wants to see how I tolerate them. After I get stable, we'll move on to an as-needed basis."

Herm went to the kitchen, drew a glass of water, and returned to the recliner with pill and glass in hand. "You better call Bellevue to see which one has the casket."

"I did, but nobody's at home. I'll keep trying."

"Too bad we're not working with James Bond. He has a tape recorder hooked up to his telephone. You could leave messages."

"In your dreams, but it's time for me to get back to the store," Irv made for the doorway. "What say you shave and get dressed? Sitting around in your bathrobe won't help you feel better. I'll pick up a bottle of wine and fix us a shrimp scampi tonight."

Herm swallowed his pill. "I don't know what I ever did to deserve someone like you. Scampi sounds great."

"Okay, see you later. Don't forget to feed the cat."

After Irv closed the door, Herm settled into his chair. Try as he might, comfort eluded him. He'd been through a lot the past week, and with Irv careening back and forth like a loose cannon, it's no wonder he had trouble relaxing. Doctor Bob told him to take it easy for a few days, and he could think of no better way than watching game shows on daytime television. He'd almost made it through *The Price is Right*, when one of the contestants won a Caribbean condo.

His newfound serenity vaporized. Herm rocketed out of the recliner. "God damn it, Irv. How could you gamble our tropical paradise away? Not only gamble it away but cut me out of the decision making."

Shaking like a leaf and concerned the Valium wasn't working, Herm made his way to the dining table, fished another pill from the container, and downed it dry. He began coughing. Convinced that the darn thing would stick in his throat, he went to the liquor cabinet and washed it down with brandy.

I've gotta not let things get to me like this.

He switched channels. Game shows were too stressful. The tribulations of the beleaguered staff of *General Hospital* kept him pleasantly occupied until the damn cat leapt onto the end table and started staring at him as if he were a stranger.

"Cool it, Koko. I'll feed you later."

Though she knew full well it was him, Koko hissed, screamed like a banshee, and ran for her hiding place in the basement. His nerves undone and intent on retrieving another Valium, Herm shifted in the recliner. The chair, locked in position, refused to cooperate. Struggle as he might, an exit from his Naugahyde prison eluded him.

"Damn stupid thing," he muttered.

Looking up, he noticed a commercial for fabric softener on the television. Snowy white sheets fluttered gently through the air as birds sang and soothing music floated in his direction. Herm felt himself relax and abandoned his difficult mission.

"Too much work," he muttered and fell asleep.

———————————

Early afternoon found Hank and Marty in her garage, looking at the fruit of their nighttime venture. They'd unloaded when they got in, and now it was time to stash the thing. Marty, her hands on her hips, smiled at Hank from the other side of the coffin. "It's a beauty. I told you we wouldn't have any problem."

"It would have been a lot easier if you'da bought it when Blackie and I tried to sell it to you."

"But I didn't, and there's nothing like twenty thousand dollars to make a girl forget she doesn't deal in used coffins."

God, Hank loved the woman's smile. "Don't distract me if you want to get anything done this afternoon," he said. "You take the foot end, and I'll take the head. I cleared a space behind that wall of boxes. It'll be good enough for a day or two."

Given that it was made of cast iron, the casket wasn't particularly heavy. Hank guessed a little over two hundred pounds. Because she had to stoop to pick her end off the floor, Marty had difficulty handling the weight. She knocked over a stack of boxes as she struggled to maintain her grip. "And to think I wanted to hide it upstairs," she grunted as they maneuvered the box into the narrow space. "It was a lot easier when this thing was on saw horses."

The task complete and the burial case hidden, Hank straightened up and wiped his hands on his jeans. "It's a little heavier without that adrenaline stuff from all the excitement at Ray's place." He gestured toward the coffee pot resting on her hot plate. "Think there's two cups left?"

Marty nodded. "Good idea. I'll reheat it."

They made for the chairs next to the pot. While Marty poured, Hank pulled his tobacco pouch and pipe from his pants pocket. "When you gonna pick up the old man's wood tools?"

"Slight problem, my business account is a little short on the six hundred dollars I'm supposed to come up with."

Hank stuffed his pipe with cherry-blend tobacco. "How short?"

"One hundred seventy-five dollars."

Hank struck a match and lit up his pipe. "Can't help you. I'm down to my last fifty. What about taking it from your personal money?"

"No way!" snapped Marty. "The one thing I learned from losing Efferding's Menswear is to keep business and personal accounts separate. I'm not about to change that now."

"Then ask your cousin Clete for a little more."

"Not a good idea," sighed Marty. "If I ask him, he might not lend me the other six hundred. Maybe I can sell that super fancy wood stove to Steel Belly. He's wanted it forever. If I cut the price, he might jump on it."

Hank settled back in his chair. "It's a good thing Ray didn't store the coffin at the funeral home. We wouldn't have been able to get it out of a house where people actually live. Strange that he owns a furniture store. You'd think there'd be enough money in undertaking to keep a man satisfied."

Marty giggled. "I like the way you get so philosophical when you smoke your pipe. Furniture stores and funeral homes have a lot in common. Back when families held wakes at home, they bought the casket at their local furniture store. Before that, the men who built furniture, built coffins too. There's a long history."

"I like it that you're smart, Marty. It makes life more interesting."

"I read a lot. When you guys first told me that you had a cast iron coffin. I did a lot of research. I never expected you found a top-of-the-line Fisk."

Hank tipped back in his chair. "That's me and Blackie for you, top of the line all the way."

"Don't get a big head. You're just lucky the thing didn't have Clovers on it."

"Clovers?" Hank leaned forward again. "Talk about weird—coffins with four-leaf clovers on 'em. Like, you're lucky you're dead. Or maybe, your family is lucky to be rid of you, you cranky old son of a bitch."

Marty snorted with laughter, nearly choking on the smoke from her cigarette. "No, Clover coffin torpedoes, and that could have been really unlucky for you."

"Kind of a curse or something?"

"A guy named Philip Clover patented coffin torpedoes in 1878. He designed them to prevent what he called unintended resurrections. Coffin torpedoes were bombs an undertaker could put inside a casket. They went off if the body changed position."

Hank whistled. "Those old-timers sure worried a lot about what happened after somebody died. Talk about afraid of vampires. Bombs beat the hell out of wooden stakes."

"They were more worried about grave robbers. Medical schools never had enough cadavers. Sometimes students helped the school by coming up with one of their own. It even happened over in Iowa City. Clover claimed his torpedoes would kill or maim anybody who tampered with a coffin. No one knows how many were produced or where they were used."

"Do you think Ray knows about 'em?"

"If he doesn't, he should." Marty glanced at her watch. "Look at the time. Big day tomorrow. I better remember to call Irving. I tried at lunch but couldn't get him."

"Even though the casket didn't blow up on Ray, I'm glad me and Blackie didn't open it all the way."

Marty arched an eyebrow. "After all that time in the river, there wouldn't have been enough explosive left to kill anybody."

"Maybe, but getting maimed doesn't sound so great either."

22

Confident I looked good, I said goodbye to Lumir and Eddie and made for the entry to Lombardi's. My tan linen suit showed just the appropriate amount of wrinkle, and my silk ascot looked phenomenal. An ascot is an accessory that separates the men from the boys. It's worn directly around the neck rather than around the shirt collar, and only a handful can pull it off. Peter Lawford and Fred Astaire come to mind.

And even then, for all their innate sense of style, these icons of fashion made the occasional gaffe, like wearing a necktie as a belt. Unbelievable. A fashion-savvy man needs to know where to draw the line between flair and outright stupidity. Any haberdasher worth his salt would have shown Lawford and Astaire the door rather than have his business associated with a blunder like that.

I entered the building as the first band, the Undecided Decision, were taking a break. The place looked crowded for a Tuesday night, but there were two adjacent seats available at the bar. I took one of them and ordered a beer. Unlike a lot of people, I don't mind being alone in a bar or restaurant. I often meet interesting folks, and since the place had a dance floor, I expected to enjoy my night.

Lumir and Eddie had promised to pick me up about midnight. I'd have been uncomfortable if Eddie had gone to the East Dubuque strip bars by himself. East Dubuque enjoyed a checkered reputation. An assortment of low dives and exotic dancer venues lined its main street. Riverbilly hangouts for sure, they featured watered-down liquor, nasty fistfights, and down-on-their-luck women. Now and again somebody would be murdered in a disagreement over the favors of a dancer or get offed from pure cussedness. The castrated remains of one of the biggest losers had been found on a sandbar just south of town a few years back. Although Eddie worked in a packing plant, I worried because he still retained a measure of boyhood innocence. The odds he'd over-imbibe were slim given the steady hand of Lumir at his side.

When my beer arrived, I turned around on my barstool and took in the scene. A nice middle-class crowd, most of the older customers looked to be married couples out for a night with their friends. The clean-cut younger folk hung out in mixed groups. No mystery in the age split. The over-forties had come to hear Razor Ray, the youngsters, the Undecided Decision. I took the honors for best-dressed. Jeans and t-shirts predominated, and as for the occasional fringed cowboy shirt, oh Lord, spare me.

You could have knocked me to the floor when Canker DeCook entered and made a beeline for the vacant barstool next to me. Did he know I'd vandalized his truck? I had no escape so turned on my stool to face the bar.

"What'll it be?" I heard the bartender ask.

"Wild Turkey," Canker grunted. "No ice."

My guts in turmoil, I stared down at the bar top, felt sweat running down the back of my neck.

Canker slapped me hard on the shoulder. "Efferding, you old asshole. I seen you down at the hotel the other night. How's it hangin'?"

"Same old." I didn't look up.

"You sure picked an interestin' time to show back up in town. That coffin thing's been a pretty big deal."

I tried not to shake. "Guess so."

"Who'd a figured somebody would try to steal it?"

I breathed a sigh of relief as it dawned on me. Canker didn't know I'd trashed his truck. I looked up from the bar top and rejoined the world of people with a future ahead of them.

Canker slammed his shot and belched. "Wouldn't mind getting hold of one myself. I heard it's a rare and valuable item. Be a heck of a conversation piece."

I still hadn't looked at Canker but made eye contact through the mirror behind the bar. "It'd be pretty hard to find one. Most of them are in the ground."

"Hell's bells, Efferding. I own two backhoes. Just wish I knew where to look."

I don't know where the idea came from. Perhaps the good Lord had chosen me as his angel of vengeance for the arson at the State Park lodge. Maybe I just couldn't help myself. "If you really wanted one, you wouldn't need a backhoe because the one at Ray's was never really stolen."

"What?"

"I was talking to Wiley McCard today. Nobody stole the coffin. They were so worried about it that they moved it out early this morning and announced it'd been stolen. They were afraid people would dig up every fresh grave in the county looking for it."

Canker ordered another whiskey. "Wonder where they took it."

Once again, I met his eyes in the mirror. "Wiley told me, but if it ever got out, he'd know I spilled."

"Christ, Efferding. You think Wiley told you and nobody else?"

His second shot came, and Canker downed it.

"You're probably right."

"So, where is it?"

I turned on my barstool to face the crowd. "Wiley says they're going to bury it in that old cemetery up at Spruce Creek, but the grave isn't ready yet."

Canker turned around too. "They still bury people there?"

"Don't know," I said. "But that's where the mystery lady goes. Right now, she's stored in a building next to Ronnie Redmond's hog shed."

Canker looked at me as if I was crazy. "Next to his hog shed?"

"It's only a couple of miles from the cemetery. Besides, who'd ever look for it in a place like that?"

"Well, I'll be." Canker rubbed a stubbly cheek, turned, and settled his account.

I noticed he didn't tip.

"Gotta be going," he said. "Can't be sittin' here all night.

"See you," I replied.

The odds were fifty-fifty he'd go for it. If he did, maybe another fifty-fifty he'd realize I'd set him up.

Not my smartest move.

As I'd expected, the Undecided Decision played pop music for the younger set. If Razor Ray didn't come up with a few two-steps, waltzes, or foxtrots, there'd be no dancing for Cletus Efferding tonight. While waiting for the Decision to finish their set, I spent the time surveying the room for potential dance partners.

A man who dances never lacks for female companionship. Though I'm an instructor, I'm not always interested in dancing with the most accomplished female in the room. My requirements are two: a pleasant personality and the ability to walk backward. I considered my best chance for a good evening lay with two women sitting at a table along the far wall. They appeared to be in their thirties. I'd been watching them while the Decision played, and my dance radar told me they were the type to enjoy a spin on the floor.

When Ray started his set with a country two-step, the look on the face of the older of the pair confirmed the accuracy of my radar. I left my bar stool, approached the table, and introduced myself. I didn't get a chance to ask for a dance. The woman just grabbed me by the hand and led me out on the floor. She danced well and passed me off to her friend when I escorted her back to the table. The trade-offs continued until the end of Ray's first set when they asked me to join them.

It didn't take long to get the lay of the land. The women were from Madison, Wisconsin. Marcie, the older one was working on a

Ph.D. in American Studies. Her younger sister, whose name I didn't catch, taught science at a junior high school. While I'm not the most perceptive puppy in the litter, it didn't take long to realize they didn't hail from the Badger State. Their accents were pure Dixie.

"Let me guess," I said. "You took dance lessons while you were in high school. I hear ballroom dance lessons for Phys. Ed. is still popular down south."

"How else is a girl going to get ready for the Southern Debutante Cotillion?" Marcie replied.

"You were a debutant?"

"Why of course, white dress, formal dinners, corsages, the whole nine yards. My folks wanted to give me a good start in Mobile society."

"Mobile, Alabama?"

She nodded.

"I'm a Double Deb," her sister chimed in. "My name's Deb, and I did cotillion too."

"What brings you to Lombardi's?"

"Marcie's researching Mississippi River ghost stories. We're going to spend some time in Bellevue to find out about the Old Hag and the coffin. You must have heard about it."

The Old Hag again.

"Actually," said Marcie, "I discovered the hag tale on a collecting trip through Jackson County last summer. As far as I know, the Old Hag is unique to the Bellevue area. Most river ghosts are variations on one of six basic stories that have passed up and down the river for generations. Linking the Bellevue hag to the coffin find represents a unique opportunity to study how recent events can change a traditional folktale."

Ah well, if you can't beat 'em, join 'em. "I'm from Bellevue. You'll want to talk to Blackie Stiles. He's the one who started the rumor that the body in the casket belongs to the Old Hag."

"I know Blackie," Deb squealed. "I met him when I went collecting with Marcie last summer. He's a real river rat."

Marcie glared at her sister. "That's not nice. Blackie belongs to a traditional river culture that is rapidly disappearing. Don't make fun."

Deb stuck out her lower lip. "Big sisters can be so bossy."

"I have a friend who calls them riverbillies," I offered.

"Oh, I like that," Marcie said. "My advisor is the type who enjoys seeing a student coin a new term. Maybe I can use it for my dissertation. Something along the lines of *The Effects of Mass Media Exposure on a Riverbilly Culture*."

I was about to offer my services as guide to my hometown when Lumir and Eddie showed up to give me a ride back to the cabin. Their abrupt entry succeeded in bringing all conversation to a halt.

"Clete, Clete, Clete!" shouted Lumir.

Heads turned.

Eddie spotted me and pointed. All too soon they were on the way to our table, the center of attention for the entire room. A red and black garter circled Lumir's head; Eddie's neck sported a pink feather boa.

"Clete," Eddie yelled. "One of the dancers couldn't keep her hands off Lumir. She kept sitting on his lap."

Lumir's voice filled the now-quiet room. "And you know what, Clete? She had really big tatas." He held his hands before him, making circular, squeezing motions. "Really, really, really big tatas."

Eddie began swinging his boa, improvising a song as he danced back and forth.

> *She had tatas, real big tatas.*
> *She was the kind of girl with real big tatas.*
> *She liked Lumir. Yes, she did. She liked Lumir.*
> *And she danced on the bar to a cha-cha.*

He repeated the verse again, and Lumir began stamping his foot and clapping to the song. No use pretending I didn't know them. I wished I were a thousand miles away.

Nothing to do but get them back outside as soon as possible. Nervous titters had begun rising from the corners of the room. We were maybe a minute from outright hostility and a visit by the owner. My tablemates' faces registered shock and disapproval. So much for snagging a date with Marcie.

"Just some friends of mine," I muttered and hopped from my chair. I bid the Debs farewell and began shooing the merrymakers to the door amid a chorus of hoots and boos.

"Clete, the stripper liked me," Lumir shouted. "She liked me a lot."

"Lumir's the man!" bellowed Eddie. "He the man."

I hustled my friends into Eddie's pickup and drove them back to Bellevue. Eddie had a giggling fit when Lumir fell asleep and began snoring. I don't know how Lumir did it. Whether eighteen or eighty-eight, women went bonkers over the guy. His wife Gladys had passed away a dozen years ago and since then, my friend had been on the receiving end of something like eight marriage proposals.

His laughing fit over, Eddie raised his fist in the air. "Lumir's my role model," he proclaimed.

"Lumir's a good man," I said. "You could do a lot worse."

"I sure could—you."

"There's such a thing as too honest, Eddie."

"Nah," he replied and closed his eyes.

23

Doing his best to ignore the ketchup bottle in Irv's hand, Herm poured milk over his cornflakes. Unaccustomed to the Valium, he'd had trouble getting out of bed, and to tell the truth, he didn't feel like going anywhere today.

"Well today's the big day," Irv announced. "By five o'clock tonight, Marty will be here with the tools and your coffin. I told you everything would work out. Maybe we should take the time to order your mortuary antiques specialist cards today. And how about some stationery? You'll need stationery."

Herm yawned. "How about tomorrow? I'm still not quite up to snuff. The Doc wants me to take it easy for a few days, so I can get used to the medication. I just got the prescription filled the day before yesterday. It's nice you want to come with me. I'd like to have your advice."

Irv covered his toast with ketchup and began carving it into pieces. "And the scampi last night, wasn't it to die for? Even if I did cook it myself. I don't know how the people down at Boston Fish manage to get fresh seafood shipped to Cedar Rapids."

Herm looked across the kitchen table. *Funny about the Valium, Irv putting ketchup on his breakfast doesn't bother me half as much.*

"Say something?" asked Irv.

"Just thinking about breakfast. You know, the newspaper said the body wasn't decayed. Anybody who buys the setup will want to display the lady inside the coffin. Until the body's dried out, she's gonna stink. We gotta find a way to make that happen."

Gulping his coffee and shoveling his toast in his mouth, Irv looked ready to tear into the day. "We can handle it. Marty's bringing our order to the warehouse. I'll have her drive her pickup inside. You can whack her then. After that, we'll put your casket in the back corner and unseal it, then each day open it a crack farther. If it stinks too much, we can come up with another plan."

"Okay, but with these pills, I don't know about whacking anybody today. I'm so unsteady, I might burn myself with the blowtorch."

"You sure you want to use the blowtorch on Marty? She seems nice enough."

"Yeah, I suppose so. Besides, she's probably a screamer, and in my condition, I couldn't handle the noise. A gag would take care of some of it, but who needs the drama."

Irv downed his orange juice. "Makes sense. You wanna go with the little .22 caliber? Be lightweight and easy to handle."

"Sure, two behind the ear, time-worn and proven true. Tell her there's a nail in her tire, and when she bends down to look, I'll clip her. The tire-trouble bit, it's such a cliché, but it's foolproof. Everybody's heard about it, but then they fall for it anyway. You'd think they'd learn."

"Dead people don't learn anything."

"At any rate, I don't have the energy for a lot of excitement. You sure she's coming alone?"

"I said no secrecy, no deal. I told her our reputation as a top-drawer operation is too important to chance things like this getting out. She understood. What say I drive her vehicle to Waterloo afterward and torch it? You gotta be clear-headed enough to follow me up. I can take over after that."

"I'll be okay as long as I drive our car."

Irv looked at his watch. "Look, I gotta run. I'll gas up the car and swing by at five to pick you up."

"Don't forget we need an oil change."

"I'll see if I can work it in. See you later."

As the door closed, Herm looked across the room at the knife-and-fork clock above the refrigerator, an American classic. The knife was on twelve and the fork on nine, a little early for another Valium. The container beckoned. He could take a few and sit in front of the TV the rest of the day.

It won't do to take them all at once. He took a sixteen-ounce bottle of cola out of the refrigerator, grabbed the medication container, and retired to the den. Under doctor's orders to relax, it made no sense fighting with the recliner when he needed another calmative.

Nine o'clock and the gray sky threatened one of those rains that lasted all day. Still no sign of life from Eddie and Lumir's cabin, so I sat at our outdoor table wondering if I should go for breakfast on my own. About ready to head for a stack of pancakes at the Anchor Inn, I watched as a red Ford Pinto turned off the street and pulled up on the gravel next to me. An agitated Cousin Marty got out and shouldered her purse.

"Pretty little car," I said.

She made a face. "Actually, it's a hunk of junk. Pintos have aluminum-block engines that melt at fifty thousand miles. I didn't know that when I bought one with thirty thousand on it. Where's Lumir?"

"He and Eddie made the rounds of the go-go bars in East Dubuque last night. They really tied one on. I expect they're still recovering."

My cousin plopped her handbag on the table and seated herself across from me. Reaching into the purse, she extracted an envelope with Lumir's name on it. "I don't want to wake him. There's four hundred twenty-five inside. I'm going out of town for a couple of days and want to make a good-faith deposit. I'll have the rest of the money before you leave."

She handed me the envelope. "Would you give it to him when he gets up? Right now, I'm so flustered, I can hardly think straight."

Marty didn't look good. Her eyes were red. It didn't take a Sherlock Holmes to see she'd been crying.

"Sure," I said, "I'll be happy to."

Looking as though the waterworks might start up again, she reached out and grabbed my hand. "Cletus, my mother really did love me. She didn't abandon me. I got a call from the police chief in Prairie du Chien this morning. My mom was murdered."

"What?"

"Mom. They found her body. A mile from our old house."

I met her eyes as the ground shifted beneath me. Aunt Kate, murdered.

Tears rolled down her cheeks. "They were demolishing an abandoned hatchery about a mile from our old house and found her under a floor. After thirty years, there wasn't much left but bones and scraps of cloth. They found a locket with the words *Our little Martha* engraved on it. Cletus, I remember that locket. She kept a baby picture of me inside."

All the family's condemnations, finger-pointing, and judgments, all ignorant and wrong-headed. "I am so sorry," I said. "I can't imagine what you're going through. It's a miracle they ever found you."

"A retired policeman was visiting the station and heard about the discovery. My name rang a bell. He remembered it from back when Mom went missing. The guy never forgot the name Martha because he felt so bad about the girl with no father whose mom walked out on her."

The emotional dam burst, and sobs wracked her body. I moved to her side of the table and put my arms around her. She put her head on my shoulder. I couldn't think of anything to say but patted her back and let her cry. When the rise and fall of her shoulders subsided and weeping turned to whimpers, I loosened my grip and fished into my hip pocket to produce a handkerchief.

"It's okay," she said reaching for her purse, "I have tissues. I'm taking off for Prairie du Chien to identify the locket. It took them four months to find me because I changed my name to Efferding. Mom's already buried."

"Are you okay to drive?"

"I don't know. My head is spinning. They think the guy who owned the hatchery did it, but he's been dead for five years. Hank wants to drive me, but I need to be alone."

"Prairie du Chien is a long way, a couple of hours, and it looks like rain. I'd be happy to take you."

She got up from the table and picked up her purse. "No, I have a lot to sort out right now."

I watched as she walked to the car. Though she'd had a big shock and had been crying, her posture seemed more erect and her shoulders straighter than usual. I had the feeling that something in Marty had changed, something positive and permanent.

I sat with my coffee, looking out the rain-streaked cabin window. Lumir and Eddie had yet to leave their cabin, and the envelope with Marty's four twenty-five in it lay on the table by my side. I picked up a pen and wrote Lumir a check for seven hundred twenty-five dollars, enough to cover the six hundred I agreed to loan Marty plus the one seventy-five she was short. After anchoring the check and envelope with a water glass, I settled back and sighed. The chances she'd repay more than a fraction of it were slim.

There'd been no real reason for Marty to bring a good-faith deposit to the cabins this morning, especially with all she had on her mind. She'd wanted me to know she hadn't been abandoned by her mother, that she wasn't a bad seed, that she counted for something. As much as I wished we might grow closer, it would never be. The coldness she found in my parents' home and my disappointment with the way she'd stiffed me on the sale of the family business would stand between us. Like the first six hundred, the extra one seventy-five had more to do with guilt for the way our family had treated her than with common sense.

Through the glass panes, I saw a woman holding a newspaper over her head run up to the door of Lumir and Eddie's cabin. She raised her hand and knocked. Eddie appeared in the entry and followed the owner's wife to the office. Several minutes later he ran back to the cabin. Having been through the drill on Monday, I expected he'd gotten a phone call. I shook my head. When I rented the cabin, it never occurred to me that there'd be no phones in the units.

I debated going over but had no doubt my friends were nursing world-class hangovers. Rather than add to their misery, I poured another coffee and picked up Max Brand's tale of the irrepressible Destry. I'd barely started when I heard thumping on my door. I looked up as Lumir's stuck his head inside.

"Come in out of the rain," I said.

Lumir entered, looking well-rested, without a hint of a hangover. "Eddie's father has taken a turn for the worse. His mother wants him to come home. This has happened before, and always the man comes through. But home is where the boy belongs, and I do not want him to be alone on the drive back. I am going with him."

"Of course. I'm happy he had a carefree birthday celebration last night. The two of you really tied one on."

"I did not drink too much."

"Yeah, and the Pope is Jewish."

My friend reached into his jacket pocket and removed the brass plate he'd been polishing the other day. "You might as well take this. There doesn't seem to be much need for it now."

I took it and turned it over. There was an inscription: a set of initials and a pair of dates.

"Is this what I think it is?"

"I am certain. I did not know when I found it in the weeds. But when I cleaned it and the letters began to appear, I grew suspicious. Do you remember when the funeral director took me to task for touching the coffin?"

"Before you gave him that mumbo jumbo about the Evil Eye?"

"Yes. I was taking a rough measure. You know, so many knuckle joints wide, or so many fingers long. The holes lined up with the ones on the casket. That's when I knew."

"Why on earth didn't you tell Ray you found the plate?"

"Look the dates on the plate."

The numbers were faint but readable, 1852-1886.

Lumir continued, "The poor woman was only thirty-four years old. When I touched the coffin, the tragedy of a life cut short came home to me. I imagined I heard the person inside talking to me. The voice was so strong, it scared the pants off me. 'Leave me in peace,' it said. 'Leave me in peace.'"

"Dim lights, an old coffin, wild stories, it's enough to scare anyone," I said. "Sometimes our imaginations get the best of us."

"Clete, the voice belonged to Gladys. She's been gone for thirteen years."

I flinched. The casket business was getting scary. First Myra appears in the fog and invites me to drown myself; then Lumir's late wife speaks to him from a century-old burial case.

Lumir cleared his throat. "I am a sensible man and know when my mind is playing tricks on me, but I decided the funeral director could wait to hear about the plate. If I had come forward on Sunday, my discovery would have generated a new round of news stories. I decided the time to tell him would be Tuesday when things quieted down."

"And then the coffin was stolen," I added.

"So now there is no rush. Unless the coffin is found, the nameplate is useless. I intended to give it to Mr. Gallagher at the end of our fishing trip, but now Eddie and I must hurry. Would you do it for me?"

"I'll be happy to," I said and set the plate next to my paperback. I removed Marty's envelope and my check from under the water glass. "Here's the payment for the Nicholson chests."

Lumir stuffed them in his shirt pocket without looking. "It is nice to see you taking your six-hundred-dollar loss like a man."

I shrugged. "Actually, I loaned her seven twenty-five. She might come through with it yet."

Lumir snorted. "There is an old Czech saying: *Až prasata začnou chcát duhu*—when pigs piss rainbows."

"We'll see," I said. "Hank Steines will be picking up the tool chests for Marty. I'll have to store them in the Nova until then. My cabin's too small."

"I have already taken care of it," replied Lumir. "The motel owner will keep them in his garage until you are ready for them."

A knock on the door and Eddie walked in, rumpled and unshaven, with bloodshot eyes. "Dad's bad. We're going back. Sorry to cut our fishing trip short."

"Lumir already told me."

"You gonna stick around or drive back?"

"I've got another week of vacation to go. I'm staying."

"Suit yourself, but nobody seems particularly happy to have you back."

"I'm swimming in popularity, Eddie. Besides, who knows when I'll get back this way. The river, the woods, the hills, I miss it all so much it hurts, and if I stayed here long enough, the people would accept me. No matter what happens, this is the only place I'll ever call home."

"Then why don't you move back?"

"The lights are brighter in Cedar Rapids. But hey, how are you feeling? You guys were soaked to the gills last night."

"I didn't drink too much."

"Find a feather boa in your room this morning?"

"No."

"Must have gone the way of Lumir's garter."

Lumir looked puzzled. "What garter?"

Since I hadn't gone along with them, the adventures of the night before were not to be shared with me. I felt a little left out but helped them load up. The task complete, I stood outside in the drizzle and waved goodbye. I returned to my cabin, saddened by the loss of companionship. In all the excitement over Eddie's father, I'd forgotten to mention the discovery of Aunt Kate's body.

Destry's adventure called and an hour later came to its conclusion. Putting the book down, I suppressed a yawn and looked up. From her place in the corner, a transformed Kissy Kathy caught my eye.

I don't know how they'd managed it, but Kissy now sported a garter headband and feather-boa shawl.

The rain kept me inside much of the day. The sky cleared in mid-afternoon, and by evening, the streets and sidewalks had dried. Wanting some exercise, I walked uptown. The rain-freshened air felt glorious, birds sang, and my earlier melancholy disappeared.

Half-way to the business district, I began to obsess over a breaded pork tenderloin with a side of French-fried onion rings. By the time I reached the hotel, my fixation with all things breaded had vanquished any illusion of moderation. I entered through the restaurant door and took a seat at the counter. The waitress didn't bat an eye at my order for a tenderloin, a basket of fries, plate of onion rings, and some deep-fried mushrooms. I topped the whole thing off with a request for cherry pie *à la mode*. At the end of my repast, I left the restaurant, a bloated and happy man.

My destination, a wooden bench overlooking the river, lay across the street from the scene of my gluttony. A dozen boats dotted the water below the dam, pole-and-line fishermen taking advantage of a magnificent evening. Screeching gulls circled and wheeled, some guys backed a trailer down the municipal boat ramp, an outboard motor hummed. All in all, a breathtaking scene, one that left me content to sit quietly and digest. I heard the footsteps before I saw the shadows approaching my bench. I turned, and there they were—the Debs.

"Oh, it's you!" said Double Deb. "We're out tonight doing interviews for Marcie's Old Hag research."

"Might we join you?" asked Marcie.

I gestured at the empty part of the bench. "Please do."

Though still embarrassed by last night's scene at Lombardi's, I'd apparently misjudged the Debs' reaction to the antics of my friends.

Marcie sat next to me, her younger sister on the outside. Most people would have considered Deb the better looking of the two, but Marcie's intelligence and legs that didn't quit had me solidly in the camp of her admirers. I resolved that whatever happened, I would not demean myself by staring at limbs lovely enough to make mortals despair and gods weep.

Deb opened the conversation. "Your older friend is cute. He looked so funny with that garter on his head."

I sometimes tire of women singing the praises of Lumir. "He and Eddie went to East Dubuque to see the exotic dancers. I'm afraid they had too much to drink. Please accept my apologies for the disturbance."

"Accepted," said Marcie with a smile.

Her drawl would have melted butter. My inner organs liquefied.

"They made for an unexpected diversion," she continued.

My reason returned. Marcie was traveling with her sister. They'd be rooming together and leave town in a day or two. Worse, she lived in Madison, hours away from Cedar Rapids. Though I felt a connection, there was no opportunity for a date. My life stinks.

I forced myself back into the conversation. "It was Eddie's birthday. He's the younger one and wanted to do it up right. I guess he succeeded. How's the research going?"

"We had a fascinating day," Marcie replied. "I've been to the fish market, both drugstores, and the Senior Center. Deb went to the public library and interviewed a group of junior high students that a teacher friend rounded up. The coffin has already become part of the Old Hag legend, and Blackie Stiles' stories have a lot to do with it. It's been fascinating to watch a century-old tale change so quickly. The first thing I noticed is that several interviewees referred to the Old Hag as Old Hag Bowman. For them, she's become inextricably linked to the coffin found on Bowman's Island."

"You should talk to Ole Olsen, Charlie Bailey, and Walt Florence," I said. "They know as much about old times on the river as anybody around."

"I already have. Walt Florence tells an interesting variant on the legend. In his version, the hag was once a beautiful young woman who had the ability to mimic other people's voices. The daughter of a fisherman and blind from birth, her eyes were covered with a white film that shut out all light. She married a homely fisherman. One day, a traveling magician came through the area and mixed up a poultice that dissolved cataracts. He gave it to her on one condition—that she use her vision to bring joy to others. When the young woman saw her husband for the first time, she despaired at the thought of spending a lifetime with such an ugly man and killed him with a meat cleaver. The next morning, she looked in the mirror and discovered she'd become an unsightly old hag. Her reflection was the last thing she ever saw because as she looked at herself, the cataracts began forming again."

"Never heard that one," I said. "Does she come out during full moons to kidnap children and feed them to snapping turtles?

"No, she haunts handsome men, speaking to them in the voice of a departed loved one, sometimes asking them to join her."

My ribcage jumped and so did I.

"Are you okay, Cletus?" Deb asked.

"Please, no more hag stories for now. A couple of nights ago my late wife came to me in a dream and turned into the Old Hag. She asked me to go into the river with her. On Sunday, something in that damn coffin spoke to my friend Lumir in his dead wife's voice."

I saw the disbelief in Marcie's eyes. "Cletus, you must have heard the Walt Florence version and forgotten it. All the talk about the Old Hag dredged it up in your subconscious. Then it worked its way into your dreams."

I realized I'd been holding my breath and exhaled. "You're probably right," I said.

"Besides," Deb interjected, "you don't fit the profile. You're not handsome. Good-looking, maybe. Handsome, no."

"Deb!" snapped Marcie.

"It's okay," I said. "The Warren Beatty look isn't for everybody. I have confidence in my appearance." I'd no sooner said this when my doubts about the Hag returned. "Of course, how do you explain Lumir hearing his wife's voice?"

"Coincidence and an active imagination," said Marcie. "Bound to happen now and again."

"It's easy to explain," Deb teased. "Lumir fits the profile."

24

Irv and Herm sat before the flames of a gas fireplace in a trendy A-frame restaurant in northern Cedar Rapids.

"Leonardo's West makes better pizza," observed Herm. "Want the last piece?"

"No," fumed Irv. "I don't know how you can eat at a time like this."

Herm transferred the last piece of the pineapple and Canadian bacon pizza to his plate. "You gotta lighten up. Little setbacks like this happen."

Irv smashed his cigarette into the ashtray so hard the contents spewed over the table. "I can't believe Marty stiffed us like that. She's a dead woman."

"We're gonna whack her anyway, remember?"

"Okay, use the blowtorch on her and make it slow. She deserves it."

Herm looked at his watch. "Oops, time again." He reached into his pocket, pulled out his vial of Valium, and took one. "Looks like I'm gettin' low."

"The way you're going through those things, you'll have to go back to Doctor Bob early."

"I already called for a refill. You never did tell me what happened when you asked Canker if he had any news about Marty. When I asked, you got mad and stalked off. I felt hurt."

Irv removed a cigarette from his silver case. "Sorry, but I'm so frustrated. Never did talk to Canker. I called the phone number for his construction business and found out he's in the hospital."

"I bet it's a heart attack. Walking around with a stomach bigger than your belt is bad for your health."

Streams of smoke poured from Irv's nose. "The guy who answered didn't want to tell me what happened, but I wormed it out of him. Turns out Canker got thumped, bad. Some farmer found him on his property, thought he was stealing pigs, and beat the livin' crap right out of him. He's got a broken arm and two fractures in his leg."

Herm shook his head. "A tough break, but what the hell did he expect snooping around a farm like that? Iowa people are nutty about their cows and pigs. We shoulda snatched the casket when we had the chance and then bought the tools from Marty. Nice and simple. Say I'm right, Irv."

"You're right."

"Say it again."

Irv tapped his cigarette on his case. "Don't press your luck. Marty must have another buyer, so we've gotta move fast."

"No, Irv. Marty can wait. Don't forget we're meeting Thomas and Benjamin for dinner tonight."

"We could lose the coffin and the tool chests. What if we wait another day, and they're gone?"

Herm took a deep breath and stretched. "The past few days, I've got myself a whole new perspective on life. If we're meant to have the casket and tool chests, we'll get them. If not, it's okay. And I don't want to blowtorch Marty. That was the old me. I've matured. The new me wants to keep it nice and clean."

Irv looked at his partner in disbelief. "You do sound like a new man. I don't know what to say."

"I do. I'm sorry," said Herm. "Sorry for pressuring you about money. Sorry for being a neurotic mess. I never realized it until I started taking Valium, but I've been a huge pain in the ass."

Irv's took a drag on his Benson and Hedges. "It's no big deal. I'm just glad the stuff is working for you."

"This Valium, it's a miracle, a frickin' miracle. So, dinner with friends tonight, worry about Marty tomorrow?"

"Sure. You want me to whack her instead?"

"No way. This is my hit."

<hr>

I took a sip of coffee and unfolded my day-old *Chicago Tribune* on the marble counter of Peely's Drugstore. The sign outside said Bellevue Pharmacy, but I couldn't remember anyone ever using the name. Peely didn't run the place anymore, but it didn't matter, people would use the name for at least another ten years. When Peely took over the business, it took that long for people to stop calling it Kranz's. The place had been remodeled since I left town. It looked brighter and cheerier. I'd come in for a chocolate Coke, but to my dismay, they'd removed the soda fountain equipment. Engrossed in a story on the disaster known as the Chicago Cubs, I didn't notice that someone had seated himself two stools away.

"Mornin' Clete."

I turned to see a smiling Hankie Steines.

"Marty's a little short on the money for the tool chests right now," he said, "but she'll have it before the weekend is over."

Not wanting to reduce the chances of repayment, I didn't tell him I'd covered the difference, and the chests were already as good as Marty's. "That's some news about her mother," I said. "I can't imagine what it's like to have something like that pop up after all these years."

"She's not takin' it too good and wants to be alone. While she's gone, Blackie Stiles and I are gonna spend a couple days scoutin' fish buyers. We're leavin' tonight."

"Over the Fourth of July?"

"I got a couple of days off from the garbage truck, and Blackie wants me to go into business with him, so I figured what the heck? Anyway, I can see you don't understand the fishin' business. There ain't no days off—even for the buyers."

Hankie wore a new straw hat covered with wooden golf tees. Since Marty had thrown its twin in the fire the night they'd come to our fish fry, I had to ask, "What's Marty gonna say about the hat? She hated the last one."

"She felt so bad about burning my favorite hat, she bought me a new one. You know, I'm staying with her right now."

Though the frizzy-haired clerk behind the counter appeared lost in a movie magazine, I noticed her doing a double take. Hank and Marty's household arrangement was about to become the talk of the town.

Hankie reached into his pants pocket and pulled out a tobacco pouch. When he did, the tattoo peeking from the sleeve of his t-shirt became fully visible. It was one of those old-fashioned designs, a heart with an arrow through it. The ink had faded, but it didn't take much effort to read the name over the top—Marty. I don't know how I could have been so dense. When Marty had spoken of a love affair with a man who fished for a living, she didn't mention a name. I should have made the connection with Hankie Steines; he was single then. He'd fathered the child she miscarried. I doubted he knew.

"See the sign?" The frizzy-haired clerk interrupted us to point to a *No Smoking* sign taped to the mirror behind her. "We sell medications and healthcare items. Smoking is a no-no."

Hank returned his pouch to his pocket, turned toward me, and met my eye. "Your cousin is a good woman, Efferding. I hope you know that. The years she spent living with you guys were the most miserable time in of her life. She was just a kid and got treated worse than dirt."

A week ago, I'd have been furious with him. A week ago, I'd have been shouting. Today was different. My mom and dad weren't perfect anymore. "I was just a kid, Hank. Younger than she was."

Though the counter clerk had her back to us, she'd nearly bent over backward to listen to our conversation.

"Did you ever stick up for her?"

I didn't respond. I couldn't defend my parents, and I couldn't defend myself. My father would turn over in his grave if he knew a commercial fisherman had belittled his family in front of a clerk sure to pass the story on.

"That's what I thought," Hank continued. "For the life of me, I don't know why she still likes you. One minute she's ready to take your head off, and the next she thinks you're okay."

The counter clerk hovered. "More coffee?"

She looked familiar, but I couldn't place her. Since I couldn't place her, I didn't know the social cost of what I was about to do, but her interest in our conversation put me over the top.

"No thanks," I said softly. "I don't remember you, but I'm Cletus Efferding, the man everybody blames for his wife's suicide. I got busted for prostitution the day before she took her life by drowning herself. Hank and I are talking about my cousin Marty, the woman most people in town think of as a slut. Marty was orphaned at age fourteen and came to live with us. Those were not easy times for her. For reasons I don't understand, my parents had trouble dealing with her, and it only increased the difficulty of her situation. Though she is my last living adult relative, Marty and I have trouble getting along, but on some level, we do like each other. Is there anything else you want to know?"

Mission accomplished. Without a word, she turned on her heel and disappeared into the back of the store.

"Nosey busybody," I muttered.

Hankie must have heard me. "Have to agree with you on that one."

Despite my anger, I regretted my outburst. My folks would have been humiliated beyond words if they'd known what I'd just done. On some level, I'd embarrassed myself, but truth be told, my tantrum felt good.

I looked over to see an unperturbed Hank Steines smiling into his coffee. He picked up his cup and raised it in my direction. "You're all right, Clete Efferding. You probably don't want to hear this, but I'm gonna tell you anyway. You're more like Marty than you know."

He had one thing right. I didn't want to hear it.

I exited Peely's, rounded the corner, and found the Debs standing alongside my Nova. Marcie stood with a pen poised over a notebook. Double Deb stood in the street, snapping pictures.

Deb put her camera down and beamed at me. "We're recording the graffiti on your car."

Marcie looked at me red-faced. "Um, uh—hi," she stammered.

"Marcie wanted to document your car in case you become a part of the Old Hag legend. You know, what with the little rhyme and all."

"Deb," growled Marcie, "put a sock in it."

Deb must not have heard. "Since your wife walked into the river, and the Old Hag lives in the river, Marcie believes pieces of the stories will merge at some point, especially since you were back in town when they discovered the coffin. Your car is important because the graffiti refers to the children's poem."

I felt confused. "Children's poem, what are you talking about?"

"Oh, you don't about know it? It goes like this."

> *Little Cletus Efferdong,*
> *Wiener wasn't very long.*
> *Wife got bored, so Cletus whored.*
> *She drowned herself. He done her wrong.*

"Almost every kid can recite it, but don't worry, the little ones don't understand what 'whored' means."

Red-faced, Marcie stared at the ground. I knew the look. She was hoping the earth would swallow her up.

"When we found out about your car, we were afraid you'd be embarrassed and wouldn't want us to take pictures," continued Deb. "When we saw it parked here, it was like a gift."

"Marcie," I said, "I thought we were friends. Why didn't you just ask me? I would have been happy to help."

She didn't answer.

Double Deb slapped her hand over her mouth. "Looks like I goofed," she mumbled through her fingers.

"You sure did," I said as I edged her aside and put my hand on the door handle. "I don't know much about southern etiquette, but contrary to what you may think, my wife's death is not a joke, nor is it fodder for a Ph.D. dissertation. If you ever see me again, please have the decency to walk the other way. You can be assured I'll do the same."

I said nothing more but got into my car and pulled away, rounding the block, making a beeline for Lampe's hardware store. I left the engine running, hurried inside, and came out with a can of black spray paint. To think that I'd once considered that calculating cow Marcie as date material made me livid. I fantasized about spraying the Debs' car, Peely's window, Canker DeCook's truck, the town's water tower, City Hall, you name it.

As I sped down Front Street, a little girl riding a pink bicycle with ribbons on the handlebars appeared out of nowhere. Focused on a friend on the other side of the street, she'd started across without looking. My unexpected appearance must have scared the crap out of her for she did the worst thing possible, she stopped in the middle of the road and stared at my car. I slammed on the brakes. The Nova came to a halt not five feet from her. Nearly sick to my stomach, I gave her a weak smile and wiggled my fingers.

Realizing I was not going scold her, she recovered quickly and gave me a 500-watt version of my sickly grin and went merrily on her way. I continued south, quaking like a leaf but with my priorities re-ordered. My self-righteous irritability had nearly caused the death of a child.

When I pulled onto the gravel patch next to my cabin, my heart rate had yet to return to normal. I exited the car and did something I should have done days ago. Removing the can of paint from its paper bag, I shook it briskly and sprayed over the graffiti. I'd left the vandals' paint job intact in hopes the townsfolk would see it and realize they'd overreacted to my return. Not my best move, my I'll-show-em stunt backfired on me when people didn't understand.

My encounter with the Debs confirmed my suspicion that the miscreants who'd sprayed my car were junior-high age. And now I knew exactly what the *Efferdong* and *little dicky* referred to. Too bad the vandals hadn't been in my gym class, they'd have seen firsthand just how wrong they were.

25

Late afternoon found me ringing the front doorbell of the rectory next door to St. Joseph's Catholic Church. A genial man with a bulbous nose, black-rimmed eyeglasses, and a 1950s haircut answered the door.

"Hello," I said, "My name is Cletus Efferding, and I'd like to speak with the pastor about taking a look at the parish records. I'm in town for a few days and trying to locate information on the August Efferding family."

The man extended his hand, his face beaming. "It's always a pleasure to meet another Cletus."

I shook his hand. "One of the best names around. After the formalities are done, I usually go by Clete."

He let out a belly laugh. "I usually go by Father Tillman, protocol you know. Come on in."

Astonished he wasn't dressed in a black suit and wearing one of those collars with a little white square in the middle, I followed him inside, thinking it a sad commentary on the state of the American wardrobe when priests and ministers quit wearing suits. Losing those cassock things had been a step forward, but a black suit commands respect.

As Tillman led me through the hall, my mind conjured up images of priests in purple leisure suits with chains and heavy gold crosses around their necks. What was next, iridescent shirts with little white squares in the collar? The priest's plaid shirt suddenly looked good.

We entered a cluttered office lined with bookshelves. Opposite a desk buried under stacks of paperwork, stood a small table, its top completely bare.

"This is where we assemble the church bulletin," the priest said.

"I knew there had to be a reason for the clean table."

My fellow Cletus chuckled and indicated I should take a chair. "I'm not much of a housekeeper," he said and turned toward the shelves to fetch three small, leather-bound journals.

"These are our earliest records. They only go back to 1881," he said. "Bellevue had a smallpox epidemic that year, and the parish priest caught it and died. They removed everything inside the rectory, even the furniture, and incinerated it. Afterward, they burned sulfur in the house for five days. So much for the older records."

He placed the journals on the table.

"Too bad," I said. "I've already checked the county courthouse. "They suggested I try here."

"How's your Latin?" he asked.

"Latin? The records are in Latin?"

The good Father Tillman smiled. "I don't think you'll have much trouble. The top volume is for marriages, the middle for baptisms, and the last for deaths. Family names are spelled as they are in English. First names are spelled in Latin but look pretty much like their English counterparts. The entries are arranged by date."

'Dubious' didn't begin to explain my reaction to his news. "Maybe this isn't such a hot idea after all."

Tillman grinned and gave me a whack on the shoulder. "Most folks manage to get by. I'll be across the hall in my study. Just put one of these slips of paper in a page that interests you, and I can answer your questions later."

"Gee, thanks, I think."

The good father smiled and turned to go. "You're a Cletus. That means you're smarter than the average bear, so I'm expecting a lot from you."

Appalled at the reality of the task before me, I pulled out my stenographer's pad and reached for the stack of books. The motivation for my project had been to put together a few pages on the Efferdings. With Tammy and Mike now named Hinkley, we were a dying line. Someday the kids would want to know where they came from. At least I hoped so. In my more cynical moments, I wondered if they'd even care.

I set the marriage book aside because it didn't include anything before 1881. My trip to the county courthouse had revealed that Grandpa Efferding married Grandma in 1876. Since they were still married at the time of his death, his other marriage would have been even earlier. With no record here or at the courthouse, I was out of luck.

I picked up the baptisms book. Good Lord, if the Latin wasn't bad enough, the handwriting and faded ink were even worse. After the first few pages I got the hang of it. The notation for October 9, 1883 brought me up short.

Octobris 9, 1883
Hodie, ego baptizavi Katharina, illegitimus filiam Augusti Efferding et Martinae Dufay. Natus Octobris 5, 1883.
Patrinus et matrina: Petrus Till, Maria Deppe.
J. N. Bies

I might not know much about Latin, but it didn't take a whole lot of brains to realize *illegitimus* meant illegitimate, and that *Martinae Dufay* sure as hell wasn't grandma Gertrude Efferding. Grandpa Efferding, my father's idol, had strayed off the ranch. I wondered if my father knew. Families kept a tight rein on scandal back then, but still, it's hard to keep secrets in a small town.

As I stared at the nearly illegible scrawl, the word *Katharina* popped out at me. Aunt Kate? Marty's mom? I thought of the unfortunate woman found dead under the floorboards of an abandoned hatchery. My head spun as the words in my Aunt Millie's last will and testament rushed back at me.

To my niece Martha Efferding, I leave nothing. Blood will out.

If Aunt Millie knew, it stood to reason that my father knew as well. They'd grown up in the same house as Aunt Kate. And what about Grandma? She'd raised the child of the woman who'd bedded her husband.

Certain I'd jumped to conclusions based on my ignorance of Latin—there were four names in the notation—I picked up the book, crossed the hall, and knocked on the door of the other Cletus. A hearty invitation to enter followed.

My namesake sat at a typewriter, pecking away with two fingers. "Just working on my July Fourth speech," he said. "Can't let the Lutheran or Presbyterian ministers outdo me at the big ceremony."

I handed Father Cletus the baptism book and pointed to the Efferding notation. "I'm having trouble with the Latin here. Can you give me a hand?"

The priest let out a long, low whistle. "A close relative?" he asked.

"My grandfather. Is it what I think it is?"

"You didn't know your grandpa fathered an illegitimate child?"

I shook my head. "Never heard a whisper of it."

The priest gave a half smile and looked at me kindly. "Omissions like this are more common than you think. Families usually edit out the scandals when passing on the family history. From the Church's point of view, your grandfather's infidelity was a serious matter, but it could have been worse, at least the child was baptized."

"What's with the *patrinus* and *matrina* business?" I asked.

"Godparents," he answered.

I'm not religious and don't get bent out of shape by human weakness, but the discovery that my grandfather cheated on Grandma Efferding upset me. I never knew him but remembered Grandma as a sweet woman whose main purpose in life was seeing I didn't lack for freshly baked cookies. My face must have given me away.

"On the plus side," said the good father, "you may have relatives you don't know about. Additional family can be a blessing." He extended the book back in my direction.

I returned to the other office. No use looking for Aunt Millie's baptism. She died at age ninety-two so was born before 1881. I found dad's baptism and went on to the death book, checking up until 1930. No joy, Martine Dufay wasn't listed.

Returning to Father Tillman's office, I held out my hand. "Thanks, you were a big help. I have all the information I need."

"I enjoyed meeting you, Cletus. See you in church on Sunday?"

He thought I was Catholic, but I didn't want to talk about it. "If I'm still here," I said and made for the door. Grandpa Efferding was once Catholic, but at some point, he and Grandma quit going to church. My father had never been inside a house of God until my mother insisted on a Presbyterian wedding as a condition for their engagement. I guess the experience took because Reverend Morehouse loved us. Our family was one of a handful who showed up for services fifty-two weeks a year.

Once back at the cabin, I pulled a beer from the ice chest, grabbed a bag of potato chips, and flopped into a chair. As I munched, I wondered what Marty knew about her mother's childhood. She'd never spoken of it, and if Marty didn't know, would it be best to let sleeping dogs lie? The poor woman had enough going on dealing with the murder of her mother.

My father's references to Aunt Kate had been uniformly negative. Had Grandma Efferding seen her as the ill-begotten fruit of a philandering husband's loins? Aunt Kate's life in Grandpa's house must have been a living hell, a situation akin to that encountered by her daughter Marty when she came to live with us.

The old quote about the sins of the fathers didn't apply in our situation. It should have been: ... *and the sins of the father shall be visited upon the daughter, and upon the daughter of the daughter, and they shall suffer the length of their days.*

Illegitimacy, rejection, murder, miscarriage; between them, Aunt Kate and Marty had it tough.

———————————

The dinner dishes cleared and deposited in the dishwasher, Irv and Herm sat quietly in the den. Irv, his feet on a hassock and pencil in hand, jotted now and again in a crossword puzzle booklet. Koko slept peacefully on his outstretched legs. Herm, upright in his recliner, sat absorbed in a book on the art deco movement. The sounds of Verdi's *La Traviata* came softly from the stereo.

Herm looked up as Irv folded the booklet and put his pencil behind his ear.

"I'm almost happy Benjamin got sick, and they had to cancel," said Irv. "Eating at home was nice."

"You did a great job picking the wine, Irv. That *Chateauneuf* was spectacular. Too bad I could only have one glass because of the Valium. A quiet night at home, a little Verdi, a nice book, who could ask for more? You know it's kinda odd how we listen to operas and classical at night and country music during the daytime."

"Not so odd at all, they're both about a good story and strong emotions. Nothing like that feces-encrusted, knuckle-dragging hard rock."

Herm rested the art deco book on his belly. "Chainsaw music, that's all it is. Instead of guitars, the guys could just stand on stage, put the back end of chainsaws against their crotches, goose the throttles, and wave 'em around. Whoever makes the most noise gets to be the star. The guitars are nothing but penis substitutes anyway."

The phone rang. Irv lifted Koko and put her on the floor. He went to the kitchen to answer while Herm turned back to his book. Irv returned to his chair ten minutes later, obviously irritated.

"That was Marty. She has the coffin, but she still doesn't have the tools. She can't buy them because she doesn't have the cash to meet the seller's price."

Herm looked up from his book. "See, I was right about two things. Marty would call us sooner or later and working with amateurs is a pain in the heinie."

Removing his reading glasses, Irv rubbed his eyes. "The woman is a real headache. She blows hot; she blows cold. And now she wants money up front."

"Why'd she stiff us?"

"Her mom got murdered."

After reaching for his vial of pills, Herm extracted one and downed it with the glass of water at his side. "Seems like a good excuse."

"It happened something like thirty years ago, and they just found the body. Twenty grand, and she lets ancient history get in the way. She kept yakkin' and yakkin' and yakkin' about it. I thought my ear was gonna fall off."

"Like I say, Irv. Never trust somebody that's not in the life. She shoulda been over it by now."

"I agreed we'd meet her tomorrow in Dubuque. She thinks we're bringing the money she needs for the buy. We'll make her tell us where the stuff is, whack her, and pick up the goods ourselves."

Herm put down his book and sighed. "I told you. When you work with somebody like Marty, you get the stink end of the stick. Tomorrow's the Fourth of July. God, I hate working holidays."

Koko leapt onto Irv's lap. He began stroking her fur. "We'll have to improvise."

Yawning, Herm picked up his book. "We've done it before. Anyway, sometimes I think we're better in a clutch."

Irv snapped his finger. "Forgot to tell you. I called that guy you told me about, the one from the gravestone society. He's interested and knows guys who will want to buy the coffin. Having the original body makes it worth double because some customers want to display the coffin with the contents intact. How did you ever hear about him?"

"Saw an article about Manny Mendez in the newsletter last year. He got kicked out of the Association for ripping off headstones and taking a body from a crypt. Poor guy got six months in the Kentucky state pen. I figured he'd be out by now."

Irv picked up his book of crosswords. "Anyway, he has a couple of customers who'd be interested. A motorcycle gang in California wants something over the top to decorate their clubhouse. Then there's this guy who runs a fake ghost town in Mexico. He wants to add an undertaker's parlor to his operation. Manny says the important thing is that the body is dry, so it doesn't smell bad. I wonder how hard it is to turn a body into a mummy."

"Should be a piece of cake. We just open the coffin and let it dry out."

"Manny will hook us up for ten percent."

"Like hell, Irv. Tell him four hundred or nothing."

"Thought you'd say that," laughed Irv.

La Traviata reached its conclusion. The speakers clicked as the phonograph arm popped in and out of the last groove on the disc. Irv looked at Herm; Herm looked at Irv. Neither wanted to rise from his chair. Sensing he was about to lose the war of the wills, Herm got up to tend to the music.

"String quartet?" he asked. "Vivaldi?"

Re-involved with his crosswords, Irv just nodded. The sounds of the composer's *Four Seasons* soon filled the room.

Herm had just returned to his chair when the phone rang. "Your turn," he said.

"Damn," Irv grumbled. "Can't a guy get five minutes of peace around here?"

He put a protesting and thoroughly disgusted Koko back on the floor and returned to the kitchen. The call didn't take long. Irv was back in five minutes.

"That was Canker," he said as he returned to his chair. "He wants us to croak some guy named Cletus Efferding. Blames him for the beating that put him in the hospital. Canker's gonna have to use a wheelchair because of the way they put the cast on his leg."

"Wonder if the guy's related to Marty. What'd you say?"

"I'm not too old to learn, Herm. I remembered our discussion and told him we'd have to confer."

A happy glow filled Herm's chest. "That's more like it. Equal partners is always the best way to go. How motivated is he?"

"Five thousand, and he wants the guy to suffer."

"Not enough to get me out of retirement. You had to do the farmer because of our lost savings, and the deal with Marty was gonna net us a real bundle. I'd say at least ten grand—twelve if he wants us to make it slow."

Irv laced his fingers behind his head and stretched. "Not only does he want the guy to suffer, Canker wants to watch."

"At one time, I'da said a man after my own heart, but now it just seems weird. We'll have to drag it out longer than normal just to put on a good show, and then we'll have to take Canker out after we get paid because he's a witness. That's two hits. Not a penny less than fifteen."

Removing the pencil from his ear, Irv picked up his puzzle booklet. "Makes sense to me. After he pays us, he's gone. I'll call him in a day or two. If that cotton-pickin' phone rings again, I'm gonna rip it off the damn wall."

Randy Roeder

26

I sat next to Lumir on the hard, wooden pews of St. Wenceslaus Catholic Church. Eddie and his mother sat at the front, and even from my vantage point three-quarters of the way back, the tension between the two was easy to spot. To put it mildly, the aftermath of the death of Eddie's father had been a disaster.

Bob Brada had passed within an hour of Eddie's return to Cedar Rapids. Not wanting to disturb his mother and not expecting the man's immediate demise, Eddie had neglected to tell her about the walnut casket he and Lumir had built. The omission had unintended consequences. His parents, having no idea of the project underway, had gone to the Janeba-Kuba funeral home and signed on for a pre-arranged service, one that covered all the details, including the casket.

Eddie's father had chosen his own coffin, a deluxe, smoky-gray model with pewter-colored trim that looked more like a full-sized Buick than a casket. His mother, adamant that the man would spend eternity in something that looked like it had rolled off an assembly line in Detroit, refused even to look at the work of art resting in Lumir's garage.

Her rejection had been as firm as it was succinct. "Bob chose his casket, and that's all there is to it."

According to Lumir, grief disrupts normal human thought processes, turning the relatively unimportant into issues fundamental to the survival of the human race. "Just as many families have been destroyed by fights over Grandma's sewing box as over money," he'd told me. He was right, of course, but a mother rejecting a son's final offering to his father raised the ante to the tenth power.

I'd arrived in town last night, too late for the viewing. Lumir gave me the details when he stopped by my apartment on his way home. He'd taken the blowup hard, believing Eddie and his mother would never reconcile. Then the other shoe dropped. Eddie had gone out of his way to avoid speaking to Lumir at the wake.

When the church service ended, Lumir rode to the cemetery with me. Eddie left his mother's side as soon as the graveside rites were over. He separated from the crowd, acknowledged no one, and began walking away.

I left Lumir's side and hurried to catch up to Eddie. "Eddie," I said, "I'm sorry your father has passed, and I'm sorry to hear about the way things went with your mother. You've got a lot to deal with, but don't let it break you. You're feeling bad right now, but you have responsibilities. Don't mess it up like I did when Myra died. I let my children get away from me, and there's a good chance they'll never want to see me again. Lumir and your mother need you, and you're the only one in a position to help them."

Eddie didn't look up and didn't answer. Since I couldn't think of anything else to say, I took his hand, patted his shoulder, then gave him a hug. "I'm so sorry, Eddie," I said and turned to rejoin Lumir.

I stared at the door of my cabin, key in hand. A hasp and padlock had been installed over the lock. Bits of wood lay on the ground. The edge of the door frame looked as if a rabid beaver had attacked it. Someone had broken in.

Hearing footsteps on the gravel behind me, I turned to find the unshaven owner holding up a key. "You'll have to use this until I can get the door repaired. Been here over ten years and never had anything like this. Two break-ins in one night. They hit the cabin where your friends stayed too. I don't know what things are coming to anymore. Drugs, hippies, losing wars, presidents getting thrown out of office. It's enough to make a man want to sell out and move to Alaska. They don't have criminals up there because they don't believe in arrests and trials. They just shoot 'em."

He handed me the key. I opened the lock and looked inside. The place hadn't been ransacked, but the open closet door caught my eye. Fearing the worst, I rushed to look inside. My suits, the most valuable thing I brought with me, hung as I'd left them. An inspection of my dresser drawer revealed the contents still present and neatly folded.

I turned to see the owner just outside the door, waiting for me to complete my inspection. "Everything looks okay. Let me check the cooler," I said.

My beer and soda, my food, intact. I went into the bathroom. My toiletries, the towels, all in place. I addressed the owner: "Doesn't seem to be anything missing."

"Just like the other cabin," he snorted. "They wreck the locks and doors, and what good does it do 'em? They get nothing, and I get to pay for the damages. Hard enough to make this place go without crap like this goin' on."

I felt sorry for the cranky old guy. Old enough to collect Social Security, but ambitious enough to run a business. Sure, the cabins weren't much but like as not, they represented his life savings.

"It'll be Monday before I can get somebody in to repair the damage. Until then, you'll have to make do with the padlock. The police will want to talk to you to see what's missing."

The owner left after I assured him I'd make a report. The violation of my privacy left me uneasy. Though nothing had been disturbed, the urge to clean house overtook me. I gathered up my once-white t-shirts and slime-covered sneakers. No way they'd touch my body again. A quick trip outside gave my fishing clothes a new home, the trash barrel. Only the blue jeans escaped execution.

I inventoried the cupboards to rid them of food left by previous tenants. Out went the canned lima beans, coffee crystals, and tins of spam. By the time I'd finished, the shelves were bare. I was preparing a grocery list when a voice came through the screen door. I looked up to see Hank Steines standing outside. Happy for the distraction, I yelled, "Come on in."

Hank opened the door and let it slam behind him. "Looks like you got broke into," he observed. "They get much?"

"They didn't take anything, but the landlord's sore about the door."

Rocking back and forth on the balls of his feet, he asked, "Seen Marty?"

I put down my pad and pencil. "I've been out for a funeral in Cedar Rapids. Just got back."

The man looked uneasy. "Blackie and I came home from our trip last night. As far as I can see, Marty hasn't been at the house since she left for Prairie du Chien on Wednesday. Nobody brought the newspapers in, the mailbox is full, and her dirty coffee cup is on the kitchen table where she left it. Wednesday, Thursday, Friday, and now, today. Seems like a long time."

Stability had never been one of Marty's virtues. She could have decided to extend the trip, take a little vacation, but given what she'd been dealing with, it seemed unlikely. Even after thirty years, a murdered mother is a big shock. I wondered if she'd gone mental.

Hank continued, "No note, no nothing. She goes out for coffee a lot, so I asked around at the hotel and drugstores. Nobody's seen her."

Marty had gone off the rails before, attempting suicide, leaving town, then wandering in a haze. I hoped she was okay. "I don't like it, Hank. She should have been back by now. How's she been?"

"Fine, until that phone call. I never shoulda gone with Blackie. Not when she was all stirred up."

I'd have asked my visitor to sit, but the way he was bouncing around, he wouldn't have been able to. "Don't blame yourself. She wanted to be alone. Remember?"

Maybe it was the worry in the guy's face. Maybe it was the ants in his pants. I started to get nervous too. "The newspapers, the coffee cup, the mail, it's safe to assume she hasn't come back yet. Discovering somebody murdered your mom would throw anybody for a loop. We should talk to the police, maybe fill out a missing person report."

Hank removed his straw hat and ran his fingers through his hair. "I don't know what to do. If she's okay, the report will make Marty ornerier than a bee-stung bullhead with a hook in its mouth."

"What if she's not okay?" I asked. "Like the time she disappeared after losing your baby?"

The words hung in the air. The look on Hank's face told me he'd been unaware of how close he'd come to fatherhood. He sat on the arm of the upholstered chair, staring vacantly, looking as if he'd been punched in the gut. I'd screwed up royally. My blunder had transformed a hyperactive Hank into a deflated poster boy for melancholy. He stared at the floor from his perch on the arm of the chair, his lip quivering. Marty would tear the tongue from my mouth when she realized I'd spilled her secret.

"She didn't tell me," he sighed. "I always wanted kids. All those years we coulda been with each other—wasted. I wanted to get married, but she said no. Now she wants me, but she's too old to have 'em. Funny how things work out."

Hank was a decent enough guy, but I suck at playing amateur psychologist. The only way I could think of to undo the mess I'd made was to get him moving. "Okay, this is what we'll do. There's no phone here at the cabin. We'll drive to Marty's and call the police department. Tell them we want to file a missing person report."

Hank nodded. An old-fashioned man, his quivering lip and twitching nostrils were as close as he'd ever come to crying in front of another human being. Though I'm a bit of a weeper myself, I've never understood the current fascination with the so-called sensitive man. Anybody with an ounce of smarts could see the guy was hurting. The fact that he chose to avoid inflicting his pain on others didn't make him an insensitive clod any more than the occasional tear turns an oaf into a model of compassion.

Who knew when we'd see Marty again? But the cabin was beginning to feel claustrophobic. We had the police to contact, and I wanted to use the trip to Marty's house to get the tool chests off my hands.

"Say, Hank," I said, "as long as we're heading up to Marty's, let's take the tool chests along. The guy who owns the cabins is here right now, and he's storing them in his garage. That way, they'll be there when she gets home."

My visitor didn't rise to join me.

"What about the money she's short?" he asked.

I waved my hand. "Not a problem. I already paid Lumir the extra one twenty-five. She can add it to the six hundred she owes me."

Hank cocked his head and looked at me. "Clete, you know Marty's not so great with money. You might not want to lend her so much. The deal could fall through."

"True, but the Efferdings weren't so great with Marty either. I'm not going to worry about it for now."

Exhaling loudly, a glum and defeated Hank rose from the chair. "You know, with Marty gone, my imagination got the best of me last night. I felt like somebody was in the house with me."

"Probably a dream. Marty's dog would have gone nuts when they tried to unlock the doors."

"She had Mabel Kilburg keep the dog for her. Besides, I didn't lock the house because I thought she might come home in the middle of the night. Not that it matters. She's probably tired of me already."

"Look on the bright side," I replied. "At least you didn't get a visit from the Old Hag."

I may suck as an amateur psychologist, but in a pinch, I can hold my own playing nursemaid.

It's the little things that make small towns so great. Hank and I sat in Marty's living room as patrolman Mac McClean leaned over the coffee table filling in the blanks on a pre-printed missing person form. Back in Cedar Rapids, you'd have to go down to the station where they'd make you feel so bad for disturbing them, you'd want to fill out the damn thing yourself.

"Bear with me," said McClean. "I've only done a couple of these before, and I want to get it right. Too bad you don't know the license number for Marty's car, I won't be able to get it until Monday. We'll get the report out tonight anyway. Maybe the bright red Pinto will be description enough."

"How do you put it out?" I asked.

McClean clicked the top on his bright yellow ballpoint and returned it to his plastic pocket protector. "We go through the County Sheriff's Office. I'll phone the most important information, and they'll put it on the teletype. Because Marty left for Prairie du Chien, I'll ask them to make direct contact with the agencies up there. Dubuque should get special attention, too. She had to drive through it in on the way up. Can you think of anything else?"

Hank pulled on his lip. "Yeah, if the County Sheriff is in the courthouse, why can't he get the license number tonight?"

McClean sighed. "Except for the sheriff, all the offices are closed for the weekend. In an emergency, we could get it from Des Moines, but I don't know that a missing person report qualifies. I'm pushing the guidelines already. An adult has the right to leave home, but since Marty has a prior disappearance and just received bad news about her mother's death, I've justified the report by saying we have reason to believe she might harm herself."

Hank's face turned red. He threw his new hat down on the table and smashed it with his fist. "A person finds out her ma was murdered and disappears. She's missing four days, and that's not an emergency?"

I held up my hand. "Easy Hank. Marty told us she'd be away a couple of days and wanted time to herself. She's been gone longer than we thought, but she's always had a mind of her own. We're doing the careful thing, but now's not the time to panic."

Hank's display of anger didn't seem to bother McLean. He stood, shifted his gun belt, and stretched. "Well, the sooner I get the report out, the sooner they'll start looking." He bent over, picked up the pages, and left through the front door.

I looked at my watch. Eight p.m. My unhappy stomach craved sustenance, and mooning around Marty's living room with Hank didn't meet my definition of a good time. "Let's unload the tool chests," I said. "Then I'd better be going."

"Okay," he replied. "I'll open the garage. The keys are in the truck. Back it up to the left side of the overhead door."

I positioned the truck, got out, and waited for Hank to raise the overhead door. He didn't. I went around to the side door and recognized the telltale signs. Somebody had jimmied it open. Hank, his back turned to me, stood inside surveying a tangle of broken furniture and tumbled stacks of boxes.

"It must'a happened last night," he said. "Everything was okay yesterday."

Whoever broke in had ransacked the place. Shattered glassware spilled from cardboard containers, tables lay on their sides, drawers had been removed from cabinets and tossed aside, antique quilts lay dirty and torn. Salvage and cleanup would take weeks.

Hank shook his head and mumbled, "I can't believe it. The dirty sons of bitches. What's Marty gonna say?"

Since Hank had slept in the house, I wondered how he could have slumbered through the ruckus. "Whoever did it must have made a lot of noise. You didn't hear anything?"

My question met with a red-faced look at the floor.

"Blackie and I met with our last buyer at the Bronco last night— old Jim Beam. I don't know how much Blackie drank, but after eight shots of Jim it's kinda hard to remember when I got home."

"I'm pretty sure of one thing," I said. "Somebody was in the house with you last night, and whoever it was didn't need to break in because you left that door open. Is everything inside okay?"

"Let's go," said Hank, motioning for me to follow.

We checked the house. Except for a few upended boxes in the basement, it didn't look as if anything had been disturbed. Our examination complete, we returned to the garage.

I surveyed the damage again. "Well, it looks like we'll have to call the police and get them back here."

"No," said Hank. "What's done is done."

"We need to file a report, so Marty can make a claim on her insurance. The company will probably want pictures too."

Stubborn is the only word I could assign to the look on Hank's face.

"No, Marty won't want that."

"Doesn't she have insurance?"

Hank adjusted his straw hat, apparently unaware of how ridiculous it looked since he'd smashed it with his fist. "No cops," he said.

"If we don't file a report within so many hours of discovery, Marty won't collect. You know, Hank, you should lose the hat. It's dead, believe me. Besides, you need something better for the shape of your face, maybe a pork pie."

He looked at the floor. "Marty won't want a report."

"Why on Earth not?" I asked.

"She won't want to tell them about the coffin. Who in the hell woulda stole the coffin from us?"

I couldn't believe my ears. "Tell me it's not the Bowman's Island box."

Hank looked at me, all innocence. "Why, of course it was."

"Are you guys insane? What were you doing with it?"

"Marty had somebody who wanted to buy it with the body still in it. So, we swiped it from Ray, and now some rat-faced puke has gone and swiped it from us."

27

The morning sun streamed through the cabin window. I'd imagined Cousin Marty as capable of many things, but coffin-stealing had never been on the list. As I sat on the edge of my bed, I thought how strange my life had become since I'd returned to Bellevue. Stolen coffins, the Old Hag, spray-painted cars, a cheating grandpa, crazy parents, underhanded folklorists, break-ins, little Cletus Efferdong...

I don't know where it came from, but deep down inside me, pressure started to build. Suddenly, without realizing it, I was laughing. Not chuckling, not giggling, but rolling-in-the-aisles, floor-pounding, convulsing, whooping, belly laughing.

My life back in Cedar Rapids had grown comfortable, so comfortable it had become more existence than adventure. The past week had destroyed the pattern, and although I stood on the line between adventure and disaster, I wasn't bored. Canker DeCook might pound me, and Marty might be in real trouble, but I wouldn't have traded the first ten days of my vacation for anything. The man known as Cletus Efferding had grown stale, and it had taken a week and a half away from his two jobs for him to realize it.

As stimulating as life had become, I felt the need to slow it down a tad. Last week's *Bellevue Herald-Leader* mentioned the public library was experimenting with Sunday hours for the summer. In anticipation of the upcoming bicentennial of the United States, it had purchased microfilm copies of the early censuses for Jackson County. The news reminded me I'd neglected my family history project. Though short on thrill and excitement, library research beat the hell out of flogging men's clothing fifty weekends in a row. I had something to accomplish. Time to get dressed and get moving.

I'd returned from Cedar Rapids with reinforcements for my beleaguered wardrobe, and after a shower and a shave, I opted for Sunday casual, pairing a Carolina blue polo shirt with tan linen slacks. An oxblood belt and loafers followed, and to top the whole thing off, I parked a snow-white straw fedora on my head. I looked in the mirror. Though I liked what I saw, something was missing. I walked to the dresser and selected a pair of Foster Grants with navy-blue frames. Too many guys ignore the fashion possibilities inherent in sunglasses. It's a shame.

After a fine morning walk and lunch uptown, I made my grand entrance into the Bellevue Public Library. Located on the second floor of the city hall, the place looked even better than I remembered. Kids perused books in the children's section, adults read in plush chairs, and most importantly, no one occupied the alcove containing the sole microfilm reader. Curious about how all this microfilm business worked, I approached an older, bespectacled woman at the main desk. Her name tag identified her as Roberta.

"Good afternoon," I said. "I'd like to look up census information for the town of Bellevue as part of a family history project. I read it's on microfilm but don't know where to start."

She removed her glasses and left them dangling from the beaded chain around her neck. "We have the records for the 1860, 1870, 1880, and 1900 federal censuses—1890 was destroyed by a fire and never released. The state of Iowa conducted censuses too. We have the one for 1885. Once you get familiar with it, using microfilm is easy."

I held up my steno pad and ballpoint. "I'm ready when you are."

She led me to a table with an enameled steel box resting on it and flicked a light switch on the gadget's side. "This is a Recordak microfilm reader. You put your reel on the square spindle to the left and thread the film onto the take-up reel on the right." She pointed to a piece of paper taped to the table. "The instructions for threading the film are on this sheet. I'll set up your first reel. After that, you're on your own."

Roberta showed me how the microfilm storage cabinet was arranged and strung up the reel for the 1860 Census. She turned a crank on the side of the machine to advance the film. "We couldn't afford the census indexes, so first you have to find Bellevue Township. There's no separate listing for the city of Bellevue. You start at the beginning of the township and scan down the column looking for the last name of the family you're interested in. By the way, they're not in alphabetic order, so it will take a while. If you have questions, I'll be at the desk."

I dug right into the task, reading the name of every person living in Bellevue Township, and didn't find a single Efferding. Though disappointed, I wasn't about to give up, so put on the reel for 1870. About halfway through, I got the hang of it and skipped the pages filled with individuals listed as farmers. The pages clustered with grocery store owners, harness-makers, and barkeeps represented the households for the city of Bellevue.

It didn't take long to find Grandpa Efferding. The census taker noted that he was a twenty-four-year-old unmarried store clerk living in the home of Charles Kuchman in what appeared to be downtown Bellevue. The dwelling next door must have been the hotel because twenty unrelated adults lived there. I glanced through occupations of my grandfather's neighbors: a salesman, a lawyer, a woodcutter, a cook, a teamster, and a profession that brought a smile to my face—lady of easy virtue. Three of them lived in the hotel.

"Well, what do you know," I said to myself. "The Whore-tel. A hundred years ago, hookers really did live in it." Though my adolescent fantasies were misplaced, they'd have been justified eighty years earlier.

The hotel merited further examination, but I was unprepared for what came next. One of the ladies of easy virtue was Martine Dufay, the mother of Grandpa Efferding's illegitimate child. My grandfather, the family scion, the apple of my father's eye, had been bonking a prostitute. I studied Martine Dufay's listing: age eighteen, born in Louisiana. Next to the letter M, the code for mulatto, the census taker had written *quadroon*. I dropped out my sophomore year in college but knew what quadroon meant. My grandfather had been shagging a quarter-black woman, a negro. Though she didn't look it, Aunt Kate was black.

There's a word for someone who is one-eighth black. I couldn't remember it and wanted to add it to my notes, so I went searching for Roberta, the friendly librarian.

"The word you're looking for is *octoroon*," she said. "No one uses it much anymore because it's considered offensive. The child of an octoroon is a *hexadecaroon*."

Librarians are amazing. "How do you remember all this without looking it up?" I asked.

Roberta removed her glasses and smiled. "I was a history major in college and wrote a paper on slavery in the Old South."

"I imagine at some point a person became white and was freed."

"Not necessarily," she replied. "It depended on where you lived. In most of the south, slave status was inherited from the mother, so children born of a slave were slaves, even if they looked white. I read an account of an auction in Kentucky where a trader sold a woman who was one sixty-fourth black."

Martine Dufay was a quadroon, Aunt Kate an octoroon, and Marty a hexadecaroon. My father and mother were anything but enlightened on race. I'd once heard Dad making excuses for a neighbor's membership in the Ku Klux Klan. Given their prejudices, it would have been better for Marty if my parents had never taken her into our home.

I walked back to the microfilm reader and flopped in my chair wondering how a prostitute would know who fathered her child and why my grandfather took the rap. I loaded the reel for 1880 and bingo, found the answer to my questions. Grandma and Grandpa had married by then, Aunt Millie was a baby, and Martine Dufay lived in the house as a mulatto servant. No hooker-humping for Grandpa Efferding, he was bonking the maid, an activity that left little doubt he'd fathered a mixed-race child.

I checked the library's other censuses. The 1885 Iowa Census listed Martine Dufay as a colored servant living in the home of August Efferding with her colored daughter Kate. By the time of the 1900 Federal Census, Aunt Kate had magically become white. Martine Dufay no longer lived in the household, and I couldn't find her anywhere in Bellevue Township.

Slumping in my chair, I thought about lies. There are two kinds: the ones you tell and the ones you don't. Pastor Morehouse had a name for the ones you don't. He called them sins of omission—the truths you don't tell even though you owe them to others. I wondered if they were worse. Though he didn't intend it, my grandfather's guilt and shame had wreaked havoc on his family for three generations.

I resolved that when my children turned eighteen, the Hinkley's lies about the man and woman who brought them into this world would stop. Though Tammy and Mike might hate me, the truth about their mother's death and my responsibility for it would become theirs. The Efferding family had been awash in lies for nearly a century, and I intended to put a stop to it.

My kids deserved no less.

I'd stopped by the Big D Super Value on the way back to the cabin and was putting a can of tuna in the cupboard when the tumblers clicked into place. Funny how a connection can be in the back of your mind tending to its own business and then for no reason pop up and smack you in the face. I should have put the pieces together last week, and if not then, earlier this afternoon.

I shoved the can in the cupboard and made for the cabin's battered dresser. Lumir's brass plate, the one I'd yet to hand over to Ray, lay on top. Though I hadn't flipped the light switch, the shadows created by the late afternoon sunlight provided all the illumination needed to decipher the lettering inscribed on its surface.

M. D.

1852-1886

I reached for the plaque, studied it, and went out to the car to retrieve my steno pad. Flipping through the pages, I came to the notation. Martine Dufay had been born in 1852. Same initials, same birth year.

After returning to the cabin, I sat in the upholstered chair considering my next move. Going to the authorities didn't make sense. They were more interested in who stole the casket than who was in it, and the tenuous connection between the initials and Marty's grandma didn't justify it. Charged up by the afternoon's discovery in the library, I was as likely to trim the pieces to fit the puzzle as make an objective judgment.

After chewing on the problem for a while, I realized the match on the initial and birth date wasn't even enough to convince me. If there were a link, more research might ferret it out. One option would be to check the Iowa census to determine how many women with the initials M. D. lived in the Bellevue area in 1885. There were likely to be several, but perhaps only one born in 1852. While such a discovery would be persuasive, I'd need more than that. In high water, the coffin could have drifted for miles.

Then it hit me, like a hammer to the head. The local newspaper. I don't know why I hadn't thought of it. What were the chances that someone could die in a small town and the death go unreported? Tomorrow I'd visit the newspaper office and ask to check the back run of the paper.

If I hit pay dirt, there'd be a lot to tell Marty. No doubt, the conversation would be strange. I imagined how it might go.

Oh, by the way, that coffin you and Hank swiped? Before somebody stole it from you? Your grandma was in it. No, not Grandma Efferding. Your other grandma, the one who was a hooker before she became a maid in Grandpa Efferding's house. He was bonking her while he was married to Grandma Efferding. Did you know your mom was an octoroon, the daughter of an ex-slave from New Orleans? I guess that means you're black, sort of.

I think that's why my folks didn't like you and your mom. Oh, and Aunt Millie, the nasty remark she made when she cut you out of her will? The blood-will-out thing? I expect that's why she wasn't so hot on your mom and didn't like you either. I don't know what life was like for your mother growing up in Grandpa Efferding's house. Maybe Grandma Efferding didn't hate her too much. I hope so, but it's hard to know. I expect you had it better at our house than she did living at Grandpa's. Your life may have sucked, but probably not as much as hers.

Of course, when Marty got back, it could be a while before I'd be able to have a conversation with her. If she'd flipped out, the news might be too much for her. If she hadn't gone nuts, she'd be pissed because I checked with the police. And, heaven forbid, if she'd gone off for a fling with someone there'd be real hell to pay. Hank would feel betrayed and maybe leave her. She'd blame me, claw the skin off my face, and rip the testicles from my body. Best to proceed with caution.

If the mystery corpse was indeed Martine Dufay, I wondered if Marty had some sort of legal interest in the missing casket. After all, she was the woman's only known descendant. That wouldn't justify breaking and entering if her involvement in the theft were discovered. I suspected she'd come out with probation if she played her cards right. That said, I doubted Marty would want to mention she intended to sell her grandmother's corpse along with the casket. The law frowns on selling dead people. It tends to get the common folk riled.

For the first time in my adult life, I wished I didn't know so much about my family. No matter. There'd be no more omissions. Marty would learn everything I'd discovered as soon as she could handle it. Of course, that'd be the easy part.

One day I'd have to tell my kids they were related to a crazy woman who stole her grandma's coffin.

28

Herm hit the button on the garage door opener and eased the pickup forward. He didn't wait for the door to clear the truck but pulled in as far as the windshield. When the door had raised enough to admit the horse trailer, he finished the job.

"What's the big hurry?" asked Irv.

"I can't wait to see it again. The tombstone completes the kit: carcass, coffin, and marker. I can't believe we were so lucky. A four-foot-tall column with a crying-angel on top and the guy only wanted fifty bucks for it."

"Are you sure that you'll be able to pass it off as original to the coffin?"

"I checked. They quit making ornate iron boxes in the mid-1880s, but it took a while for all the inventory to get used up, so the dates on the stone make sense. As of today, the lady in the casket gets a new name, Frances Mahoney, born 1859 and died 1887."

Herm pushed the button to close the garage door behind them. He opened the truck door and hopped out. His feet had yet to hit the concrete when the pungent odor of decay assaulted his nostrils.

Irv slammed the door on his side of the truck. "Whoa, her name may be Frances, but she stinks worse than yesterday."

Herm crossed the front of the truck to join his friend. "It's pretty bad. Time to seal her back up. Good thing most of our sales happen at the store. We won't be able to bring customers in here until the smell goes away."

The men walked to the far corner of the warehouse where the cast iron coffin rested on a sturdy oak table. A dozen houseflies circled in the air above the casket.

Herm withdrew a handkerchief and held it over his nose. "Good thing you thought to cover the box with a mosquito net."

"Wouldn't want Frances to come down with a case of maggots, would we? I left the socket set on the Stickley buffet. Why don't you go fetch it?"

Happy to put distance between himself and the source of the odor, Herm left in search of the socket set. It took a while because Irv had left it alongside a French armoire. He returned and passed the metal box to Irv. The man was good with tools. He accomplished the closure in something like five minutes, but exposure to the stench emanating from the coffin left Herm queasy. "I need to go outside and get some fresh air. I can take the smell of burning flesh, but Frances here isn't doing much for my stomach. Throw the mosquito net back over the box. We don't want it covered with fly poop."

Irv shrugged. "Have it your way, but I don't think flies crap that much."

Herm made for the fresh air and sunlight. Once outside, he took a seat on a wooden bench next to the side entrance. As much as he hated to admit it, his entry into the mortuary antique business had been a fiasco. He shouldn't have listened to Irv and insisted they steal the coffin themselves. There'd been no need to involve an unreliable Marty. The way things worked out, they had to snatch the casket anyway, only from Marty's garage instead of the funeral director's. And that rotting mess inside the coffin. Now that they had buyers who wanted the body, it made no sense to dump it. He didn't have a solution for mummifying the thing, but if Frances had been in the box for a hundred years, she could wait a while longer while they figured it out.

And then there was the reality of those heavy Victorian tombstones. They'd been unbelievably lucky when that farmer came into the shop to offer them one, a stone already loaded on a four-wheel dolly. The guy had taken it and a half dozen others from a farm cemetery that he wanted to plow over. The angel stone was the only interesting one. When the business needed more gravestones, he and Irv would have to steal them or hire some brain-damaged goofus to do it. The damn things were heavy, and he and Irv weren't getting any younger. He heard the door open. Irv came out and lit a cigarette.

"I'll call Canker tomorrow," he said. "The guy doesn't farm, but he lives out in the country and probably has some godforsaken outbuilding we can use to dry Frances out. I need to talk to him about hitting the Efferding guy anyway. We can give Canker a discount for the use of the building. The sooner we get the corpse out of here, the better."

Herm sighed. "I don't know about the mortuary antique business anymore. I mean, we can get a coffin every once in a while, but I doubt we'll ever get another corpse again, and I'm not sure I want to. And the stones, they're so heavy. It's a young man's game."

"Already thought of it. You can deal in children's stones. They're smaller and have all those cute carvings. And then don't forget all those cast metal markers."

Herm felt his face break into a smile. "That's right, those white zinc markers are just as fancy but wouldn't be all that heavy. We could handle them, no sweat. The stuff like embalming tools, wreaths, and post-mortem photos would be the bread and butter between the big sales. Civil war headstones and G.A.R. markers wouldn't weigh all that much either."

"You know Herm, coming up with Frances, stumbling into a crying-angel stone, and finding a Fisk coffin, luck like that won't come together again. What we have is a once-in-a-lifetime opportunity. As far as I'm concerned, anybody who wants the setup is gonna pay through the nose. Gotta be worth at least as much as the tool chests."

"I really like it when you see opportunities instead of problems, Irv."

"And you know what I like? I like not being in the business of taking people out. After we're through with Efferding and Canker, I want us to go back into retirement and sell antiques. Whacking people, lifting bodies, dodging cops, it's a lot of work and a lot of stress."

"I'm with ya," said Herm. "It's like moving marble stones, a job for younger guys."

Irv looked at his seated partner and shook his head. "I don't know what got into me. It didn't make sense to be so paranoid about that little river town. If I can come to terms with Canker, we'll drive back to Bellevue with the coffin and scout out Efferding."

Herm nodded. "Cletus Efferding—what kind of a name is that? The schmuck oughta thank us if we whack him."

After a beer and a couple of tuna fish sandwiches, I repaired to the upholstered chair with the bestseller I'd picked from the rack at Peely's drugstore. Repeated checks of the cabin's TV had revealed that poor picture quality was a constant rather than the exception. For that reason, I chose a book with nine hundred pages: James Michener's *Centennial*, a story about a town of that name in Colorado.

They always say the place to start a story is at the beginning, and Michener took it to heart. He began with the formation of the earth's crust some 3 billion, 600 million years ago. I guess a guy's gotta do what he's gotta do to turn out nine hundred pages, but the geology lesson lasted for forty-six. The King James version of *Genesis* managed to do the job in twelve sentences. Michener should have taken a hint.

He got going on the dinosaurs on page forty-seven. I'd just gotten inside the mind of a swamp-loving *diplodocus* when I heard a knock on the door. I got up to see who it was and found patrolman Mac Mclean standing in the twilight. It didn't take a whole lot of perception to see he was the bearer of bad news.

"Cletus," he said, "we got a hit on the missing person report. The Dubuque police just contacted us. They found Marty's car outside the Bridge Restaurant. It was sitting there for three days. The owner called to have it towed. The tow truck operators give law enforcement a call whenever there's an abandoned vehicle."

"No sign of Marty?"

"None, but a vehicle abandoned by a missing-person driver moves up the priority list. They'll put a team of detectives on it who'll interview staff and neighbors in the area of the restaurant. There'll be radio bulletins and lots of contact with other law enforcement agencies. The works."

I rubbed my face, felt a nine o'clock shadow. Marty was a free spirit, but I couldn't see her abandoning her Pinto to party with friends. Though upset to learn of her mother's murder, the situation didn't seem like a recipe for suicide. She had new reason to believe the woman loved her. Still, the shock could have been too much for her.

"Does Hank know?" I asked.

"We don't have a policy for this sort of notification, but I came here first. Near as I can figure, you're next-of-kin."

Next of kin. Whether I liked it or not, other than my kids, Marty was my closest relative. Mclean made it sound as if she were already dead. Seemed like rushing things a bit. After all, she'd wandered off before when she lost Hank's baby.

"Mac, Marty's still alive," I said. "I can feel it."

He pushed back his cap. "Who said anything about her being dead?"

"Criminetly, you come here and talk about next of kin. Makes it sound like she's already dead."

"Sorry. Is there someone else I should be talking to? You didn't mention other relatives."

Next of kin. Though Marty and I were estranged, I'd lent her money, and we'd begun talking to each other. She'd driven over to share the news about her mother with me, and I'd consoled her. I had obligations: to the child my folks pledged to care for, to the teenager who'd been part of my childhood, to the volatile woman unable to make a go of the family business. I couldn't duck them.

"No," I said. "I'm next of kin. There's just Hank and me."

Though I'd spent only a few hours with him, I knew Hank would be devastated. He was closer to Marty than I could ever hope or want to be. "I'd like to be the one to tell him," I said.

"Fine with me. He would have been a courtesy visit. You're the official contact."

"Look, I know it's part of your job, but thanks for stopping by. I mean it."

Mclean smiled and headed for his patrol car. "We'll keep you informed if we hear anything," he said and climbed into the vehicle.

I went back to my chair, sat, and stared at the wall. Unable to form a coherent thought, I picked up Michener, hoping the story would distract me. My concentration was shot, so it was slow going. I eventually made it to page ninety-six, a task that took three hours. By then, I'd finished with the *diplodocus* and gotten insight into the worlds of a prehistoric horse, giant bison, and primordial beaver. Though I was sure all of this would somehow tie into a greater understanding of the town of Centennial, I wasn't in the mood to wait for Michener to get around to his story.

I put the book down, got a few beers from the ice chest, and put them in a paper sack. After using the padlock to secure the door behind me, I left the cabin and headed up the street in the direction of Myra's picnic table. I could read a book back in Cedar Rapids, but in Bellevue, there's nothing better than staring at the Mississippi when you're trying to get the big picture.

On the way up, I noticed fish bugs clustering around the lights. They weren't thick enough to justify turning the streetlights out. Razor Ray had mentioned that the hatches weren't as big as they once were. If tonight's hatch was any indication, the dynamics of the river had changed considerably.

When I arrived at Myra's picnic table, I took a seat and popped a beer. A partly cloudy sky blocked the moon and a bunch of the stars. As I sipped, I hoped that somewhere Marty was doing the same.

29

Fortified with coffee and a sweet roll from Peely's, I armed myself with my stenographer's pad and pushed open the doors to the public library. My visit to the newspaper office revealed the library had recently microfilmed the back issues. Roberta sat at the desk again, filing cards in one of those wooden drawers that make up the catalog. As I approached, she looked up from her work and greeted me with a cheerful good morning.

"You're back again," she commented as she removed her glasses. "Two days in a row, you must be enjoying your project."

"I want to finish before my vacation is over. Do you have copies of the *Bellevue Herald-Leader* for 1886?"

"We have microfilm for both, the *Herald* and the *Leader*," she replied.

"Both?"

"One for each political party. Back in the day, small towns often had two newspapers."

"H-m-m, what do you know? Republican news and Democratic news."

"I think it had more to do with the editorials," she said. "Let's go over and get you started."

Roberta located the films for me and left me to my own devices. Since the papers came out just once a week, I'd have, at most, one hundred four issues to scan. I started with the *Herald*. The paper came across as weird, with lots of ads and wire service stories from Europe on the front page. Local news wasn't as plentiful as I'd expected, but I hit the jackpot with the first issue for March.

Commits Suicide by Drinking Lye

A servant in the home of August Efferding committed suicide last week by ingesting a large quantity of lye. The poor woman suffered horribly, lingering for five days. The attending physician reports the caustic solution severely burned her mouth, throat, and esophagus. No amount of medical care could save her.

Eighteen eighty-six. The death date matched the one on Lumir's brass plaque. Marty's grandma, Aunt Kate's mom, a suicide, and not even given a name. In scanning the earlier issues, I'd learned that obituaries, as I knew them, were rare. Most deaths got a line or two. I guess colored servants didn't merit enough attention to be identified. I checked the next issue, but the *Bellevue Herald* had lost interest in the story and moved on.

Hoping for something more informative, I rewound the microfilm and loaded the reel for the *Bellevue Leader*. The first March issue made no mention of the suicide. Though the second issue contained no death notice, I found a paragraph that proved interesting. There was no headline, just a short report in a section called "Local News."

Bellevue's lack of a cemetery for coloreds made for an interesting situation last week following the death of a maid in the home of August Efferding. The woman's suicide precluded her burial in the Catholic and Lutheran grounds for religious reasons. The trustees of the town's remaining cemeteries refused to allow the interment of a negro. A location for the disposition of the remains has yet to be determined.

I reread the article before moving on. The next issue of the paper contained no further information. Martine Dufay had left this earth with very little notice. Her daughter, Marty's mom, was three years old at the time. I doubted my grandparents ever told Aunt Kate about her mother, but in a small town, she'd have learned the truth sooner or later. Aunt Kate left Bellevue long before Marty was born, maybe in the interest of a fresh start. If she chose to, it would have been easy to hide her background from her daughter.

I thought about my kids, raised by a well-meaning woman who believed shielding them from their mother's suicide would protect them from heartache, a sad commentary on history repeating itself. I didn't believe in the supernatural, but the Efferding family must have been cursed, condemned to repeat the same unhappy story over and over again.

I filled my steno pad with more notes, carefully documenting the names and dates of the newspapers in case my kids ever wanted to follow up and then clipped my pen to the back cover. On my way to the door, I passed by a low table with the most recent copy of the Bellevue paper on top. I'd finished with the microfilm early, so sat down to see what was new. The Jaycees were sponsoring a toy drive and were looking for gently used playthings to be sent to a Missouri town devastated by a tornado. A metal bin had been set up behind the carwash so citizens who wished to donate could drop off their toys twenty-four hours a day.

Kissy Kathy still rested in the corner of my cabin. She was new in the original container when my accidental bid brought her my way. I no longer had the box, but Kathy was unused. I'd remove the garter and boa, drop her off at the carwash, and let the Jaycees send her where she'd do some good. The rest of the paper was newsy: the owner of the Rexall drugstore wanted to find a buyer, the city was squabbling with a citizen who wanted to erect a metal building on Front Street, and the Conservation Commission planned to change the limits on largemouth bass.

I finished the newspaper and left the library. I had more important things to accomplish. The day's discoveries had taken a lot out of me. I needed a nap.

The elevator doors opened. Irv stepped out into a sixth-floor hallway at the Hotel Blackhawk. They'd driven to Davenport to check out a big collection of Red Wing crockery, an opportunity that didn't come along every day. Too bad Herm had gotten sick and stayed in the room. The seller didn't want to split it up. Herm knew a lot about pottery and would have known if they'd make out on the deal. Unsure of a profit, Irv had passed.

Sick or not, Herm would have to ride up to Bellevue with him tonight. After all the arguments they'd had about the need for better communication, agreeing to hit Efferding would have to be a joint decision.

Canker agreed to let them use a corner of a dilapidated barn to dry Frances out. The isolated location meant that they'd need more than mosquito netting to protect her. They'd use the netting, but additional safeguards would be required to protect against the occasional rat. The arsenic used to embalm the body might be lethal, but an animal could do a lot of damage before it ingested a fatal dose. A chewed-up Frances wouldn't be worth much.

He and Herm planned to price the coffin, corpse, and headstone at ten grand. Though a guy could buy a couple of cars for that, one of Manny's rich freaks would be happy to pay it. Not a bad profit when you figured they had fifteen hundred in it. The money more than justified the aggravation involved in hauling the casket back to Bellevue. The tool chests might be worth more, but only a fool would sniffle at the return on the coffin.

He retrieved the key to room number 612 from his pocket and opened the door. Herm must have decided on a nap. The poor guy had closed the curtains and fallen asleep watching television. When Irv flipped the light switch, he didn't like what he saw. A half-empty pint of Canadian Club rested on the night hand, next to an open Valium container.

"Damn it, Herm. Wake up!"

Herm stirred. "Hmm, Irv? Um, uh . . . sleepy."

Irv reached for the vial. The pills reached three-quarters of the way to the top. "How many did you take?" Herm grunted. Irv shook his partner and slapped him. "How many did you take?"

"Um, three. Why you mad?"

"Get up. Now! We're going to visit Canker."

Herm drooled, "Can't . . . sick."

Disgusted, Irv let go of him. "Sick, schmick. You're loaded. That stuff's turning you into a goddamned junkie. You're a doper, Herm. A two-bit doper."

His accusation met with a snore.

Irv picked up the vial, walked to the bathroom, and dumped the Valium into the toilet. "Sonofabitchin' poison," he muttered as he flushed. He dropped the vial to the floor and stomped it to pieces, in his imagination substituting Herm's head for the container. The destruction complete, he picked up the pieces and disposed of them. Standing in place, he started the deep breathing exercises the prison psychologist had taught him.

It took five minutes for his anger to subside, only to be replaced by guilt for his partner's symbolic destruction. He couldn't help but like the guy. What with his square face, flat-top hair, and horn-rim glasses, Herm was beyond cute. And that crooked smile, it'd win anybody's heart. Still, if he didn't shape up, Herm would become a full-fledged addict. Irv resolved to send his friend to rehabilitation before the situation got out of hand. Tears rolled down his cheeks. The whole thing was so sad. The Blowtorch, the scourge of the Chicago Outfit, slobbering in bed like a skid-row drunk.

Irv wasn't about to drive Herm, Frances, and her coffin back to Cedar Rapids. He'd leave his partner to sleep it off and make the trip to Bellevue by himself. Given Herm's behavior, he no longer deserved a voice in the contract decision. If Canker had the money, the Efferding hit was on. Irv decided to contact Doctor Bob when he and Herm returned to Cedar Rapids. One more prescription refill and the doctor would be taking a little vacation. No place special, just an everyday resort where he could play with the angels.

30

I sat on the side of the bed, yawning as I stretched. Although the cabin's furniture wasn't anything to brag about, the bed felt comfy, and thirty minutes makes for an excellent nap. Any less and a guy doesn't get enough rest, any more and he gets groggy. The only flaw with the napping business is that I wake up hungry. I rummaged through the cupboard and ice chest, came up with a Budweiser and a cheese sandwich, settled into the upholstered chair, and picked up Michener's book.

I didn't open it but sat there reviewing my library discoveries. I'd come up with enough evidence to convince any thinking person that the body in the mystery coffin was Marty's grandmother, a woman named Martine Dufay. The initials on the brass nameplate matched, and the dates corresponded with the information I got from the censuses and newspapers. There'd been a dustup over her final resting place, and she'd ended up in the river.

I didn't know enough physics to determine if the coffin was buried in a non-traditional cemetery and washed into the river or if it was dumped, similar to a burial at sea. The burial-at-sea option seemed unlikely because the coffin floated in last Monday's test. Maybe the box sank when dropped into the river and floated later because of gas or something. I'd have to ask around to find somebody with enough science background to know.

The family dynamics at the time of Martine Dufay's suicide presented another puzzle. Although the decision to take her life didn't speak to a happy situation, the woman had a three-year-old daughter to live for. Maybe Grandma Efferding hated Dufay, maybe not, but my grandfather must have cared for her. After all, he'd ponied up for a deluxe casket. I wondered if he and grandma argued about the expenditure.

Given the events of the past few days, my disdain for Marty felt petty. For the first time since we were kids, I wanted to know her better. Marty was flighty, couldn't handle money, and had a butt load of rage inside her, but a fundamental decency prevailed. In my heart of hearts, I knew she was out there somewhere, confused and lonely. When she came back, things would be different. No two ways about it, I'd see we'd get along.

Michener and I were up to 9,000 B.C. when I heard the knock on the door. I sighed, got out of my chair, and found Wiley McCard, dressed in his civvies, standing outside. I swung the door outward and invited him in.

He stepped into the cabin and got right to the point. "Clete, they found a woman's body tangled up in a trotline at the mouth of Catfish Creek just south of Dubuque. She wasn't carrying any identification but with Marty missing and all, they'd like you to take a look at it. That doesn't mean it's her. I can drive you up if you like.

I don't know how long I stood there. "Damn, I didn't think she'd do it. I should have gone to Prairie du Chien with her."

Wiley pulled on the corner of his mustache. "Now don't jump to conclusions. Dubuque is just one of a lot of places she might have visited."

"When did they find the body?"

"Early this morning. Jurisdiction belongs to the Dubuque County Sheriff. The Department of Natural Resources has an interest, but they're low on the totem pole. The sheriff's office isn't telling us much, but that's typical in a case like this. They don't want to taint the investigation."

I dropped into my chair. "Taint the investigation?"

"Any unusual death is investigated: accidents, drug overdoses, murders, suicides."

Wiley was trying hard not to fall into his official cop persona, and for that I was grateful. I liked the guy back when I sold him suits, and I liked him now. The civilian clothes instead of a uniform were a nice touch.

"I'll gas up the car and drive myself," I said. "Where's the morgue?"

"They took the body to Mercy Hospital. Dubuque's not big enough for a municipal morgue."

I drummed my fingers on the arm of the chair. "That's all you know?"

"That's it," he said.

"They won't care if I take Hankie with me, right? It's better than going alone."

"Most people take someone with them when they make an identification. It's okay. I'll call ahead and let them know you're coming."

After a moment's silence, I realized Wiley didn't have any more to say. "Well, I guess that's it," I said.

"Hang in there, Clete. If it is her, it'll be rough for you even though the two of you didn't get along."

"Didn't get along?"

"The fight you guys had at Portz's Tavern. It was the talk of the town last week."

"Oh, right," I said. Embarrassed by my behavior, I'd been trying to put the incident behind me. "Take care, Wiley."

"Will do," he replied and left.

I didn't get up but remained in the chair, mentally preparing for the trip. Wiley was right when he said I shouldn't assume Marty had taken her life. No use hanging crepe if it wasn't called for. After fidgeting a half hour, I realized preparation was impossible and put aside the comfort of the chair, added an extra twenty to my billfold, and shaved. Since I didn't have a dark suit with me, the gray I wore would have to do. With luck, Hank would be at Marty's. I could swing by and pick him up on the way to Dubuque.

I stopped for gas at the Texaco station and arrived at Marty's house a few minutes later. Hank wasn't there, and I didn't know where to find him. It made no sense to drive around town to hunt him up, and the folks in Dubuque were waiting for me.

I made the drive alone.

———

The tiny candy striper, or whatever they're called, led me to the hospital basement. She stopped outside a pair of fire doors.

"This is as far as I go," she said. "Just continue down the hallway and take the last door on the left."

"Thanks," I replied. "I think I'll wait here a while before I go in. Kind of get ready."

"Of course," she said.

I leaned against the tiled wall and watched as she ascended the stairs. Though I'd used the half-hour drive from Bellevue to prepare myself for the ordeal, I wasn't ready for what lay ahead. Even if the body wasn't Marty, looking at a drowned person doesn't make for a great day. I didn't know how long the body had been in the water. If the river water had left her face bloated and discolored, I might not even know if it was Marty.

Steeling myself, I reached for the door handle and pulled. The hallway ahead brought me up short. Hospitals don't put a morgue in prime real estate. A dimly lit corridor with an unpainted cement floor lay before me. The half-dozen doors that broke up the gray concrete walls were shut. Steam pipes and electrical conduits hung from the ceiling overhead. A galvanized bucket on wheels stood halfway between me and the sign at the end of the corridor. The mop in the bucket leaned against one wall, narrowing the hall by half. I couldn't read the morgue sign in the dim light.

My footsteps echoed as I plodded down the hall. When I got close enough, I could read the sign. *Viewing Area—Please ring bell for ser-*

vice. They'd mounted an ordinary doorbell button on the doorframe. I pushed it and heard a buzzer go off inside. A guy in green scrubs opened the door.

I announced myself. "I'm Cletus Efferding. I've been asked to look at the body of a drowning victim."

The guy in the scrubs looked puzzled. "Drowning victim?"

"The suicide. The woman they found near Catfish Creek."

"Got it. Please, go over to the desk. There's some paperwork to fill out, and I'll need to see an ID. If you can identify the body, there'll be more paperwork later."

I showed him my driver's license and felt him watching me as I walked to a small steel desk with a clipboard and ballpoint on top. I picked up the paperwork—a single page. I settled in and started filling in the blanks. Routine stuff: name, address, phone number, and so on. When he saw that I'd finished, he motioned me toward a set of double doors.

I must watch too much TV. I'd been expecting one of the setups where the body is behind a window with its head on a pillow, and they pull the curtains so you can look. Instead, a gurney stood in the middle of a room with a checkerboard floor. If the operation had any of those little iceboxes where the body slides out on a tray, they were in another room. The place gave me the feeling that the hospital cared for the living rather than the dead, and they weren't about to spend any money to spruce things up.

A white sheet covered the cadaver. The smells of death and disinfectant nearly overwhelmed me. I felt wobbly but ignored it.

The attendant led the way and planted me on one side of the body. He took the other. "Ready?" he asked.

"How bad is it?"

He met my eye. "It's not pretty."

"Okay," I said.

The attendant lifted the sheet. It was bad, and it was Marty. Try as I might, I couldn't take in the details. My mind refused to cooperate. The thing that got me most was her hair. She liked to wear it big and puffed up. The hospital hadn't even taken the trouble to comb it.

I found my voice. "That's Martha Efferding, my cousin."

"Are you sure? he asked.

I was about to answer when my knees gave out. Things got a little fuzzy after that. I know I went down and the attendant helped me into the other room where he propped me sitting against a wall. He said something about no chair until I was steady and got on the telephone. A nurse came, asked some questions, and took my pulse.

By the time she left, I was ready for the chair. Miracle of miracles, I hadn't hit my head when I fell. "You guys need to work on your viewing procedures," I complained. "Somebody could pass out and get hurt."

"As far as I know, you're the first one who's fainted," the attendant said. "You're sure of the ID?" he asked.

I nodded. "I'm her only living relative."

He picked up a set of papers from the counter and handed them to me, indicating that I should return to the under-sized desk and fill them out.

As I made my way through the paperwork the reality of the next-of-kin business began to sink in. There'd be a funeral to consider. A form asked for instructions on where to send the body. Though Ray Gallagher was a nice enough guy, the decision was a no-brainer. I'd be sending the body on to Johnny Dye. Ray took care of the Catholics; Dye Funeral Home did everyone else.

I'd have to come up with the funds for the funeral but wasn't about to cheap out. There'd be no way to tap the estate for expenses. By the time the lawyers raked off their cut, Marty's few assets would be gone. I'd be making payments for years.

I finished with the forms and handed them to the attendant. "I need to make arrangements with the funeral home. When will you release the body?"

"A few days. The medical examiner hasn't scheduled the autopsy yet."

The final insult. Marty had been through a lot, and now they wanted to cut her up. "Is that really necessary?" I asked.

The attendant looked uncomfortable. He started to speak, hesitated, and started again. "The medical examiner makes the decision on suspicious deaths."

Seemed like overkill, but apparently a suicide was considered a suspicious death.

"I guess I'm done here," I said.

"Not quite yet. A deputy is on the way, and he'll want to ask you some questions."

"A deputy? Some questions?"

"Standard in a case like this."

I didn't get one deputy. I got two, a young guy with a butch haircut, and an older one with a gut that strained the buttons on his shirt. Things started out okay, with introductions and a bazillion routine questions, most of which I don't remember. I got uncomfortable when the big gut asked me about where I'd been and what I'd been doing for the past week. It didn't take long to go from uncomfortable to angry.

"What, you guys think I drove to Dubuque and drowned my cousin?"

The butch haircut answered my question with a question. "Who said anything about drowning?"

"I did," I snapped, "and it's bad enough to come down to this dungeon and see what she looks like without being harassed by guys like you. I didn't push her into the river, and I didn't drown her."

The big gut held up his hand. "Of course you didn't. Your cousin died from a gunshot wound."

I shook my head, trying to clear it. Gunshot wound?

The young one chimed in, "Two shots at close range, .22 caliber. Do you own a .22 caliber firearm?"

It couldn't be. Marty didn't look like somebody shot her. "No," I answered.

Big Gut stepped back in. "Can you think of any reason why someone would want to kill your cousin?"

I couldn't. I really couldn't. "No," I said.

The butch haircut cut in so quickly I barely had time to think. "What about you? How did you get along with your cousin? Did you have any family problems?"

That was it. I folded my arms across my chest and didn't answer.

Big Gut sighed. "Mr. Efferding, we're trying to investigate the death of your cousin. I'm sure you want answers, and so do we. Your lack of cooperation looks suspicious and will only hamper the investigation."

"Look," I said, "I've had a bad night. I find out somebody killed my cousin, and to top it off, I had to look at something that will haunt me the rest of my life. Am I free to go?"

"Is he free to go?" the young guy asked his companion.

"I don't know. If he isn't, trying to leave would be a big mistake," replied Big Gut.

Hearing no Miranda rights and tired of the charade, I got up and made for the door.

Butch Haircut didn't like it and took a step toward me. "Where you going? We didn't say you could go."

"You didn't say I couldn't."

I kept walking, through the door and down the dreary hallway with the deputies keeping pace, ten steps behind me. They followed me up the stairs, through the lobby, and out to my rusty, spray-painted Nova. I got in. They stood behind the car, so I couldn't pull out of the parking space. The fat guy lit a cigarette while young one stood with his hands on his gun belt. They chatted, and I waited. Fifteen minutes later, they got bored with their game and stepped aside, one to the right and one to the left.

The situation forced me to pull out by driving between them. The older guy stood on the driver's side, and as I came even with him, he motioned that I should open the side window. I did.

"Nice paint job," he said.

"Nice way to treat a guy who just lost a family member," I replied. "Trying to pin a murder rap on somebody when they're in a state of shock. Talk about a cheap shot."

His face hardened. "You weren't a suspect, asshole."

I felt myself relax.

"... until you got weird," he hissed.

I cranked up the window, backed out carefully, and continued on my way, using the turn signal at every corner in the parking lot.

31

I drove back to Bellevue and hit town as twilight settled into night. The fish bugs were out and had begun clustering around the streetlights. I turned right at the Municipal Power Plant and made straight for Marty's house. Not a light in the windows. Though I didn't expect anyone to be home, I went to the front door, rang the bell, and knocked loud enough to wake the dead. The outside light came on, and a disheveled Hank Steines opened up. I didn't know how I was going to tell him, but he didn't deserve to hear about Marty from the news.

He let me in. "Been watchin' television in the dark and worryin' about Marty."

A bottle of beer on the coffee table stood silhouetted against the blue light of the TV, and the haze-filled room smelled of cherry tobacco. I looked down and noticed a smoldering pipe in Hank's hand.

I wanted to break it to him easy. "Got a beer?"

When Hank walked out to the kitchen to fetch a bottle, I turned down the volume on the television and seated myself on the couch. He returned a minute later and handed me a bottle and opener. I popped the cap, took a long swallow, and waited for him to sit. Images from a police show played across TV screen. As the barely audible sound of fake gunshots came from the set, I struggled with how to break the news.

I was about to begin when he beat me to it. "You're here about Marty. I can tell by the look on your face. Something's happened to her."

"Marty's dead." The words coming from my mouth sounded muffled, as if spoken by someone under a blanket in the next room. I waited for my lungs to refill before continuing. It took forever. "They found her near the mouth of Catfish Creek, tangled in a trotline."

Hank's broad shoulders slumped.

As bad as the first part was, it'd been easy compared to what I had to tell him next. "She was murdered, Hank. Shot."

He said nothing but got up from the chair and put his fist through the wall. Marty's house was pre-wallboard. Chunks of plaster fell to the floor. He'd punched clear through the wooden laths. In the dim light of the TV, I could see him bleeding.

"You messed yourself up pretty good, Hank. You're lucky you didn't hit a two-by-four. You'd have so many broken bones in your hand, it'd never be right again."

Hank returned to his chair. "Murdered," he muttered, "Marty got murdered."

I left the couch, turned the lights on and the TV off. Bits of plaster had embedded themselves in Hank's hand. Blood trickled onto the upholstery. I worried he'd get blood poisoning. "Tetanus shot up to date?" I asked. As soon as it was out, I wanted to kick myself. A guy loses his girlfriend, and I ask him about his inoculations.

He looked down at his hand as if he'd never seen it before. "I work on the garbage truck. The city makes us take the shots. Why would anybody shoot Marty?"

"I don't know. It doesn't make sense. But you need to get that hand cleaned up. Go into the kitchen and wash it. You might need stitches."

Hank went into the kitchen, while I stayed behind and downed the rest of my beer. When he didn't return, I got worried and went to check on him. A roll of white adhesive tape and bottle of mercurochrome lay on the counter next to a bloody towel. Water ran from the faucet. I shut it off. When I did, I could hear Hank making his way up the basement steps. He reappeared with his hand wrapped in a towel and holding a small package. Blood oozed through the fabric. I'd have to take him to get sewn up.

"Just lookin' for glue," he said and walked to the sink where he unwrapped the towel. His fingers and knuckles looked like somebody had used coarse sandpaper on them. There was a nasty cut on the back of his hand.

"You're going to need stitches," I said.

"Nope," said Hank. "The city's insurance ain't so hot, and doctors cost too much. Gonna glue it." He handed me a three-pack of super glue.

"I don't think that's a good idea. It could get infected."

"Do it all the time."

There was no talking him out of it. I squeezed glue into the cut as he held the skin closed. The wasn't as bad as I thought, maybe an inch and a half long, but it was so bloody it was hard to get the glue to bond. Halfway through the second tube, we finally got the cut sealed. When Hank went to see if Marty had any cotton, I checked the refrigerator for beer. Only two bottles remained. I left them for Hank.

Hank returned with a box of cotton balls and a fifth of Wild Turkey. I didn't see any reason for it, but he mashed the cotton into a makeshift pad and taped it over the cut. The hand looked like it belonged to a mummy, but Hank wasn't taking any chances.

I was about to return to the living room when Hank picked up the liquor bottle and wiggled it in my direction. "Let's go sit out back." He said. "You can tell everything you know about what happened to Marty."

Outside, two lawn chair chairs rested on the grass. We grabbed them. Hank put the bottle on the ground and unthreaded the cap with his good hand. As we talked, I realized I didn't have much to tell him. Storming out of Mercy Hospital saved a lot of unwelcome questions, but I wondered if I'd made a mistake. I didn't have half the information Hank wanted to know.

"Do they know when she died?" he asked.

"I didn't ask."

"Where did they shoot her? Did she suffer?"

"I don't know."

"They have any idea who did it?"

"I don't think so."

"You shoulda asked more questions," he said as he passed me the Wild Turkey.

Hard liquor isn't my thing, but tonight I made an exception. I tipped the bottle and took a healthy belt, the first in a decade. The bourbon felt as warm and friendly as a fireplace on a snowy night.

"Look, Hank, I wanted to get out of there as soon as possible. I passed out when I saw her and felt woozy afterward. They were asking me stuff like did I own a .22 caliber firearm. Did Marty and I get along? It sounded like they were trying to set me up, so I bailed."

Hank wasn't happy with me. "Sounds like you don't know much."

I couldn't blame the guy. I'd panicked, but sure as the sun rises, I'd be on the shortlist when they found out Marty and I had squabbled at Portz's Tavern. Not only did we argue, but I'd accused her of ripping me off on the sale of Efferding's Menswear. Talk about motive.

"I may not know much, Hank, but I'm sure of one thing. You're in for a hard time too. The boyfriend is the first one they think of."

"It'd help if I knew more," he said. "It'd make it harder for them to trap me."

"The less you know, the better. It makes you look innocent."

"I suppose you're right."

The stars were coming out. In the distance, I saw clouds of fish-flies congregating around the lights downtown. We were in for a hatch larger than the one last night. Hank reached for the Wild Turkey, so I handed it back. He tipped the bottle, took two prodigious swallows and passed it to me. I sat quietly, waiting for him to speak.

At length, he broke the silence, "What happens next?"

"They'll do an autopsy and after that, send her to Johnny Dye."

He nodded, "I'd like to pay part of the funeral, but until I get my check next month, I won't have money or even a place to live."

"No problem, the funeral finances will work out somehow, and as far as I'm concerned, you can stay in the house until the bank decides what to do with it."

"I was gonna quit the garbage route and partner up with Blackie. Marty was all for it. Guess none of that's gonna happen now. Poor Marty, she didn't deserve to get shot."

"She sure didn't. Think it had anything to do with the coffin?"

Hank folded and unfolded the fingers of his damaged hand. "I don't think so. Nobody knew she had it except for a couple of Cedar Rapids antique dealers, and they were going to buy it. A package deal along with the old tools. Now that Marty is gone, they won't get any of it."

The bottle in my hand slipped a bit. I recovered in time to keep it from dropping and took a second drink. It tasted even better than the first. "There's a reason I don't drink the hard stuff," I said. "I like it too much. This is the last one for me."

Hank reached for the bottle and tipped it up. "I'm gonna miss her, Clete. She was the one I shoulda married."

He handed the bottle back, and I put it on the ground.

My heart went out to the guy. He really loved her and needed the company, but I'd been through enough for the night. I stood, put a hand on his shoulder and said, "I know she felt the same way about you, Hank. She told me."

Guilt set in halfway to the car. Hank needed company, but the liquor sang a song I couldn't resist. It had taken all my reserves to walk away. No way Cletus Efferding was going down that path again.

In the gravel lot of a roadside steakhouse, Irv Kaplan checked the hitch and chains on his horse trailer. Satisfied they were secure, he went around to the driver's side, opened the door of his Ford F-100 pickup, then slammed it closed as hard as he could. Finding no relief in the activity, he opened and slammed it again. He'd just completed the action yet another time when he noticed the nerdy guy in the car parked next to him. The idiot just sat there staring at him. Irv stared back.

The wide-eyed numbskull recovered from his stupor, locked his door and began to roll up the window. Irv smiled disarmingly and asked, "Do you know anything about locks on Ford pickups? I can't seem to get mine to work. Seem like it's stuck in the open position and the latch won't go all the way closed. Truck's only three months old. Seems like everything they build these days is crap."

The man stopped rolling his window. "Ain't it the truth? Can't say as I know anything about locks, but when I need somebody, I use Quad-City Lock and Key."

Irv sauntered over, closing the gap between them. "Is that in Moline?" he asked as he lowered his face toward the window.

"Davenport," the guy replied. "I don't know if they can help you or not."

"No, but you can," Irv snarled. Reaching into the half-open window, he grabbed the hair on the back of the guy's head and slammed his face into the steering wheel. Irv pulled back and repeated the action. Blood ran from a cut in the wimp's forehead. *One more*, Irv thought and slammed him yet again.

Sensing the guy was too out of it to honk the horn, he reached into the car, unlocked the door, and pulled the hapless driver from the seat. When the guy cleared the car, Irv let go and kneed him in the ribs. The candy-ass hit the blacktop like a sack of wet sand. "Sayonara, sucker," he muttered and kicked the guy's head hard enough to send it into orbit.

Irv pulled his handkerchief from his pocket and wiped his brow. He felt much better. Calm and in control, he could appreciate Herm's valium abuse was an irritant rather than a crisis. Humming to himself, he went back to his pickup.

He exited the steakhouse lot, turned on the car radio, and searched for the Maquoketa country station. Though he'd found contentment in the life of an antique dealer, like Herm, he sometimes missed gang life. The hardest part of the whole middle-class *schtick* was finding ways to let off steam. While the prison psychologist's breathing exercises usually worked, they'd failed tonight. He'd tried to decompress by watching the Mississippi flow under the Interstate 80. All he got for his three hours was a neck covered with mosquito bites and a few stupid fishflies hitting him in the face. A banana split hadn't helped, and neither did a steak and baked potato dinner. No matter how he tried, it sometimes took the proven-true stress relievers from the old days to do the job.

His route tonight would take him from through Sabula, and then on to Bellevue and Canker's shed in Cottonville. Since Canker was confined to a wheelchair, he'd promised he'd have somebody there to assist, yet another witness to deal with. No two ways about it, this coffin job was big-time cursed. Efferding, Canker, and the new helper would all have to go, and Herm was in no shape to pitch in.

He and Herm had only been cutting legal corners for a little over a week, and already they'd accumulated a backlog of hits. The workload was worse than when they'd been with Angie.

If Canker had the down payment, Efferding would go bye-bye tonight.

What do you do when sleep is impossible? I'd fallen into the habit of walking up the street to sit on Myra's picnic table, but the fish bug hatch foreclosed the option. The last thing I wanted was to sit outside and feel a thousand of the damn things land on me. People from away think Mississippi River mayflies are those delicate little white things that come out a few hundred at a time on quiet summer nights. Ha! When it comes to bugs, the Father of Waters doesn't mess around. Big Daddy's bugs are two and a half inches long, black, smelly, and squishy. When they hatch, sensible folk go home and close the windows.

Going out for a midnight beer might result in having to make conversation, but after my trip to the morgue, the thought of idle chatter didn't appeal to me. Hoping James Michener's meandering tale of eastern Colorado might put me to sleep, I looked up from my chair to locate the volume.

Kissy Kathy met my eye. When she did, I remembered the Jaycee's twenty-four-hour drop-off behind the car wash. The mundane task of contributing to the toy drive seemed preferable to sitting with Michener, so I grabbed the doll and headed for the Nova.

Thank God, the owner of the cabins had turned off his outdoor sign. The mayfly hatch was a doozy. As I ran to the car, Kissy's light pink dress picked up a half-dozen of the sickeningly soft hitchhikers. I knew better than to take time to brush them off, so I snapped the driver's door open, tossed the doll across the seat, and dove in.

I turned on the headlights, illuminating a virtual curtain of bugs. I'd never seen anything like it. The air breathed fishflies, hundreds of millions of ghost-like creatures attracted by the town's lights and intent on two things: mating and dying. We tell humans to go for the light as they cross the great divide. Somebody must have given fish bugs the same advice because that's what they do: fly to the nearest light and cash in their chips. By morning, the town would be littered with dead bugs, in places a foot and a half deep.

I drove down Front Street. The invasion limited visibility to something like a dozen feet. I was doing all of ten miles an hour, but the bugs plopping against the windshield splattered anyway. Though the wipers helped, I had to use the washer every block or so. The corner at the hotel nearly did me in. When I hit the brakes to slow for the turn, my tires slid on an oily layer of crushed fishflies. I almost bumped a parked car but managed to pull out at the last minute.

Although the bugs thinned as I got farther from the riverbank, tens of thousands flitted in the air at the carwash, a location eight blocks from the water. Too bad for the owner. The staff had neglected to extinguish the lighted outdoor sign when they closed for the night. Once white, a two-inch layer of fishflies covered the board so thoroughly it had become almost invisible. Either the *Bellevue Herald-Leader* got it wrong, or I was too late for the toy drive; a pass around the building revealed nothing that resembled a collection box. Kissy Kathy would be returning to the cabin with me.

I decided to drive back through the less brightly lit part of town. As I approached the corner at the Catholic cemetery, a solitary street light stood awash in a cluster of fish bugs. A wraithlike figure danced in the cone of its illumination. Closer inspection revealed the dance was anything but. A panicked figure swatted desperately at the flies, an older woman who must have had an intense fear of insects. I came to a full stop so as not to hit her. She made a beeline for the Nova. As she approached, I recognized the terrified face of Ardelia Krumbatey, the woman local kids referred to as the Underwear Lady.

I put the car in park and rolled down the passenger side window. "Miss Krumbatey, is anything wrong?" I asked.

"Please, give me a ride," she panted. "The fishflies, it feels like they're trying to get me."

What the hell, I already had a half dozen bugs in the car. One more couldn't hurt. "Hop in."

She yanked the door open, picked up Kissy Kathy, and hopped in.

"Thank you," she said. "I shouldn't let the fishflies get to me like that. It's kind of you to give me a ride."

Though Ardelia certainly looked it, she didn't sound wacky. I wondered if she was as off-kilter as people claimed. "Where to?" I asked.

She made a vague gesture toward the southeast side of town. "Over there. I know the way."

Not much for directions, but it's hard to get lost in Bellevue.

"Go down to Front Street and turn right?" I asked.

She didn't answer the question but squeezed Kissy Kathy. "What a nice-looking little girl. I don't have one like her, but I just know she'd like to live in my house. You know, I've taken in over four hundred homeless dolls. Every night I take ten or fifteen to bed with me, so I don't get lonely."

Yup, totally wacko, bananas, one hundred percent bonkers. "Her name is Kissy Kathy," I said, "and you can have her if you want."

"Thank you, she'll make a nice addition to my home."

I turned the ignition switch and headed downtown. Since this part of Bellevue was not as well lit, the flies were fewer. I rapped it out to thirty miles an hour.

Ardelia scooted over, positioning the doll between her and the door. The stench of lilac perfume engulfed me. For the first time in eight years, I wished the Nova had bucket seats.

"You're such a nice-looking man," she cooed and moved a little closer, ". . . and a sweet one. Do you get lonely sometimes? Even though I have my doll friends, sometimes I do. Would you like to see them?"

I felt sorry for the old gal. So socially inept that she didn't have any friends and too naïve to understand her amateurish attempt at conversation sounded like a come-on. Still, the woman made me uncomfortable, and I intended to get her out of the car as so as possible. Despite the fish bugs slapping the windshield, I picked up speed.

"Look at me," Ardelia said.

"What?"

"Just look at me. I won't bite."

I glanced to the side and saw a face so caked with makeup it looked like a mask from a horror movie. Worse yet, her vampire-red lips seemed to be mouthing the words *kiss me*. Probably my imagination. Seeing Marty at the morgue, the fish bugs, the dim dashboard lighting, my nerves were shot.

I averted my eyes, but not before she pursed her lips a second time. At least I think she did. "How much farther Miss Krumbatey?"

"We should go little farther," she replied putting a hand on my forearm.

I gave Ardelia a ride because I felt sorry for her. Though she may have had a sad life, I didn't like the turn of events. Unsure of what to do, I told a white lie. "Miss Krumbatey, please stop. I have a wife."

"Well la-di-dah," she snorted. "Maybe she can spend a night alone."

My rider was not only nuts, but she had a bad attitude. Then I felt her other hand snake across my thigh. My stomach turned.

Eager to deposit her at her house, I sped up. A rapidly thickening layer of bugs covered the windshield. I hit the wipers as we sailed down Jefferson Street. When I realized the desire to get rid of my companion had trumped all sense of automotive safety, I resolved to pull over and get her out of the car.

Easier said than done. She kept coming at me, licking my ear and massaging my groin. I should have braked, but panic set in and priority one became getting Ardelia off me. "Stop that," I insisted.

She didn't, and when I tried to take her hand off my arm, she hung on for dear life. "Feels like your willy likes me," she whispered as she continued the massage.

When I elbowed her in the rib cage, she grunted and began to disengage. Wanting to speed the process, I pushed her away with my right hand. My adrenaline must have been over the top. My palm smashed into her breast with a force that astonished me.

Ardelia bellowed, "That hurt!" and began pummeling me with both hands. "What's wrong with you?" she cried.

"I didn't mean to—"

A blow to the side of my mouth made my head spin. The old lady had muscles.

"You hit me," she howled. "I was nice to you, and you hit me."

The Nova hit the Second Street railroad crossing so hard, we became airborne. As I struggled to keep the car under control, Ardelia slugged me again, hitting my nose. "Stop," I pleaded. "It was an accident."

"Accident, my ass," she shouted and unleashed a kick that hit my shin and forced my foot against the accelerator.

The increase in speed spattered fish bugs left and right. Still struggling to clear my head, I focused on visibility rather than my speed—a mistake. The wipers revealed a pickup traveling up Front Street, entering the intersection from my right. The last thing I remember was checking the speedometer and looking up to see the letters "F100" as we T-boned a pickup at thirty-five miles per hour.

I tried to open my eyes, but the beam of a powerful flashlight shone in my face. A disembodied voice floated toward me. "He's awake. Let's get him out." I reached to touch my forehead. It felt wet. Somebody put their arms around me and lifted.

"Okay buddy, just relax," another voice said.

Somehow, I ended up inside a station wagon strapped to a bed with rails. An ambulance. My head hurt. I wondered if I'd die or be crippled. I tried to talk but couldn't hear my voice.

"We're going for a little ride now," a woman said as she stuck something into my arm.

After that, I didn't remember anything but pain. I hurt so bad I couldn't tell where it was coming from. Opening my eyes would have helped me get my bearings, but the lids wouldn't work. After a few attempts, I gave up. It didn't make that much difference, because I knew where I was now—a hospital room. My brain disengaged again, and the nightmares fired up. When I came around, the lights were on, and a nurse was holding my wrist, taking my pulse.

"Good morning," she smiled. "How are you feeling?"

"I hit a truck," I mumbled. "My head hurts and my chest doesn't feel so good."

"They put seatbelts in cars for a reason. The doctor says you hit the steering wheel and windshield. Your head spiderwebbed the glass. You have a concussion and a broken nose, but no internal injuries. Your head is bandaged because you have thirty-five stitches."

I reached up, felt a big wad of gauze, and put my hand back down. "My car doesn't have seatbelts." Oh God, Ardelia, I had to know. "The lady in my car," I asked, "she okay?"

"She's down the hall, and they're still not sure. The last I heard, she had massive bruising, lacerations, and a broken arm."

I touched my nose. Ardelia must have done a real number on it.

"You were lucky. Your nose didn't need splints."

"I think I'll rest some more."

"You can have breakfast if you want."

"No. Hurts too much."

She left. I suppose I drifted in and out, but what I recall is a pounding head and aching body doing their level best to kill me. I lay with my eyes closed until the part about the stitches came back to me. I reached up and felt around the edges of the bandages. They'd shaved part of my head. You'd think they'd have done it all, but no, they decided to leave me looking like something from a horror movie.

Though I hurt, my head had cleared. It occurred to me that I hadn't asked about the driver of the pickup. It took a while, but the struggle to pull the moment before the crash from my memory bank paid off. I'd hit the driver's side but just in front of the door. The Ford was a truck and my Nova a light-weight compact. The driver would have been knocked around but be in better shape than Ardelia and me.

I owed the guy. If he hadn't come along and blocked us, Ardelia and I would have sailed through the intersection and gone over the riverbank drop-off. The rapid descent wouldn't have done either of us any good. Bruises, lacerations, a busted nose, a broken arm, these minor injuries were nothing compared to what would have happened if we'd gone over the edge. Insurance would cover most of the other driver's expenses. Given the state of my bank account, there didn't seem to be anything more I could do.

No two ways about it. The Nova had gone to the great Chevyland in the sky. My car had been good to me, but it was high-mileage, spray-painted, and rusted out. I'd have to figure out some transportation: first back to Bellevue for Marty's funeral and then back to Cedar Rapids for my jobs. Credit is a wonderful thing but has its downside, what with the expenses for Marty's funeral and a replacement vehicle, I wouldn't see the light of day for a decade.

A youngish doctor came, raised my eyelids, and burned my irises with a too-bright light. When he'd finished with the torture, he asked me how I was doing.

"Okay," I said. "When can I go home?"

"Ready to hop up and get back into action?" he laughed.

"Not really."

He put the light back in his pocket. "We'd like to keep you until later this afternoon. Then, if you're not dizzy and can walk on your own, we'll release you. We'll give you enough medication to help with the headache for the next day or two. Since you're not from town, you'll want to check with your family doctor to have the dressing looked at. He can decide when the stitches come out.

The doctor returned mid-afternoon to give me the go ahead. As he left, a pair of uniformed sheriff's deputies entered the room. They didn't look familiar, but then I realized they were from Jackson County, not Dubuque. One stood in the doorway; the other approached the bed and put his hands on his hips.

"Cletus Efferding," he announced, "you're under arrest for involuntary manslaughter."

32

There's nothing like spending the last day of vacation in jail. Though the drive to Maquoketa had taken forty minutes, I invoked my right to be silent, so the deputies wouldn't tell me a thing. It wasn't hard to figure out what had happened. Ardelia, the Underwear Lady, didn't make it. Though surprisingly strong, she was an old squeaker, and it wouldn't have taken much to finish her off. My nurse had mentioned something about massive bruising. The poor woman must have died of internal injuries.

I felt sorry for Ardelia, but the irony of the situation galled me. She feared fish bugs, so I offered to give her a ride home. When her erratic behavior caused me to lose control of my vehicle, I got blamed for the resulting accident and ended up in the hoosegow.

I made my one phone call as soon as they'd finished processing me. Since I didn't know any of the local lawyers, I called my assistant manager at the dance studio. Thank goodness she wasn't with a student. She picked up on the second ring.

"Sharon," I said, "I'm in the Jackson County Jail in Maquoketa. They've got me on a bogus involuntary manslaughter charge. I need you to get me a lawyer. The place is a county seat, so there should be scads of them. Just call Directory Assistance. When you get hold of somebody, find out how much he wants on deposit and wire him the money. Take it out of the studio account."

The most reliable dance instructor I'd ever met, I would have made Sharon full-time manager of the Efferding Dance Studio if she'd have let me. Unfortunately, she had kids in elementary school and didn't want to be tied down. As an instructor, she was just average, but her students would have walked over hot coals for her. Though it was late in the day, I had no doubt she'd find a lawyer for me, a good one.

I also asked Sharon to contact Killian's Department Store and tell them my cousin had passed. Thank God, I was a good salesman and had banked an unbelievable amount of vacation. Though entitled to funeral leave, word of my arrest would eventually get back to them. They weren't so hot on employees with legal issues, but I hadn't been convicted yet, and most of the store's big spenders came to me for clothing advice. I'd have been surprised if management didn't cut me some slack.

My phone call over, a deputy led me to a cell. Nothing to do but wait until my lawyer arrived, so I settled in for a relaxing stint of staring at the ceiling. They took my suit jacket, belt, necktie, and shoestrings. My shirt and pants were bloodstained and torn.

A prisoner's uniform would have been an improvement.

––––––––––

Harriet Groves wasn't quite what I expected. Overweight and nearly sixty, my lawyer looked like an escapee from a school of cosmetology. Whoever cut her hair must have used garden shears, and whoever permed it, burned it. After shaking hands, she took the chair opposite me, laid a legal pad on the table, and pulled a pen from behind her ear. The lady didn't look like much, but she knew the details of my case and didn't beat around the bush.

"You're charged with involuntary manslaughter," she said. "Since you caused a death while committing other offenses, in your case speeding, running a stop sign, and reckless driving, the county attorney will likely pursue the case as a felony. It's no accident the deputies showed up at the hospital when you were released. The sheriff's office arranged it ahead of time. It's standard practice with felony cases."

Felony. I felt the walls close in on me. I'd been angry about the bullshit charge, but now I felt scared. Really scared.

"You had alcohol on your breath, but they didn't charge you with drunk driving. That's because Iowa doesn't have a blood-alcohol law, and they had no evidence you were impaired. They know you were speeding but will have to prove it, and they'll have a hard time with the reckless driving charge because of the poor visibility and lack of witnesses. Unless of course, the lady in your car testifies against you. In any event, the charge you can't beat is running the stop sign, and that's enough to justify involuntary manslaughter."

"Ardelia is alive?" I asked. "Who died?"

"The driver of the pickup truck. When you ran the stop sign and hit the pickup, he lost control and went over the riverbank. On the way down, the trailer he was towing broke loose, and the truck flipped. The guy died of a broken neck. They're not sure who he is because he carried IDs and credit cards under two different names."

Though he'd gone over the rock-strewn embankment next to the International Harvester dealership instead of me, I no longer felt I owed him one. A man doesn't carry two sets of ID unless he's a spy or a lowlife. The happy discovery that Ardelia survived the crash blocked any remorse I might have felt about the fate of the other driver. Though guilt might come later, my plate was full. I'd deal with it then.

My attorney removed a pack of spearmint gum from the pocket of her blazer, extracted one, and unwrapped it. "The interesting part is what was in the trailer—the fancy iron coffin that was stolen last week. The guy you hit was no angel. He was transporting stolen property, and five will get you ten that both IDs are phony."

"Does that help me out at all?"

She put the stick in her mouth and masticated before answering. "Too early to say. Depends on what they find out, but my guess is it won't make any difference. But what about you? Do you have an arrest record?"

"Drunk and disorderly in Linn County, prostitution bust in Dubuque."

"Pandering?" she asked.

"No, I was the customer."

Her mouth worked the gum as if her life depended on it. She noticed that I'd noticed. "Trying to quit smoking," she explained. "It'd be better if you were Snow White, but a couple of misdemeanors won't hurt much. Anything else?"

I went into a long explanation about Marty's death and what had happened when the Dubuque County sheriffs tried to interview me at the morgue. When I finished, she looked at me as if I'd just passed gas."

"Got a lawyer on that one?" she asked.

"Haven't been charged and no time to find anybody."

"I don't do murder cases, so don't ask. With a rap like that hanging over your head, you're a big risk for non-payment, so if you want me to represent you on the manslaughter charge, I need my fee up front. The money you've put down guarantees I'll be there when you go before the magistrate tomorrow. You can be sure he'll find probable cause for manslaughter, and he'll set bail. If you want me to represent you after the hearing, I'll need my fee up front."

The lady was a hard-butt. "I have a funeral to pay for and need to pick up another car, so the money might take a while. If you can't wait, I'll ask for a court-appointed attorney."

"Cletus, there's a word for people represented by a court-appointed attorney—guilty."

I still hadn't explained the situation with Ardelia, that she was crazy as a loon and her actions had caused the accident. I began telling her about it.

"Not interested," she cut in. "It's not relevant to tomorrow's proceeding. I'll have time for it when I see my fee up front."

"That's all you're doing for me?"

"Hey, I'm an honest woman. The deposit your friend sent me more than covers my fee. If you get the standard thousand-dollar bond, there'll be enough left over for the bail bondsman. I'll see he gets it."

"Gee, thanks," I said.

She paused to work on her gum, then spoke. "I'll give you a freebie. Even if your passenger is as crazy as you say, it won't help much. I'm probably the only lawyer in the county with the smarts to get you out of the situation you're in."

"Nobody's as good as they think they are," I snapped. "After tomorrow, we're through."

"Okay Cletus, but without me, you're screwed. Really screwed."

It must have been noon when the guard came to fetch me and took me to the same room and table as last night. Harriet sat silently, scribbling on a legal pad. Today she wore a red blazer. A cigarette smoldered in a pasteboard ashtray.

"No gum today," I observed.

She chose to ignore my comment. "Cletus," she said, "I have some bad news, some good news, and some worse news. I'll start with the bad news."

"Thanks," I replied.

"When you leave the magistrate's courtroom today, an investigator and a deputy from the Dubuque County Sheriff's Department will be waiting. I don't know if they have a warrant or simply want to question you."

I should have panicked but didn't. Things looked so bleak I'd have willingly put my head in a guillotine and waited for the blade to drop. "How about the good news?" I asked. "I could use some."

"On my way into the building this morning, I ran into Melvin Osterman. He heard that I was representing you today and said you're originally from Bellevue, come from good people, and I should do my best for you."

I remembered Melvin Osterman. His son Mike went to high school with me, and the two of us worked backstage on plays and musicals. Efferding's Menswear had dressed the males in the Osterman family since my grandfather opened his shop.

I watched Harriet stub her cigarette. "So, knowing the Ostermans changes things. I wouldn't have guessed."

"Yesterday, you were a bozo from Cedar Rapids, today you're a representative of an old family from Bellevue. Besides, when the best-looking lawyer in Jackson County asks a favor, I give him what he wants. I've had my eye on the man for years."

Judging by Harriet's appearance, she'd have to settle for eyeing. The lady had too many brains to be unaware of her physical shortcomings. "There's more to it than an old Bellevue family," I replied.

She leafed through her legal pad and extracted several forms. "I found out you can pay. Osterman tells me he took care of your cousin Marty's civil matters. Your inability to handle money must be legendary because he seemed concerned you'd worry about legal expenses. Your cousin made a will last month, leaving you her entire estate. Since I contracted with you on an unrelated issue prior to any murder indictment and Iowa doesn't have a slayer rule, I'll see my money whether you go down for your cousin's murder or not."

Melvin Osterman must have been confused. Marty was the one who couldn't handle money.

"What's a slayer rule?" I asked.

"A law that says you can't inherit from someone you've murdered. It's an old legal principle. A slayer rule just tightens it up."

Marty's will made for a nice gesture, but I'd have been surprised if she had twenty dollars to her name. No sense telling Harriet. I needed the lady's help and didn't want to discourage her.

She pushed the typewritten forms toward me. "Sign the first form, and you agree to representation on the manslaughter charge at my standard rate. It also states I can attach the estate if you don't pay. The document applies to anything I do for you after the magistrate's hearing today. The second form instructs me to represent you on criminal issues related to the untimely death of your cousin. The terms are identical, and it's valid until such time as charges are filed. Basically, you're instructing me to represent you if Dubuque County law enforcement interviews you today. If you're charged in your cousin's death, it will almost certainly be a murder rap, and I'm out. Two bullets to the head are hard to explain away."

"Marty was shot in the head? How do you know? I saw her, and it didn't look like it."

"You hang around a courthouse as much as I do, you learn a lot. Dubuque's been leaning on Jackson County to hold you while they work on the investigation. Jackson County is obliging by stretching things out, but they can only hang on to you for twenty-four hours. That's why your appearance before the magistrate is delayed until 3:30 this afternoon."

I signed the documents without reading them and shoved the pen and papers back across the table. "So much for the good and bad news," I sighed. "What's the worse news?"

Harriet held a lighter to the tip of another cigarette and puffed. "The worse news is the same as the good news. You're inheriting Marty's estate. Unless something has changed in the last four weeks, it includes three thousand in certificates of deposit, five hundred silver dollars, and a paid-off house and vehicles. Melvin figures it will add up to something like thirty thousand."

"Thirty thousand?"

"Not a bad motive for murder, Cletus."

I ordered a Stromboli sandwich and glass of draft while Harriet walked to the cigarette machine. She came back with a pack of Marlboros.

"Would you like a drink, Harriet?"

We'd come to a bar near the courthouse after the Dubuque County Sheriff's deputies interviewed me.

"No. Besides I'm still on the clock. I doubt you want to pay me to get sloshed with you. And before you ask, it would be stupid for me to drive you back to Bellevue, because I'd charge a minimum of two hours. Any of the guys here in the bar would be happy to do it for a twenty."

I wasn't so sure. Though Harriet had managed to get me a clean prisoner's outfit for my appearance before the magistrate, it was taken away when they released me. I was back to the blood-stained clothes I'd been wearing at the time of the accident.

I'd bonded out on the manslaughter charge only to be met at the door by the deputies from Dubuque. Although the deputies hadn't arrested me, I remained more worried about the possibility of a murder charge than the near certainty of an involuntary manslaughter conviction. Harriet had thought it best to cooperate with the Dubuque County officers, rather than stiff them, and insisted I mention my argument with Marty at Portz's Tavern because they'd find out if they didn't already know. I'd done as directed, careful to refer to the event as "a disagreement" rather than the screaming match it had been.

She also wanted to disclose the contents of Marty's will but controlled the situation by revealing it herself. That way the interviewers were looking at her, rather than me, when the news came out. My role was to act as if I was aware of the will but surprised by the details. I didn't have to act; the shock of my inheritance had yet to wear off.

I spent the entire interrogation watching Harriet's index finger. Every time she tapped the table, I was to shut up immediately, even if in mid-sentence. She'd warned me the deputies would be more interested in closing the case than continuing to look for a person or persons unknown. It didn't take long to see she was right.

Harriet's voice brought me back to the bar room. "Pay attention. They have you for motive, but not means. They can't connect you to a .22 caliber handgun. Expect your home, business, and the cabin in Bellevue to be searched if they haven't already done so. They'll be checking to see if you had the opportunity to kill your cousin. Do yourself a favor and make a list of every place you've been and everyone you've talked to since Marty left town. You may be seeing deputies from Dubuque again. You've given your statement, so don't talk to them without me."

As far as Harriet knew, the investigation into the involuntary manslaughter charge had yet to begin. No one had come for my statement, and I was to speak to no one from law enforcement without Harriet present. Law enforcement was certain to interview crazy Ardelia, but since she was bats they'd get nothing useful.

"If we go to trial, I hope to put her on the stand," Harriet offered. "If she's as nutty as you say, it'll be obvious and make your story more believable. At that point, it becomes poor Cletus Efferding, he tried to help a crazy lady, and it turned around and bit him in the butt."

"What about the guy in the truck?" I asked. "If the street hadn't been covered with fish-bug grease, he wouldn't have lost control of this vehicle when I hit him. He had a stolen coffin in his trailer and carried fake IDs. The man was no boy scout."

Harriet squinted an eye and answered without taking the cigarette out of her mouth. "The fish flies didn't cause the accident; you did. As for the phony identification, he'd have to be one bad *hombre* before it'd make any difference. County attorneys take manslaughter seriously."

"I wonder if they'll ever identify the guy."

"If he has a record, they will. Bill Ehler, the acting sheriff, has a brother who works in the FBI crime lab. Bill pulled strings to get a quick ID on a suspicious hit-and-run when he was an investigator, so I expect he'll hit his brother up on this one as well."

When Harriet left, I went to the bar, got change for a five, and lined up the quarters on the shelf below the phone. No sense using dimes, my calls would be long distance. An unused, hand-made casket rested on a table in Lumir's workshop, and I hoped to use it for Marty. I couldn't believe my luck when he answered the phone. We had a lot of catching up to do. Lumir didn't know of Marty's death, my being a murder suspect or the manslaughter charge.

"How one man can get into so much trouble is beyond me," he said. "You should have come back to Cedar Rapids with us."

"Hindsight is twenty-twenty," I replied. "Are you and Eddie speaking yet?"

"Eddie has not phoned or visited me. I think the best thing is to wait for him to make the first move."

"I have an idea that might get the two of you talking. The casket in your workshop would make a beautiful addition to Marty's funeral. She had a hard life and deserves the best. You and Eddie have a personal connection with her—you chatted around a campfire with her on a starry summer night. Seems like the right thing to do.

"It is too soon, Clete."

"You might not want to wait too long," I advised. "Sometimes it gets harder to re-connect as time passes, especially if people are embarrassed they've let something come between them."

"I was not born yesterday. Already, I don't know what to say to Eddie."

"He might have the same problem. You'll have something to talk about," I counseled. "The funeral will likely be Saturday or Monday. That means the funeral home could need the casket as early as Friday morning. You have a good excuse for calling."

We ended the conversation with Lumir agreeing to call Eddie. I phoned the Dye Funeral Home next. The coroner had released Marty's body. They'd be picking it up Thursday. We scheduled the funeral for Saturday morning. I called Marty's house to see if Hank was in, but nobody answered.

Harriet had been right. The first guy I asked agreed to drive me to Bellevue for twenty bucks. Neither of us was inclined to talk, maybe because my banged-up head and blood-stained clothes made me look like a deranged killer. I spent the time brooding. Three days ago, I sat on the edge of my bed laughing like a hyena because I'd been bored and now my life had become interesting.

I was a fool.

I stopped by the owner's office when I got back to the cabins. The guy had wanted me to check out by noon, but my time in the clink had delayed my exit. He'd been about to pack my belongings when a pair of Dubuque County deputies arrived with a search warrant.

"All they took was a book, but they made quite a mess," he informed me. "I put everything together as best I could. If you ask me, they should give you a medal for taking out the kind of guy who'd steal a coffin."

My landlord thought the search had something to do with the manslaughter charge. That meant two things: the Dubuque County Sheriff's office was pursuing its murder investigation quietly, and my home and business in Cedar Rapids had been searched. I had no idea why they took Michener's novel, but I doubted I'd miss it very much.

"Sorry to hear about the death of your cousin," he added. "I didn't know her to talk to her, but she seemed like a nice gal."

"Thanks. Do you get the Dubuque paper?"

"I got everything since Sunday behind the counter, and you can read 'em. I expect your cousin's funeral will be coming up in a few days. Your cabin is booked, but the big one is vacant until the middle of next week. You can have it for the price of the economy cabin if you want."

"Thanks, I'll take it." I re-registered and schlepped my stuff over to my new cabin. The task completed, I returned to the office and asked to see the newspapers.

"Take 'em with you," he offered. "I finished up. By the way, you should get a haircut and bandage change. You look awful."

I returned to the new cabin, one with a real bedroom, a couch and a chair with a hassock. A guy could get used to that kind of luxury. I made for the couch, reached over to the end table, and switched on the lamp.

Tuesday's *Telegraph-Herald* reported the discovery of Marty's body with a half column on the front page but no picture. The piece didn't mention the cause of death. The reporter wrote the story from the viewpoint of the trotliner who found the body. The man seemed more upset about the trouble he encountered locating the buoy that marked his trotline than the fate of the woman entangled in it.

"You don't go out in the morning and expect to pull in a corpse," the guy complained. "I had a heck of a time finding my line. The current caught the body just right and dragged my setup a hundred fifty feet downstream. On top of that, the weight of the corpse had the buoy floating a foot and a half below the surface. Just dumb luck I found the trotline at all. They wanted to cut my line, but I said, 'Like hell you will.' Guess I can't complain. After they untangled the body, I finished pulling the line and found three channel cat on it."

I made the front page of Wednesday paper, above the fold for the second time of my life. A photo of the pickup I hit, overturned at the bottom of the bank, occupied center stage, but the article focused on the contents of the trailer.

Freak Accident Reveals Stolen Coffin
Mayfly Hatch Contributes to Crash

The mysterious cast iron coffin stolen from a Bellevue, Iowa, furniture store last week has been discovered in the wreckage of a fatal motor vehicle accident.

The Bellevue Police Department, still embarrassed by the theft of the valuable casket, remains mum on its current location. The larceny occurred when the officer responsible for keeping watch on the furniture business left the scene to respond to a call about a fire in another part of town. His departure allowed thieves to make off with the antique burial case.

Reduced visibility due to a massive mayfly hatch may have contributed to the collision, which killed an unidentified man when a car driven by Cletus Efferding, of Cedar Rapids, hit the side of a pickup pulling a horse trailer. The driver of the truck was declared dead at the scene.

Police believe the impact of the crash caused the driver of the truck to lose control and plunge over a steep embankment bordering the Mississippi River. The pickup overturned as it descended the rocky incline, killing the operator. The horse trailer broke loose as the vehicle hurtled down the bank and came to rest in shallow water with its doors open. Inside, authorities discovered the ornate casket stolen from temporary storage at Gallagher's Furniture Store, undamaged despite the tumble.

Unable to identify of the truck's operator, officials can think of no legitimate reason for its driver to be in possession of the coffin. Efferding was transported to an area hospital for observation. A passenger in Efferding's car, Ardelia Krumbatey, suffered lacerations, contusions, and a broken arm.

Although the mayfly hatch, perhaps the largest on record, had reduced visibility to several feet, charges against Efferding are pending.

"When a small car like a Nova hits the side of a pickup hard enough to cause the driver to leave the road, you can be sure excess speed was involved," police spokesman 'Mac' Mclean explained. "We couldn't use our normal estimates for braking distance because the oily residue of crushed fishflies acted as a roadway lubricant, but there's no doubt the driver of the car was traveling too fast and ran a stop sign."

Though the occupant of the mysterious burial case remains unidentified, some local residents believe it houses the remains of the 'Old Hag,' a legendary figure on whom disaster and bad luck are blamed. "That coffin is jinxed, and there's more to the Old Hag story than people want to admit," said Ella Burmeister, clerk at Lampe's Hardware, a business near the scene of the accident. "We have freak car crashes, stolen coffins, and get invaded by hordes of fish bugs. The whole town is going nuts."

They'd bumped Marty to page two, though she got the upper left-hand corner, not a bad spot. They'd come up with a picture of her that looked to be ten years old. The lead for the article stated she'd been murdered execution style and was last seen dining with two men at the Bridge Restaurant. Although the eatery's staff were able to identify Marty, they'd been unable to describe either of the men. I can't say I was surprised. With her big hair, vivid makeup, and tight jeans, Marty attracted attention. Anyone with her faded into the background. The story mentioned she operated an antique business in Bellevue, and the police had no suspects. Though the 'no suspects' business amounted to no more than a convenient lie, it beat the heck out of seeing my name on a murder warrant.

33

Standing unsteadily on the porch of the Queen Anne home he shared with Irv, Herm Cohen fumbled with his wallet as he tried to extract enough cash to pay the cab driver. The billfold fell to the ground, and he nearly passed out as he bent over to retrieve it. The wallet retrieved, he found himself unable to do the math and handed it to the driver.

"Just take what you need," he said.

The driver extracted some cash and returned the billfold. "I don't know what you've been takin'," he said, "but whatever it is, you better quit. It's really messin' you up."

"Do me a favor," Herm said extending his keys to the man. "I'm a little under the weather. Could you unlock the door?"

The cab driver shook his head, unlocked the house, and returned the keychain. "Listen, Bud, you better get some help before you kill yourself. Do yourself a favor, go in for a detox."

"I'll think about it," Herm said and turned to watch the driver descend the steps. "Thanks," he yelled after him.

After struggling to get the bags in the hallway, Herm wandered through the house, checking both floors and the basement. No Irv.

Yesterday was the worst day of his life. He'd waited and waited for Irv to show. Waited in vain. He'd held on to the hope that Irv was trying to teach him a lesson and that he'd find Irv at home today, prepared to give him a lecture. His walk through the house and the tableware still in the dishwasher confirmed his worst fears. Irv had gone, taken the truck, and started a new life.

The last thing he remembered was something about Irv calling him a junkie. Overcome with emotion, Herm flopped into his easy chair. Irv had left him, left him because he'd been too needy, left him because of the Valium. That damned crap. He recalled almost nothing of the time he'd spent at the hotel. Without his medication and stressed beyond belief, he drifted into a nightmare state somewhere between sleep and wakefulness, a place he hoped he'd never visit again.

His repeated attempts to pull himself out of it failed. He was about to give up when a deafening meow brought him back to the present. An unhappy Koko sat on his chest, and he couldn't blame her for being upset. She would have run out of food yesterday. Happy that she'd rescued him from his dream-like trance, Herm went to the kitchen and put out cat food. He returned to his chair determined to stay awake.

Though he knew he couldn't get addicted in a little over a week, quitting Valium would be a cakewalk compared to withdrawing from Irv. He sat, cried, and shivered until the sky grew dark and then dozed off. When he awoke, he realized that he'd been sprawled in his recliner, plagued by fearful dreams, for the better part of four hours. Though his neck and joints ached, he managed to haul himself upstairs for a cleanup.

His bath finished, Herm put on fresh pajamas and a bathrobe and returned to the den downstairs. No way he wanted to eat, so he brewed up a cup of tea and set it on the smoking stand next to Irv's chair. The lineup of guests on the *Tonight Show* looked second-rate, so he retrieved the newspapers that had accumulated since Monday, opened one, and fell into yet another agitated, dream-filled sleep.

Herm awoke with a start at 4:00 a.m. and returned to the newspapers. Between the occasional shakes and problems focusing, the newspapers were slow going. He was about to give up when a report on an antique coffin discovered as the result of a car accident caught his eye.

It took a minute to sink in. Irv didn't leave him. He'd been in an accident. Maybe he was in the hospital. Maybe he was … dead?

Cold type, but colder truth. Some guy ran a stop sign, and Irv died. He forced himself to look at the article again. Cletus Efferding, the guy they were going to whack, drove into Irv's pickup and killed him.

Herm slammed his fist on the smoking stand. "Goddamn you, Cletus Efferding! Damn you and the whore who brought you into this world. You're dead, puke. I'm gonna burn you and do it a little at a time. By the time I'm done, there won't be enough of you left to burn in hell."

The punishment didn't come close to paying for the crime. He hit the smoking stand again, so hard its joinery failed, and it collapsed to the floor in pieces, taking the teacup with it.

"You got a wife, kids, a dog—I'm gonna hurt 'em so bad they'll wish they never were born. I'll torch your house and gut your friends. You're gonna burn, Efferding. And when you can't take it anymore, I'll cut you up and watch you die."

34

Thursday morning brought with it a list of chores long enough to keep me busy all day. Eager to get started, I showered and paired my tan suit with a pastel yellow shirt and dark blue tie. My stitches itched like the blazes, and the bruise over my nose had grown to encircle both eyes. I covered the mess on top of my head with my reliable fedora and my eyes with Foster Grants then went to the kitchen table and reviewed the tasks before me. I'd been so worried about fitting them into the day that I'd started the list with "eat steak and eggs at the hotel" and finished with "plan funeral." Not wanting to get off to a bad start, I walked uptown and got working on item one.

I'd just finished an egg and ribeye steak breakfast when Hank Steines and Blackie Stiles approached my booth and asked to join me. Their arrival proved fortuitous since it allowed me to put a check mark against item number three—talk to Hank. I ordered a second cup of coffee and settled in.

Hank started right in. "I did us a favor Clete. When the deputies asked me if I owned a .22 caliber handgun, I told them I hadn't seen it since the day my wife and Marty got into a big fight and got arrested. Then I said I left it behind when the old lady kicked me out and went to stay with Marty. The best part is that it's the truth."

"That's right," Blackie agreed, "the best way to lie is tell the truth."

I had to laugh. Leave it to Blackie Stiles to accidentally hit the nail on the head. Though colorful and irascible as they come, I found it hard not to like the man.

"I gave 'em a picture of Marty to use in their investigation," continued Hank. "They grilled me pretty good, but since Blackie and I were out of town working up fish buyers, I'm in the clear. What about you?"

"I'm a suspect because Marty and I had that fight at Portz's Tavern, and I don't have an alibi because I spent a lot of the time by myself. They searched my cabin. I suppose my apartment and business are in for the same. Not only that, but the County Attorney charged me with manslaughter in the car wreck."

"You look like hell," said Blackie. "You must have been pretty desperate to have Ardelia Krumbatey in your car. She's a lecherous old bat. I hope it was worth it."

"You're just jealous you didn't think of it yourself," I replied. "Ardelia wanted a ride because she was afraid of the fish bugs. She caused the accident when she went nuts in the car and started beating on me. Ardelia's a strong old bird."

Blackie looked me over and grinned. "Maybe not so strong. You ain't what I'd call a fine physical specimen."

"Never said I was. You try driving when somebody's kicking and hitting you, and your windshield is covered with bug guts."

"Biggest hatch I ever seen," said Blackie. "Bigger than even before they put the lock and dam in. Probably the biggest in history."

"They brought snow plows in for the cleanup on Front Street," Hank added. "Just pushed the stinkin' carcasses into piles and brought in a loader to scoop 'em into trucks."

Loretta refilled my coffee when she brought Hank and Blackie theirs. A healthy swallow burned my tongue and tonsils. "Damn that's hot!" I protested. Loretta sniffed and left.

"Strange they didn't turn out the streetlights," I observed. "Talk about a blunder."

Hank cocked his head. "You didn't hear? Billy Babich was supposed to do it. Had a heart attack. They found him dead on the floor next to a push broom."

Blackie rubbed his unshaven chin. "Blunderin' Bill Babich never did anything right, not even in grade school. Figures he'd pick the wrong time to die."

"At any rate, fish won't be hungry, so your trotlines will be slow next week," Hank noted.

"That's why I'll be settin' hoop nets for snapping turtles," Blackie replied. "My fish traps will be okay too. Say, Hank, what say we go giggin' bullfrogs tomorrow night. Reed's Pond is full of 'em."

"Sounds like fun. Wanna go Clete?"

I didn't know what they were talking about. "Gigging frogs?"

Blackie lit a Lucky Strike. "You spear the suckers, and when you get home, you cut off the legs. Then you wash the blood off 'em, cover them legs with eggs and cracker crumbs, and fry the little suckers up."

I didn't know frogs had blood. "I think I'll pass."

Hank pulled out his pipe and lit up too. "Reed's Pond, a wild place, but close to the road. So many frogs, but never hunted out. I wonder why nobody goes there."

Because nobody wants to eat frogs. I kept the thought to myself.

I blew on my coffee and took a sip. "There's got to be a connection between Marty's murder and the break-ins at her garage and down at the cabins," I said. "The tools and the coffin were worth a small fortune."

Hank puffed on his pipe. "Marty said the tools were worth a lot more than the iron casket. Some guy named Irv wanted 'em in the worst way, but his partner didn't want him to spend the money unless he got the coffin too."

I nearly spit the coffee from my mouth. "What? Marty eats dinner with two men at the restaurant before she gets killed, and two guys wanted the tools and coffin. You knew their names and didn't tell me?"

Loretta appeared from nowhere. "One of our customers is complaining about your pipe, Hank."

Hank smothered his pipe, and Loretta left. "Course I know about the guys who wanted the stuff, but you never asked. And I don't know their names. All I know is one is from Cedar Rapids and is called Irv."

"Did you tell the investigators?"

"You think I'm that dumb? I might'a helped 'em out with an old picture, but Marty and I took that coffin. Stupid thing's been in the news too much for the cops to ignore it. I don't need that kind of trouble, and on top of that, they'd want to take away the tool chests for evidence. If Marty was alive, she'd be mad if I let 'em get away like that."

"Those guys probably killed Marty, and you're worried about what she might have thought about the tools?"

"Ain't no probably, they did it, and thanks to your car accident, one of 'em is dead already. Goes a long way to even up the score."

"What about me?" I asked. "Dubuque wants to pin a murder charge on me, and you didn't say anything."

Hank smiled. "I woulda said somethin' if it came to that. Besides, they'll be botherin' my old lady about the .22 and the fight she had with Marty. That'll keep 'em busy for a day or two."

Blackie snorted and chimed in, "Don't get your underwear in a bundle. The less the law knows about anybody, the better. I can tell you ain't been in much trouble before. Getting' panicked before you're charged is a waste of time."

"Blackie's right," Hank added. "You're actin' like an investigation is a big deal. A man ain't lived unless he's been investigated for something."

My head spun. I decided to move on because Hank and Blackie's down-home logic was beginning to make sense. I wasn't about to bring it up, but I'd had issues with the police before and wouldn't wish it on anybody.

After securing a pledge from Hank that he'd wait for me at Marty's house after his shift on the garbage truck, I made for the door.

My to-do list included making arrangements at the Dye Funeral Home, and come hell or high water, he was going with me. I had no idea of how to plan a funeral service and had no intention of going it alone.

My next stop lay across the street—Wolfie Till's Pontiac dealership. I needed wheels, and between Wolfie and his father, they'd patronized Efferding's Menswear for something like fifty years. Add in their kids and grandkids, and the Till family must have sent something like thirty customers through the door. No doubt about it, a Pontiac it would be, and not just any Pontiac would do. I wanted a big, good-looking car, one large enough to transport well-heeled customers to dances.

I worked with a salesman named Willie, and it didn't take long to settle on a loaded 1973 Bimini Blue Bonneville. A low-mileage car, the shop had just taken it on trade. My selection made, Willie led me to his cubby, a desk and two chairs under an overhead sign displaying the dealership's timeworn motto.

Other dealers sell cars. We sell automobiles.

Coming to a price wasn't a problem, but convincing Willie I had the financial wherewithal to purchase the vehicle proved difficult. I'd provided him with information about my job, the business I owned, and the inheritance from Marty, but Willie remained unmoved.

Our discussion grew loud enough for our voices to drift across the room and over to the service counter, where Wolfie leafed through paperwork. I heard him thump a clipboard on its hard surface and clear his throat. "Jesus Christ, Willie, sell the man a car. He's good for it."

Within ten minutes, I had the keys in hand. Despite my wife's suicide, Wolfie had treated me with respect. He must have heard about the manslaughter charge, but our shared history trumped petty gossip. I could have hugged him, but hey, no sense in weirding the man out. A car with an air conditioner, I never imagined I'd own one. I turned it on full blast and drove the few blocks to Razor Ray's barbershop listening to the Bonneville's magnificent AM/FM radio. I may have been a suspect in a murder case and charged with involuntary manslaughter, but for the moment life felt good—very good.

I removed the bandages from my head before I entered Ray's. He raised his eyebrows when it was my turn to get into to his chair. "Cut off the long stuff," I explained, "then shave my head as best you can. Don't worry you'll nick a stitch. I'm going to Doc Fredrickson's to get re-bandaged after I leave here."

It took Ray all of ten minutes to remove my remaining hair. When he finished, I gave him a fifty-cent tip and headed out the door feeling good about what I'd accomplished. My watch said 10:30, and I'd already checked four items off my list.

I walked to Doc Fredrickson's office. I didn't know what to expect. Doc would be nearly seventy by now. He'd brought me into this world, and I wanted to return the favor by giving him a little business. I got lucky; an empty waiting room greeted me. I was in and out in something like fifteen minutes. Doc changed my dressing, rubbed some ointment on the stitches to help with the itching, and charged me fifteen dollars. In Cedar Rapids, the same visit would have cost twenty-five.

Back at the cabin, I was putting the finishing touches on a ham sandwich when the owner knocked on the door. Another telephone call for me at the office. I ate the sandwich as I followed him over and picked up the receiver to discover Lumir on the line.

My friend was in an expansive mood. "I talked with Eddie, and he wants you to use the coffin for Marty."

"That's great," I replied, "but I still don't know whether the funeral will be Monday or Saturday. When are you coming over?"

"I do not know yet, but Eddie will not be with me. The packing plant has a big order, and he will work this weekend."

"Too bad," I said. "Everything okay between the two of you?"

My question brought a blow-by-blow description of their reunion. My efforts to change the topic failed to deter him. He'd regret his rambling monologue when the long-distance charges showed up on his phone bill.

As for me, I'd killed two birds with one stone: located a casket for Marty and restored Lumir and Eddie's friendship. Not bad considering the effort I'd put into it, but then again, to be expected. Except for my inadvertent brushes with the law, mere mortals couldn't hold a candle to me.

Lumir's phone bill aside, I had one more thing I wanted to go over with him. "You know the Nicholson tools chests you sold Marty? She never paid the seven twenty-five she owed me. As far as I'm concerned, they're yours."

"I warned you, Clete. I said you would never see the money, and you have not. I made a thousand percent profit on the deal, and you managed to go down over seven hundred dollars. You must learn to handle money."

"I do fine with my money. It was hard for you to part with the tools, so I'm giving them to you—no strings attached."

"I do not want them. Their magic is gone. They would remind me of Marty's death. No."

I didn't want them either, for precisely the same reason. I didn't want to see them, touch them, or be in the same room with them. I'd give them to Hank. Maybe he could make some money on them.

By the time I told Lumir about my new car, we'd been on the phone for fifteen minutes, and somewhere in a corner office on the thirty-fifth floor, I could hear a Ma Bell executive laughing himself silly about the way they were sticking it to the little guy for a service that cost them almost nothing. With that happy thought in mind, I promised my friend I'd contact him when the funeral plans were in place and hung up.

I knew better than to ask the cabin owner if I could make a long distance call on his telephone, so left the office and headed over to Milt's Conoco to use the pay phone. After exchanging a couple of bucks for a stack of quarters, I waited for a talkative teenager to finish a conversation with someone who could only have been her boyfriend. The drama went on for something like ten minutes, her voice going from cheerful, to incredulous, to concerned, and finally, to tearful. Visibly shaken, she hung up the receiver and staggered to the door. Though the course of young love seldom goes smoothly, I expected she'd survive the experience.

I fed a buck's worth of quarters into the phone and called Sharon, my assistant manager at Efferding Dance. A Nervous Nellie, she tended to overreact when stressed. Best to warn her in advance. When she answered, I got right to it. "Hello Sharon, Cletus here. I think there's a warrant out to search the studio."

"Already happened."

"Are you okay?"

"I'm okay but confused. I thought you were charged with manslaughter because of a car accident. They were looking for a handgun. I didn't know you shot someone."

Yeah, Cletus. Explain your way out of this one.

"I can explain," I said.

"What's going on over there?"

And this is where your assistant manager resigns.

"Well, I didn't shoot anybody, but the Dubuque County Sheriff thinks I murdered my cousin."

"Cletus, how many people are dead?"

"Just two. My cousin Marty and the driver of the truck I hit."

"Only two? That's one a week. Police raids, manslaughter, murder, I don't think I can work here anymore."

"I can't talk you out of it? There's a hundred-dollar bonus in it if you stay."

"No way, the job's too stressful."

"Can you at least put a closed notice on the door, and wire me the entire balance in the shop account?"

"I'll do both and mail you the key."

She hung up without saying goodbye.

When I returned to the cabin, I pulled my to-do list from my pocket. Breakfast, check. Talk to Hank and Lumir, done. Buy new car, accomplished. Have doctor examine stitches, yup. Get head shaved, bagged it. Call studio, blew it. I added 'update car insurance' to the list and circled the notation 'plan funeral with Johnny Dye.'

The morning's activity had taken its toll. A well-deserved nap beckoned, so I headed for my bed and wandered off to the Land of Nod. I feel no sympathy for people who don't take naps. They're a cranky lot, responsible for most of the world's misery.

35

Johnny Dye's office, done up in dark wood and deep blue fabric, looked as if a magazine article had inspired it. I found it easy to imagine him, feet up on his spacious mahogany desk, browsing an issue of *Modern Funeral Director*. I thought the bag of golf clubs in the corner a nice touch.

Hank Steines occupied the chair next to mine. We'd just delivered the news that we'd supply Marty's casket. For a guy who'd just lost a good chunk of his cut of the funeral, Johnny took it in stride.

"Since the funeral will be on Saturday," he said, "I'll need the casket by noon tomorrow. If you can't get it here by then, we can take one from inventory, but selection will be limited. Did Marty have a plot?"

"Not that I know of," I replied. "My family was Presbyterian. Can we get her a plot in the cemetery south of town?"

"Shouldn't be a problem. I ran into Pastor Stewart a couple of days ago. He mentioned he'd be leaving for vacation. Of course, there'll be a backup for Sunday services. If he can't come a day early, we might have to postpone until Monday."

I looked at Hank, and he looked at me. We knew what we wanted, and a church service was not on the list.

"Actually," I said, "we aren't interested in a church service. We'd just like something here and a few words at the graveside."

"So, visitation, something simple here at the home, and then off to the cemetery?"

Hank nodded, and I said, "Yup."

"No minister, then who's speaking?" he asked. "I can read some scripture, but that would be religious. I didn't know the lady well enough to say anything meaningful."

His question brought me to item seven on my list, a notation with a checkmark next to it. The world doesn't have many Cletuses in it, but when we meet, we tend to bond.

"It's not that we have anything against God, but we're not big on church services," I explained. "I've asked Father Cletus Tillman to say a few words. He's happy to do it because it's ecumenical."

Johnny nodded. "Ecumenical is very big with the Catholics these days."

"After he's done, I'll say a few words. Hank will read from the Bible at the cemetery."

"You understand," Johnny added, "the service will be very small. There's been no obituary. I might be able to get a short notice in tomorrow's Dubuque paper, but more than likely, it'll appear Saturday."

"Hank and I already thought of it. We'll check in at the drug stores, grocery stores, hotel, and barbershop. Visitation at nine, memorial service afterward, followed by the cemetery. The whole town will know."

"Yeah," added Hank, "and we're paying the Cedar Rapids and Maquoketa radio stations to put it on the air—a dozen times each. We didn't think their ordinary community service notices would do the trick."

I could see Johnny working hard not to break into a smile. "An advertising campaign for a funeral," he remarked, "I must say that is unusual."

"Nothing but the best for Marty," said Hank.

The rest of the planning came off without a hitch. I'd make a down payment with the money Sharon sent from the shop account. We went for the deluxe, leak-proof vault, gave Johnny a photo of Marty to place on the closed casket, and had him arrange for a generous assortment of flowers. The photograph was a larger version of the one Hank gave the Sheriff's deputies. Marty hadn't changed much in the past decade, except for her hair. She'd been wearing it twice as big as she did back then.

Lumir showed up with the coffin at ten. He'd hauled it in the back of his pickup, cocooned in a roll of quilts. We drove both the Pontiac and the pickup to the Dye Funeral Home so we wouldn't be stuck there if Johnny didn't have anybody to help unload the box. He didn't, so we left the truck and took the Bonneville, cruising in sweet luxury to the Anchor Inn, a lunch spot north of town.

"You have a fine car," Lumir remarked as we settled into a corner table. "I can see why you paid the man at the cabins for the use of his garage. It would be a shame to see your new car spray-painted."

"Automobile," I insisted, thinking back on the sign in Wolfie's dealership. "When a guy moves up to a vehicle like this, it's an automobile."

"I guess that makes my pickup truck a hearse," laughed Lumir.

"Not in this lifetime."

I'd asked Lumir to stop by my apartment in Cedar Rapids to pick up my black suit for Marty's funeral. He told me the place had been searched but hadn't gone into the details. I was curious. "So how bad did my apartment look?"

"They tossed it. Just like on television. Nothing looks broken, but it will take you a half day to put it back together. They piled your suits and shirts on the floor. I expect many of them will have to be pressed. If you hang your black suit in the bathroom while you shower, it will look good enough for the funeral."

Not good enough for Cletus Efferding. I intended to buy a steam iron at Lampe's Hardware and touch it up on the kitchen table. "They break the lock?" I asked.

"No, your landlord must have let them in."

I sighed. Still a murder suspect. The Dubuque County Sheriff's office had me in the crosshairs, and Jackson County wanted to jail me for accidentally slaughtering one of Marty's killers. I wanted to get my friend's reaction to the situation.

"By the way," I said. "I killed one of the guys who shot Marty."

Lumir paled. "Another one? You are going to prison, Clete."

I should have eased into it. "No, the same one. The guy who went over the bank in his pickup, he helped kill Marty."

"So, it wasn't an accident?"

"I didn't know he was involved in her death. I got lucky."

"A manslaughter charge is not lucky. How do you know the man did it?"

"When Marty and Hank stole the coffin, they had a pair of buyers for it."

The arrival of our waitress brought me up short. The look on Lumir's face told me I'd neglected to mention my cousin's role in the original theft of the burial case. We had so much to talk about that I'd forgotten. After we ordered our coffee and donuts, I remedied the situation.

"Marty had a pair of buyers for the Nicholson tool chests, but they only wanted them if they could get the coffin too. The guys offered big money so Marty and Hank swiped the coffin from Ray's garage."

Lumir leaned forward on the table and looked both ways. "That is crazy. What do old tools have to do with coffins?"

"I asked the same question, but that was the deal. Anyway, Hank and Marty stored the coffin in her garage. Last Saturday, somebody broke into the garage and stole it. The same night, somebody broke into my cabin. It must have been Marty's buyers looking for the Nicholson chests. They didn't find them because you asked the owner of the cabins to store the tools in his garage."

"Someone broke into your cabin?"

"Yours too. If you hadn't asked the owner to store the chests, they'd be gone."

Our coffee and four glazed donuts arrived. I'd ordered three of the donuts for me.

Lumir didn't look convinced. "Why would they kill Marty? She got the coffin and tool chests for them."

"Greed," I said. "They didn't want to pay her."

We let the thought sit and went to work on our donuts. I'd just finished my second when Lumir observed, "They would have to be hard men to kill a woman over a rusty coffin and a bunch of old tools, but I believe you are right. Marty's buyers killed her, and you accidentally killed one of them."

"The coffin wasn't that rusty, and Marty told Hank the tools are valuable because the Nicholson guy who made them is famous."

"Those tool chests are cursed," Lumir grunted.

"Well, one slime bag down, and one to go," I joked. "Hank knows they were from Cedar Rapids and that one is named Irv. I wouldn't be surprised if he wants to even the score. How many antique dealers named Irv could there be in Cedar Rapids? It would take all of an hour to find his partner."

Lumir wiped coffee from his mustache. "This is not a joking matter. These men are murderers. Hank could get himself killed. I will attempt to talk him out of it, even though it might not be so good for you."

"Not so good for me? How so?"

"If the surviving bad man is as mean as I think he is, he may seek revenge for the death of his friend."

"Nah," I said. "He'll lay low, and when nobody is looking, crawl back into a hole somewhere."

"You have a target on your back, Clete."

After a quick drive to Dubuque to secure the funds Sharon wired me, I dropped Lumir at the cabin and walked to Milt's Conoco to use the phone. I wanted to get in touch with Harriet, my lawyer, before the weekend. She picked up on the fourth ring, and I could have sworn I could smell the stench of the Marlboro in her mouth coming through the receiver.

"Harriet, Cletus Efferding here. Any news on the involuntary manslaughter investigation? I'm leaving for Cedar Rapids on Sunday and haven't heard from anyone in the Sheriff's Department."

"I didn't expect them to contact you. They had most of what they needed to convict. It was just a matter of taking a statement from Ardelia and interviewing the Bellevue cops. I warned you not to talk to them without me, just to be on the safe side."

"That's reassuring," I said.

"My sources tell me they've already interviewed Ardelia, and it was a disaster. She said you lured her into the car under false pretenses and groped her."

"Harriet, I swear I didn't. She groped me."

Harriet chuckled. "Whether you did or didn't, the disaster was theirs, not yours. Her story was so filled with loopholes and exaggerations they'll never put her on the stand."

Things were looking up. Though I might get charged with murder, convicted of manslaughter, or killed by a deranged antique dealer, a sexual assault charge was not in my future.

"Wanna hear the really good news?" she asked.

"Fire away."

"I think we can plea bargain down to reckless driving and running a stop sign. Bill Ehler's brother at the FBI came through for him. The guy you killed, turns out his real name was Irving Kaplan, and he worked as an enforcer for the Chicago mob. Did time in Joliet for attempted murder, got paroled early, and dropped out of sight. They could never get anything more on him, but he's a suspect in something like thirty homicides. Good news, huh?"

I felt my guts slip to the floor and wondered if I should just shoot myself and save Kaplan's partner the trouble.

"Cletus?" Harriet asked. "You still there?"

"Sorry, my mind just wandered."

"The Medical Examiner said no one has claimed the body, and he doesn't expect anyone to. That means no friends or relatives pushing the County Attorney to throw the book at you."

"I'm off the hook because I crashed into the right guy?"

"Looks like it. In all my years of practice, I've never seen a victim so nasty a prosecutor was willing to back off on a fatality. Too bad you didn't hit the guy he used to hang out with—disappeared about the same time. I might have been able to bargain it down to just the stop sign. They called his buddy the Blowtorch because he burned his victims alive. How are you making out with the Dubuque County Sheriff? You haven't called, so I assume they didn't question you again."

"Nothing yet."

"Now that you're going back to Cedar Rapids, you need to get a local attorney with experience in murder cases. I recommend Don Mellick. I expect to have your plea bargain on the traffic accident completed sometime next week. You'll still need to go to court, but until then, we can do what we need to by mail. I'll send a couple of papers for you to sign; one will have to be notarized. Got that?"

"I've got it, Harriet."

"Your bill is due at the end of the month. If you don't pay in full, interest on the unpaid balance accrues at nine percent. It's in the documents that you signed without reading. If you'd read them, you'd also know that if I'm forced to attach your cousin's estate to get payment, I'm allowed to add the costs and hourly charges for doing so to the outstanding balance. You might think I'm hard-hearted, but compared to the guys at the Fort Madison prison, I'm a cupcake."

"Yeah, a cupcake who eats nails. You're all heart, Harriet. Hard-hearted, and a hard butt too."

She laughed. "You should be kissing my feet, awed by my ability, and overwhelmed with gratitude."

"Okay, thanks, you did good. I'll look for the bill."

I hung up and should have been ecstatic but didn't feel like celebrating. Lumir's warning about a target on my back had begun to make sense. I'd killed the friend of a sadistic psychopath. The news took the thrill off beating the manslaughter charge.

Randy Roeder

36

I sat in the recliner in Marty's living room waiting for Hank to get dressed for the funeral. Lumir stood at the picture window whistling to himself. For someone on his way to a wake, he seemed much too cheerful. His sunny disposition didn't match mine. I didn't get my beauty sleep last night because he'd discovered Woody and the Stump Jumpers were scheduled to play a dance nearby.

"Just think, Clete," he'd insisted, "Woody and the Stump Jumpers, the best polka band in Wisconsin, is playing in Lamotte. It's just thirteen miles away. I will never get this chance again."

The fact that the best polka band in Wisconsin had booked a Thursday night gig at the KC Hall in a village of four hundred hadn't impressed me. "Lumir," I said, "my head is bandaged, my nose is broken, I have thirty-five stitches in my scalp and two black eyes. Does it look like I belong at a dance?"

"Think of the wonderful polka music. Woody is the best button accordion player in the country."

I remained adamant, resisting his pleas and arguments until he struck a low blow. "We could take your new car and ride in style, listening to the FM radio, and enjoying the air conditioning."

We'd gone, and Lumir had the time of his life, dancing almost every dance and getting pawed by women half his age. I sat at the table sulking. Bandaged and bruised, I felt ugly and unwanted. We stayed until closing, and I didn't get the rest my battered body needed.

I returned to the present as Hank walked in wearing a brown checked sports coat and gray-striped pants. He held a burnt orange tie in front of his yellow dress shirt. Short and wide, the tie must have been twenty-five years old. I remembered my father seeing one on an usher in church and referring to it as a "Fat Max." All the rage for fifteen minutes in the late 1940s, Hank's cravat took the cake. It was one of those hand-painted jobbies, decorated with the image of a Texas longhorn. Whether from an unfortunate trip to the dry cleaners or just plain wear, one of the horns had vanished. Perfectionist that I am, I found the asymmetrical, one-horned steer vaguely upsetting.

"Does this tie go with this shirt?" Hank asked.

The man looked so hopeful. I didn't want to rain on his parade. He'd been through enough. Swallowing a lifetime of haberdasher's pride, I ignored everything that was wrong with his outfit and accentuated the positive. "Burnt orange and yellow are a fine color combination."

"Good," he said. "Can you help me? I don't know how to tie a tie."

I needed no further proof to know I'd returned to my hometown. For all their good points, Bellevue's mothers were woefully wanting when it came to teaching their male offspring this simple skill. My father considered his inability to make a dent in the deeply entrenched deficit his biggest failure. I removed the tie from Hank's extended hand, placed it around his neck, and recited the instructions I'd been using to teach seven-year-olds for over thirty years. "The fox chases the rabbit around the tree twice, hops under the bush and goes into the hole." The knot complete, I snugged it up to Hank's neck.

"What happened to the fox?" he asked.

"Never mind," I sighed. "Let's get going so we'll have time to do the preview before the guests show up."

We drove to the funeral home, Bonneville style. When we arrived, I saw Blackie waiting for us near the front steps. I couldn't believe my eyes. If I hadn't seen the guy the day before yesterday, I wouldn't have recognized him.

The man looked fantastic. He'd shaved and gotten a haircut. From the classic elegance of his conservative suit to the shine of his well-polished wingtips, Blackie Stiles looked every bit a candidate for membership in the Harvard Club of Boston. His well-cut jacket, a dark charcoal with gray pinstripes, sported moderate-width lapels and fit like a glove. From commercial fisherman to a prince, Blackie proved the wisdom of the axiom "clothes make the man."

I had trouble squaring Blackie's appearance with the rough-spoken, hackle-raising character I'd become acquainted with. As much as he must have hated it, Blackie had dressed in his best to show respect for Hank. My regard for the man took a huge leap. I've never understood the idea that dressing up for a funeral is an imposition. Compared to dealing with the loss of a loved one, the effort required seems trivial. I shook Blackie's hand and complimented him on his suit.

"I bought it from your daddy thirty years ago. Don't know why I kept it all these years, never enough closet space, and I moved so many times. Last time I wore it was my brother Jake's funeral."

Efferding's Menswear had done well by Blackie. I imagined my father presenting him with the accumulated wisdom of the family's seven decades in menswear. "Buy a conservative suit with medium lapels and a medium-width dark tie. You'll never be out of style." Blackie served as proof positive the old man was right.

Blackie joined us as we ascended the front steps and entered. I went last and closed the door. Though we were barely inside, syrupy music floated from hidden speakers and the overpowering smell of tropical flowers clogged the air. I've never understood if funeral flowers really smell that way or if undertakers pump an artificial *odeur de fleurs* into the air to mask the smell of death.

Unsure of what to do next, Hank, Blackie, Lumir, and I stared at each other. We might have spent a half hour in the entryway, had not Johnny, by some sixth sense known only to funeral directors, ascertained we'd arrived and appeared out of nowhere.

"Before we go in, why don't you sign the guestbook?" he said and pointed to a stand featuring a small volume.

I had no idea what Hank and I would ever do with a guestbook, but thankful to have something to do, I led the way, signed my name, and watched my colleagues do the same. When we finished, Johnny ushered us into the viewing room.

I didn't know what to expect, but Johnny had pulled out all the stops. Surrounded by mountains and mountains of flowers, the lacquer-finished walnut casket shone. Although the setup looked more appropriate for a film goddess than a small-town antique dealer, I almost felt like the Efferdings had finally come through for Marty. The fact that her estate had financed the impressive show kept me from going overboard on self-congratulation, but on one level or another, most funerals are financed by money from the deceased.

"I used three coats of furniture polish on the casket," Johnny said with pride. "The wood is so beautiful I didn't want to put Marty's picture on it. That's why she's on the tripod. If you want her on top, I can move it."

"It's fine, John," I said. "You really outdid yourself. Everything is beautiful."

"Thanks, I have a few more details to take care of. I'll leave you alone for a few minutes."

Johnny left. I looked at Hank. Hank looked at Blackie. Lumir looked at me. We stood in silence, shifting from foot to foot, utterly uncomfortable, not sure of what to do. If there were a fish-out-of-water prize for the biggest oafs ever to host a funeral visitation, we'd have won hands down.

Maybe it was the stress, maybe not, but for some reason, the weepy background music started getting to me. Even though Marty and I weren't on the best terms, tears started working their way toward my eyes. I excused myself and went looking for Johnny.

I found him in his office. "John," I said. "You've got to do something about that music. Hank is going to lose it completely. Do you have something less emotional?"

"I can put some hymns on the system. They're a popular alternative."

I tried not to grimace. "You've got some Sinatra?"

"I'll check, but the system is limited to tape. I might have something in private quarters."

While Johnny left in search of a tape, I sat in his plush office and worked to get control of myself. I'd just succeeded when he returned with an eight-track tape in his hand.

"I'm not familiar with this one, Cletus. It's labeled *Sinatra at the Sands*. You know, Frank Sinatra might be a bit of a stretch for some of the guests."

Johnny might not have known about the greatest live recording of the twentieth century, but I did. Accompanied by the Count Basie Orchestra in the Copa Room of the Sands Hotel, it featured Sinatra at his peak. In on the backbeat, stretching notes when the band had moved on, his voice danced its way through lyrics and melody with a free-wheeling authority that had no equal. With Basie on piano and Quincy Jones conducting and arranging, *Sinatra at the Sands* set the standard for everything a brassy big band performance should be.

"Marty would love it," I replied. I had no idea of what kind of music Marty liked, but anything was better than the Simpering Strings playing all-time funeral favorites. "There's just one catch, Johnny. It's a live album, so some of the songs have spoken introductions."

He appeared a bit uncertain but ready to take it in stride. "No problem, we'll turn it off when the service starts."

Time to hit him with the bad news. "There's a monologue in the middle, so when Frank starts talking about getting wasted at Dean Martin's house, just stop the tape and go back to the beginning."

Johnny paled. "Cletus, I have a reputation to protect. An advertising campaign for a funeral is one thing, but nightclub jokes during the visitation is another."

"Stick with me, John," I quipped as I rose to leave the room. "You're going to be the talk of the town. You can't buy exposure any better than that."

Johnny didn't look convinced.

Hank, Blackie, Lumir, and I stood in a private room just off the viewing area waiting for Johnny to lead us to the cemetery. The morning had been a roller coaster ride. Something like one hundred sixty people showed up to pay their respects. As far as I could determine, fifty were Marty's friends and the rest curiosity seekers. Nothing like an execution-style murder to bring the roaches out of their nooks and crannies.

Johnny dutifully played the Sinatra tape, a calming touch that may have saved me from an assault charge. I'm not deaf, and I almost waded into the crowd swinging when I overheard a blue-haired senior citizen say, "I always knew she'd come to a bad end."

I made myself scarce when Ardelia Krumbatey arrived, her arm in a sling. Unsteady, and disheveled, the lady looked a lot worse than when I'd last seen her. I don't know if she was looking to confront me or not, but when she disappeared before the service, I attributed my good luck to Father Cletus's influence with the Big Guy. I did my spiel before he did his and managed to get through it with nary a tear. I hate my emotions. Nothing good ever comes of them.

After reminding the gathering of Marty's unfortunate childhood, I brought up her distress over the recent discovery of her mother's murder. Judging by the looks of shock on the assembled faces, most of them hadn't heard the news. I hoped at least a few would remember her as a lonely teenager caught up in a bad situation rather than the town slut. An angel she wasn't, but most of us had misjudged her.

The good Father Cletus gave a touching homily on the role of grace in helping us understand the struggles of the unloved, friendless, and weak. Not that I'm vindictive, but I hoped the smug bluehair in the back, the one who thought Marty got what she deserved, would choke on her self-satisfied moral superiority. Not very Christian of me, but I suspected the lady lived a life so devoid of grace she wouldn't have recognized it if it came up and bit her in the ass.

Johnny walked into our room. "Ready to go boys?"

We followed him out to the Bonneville. Dye Funeral home didn't provide limousines, so Johnny had one of his pallbearers-for-hire park my Bonneville behind the hearse and put one of those little funeral flags on the front fender. I drove us down to the cemetery. Only a few cars followed. One of those carried the rented pallbearers. When we got to the gravesite, they carried Marty to a platform over the excavation, then stood to one side. AstroTurf covered a nearby mound of freshly turned dirt.

Though there were people at the graveside I didn't recognize from the funeral service, we were a small group. Johnny had asked if I wanted him to read some poetry before Hank did his reading. Worried that the committal would be over in something like three minutes, I agreed. Johnny read a couple of sappy things that had nothing to do with Marty's situation. I didn't care for them, but Hank seemed affected, so I knew the funeral director had done the right thing. Johnny's poems over, Hank stepped up and began reading.

> *Forasmuch as it hath pleased Almighty God in his great mercy to take unto himself the soul of our dear sister Marty here departed, we therefore commit her body to the ground; earth to earth, ashes to ashes, dust to dust …*

The ashes-to-ashes reference took me back to the misery of tenth grade.

> *Ashes to ashes, dust to dust*
> *With a girl like you, my lips would rust.*

Specifically, back to my unrequited crush on Ruthie Sawyer, the girl who sat behind me in homeroom. Rusty lips, hell. Young Cletus Efferding would have settled for an inviting smile. I snapped out of it when Hank got to the part about "comforting ye one another" and brought the service to an end.

That was it. A couple of people came up to shake my hand. The gossip mill was efficient enough for them to know about Hank and Marty's rekindled romance, but a one-week relationship didn't qualify him for special attention. Too bad, the man had taken it hard. The torch he carried from his affair with Marty ten years ago still burned as brightly as it had back then.

The crowd, if you could call it that, filtered away. We were down to two stragglers when one of them came up to offer his condolences. "I take it you're the deceased's next of kin?" he asked.

"I'm her cousin, Cletus Efferding. Our family is small."

"I'm a reporter from the *Telegraph-Herald*, and I'd like to get your thoughts on your cousin's untimely death."

I dislike violence and think of myself as an easy-going guy, so I watched in shock as my fist shot forward and made contact with his jaw. There'd been no decision on my part: one minute he was trying to interview me, and a split second later, I felt my hand smash into his face. He stumbled.

I felt good and wanted to do it again, but behind him, a short man sporting a flat-top haircut stuck out his foot. The off-balance reporter caught his heel on it and went down backward. The little guy's action snapped Blackie and Hank out of their state of stunned disbelief. They picked the guy off the ground and gave him the bum's rush, with Blackie repeatedly asking, "Where's your car? Where's your car?"

Back at the hearse, Johnny and the pallbearers looked on as my colleagues forcibly walked the would-be reporter to his vehicle. They couldn't have heard the clod's attempt to interview me, so I can't say for sure they lent us a hand, but the hearse and pallbearers' car followed the ace reporter out of the cemetery.

"What a jerk!" the flat-topped man exclaimed as he stuck out his hand. "Sherman Colton's the name. I grew up next to Marty back in Wisconsin. Sorry I missed the service at the funeral home."

The square-faced man facing me looked to be five-foot-five and wore tortoise-shell glasses. The wide lapels on his navy-blue suit didn't do much for me, and his generous floral-print tie hinted at the type of guy who'd wear a pinky ring. After our handshake, I re-checked the small digit of his right hand. Bingo! A diamond the size of a golf ball flashed in the sunlight.

"I tripped the guy," he said. "You should be more careful. He was younger and bigger than you are. You coulda been hurt worse than you are already. Your friends saved your bacon."

I'd been feeling manly, but he was right. "Pleased to meet you," I replied. "My name's Cletus Efferding. Marty lived with my family after her mother passed away."

Sherman Colton smiled. "Marty used to talk about you all the time. I'm an antique dealer too. Kind of interesting, how both Marty and I ended up in the antiques business. We had bottle cap collections, rock collections, coin collections, stamp collections, you name it. We'd still see each other at auctions once in a while and do a little trading. In fact, that's one of the reasons I'm here. I owe . . . owed Marty two hundred dollars and need to contact the estate."

"I'm the executor," I said and pulled a pen and copy of the funeral program from my coat pocket. I wrote down my address and phone number and handed it to him. "When you write the check, make it to the Martha Efferding Estate."

I was about to tell him Marty's mom hadn't abandoned her when Lumir approached us.

"What got into you Clete? The man could have taken you apart."

"I can take care of myself," I insisted.

Back from his mission, Blackie snorted, "We just saved you from learning it ain't so. Time you bought us a drink."

"Just a round or three," Hank added. He nodded to Sherman. "You should come with us."

I can't say I wanted Sherman's company but could hardly uninvite him. "We're going to send Marty off Irish-style down at the Bronco Inn," I said. "It's on the street that runs along the river, just south of the liquor store. I'm buying."

"Call me Sherm, and I'd be happy to have a drink with you."

Hank turned to Lumir. "And what about you?"

"I have had enough of you riverbillies. I'm going back to Cedar Rapids."

"Lumir has a dinner date with a widow lady tonight," I explained.

A widow in her early fifties, not bad for a guy who'd just turned seventy-five.

37

Blackie, Hank, and I sat at one of the Bronco's well-worn oak tables. We'd chosen a spot toward the back of the room, a location Blackie described as "close enough to the toilet but you can still see who's comin' in the front door." We were waiting for our first round. Sherman had yet to arrive.

I'd loosened my tie an inch, just enough to reflect the Bronco's casual environment. Blackie and Hank had shed theirs before arriving. Though doing so had taken Blackie's appearance a step backward, the absence of Hank's one-horned steer made for a real improvement.

"That Sherman," said Hank, "he's one heck of a guy. Owes Marty a couple of hundred bucks and drives all the way down to the funeral to make sure he knows where to send the money."

"Something about him is off," scowled Blackie.

"You're just not used to being around somebody with class," Hank replied. He looked up from his drink and nodded toward front door. "Here he is now."

Sherman greeted us, pulled out a chair, and sat. Though the man barely knew us, he seemed comfortable talking to strangers. He joined Hank and Blackie in a whiskey, while I stuck with beer. After a few minutes of getting acquainted, the talk drifted on to Marty.

"I can't believe that somebody would do that to Marty," Sherman offered, "Shooting her execution style and then dumping her into the river. It's the work of two men. The guys must have been professional."

"Professional maybe, but not very smart," scoffed Blackie as he touched a match to a cigarette.

Sherman seemed taken aback. "Smart enough. You can tell by the newspaper write-up the cops don't have much to go on. I doubt they'll catch 'em."

"They might get away with it, but they're still dumb."

Sherman moved his chair a few inches to avoid the smoke coming from Blackie's direction. "How's that?"

"It's the way the current runs up there. She ended up at Catfish Creek. That means they took the trouble to put her in a boat and dump her in the middle of the river. It's the only way it could happen. Somebody smart woulda dumped her from the Illinois side. She'd float for miles, and nobody woulda found her for weeks."

I was about to change the topic when Hank jumped in, "It's gotta have something to do with the antique business. Somebody broke into her garage last week because they wanted some cast iron she had. I never knew trading antiques could be so rough."

Sherman cleared his throat. "I guess it takes all kinds. Some of the traders are cutthroat when there's something they want. I've never heard of violence, though."

"The guys who killed Marty might think they're pretty smart, but only because they're so damn dumb," replied Blackie. "Goin' to all that work to kill somebody and the body gets found anyway. Hell, just as easy to take somebody down to Reed's Pond, shoot 'em, and throw the gun away. Just five miles south of town, blacktop all the way. Easy drive, no body to haul, no boat to mess with."

All in all, a strange conversation considering we'd just come from Marty's funeral. Blackie made it sound so simple that I decided to call him on it. "Reed's Pond is right along the road to Sabula. Way too public, if a guy didn't get caught in the act, the body would be found the next day."

"Shows how much you know," Blackie snorted. "Pull up on the dirt lane to the west side. With your headlights off, nobody would guess you were there. Shove the victim out of the car, plug him, and throw some brush over the body. Nobody goes there because there ain't no fish worth catchin'. The body could lay there a week or two before anybody noticed. A man could do it without a partner and never get caught."

"Sounds like you've given it a lot of thought," said Sherman.

"It's like this, Sherm. I ain't never killed somebody for raidin' my nets or fish traps, but I thought about it enough. And if I ever do, I sure as hell ain't doin' a lot of extra work. Best part about Reed's Pond is it's so close to the road, nobody will think to look there."

Leave it to Blackie, his gruesome line of bull must have gotten the best of Sherman. Our mild-mannered guest finished his drink and pushed back his chair.

"Well, I have errands to run. Cletus, I left my checkbook back in my room at the Harbor Motel. I'm free about ten o'clock and would like to clear the debt."

"No need, Sherm, you can just mail it, but if it will make you feel any better, I'm in the biggest unit at the Log Cabin Motel on the south end of Front Street."

"Clete, it's Riverview, not Front Street," said Hank, "just like it's been for thirty years. You say Front Street and strangers can't find it because they're lookin' for a sign that says Front Street."

"Listen to Hank," I smiled. "Not me."

Sherm rose and left the bar.

"Nice guy," said Hank.

I reached under the bandage on my head and scratched. Blackie was right. Something about Sherm didn't add up. As far as I knew, Marty never collected anything as a kid—especially not rocks or bottle caps, and I doubted that she ever talked about me "all the time." What earthly reason would the guy have for lying about how well he knew Marty?

I'd just readjusted my bandage when it hit me. Irving Kaplan's partner had disappeared at the same time he did. They hadn't split up but became antique dealers, and I'd accidentally eliminated half the team.

"Nice guy, hell," I said. "He's the Blowtorch, one of the guys who murdered Marty. He's not coming over tonight to settle a debt but to settle a score. The guy is planning to kill me."

———

There are few justifications for taking a life, and revenge is not one of them. When I left Hank, he was hell-bent on killing Sherman and found a willing partner in Blackie. I should have tried to stop them, but I had a vested interest in the outcome. As sure as night follows day, Sherman would eliminate me because I'd caused the death of his partner.

Joe Citizen likes to think otherwise, but law enforcement personnel can't prevent deaths. They may be efficient at solving crimes, but even there, the success rate is less than impressive. Sherman had been involved in a series of the most gruesome homicides imaginable and still walked free. I had little desire to burn to death at the hands of a maniac with a blowtorch, so I waited in my cabin, bait for Hank and Blackie's plan to capture and execute another human being.

Self-defense, not revenge, a desire to live rather than kill, lay behind my participation in the plot. The legal system wouldn't condone my part in the conspiracy, but no matter what I did or where I went, a professional killer would follow me, not resting until he'd extracted his horrific revenge. Kaplan's partner had to go.

Happy my role in the operation didn't involve violence, I sat on the floor, away from the windows. I didn't want to wait in the cabin, but Hank and Blackie insisted Sherm would smell a setup if I didn't. When he came to the door, they'd approach with guns drawn, disarm him, and spirit him away to a place of no return. A quarter of an hour before Sherman's scheduled arrival, I grew nervous, snuck to the kitchen, and slipped a small paring knife into my pocket.

The knock came at ten minutes to ten. Sitting on the floor of the locked bathroom, I listened for voices or sounds of a scuffle.

Heard nothing. A second knock. Where were Hank and Blackie? There was no third knock. I waited and listened. Heard nothing.

For a couple of rivermen, the boys were good. The operation had gone off like clockwork. After waiting an extra fifteen minutes feeling generally lousy about my role in Sherman's destruction, I knew the coast was clear and exited the bathroom wishing the police hadn't seized my copy of Michener's *Centennial*. Between guilt and excitement, there'd be no sleep tonight.

On my way to the kitchen, something crashed into the side of my head. Stars circled. I fell, but I didn't pass out. Not understanding what had happened, I was about to stand when I looked up and saw Sherm standing over me, holding an automatic pistol with a barrel the size of a cannon.

"You got one chance to live, Dickbrain. Do what I say, or I'll blow your brains into the next county. Put your hands on your head, get up, and face the wall."

Cursing Hankie and Blackie, I did as instructed. I'd no sooner turned to the wall when I felt the pistol jab me in the kidney.

"One peep out of you, Dickbrain, and you can say goodbye to your guts."

I wasn't about to peep. Though death appeared almost certain, I'd do anything to prolong my life. While there's life, there's hope, and I had a paring knife hidden on me.

The pressure on my back increased, and I felt a hand come around and probe my front pockets.

"What's this?" He extracted my weapon. "Think the little knife is gonna save you?"

Not sure if an answer would qualify as the peep that would get my guts blown out, I chose not to answer. Sherm clocked me with his free hand. I lost my balance and fell. He kicked me in the ribs, knocking the wind out of me. "Roll over on your belly and put your hands behind your back."

I did, and he duct-taped my hands. A mistake—I should have fought back. With my hands bound behind me, my chances of survival were nil. Sherm grunted and rolled me over. He laid the pistol on my chest with the barrel pointing at my chin, then pulled a strip of duct tape off the roll and slapped it over my mouth.

My heart pounded. I couldn't get enough air through my nose and struggled for breath. My chest felt like it would collapse, and my head like it would explode. I felt the eyeballs protruding from my face and bucked, sending the pistol to the floor.

"Having a little panic attack, are we?" My assailant smiled as he retrieved his gun. "No worry, it won't kill you. At least, I hope not. I have bigger plans for you. Take some deep breaths through your nose and get on your feet. Make it snappy, or I'll kick you in the jewels until your eardrums blow."

I got control of my breathing and rose. Sherman jabbed the pistol into the base of my skull.

"It's like this, Dickbrain. You're gonna walk across the room. I'll open the door, and you walk straight to the black Oldsmobile. Stop at the front passenger door. I'll open it, and you get in. No monkey business. My gun will be six inches behind you. You try something, and I shred you with seven bullets. Me? I don't care if I live or die as long as you go first."

I did as commanded, hoping Hank and Blackie waited outside. No dice. A few minutes later we were on the blacktop south of town. It didn't take any brains to know where we were headed—Reed's Pond, the place Blackie described as the ideal spot for a murder. Sherm must have checked it out after he left the bar. I cursed myself for putting my fate in the hands of a couple of yo-yos like Blackie and Hank. They'd chickened out, leaving me to die. My heart jackhammered again. I understood only too well that Sherman intended to burn me to death with a blowtorch.

My captor took no chances. He got behind the wheel, placed his pistol under his left leg and drove carefully. When he noticed headlights in the rearview mirror, he slowed to let the vehicle pass. "No monkey business," he warned. "I'm gonna slow down and let this farmer go around me. You should thank him. He just gave you an extra thirty seconds before the fun starts."

My stomach lurched, but nothing came up, good news considering my taped mouth. A battered pickup pulled by us. I could make out a figure in the passenger seat, but a hat covered most of the face. The truck swerved and hit our front fender before I had time to process the image. Sherman lost control, and we rocketed into the ditch, plowing through a fence and making a hard landing against a tree. My door popped open, and as Sherm fumbled, trying to locate his gun, I kicked the door to open it farther and made a break for it.

Running with my hands taped behind my back wasn't easy. I made a beeline for a field of waist-high corn but stumbled as I tried to climb out of the roadside ditch. Righting myself, I turned to see if anyone followed me.

The vehicles were about one hundred and twenty feet behind me, their damaged headlights turning night into day. I saw Hank standing in the roadway, bringing a long gun to his shoulder. Sherman stood several car lengths away, frozen just outside the door of his car. Hank's gun fired before he got it into position. Its payload passed harmlessly over the top of Sherm's head. The blast of the shotgun was followed by seven rapid-fire shots that could only have come from a semi-automatic pistol. I saw Hank go down. Blackie dropped what looked like a sawed-off shotgun, turned, and ran, making for the ditch I'd just exited.

I hurtled through a rundown barbed wire fence and fell again. Blackie made for the same spot and stumbled over me. I screamed into my duct-tape gag. Blackie rolled me over and ripped the tape from my mouth.

"Blackie," I hissed. "My hands are taped."

He didn't reply but came up with a penknife. He cut as much skin as tape.

"You should have shot him," I said.

"No ammo. Every man for hisself," he grunted, then got up and ran.

I looked back to see Sherm bending to pick up Blackie's stubby shotgun and head in my direction. I didn't know if he could see me but had no time to waste. Bending over to minimize my profile, I ran for all I was worth. I wasn't worth much. I hurt my ankle stumbling out of the ditch and began crawling on my hands and knees.

Ignoring my pursuer, I crawled as fast as I could. I didn't have time to wonder why Sherm stopped for Blackie's shotgun and didn't have time to see if he'd gone to get more ammo. Did he have another clip for his pistol? Curiosity would get me killed, so I tried to lose myself in the rows of corn before he spotted me.

The guy knew I was in the corn and wouldn't give up. As we played hide and seek in the rows, I realized my field was more of a plot, a three-sided corn patch not big enough to hide me for long. My pursuer worked methodically, moving a few feet at a time—pausing and listening. I pictured him looking up and down the rows. If I stayed in the corn much longer, he'd work me to one of the corners and find me.

The half-moon shone like a spotlight. If I cut across the rows, rather than crawling up or down them, he'd detect the movement of the stalks and come nearer. The frogs over at Reed's Pond made for my only advantage. Though a quarter mile away, their incessant croaking made it all but impossible to hear my movements.

I realized salvation lay in doubling back toward the truck, into the area Sherman had already checked. The way to do it was to crawl to the end of a row and hide in the grasses along the fence. With Sherm preoccupied in the corn, I might be able to work myself closer to the scene of the accident. Sooner or later, a passing motorist would stop to render assistance. I'd make a run for it, hop in his vehicle, and tell him to get moving. He might get shot at, but my survival came first. Call me a user, but a chance for life beats the heck out of certain death.

Ten minutes went by. Two vehicles passed, but nobody stopped to check on the wreck. I heard rustling behind me. Though I'd worked my way closer to the accident site, my location was no longer secure.

"I can see you, Dickbrain!"

Though I doubted it, I broke for the road. Everybody in Bellevue leaves their keys in the ignition, and Blackie and Hank had left the pickup in a hurry. The chance I could use it to escape beat the odds I'd face if stayed put. I ran as best I could, but my injured ankle limited me to a fast hobble.

I looked up as I reached the back of the pickup and saw Sherman a hundred feet away, running toward me full bore. No time to get to the driver's seat. If I was going to die, I intended to go down fighting, even if it meant bare hands against a firearm. Desperate for anything, even a two-by-four, I spied a six-foot wooden pole in the box of the pickup. I had it in hand by the time Sherm reached the front fender.

"Drop it!" screamed Sherm, pointing the shotgun at me.

"Like hell," I muttered and feinted with the pole.

The gun clicked, and I remembered Blackie's "no ammo" comment. Sherm jumped back, flipping the stubby shotgun to use it as a club. He made a run at me, but I sidestepped and swung my pole, catching him on the shoulder. The blow knocked him off balance, and he dropped Blackie's gun as he fell. As I repositioned my hands, I felt something metallic. I'd picked up one of the fishing spears that Blackie and Hank used to gig bullfrogs.

I righted the spear to put the business end first as Sherm reached toward his foot and pulled something that looked like a derringer from a sleeve on his ankle.

"Die, Bastard. Die," he bellowed.

The barrel of the gun was six feet from me, and I was in mid-air when he fired. The flash blinded me, my ears roared. Momentum carried me forward until the spear head hit something soft. Unable to see and nearly deaf, I fell forward, pushing on the shaft as Sherm struggled.

My eyes recovered, and I realized I'd caught him in the abdomen. The spear wasn't barbed, but I managed to right myself without freeing him and levered the shaft back and forth to inflict as much damage as possible. I bore down with everything I had, but it wasn't enough. I pulled out to strike again.

Sherm rose on his elbow and reached for his side. I couldn't see if he had his little gun and didn't know if it had another shot in it. In no position to hesitate, I went for his upper ribcage but thrust too high. The spear caught him in the throat, and I twisted as hard as I could. Blood spurted, then poured from the wound. When my attacker quit moving, I let go of the shaft and checked myself for a gunshot wound.

Sherm had missed.

38

Three months after a Chicago hitman named Herman Cohen tried to take my life, I returned to Bellevue to take care of the last piece of business from my summer vacation—the reburial of Martine Dufay. The arrival of autumn had turned the trees bordering the cemetery orange, but I barely noticed them as I stood at the edge of the plot my father gave me for my tenth birthday. If he'd known what I'd do with that bit of real estate next his father's grave, he'd have thought better of the idea. The infamous cast iron casket containing the mortal remains of Aunt Kate's mother rested at the bottom of a hole thirteen feet deep.

The Hinkleys hadn't marked Myra's grave, and I wasn't about to let the same thing happen to Marty's grandma. When my kids came of age, I'd fix the situation with Myra, but until then, the simple, grassy plot would have to do. Maybe it had something to do with family guilt, but I'd ordered an elaborate granite headstone for Martine Dufay.

Her marker would arrive next week. I'd asked that some Victorian-looking flowers be carved on it. The sample lilies the purveyor of monuments showed me looked fine, but to tell the truth, I'd been more concerned with the inscription. My lengthy text threw the salesman for a loop, but the Efferding family had been so cursed by its sins of omission that I didn't want to leave anything out.

MARTINE DUFAY

Afro-American mistress of August Efferding
Born 1852, died by her own hand 1886
Mother of Katherine Efferding, murder victim
Grandmother of Martha Efferding, murder victim

It had taken the brass plate from the iron casket, all my genealogical notes, and a court order to get Martine Dufay exhumed from the unmarked grave where'd she'd been buried following a media circus, two thefts, a car accident, a pair of murders, and a justifiable homicide. The task had been simple compared to that of convincing the trustees of the Presbyterian cemetery the grave would remain unmolested if covered by eleven feet of concrete with an earthen cap. A Ready-Mix cement truck from Maquoketa would arrive in a half hour, and after witnessing the fill, I'd be driving back to Cedar Rapids.

On Monday, my Bonneville would get a three-month vacation. Though Harriet had done her best to get me off the hook, the magistrate revoked my license for ninety days on the reckless driving charge. No one claimed the body of Irving Kaplan, the man killed when my car forced his pickup over the river bank, so the Board of Supervisors buried him in an unmarked grave on the grounds of the Jackson County Poor Farm.

The same fate befell psychotic hitman Herman Cohen. Although Blackie and I hadn't had an opportunity to coordinate our answers, we'd given such similar explanations of Cohen's death that Jackson County authorities decided I'd acted in self-defense. I'll never understand why they bought the part about Hank and Blackie stumbling onto a kidnapping, but I wasn't complaining.

With Hank dead, the need for secrecy about his role in the original theft of the iron burial case had disappeared. I told all. The Dubuque County Sheriff's subsequent investigation into Cohen and

Kaplan absolved me of any role in Marty's death. In the process, they turned up phone records linking the hitmen to Canker DeCook. Though I'd reported DeCook had expressed an interest in digging up the coffin, they found no direct evidence linking him to Marty's death. Their grilling must have been intense. He planned to sell his construction business and move to Alaska.

I stepped back from the edge of the excavation and began to walk the few hundred feet to Hank's grave. His death bothered me more than expected. I'd taken a real liking to the guy, and he died trying to save my life when he fumbled the hammers on his old-fashioned shotgun, discharging it prematurely. Only one of Cohen's seven shots hit him, but it had been immediately fatal.

The day after the shooting I spoke to Hank's siblings and offered to buy him a plot next to Marty's. Though a strange request for an outsider, they were moved I liked the man so much and agreed. The fly in the ointment turned out to be Hank's estranged wife. Though she had no love for the man, the thought of him buried next to the town hussy provoked all manner of protestation. Her concerns evaporated when I wrote her a five-hundred-dollar check.

When I reached the site, I discovered someone had erected a wooden cross in the space between Hank and Marty's markers. Constructed from four-by-fours and three feet high, the ends of the arms had been trimmed into tapered pyramids. Hardwood letters, cut with a jigsaw, had been attached with tiny nails. I read the inscription:

M

Y

OLD FRIEND

H

A

N

K

No one needed to tell me it was Blackie's work. I sank to my knees sobbing. Though it would have been easy to blame Blackie for leaving me in the corn after he'd freed my hands, it would have been unfair. He and Hank had risked their lives to save me, and given the circumstances, his "every man for himself" declaration had been spot on.

Irascible Blackie and easy-going Hank with his smashed-down hat had achieved a friendship that few could hope for. Despite the tears on my cheeks, I found myself laughing. Going after a professional killer with an antique double barrel and a single-shell shotgun, late to arrive at the cabin because they'd misplaced Blackie's sixteen-gauge ammunition, crashing into Sherm's car when they didn't know what else to do—blunders aside, the guys had hearts if not smarts. And who was I to judge? I'd renounced any claim to superior intelligence when I locked myself in a flimsy cabin as bait for a psychopath.

I owed Blackie; he'd saved my life. I gave him the contents of Marty's house and garage. He'd consigned the Nicholson tool chests to a New England sales firm specializing in antique tools and put a fifteen-thousand-dollar reserve on them. They were expected to bring at least that. When I asked him what he planned to do with his windfall, he looked at me as if I was daft.

"Fish," he said.

I'd ordered my cement from Maquoketa since Bellevue didn't have a concrete plant. It took a quite a bit of maneuvering for the guy driving the cement truck to make his way to the excavation. He'd brought two junior-high boys with him, and though they seemed more excited about the coffin at the bottom of the grave than the task at hand, they helped him find a path through the maze of tombstones and directed him through it. After studying the coffin from the top of the pit, they disappeared, intent on exploring a pair of distant mausoleums.

The driver appeared undisturbed by their sudden absence. "Nice kids," he said. "The tall one's my boy. The other one lost his father a few months back. He's been taking it pretty hard, so it's nice to see him all fired up about this antique coffin business. When they found out I was scheduled to pour a plug over the coffin, they begged and begged to ride along. It's against the rules, but I told 'em they could come if they helped me get the truck in place. Not that I needed 'em. Hope their bein' here ain't a bother."

"Actually, it's nice to see kids enjoying a sunny Saturday."

"Yeah," he smiled and donned work gloves. "Better get on with it, I'm supposed to help a neighbor with his hogs this afternoon."

After unlatching the chute, he placed it over the excavation, and double-checked the setup. Assured all was copacetic, he walked to the far side of the truck and pulled the lever releasing the cement. The truck growled, and the sounds of the flowing mix filled the air. The pour took all of three minutes. The task complete, the driver monkeyed with his controls and walked the chute back to its storage position. After finishing, he retrieved an Igloo cooler, drew off a cup of liquid, and gestured in my direction. "Lemonade?' he asked.

"Sure."

He handed me a cup, filled one for himself, and gestured toward the site of his work. "That plug oughta keep her in place. Smart to plan for two feet of fill over the top. Otherwise, grass wouldn't grow."

Our conversation moved on to the events that followed the discovery of the coffin and the Cubs missing the playoffs. When we'd exhausted our small talk, he pulled off his cap and scratched his bald head.

"Well, If I'm gonna make it back by three, we'd better get going." He replaced his headgear, and raising his hand to his mouth, called for the boys, "Hink, Larry, come on in."

"Hink?" I asked.

"Short for Hinkley. His name's Mike. His dad was county sheriff."

I stood mute, unable to take in my surroundings as the cemetery dissolved into an image of Myra holding my infant son, a picture so vivid I could have reached out and touched them.

"Smile, Mikey. Smile," she cooed.

My legs turned to jelly. Fearing I'd lose my balance, I stepped back to steady myself and encountered a marker. The unexpected obstacle nearly upended me, but the experience brought me solidly into the present.

"Better watch yourself," my driver warned. "You almost fell."

He might as well have been speaking Chinese. Mikey! I watched as the boys ran to the truck. My son running toward me, the stuff dreams are made of but better than a dream because it was real. I imagined myself running in his direction and sweeping him up in a gigantic bear hug.

The illusion didn't last. Mikey blew by me without a glance. He and his friend appeared to be racing each other to the truck and reached the door neck and neck. A good-natured argument ensued. Apparently, a victory earned the right to the window seat. My heart swelled with pride as Larry got in first and my son took his rightful position.

"See ya," the driver said and turned toward his truck.

I nodded. My son, just twenty-five feet away. I wanted to talk to him.

The driver walked to the other side of the truck. I heard him open and close the door. The vehicle's engine turned over and settled into its rhythm. The hell with self-denial.

"Hey, Mike," I yelled and took a step toward the truck.

He turned to look at me, the sweetest sight on the face of the planet, a vision I'll treasure the rest of my life.

The grating voice of the man claiming to be my psychologist ripped through me like a speeding freight train. "Tearing your children's lives apart is irresponsible—especially after they've just lost their father."

I stopped in my tracks. "Nice race," I said

He gave me a puzzled look, smiled, and waved.

I waved back and watched as the Ready-Mix truck slowly threaded its way through the rows of tombstones, taking my son away.

Author's Note

Sins of Omission is a work of fiction. The 1975 discovery of a Fisk burial case on Bowman's Island, south of Bellevue, Iowa, served as inspiration for the story. Though the discovery became a media event and hundreds of curiosity seekers viewed the coffin, readers expecting anything remotely similar to actual events are sure to be disappointed.

While a commercial fisherman named Blackie Stiles plied the trade in mid-twentieth century Bellevue, the historical figure has nothing in common with the character depicted in this book. The name was simply too good to ignore. The same goes for patrolman 'Mac' Mclean, auction assistant Hickory Smith, funeral director Johnny Dye, and car dealer 'Wolfie' Till. Actions attributed to them are fictional as well. I have no idea if the Undecided Decision, an area band popular in the 1970s, ever played at Lombardi's.

Citizens of Bellevue would recognize Goose, Steel Belly, and Skillet as nicknames attached to Steve Roling, Tom Cox, and James Kolker. Razor Ray Theisen, Bub Ruff, and Buzzy Lucke once cut hair on Riverview (Front) Street. Helen Nicholson inspired a generation of young readers at the public library, and a Catholic priest named Cletus served St. Joseph's Church for eleven years. Walt Florence, Ole Olsen, and Charlie Bailey were names once associated with the Bellevue fish trade. Actions attributed to these characters are the product of the author's imagination.

The same goes for funeral director Ray Gallagher, who in 1975 stored the Fisk coffin at his furniture store pending the official investigation. Several quotes attributed to Gallagher appeared in reports by news organizations. Again, those looking for historical accuracy will be disappointed to learn the author has merged quotes from several sources, enriched, and edited them.

The arson of the historic lodge at Bellevue State Park occurred in 1973. No one was charged with the crime. Other Bellevue-area locations and businesses mentioned in *Sins of Omission* existed within a year or two of the story's time frame. Efferding's Menswear is an exception. Though inspired by the multi-generational Lucke Brothers clothing store, Efferding's is fictional. Canker DeCook's construction operation, Marty Efferding's antique business, and Hap Herrig's farm never existed. Once surrounded the trees on three sides, the area around Reed's Pond was more rugged than it is now.

Sadly, references to the town's shabby treatment of its commercial fishermen have a basis in fact. I've changed the name of the neighborhood in which many of them lived to Fishville. By the late 1990s, the occupation was all but extinct.

A nineteenth-century Federal Census for Bellevue Township tags several women as 'ladies of easy virtue.' None were African-American. Prior to the American Civil War, individuals who were three quarters, seven-eighths, and fifteen-sixteenths white were regularly sold as slaves. Abolitionist minister Calvin Fairbank reported the sale of an individual in Lexington, Kentucky, believed to be 1/64th black.

The 1881 Bellevue smallpox epidemic is not fictional. Among others, it carried away Catholic priest Peter Portz who caught the disease while tending the sick. When the contents of the rectory were burned to prevent the spread of the disease, the early parish records were destroyed. Officials decontaminated the structure afterward by burning sulfur in it.

Acknowledgments

I am indebted to retired Benton County Magistrate Anders Norgaard for his insights into the administration of justice at the county level. Background on the 1975 Bellevue Police Department is courtesy former patrolman Eldon Wholers. Razor Ray Theisen and his sons Jim and Jerry kindly provided information for the barbershop scene, and Kathy Gallagher shared unpublished details on the 1975 coffin discovery. A shout goes out to the wonderful staff of the Bellevue Public Library for providing much-needed assistance with local history resources. Helen Nicholson would have been proud of them.

The cover of this volume features an illustration of a Fisk coffin virtually identical to that found on Bowman's Island. (The Bellevue coffin lacked the protective cast iron cover for the viewing window.) The helpful staff of the Kibbe Hancock Heritage Museum in Carthage, Illinois, bent over backward to facilitate photographing the example in the institution's collection. The Kibbe Hancock's Fisk, discovered during a mid-twentieth-century road improvement project, made its way to the museum some dozen years ago.

I'd like to thank my editors, Shannon Ryan and Ronda Swolley for wrangling my prose, and those who commented on the draft: Jeremiah Chublik, Ciuin Ferrin, Logan Giese, Bill Hart, Stacy Holsinger, Nancy E. Kraft, Dylan Moonfire, Riley O'Conner, Nathan Schmidt, Stacie Sugioka, Nick Tharalson, Dakota Trace, Aime Wichtendahl, and Laura Bosley Whitmore. Bill's comments were on target and spectacularly thorough. Dylan's did much to tighten up a wandering storyline.

To learn more about the Cletus Efferding series visit:
http://randyroeder.com